GOLEM

QUILL AND BIRCH

PD Alleva

Published By:

Quill & Birch Publishing

Treasure Coast, Florida

Quillandbirch.com

ISBN (eBook): 978-1-7351686-4-7
ISBN (Paperback): 978-1-7351686-5-4
ISBN (Hardcover): 978-1-7351686-6-1

Graphic Content Warning: For a list of graphic content including potential trigger warnings associated with *Golem*, please go to the authors website at:
pdalleva.com/golem-graphic-content

"Pleased to meet you
Hope you guessed my name
But what's confusing you
Is just the nature of my game
Just as every cop is a criminal
And all the sinners saints
As heads is tails
Just call me Lucifer
'Cause I'm in need of some restraint
So if you meet me
Have some courtesy
Have some sympathy, and some taste
Use all your well-learned politnesse
Or I'll lay your soul to waste"

~ The Rolling Stones
Sympathy for the Devil

Part I

John Ashton
1

Long Island, New York
Halloween
1951

Annette Flemming sat on a wooden stool with a large round salad bowl filled with candy—Charleston Chews and Tootsie Rolls— at her feet waiting for the next trick-or-treater. Daylight had been gone for more than a few hours and, with it, autumn's tranquil crisp air gave way to a cold and bitter winter like wind.

Her street had been bustling with trick-or-treaters and their parents as sounds of joy, excitement, scares, and laughter reached to every doorbell with a life of their own. The costumes—mostly skeleton prints on white sheets and Alice of course (Wonderland had never been more popular), with a few Dorothys, Tin Men, and Scarecrows but no Lions (no one likes to play the coward)—brought a smile to Annette's trembling lips. The neighborhood was drenched with Halloween decorations—scarecrows hanging from trees, cardboard ghosts, ghouls and goblins taped inside windows, and of course, pumpkins. Annette's house was the only home without said decorations with the exception of the pumpkin she'd carved on her own a few hours before. She wasn't much for Halloween, never had been, but tonight was different. She couldn't stand being in the house alone. Annette's husband, Noel, had been gone for more than a week - California hoping to open another company, Cinema Production this time, to add to his already growing empire - and she just hadn't gotten over the language barrier shared with Camilla, the help they'd hired a few months prior. Perhaps Annette required some semblance of normalcy, prompting her retreat outside.

She didn't mind that Sam—her golden retriever—barked his overgrown snout at every child and parent who offered a smile for a chew or roll. She remained on that stool for hours making sure to only give one candy to every large smile and soft-spoken Trick-Or-Treat, so she wouldn't have to go back inside. Her house seemed like a vast black hole that sucked the life from her bones. There was madness waiting in the living room, in the kitchen and dining room, and of course, in Noel's study. A still, eerie quiet she couldn't shake off.

So much better to be out here, where it's safe and there are people—living people and not statues of lions and replicas of David staring and watching every move I make.

But the crowd had thinned over the last hour (it was a school night after all), and she started to feel restless, hoping the night wouldn't end. Hoping someone would choose to come over and converse until the rising sun shed light across November.

She looked to the left for a long while, the insipid cold air restricting her skin, freezing the tip of her nose. Her chest tight, bones constricted, staring at the sidewalk beneath the streetlight across the street.

Is someone there?

No one. The street was empty, and Annette took the flask from her coat pocket, twisted the cap, and took a long gulping swig of scotch. Cleared her throat while replacing the cap and flask as quickly as possible before any nosy neighbors looked through the window as they had been all evening. She heard a rustling from across the street and stretched her neck to see beyond the trees with their barren limbs stretching into the moonlight like dark veins possessed by the night. What little leaves remained on those limbs were on the brink of making a final descent (a good rain right now would make sure of it), as they rustled with a slight sway when the cold wind blew smooth and delicate across the neighborhood. Her eyes roamed, tension in her bones, her chest tight, looking, staring, to find….no one. Only quiet hiding inside a cold wind. Then she turned to the right, and an immediate smile crossed her lips. Eight-year-old Ivan, dressed as a scarecrow, with his pudgy little hands gripping a pillow case filled with so much candy she could tell he was laboring to make it to his final destination, waddled down the sidewalk with his mom in tow.

"Hi, Meredith," said Annette with a slight wave, then bent down to pick up her bowl. Gonna make Ivan's night, she thought. The last trick-or-treater either made out the best or suffered the most—depended on the amount of candy in the bowl, and this year she'd gotten enough to feed the entire town and not just a few simple blocks.

"Annie, how are you?" Meredith greeted. "Didn't expect you at this late hour." That was bullshit; Annette knew Meredith didn't expect her at all. Annette, over the last few years, was that asshole adult that turned off the porch lights on Halloween night. Loneliness does make us go to extreme lengths to not be lonely.

Annette didn't offer a response; instead, she gave her attention to Scarecrow. But seeing Meredith and hearing that numbing judgment made Annette wince, shudder, and think, *Your husband's a loser, Meredith. How many oil changes will he complete before he sinks down that hole called alcoholism? Not very kind, Annette, but definitely time to move to a better neighborhood.* Instead, she sang (in a voice as nervous and shaky as the leaves), *If I only had a brain.* Again, not very kind, considering she stressed the words *had a brain,* but he's the one wearing the costume. Maybe next year he'll choose one of those white sheets with the skeleton print. The song brought a disgusted stare from Meredith. A gesture Annette let go.

"Well, you look absolutely darling," said Annette stretching that nervous smile ear to ear.

Little Ivan just about bounced when he said "Twick or tweet," eyeing that less than half full salad bowl of candy.

"Of course, it's treat time." She shook her head when she said, "Do you have enough strength in those straw arms to carry all this candy?"

Maybe I shouldn't have kids, she thought. I'm not very good at this. He's been here for less than thirty seconds and already two insults. At least she didn't make fun of his speech impediment. When little Ivan started nodding in apt anticipation, Sam started barking and howling as if the retriever was suddenly struck with a fever of anxious trepidation.

"Oh, wonderful. Because I've got all this extra candy and no sweet tooth to eat it with. Open that pillow case as wide as you can because it's all coming your way."

"Oh, thank you, thank you," said Meredith, a certain prideful tone in her voice. Little Ivan would have candy for the next month.

He stretched the pillowcase, and Annette could see his grip tighten as she dipped the bowl over the case, sensing Meredith's eyes on her, watching, assessing, judging. "There you go," she said, stretching her back as she dropped the last piece to little Ivan's satisfaction. She caught Meredith's stare, and Meredith smiled as if she felt some inkling of pity for Annette. As if Annette was someone to be pitied, all alone in that house. All the neighbors knew she was alone— husband's off on another adventure and little Mrs. Pristine is out serving the public with gifts of cavities and tooth decay. And doing it all with a nervous grin.

She can smell the scotch. I know it.

"Thank you." Meredith smiled, a knowing dark grin.

She definitely can.

Annette turned from Meredith's smiling façade, while catching a glimpse of Sam yipping, barking, and shuddering. "No thank you necessary," she said then caught Meredith's stare again. This time her eyes were darker— maybe it was the overcast sky that now botched the silvery glow of the moon. Definitely sinister, Annette thought, as if Meredith was enjoying Annette's apparent nervousness.

This'll get around tomorrow, she thought. The lonely wife's inability to settle in and be normal like the rest of them. Annette was the topic of conversation over the last few years since she and Noel moved into the neighborhood, among the stay-at-home moms that literally *ran* the neighborhood during weekly get-togethers that always consisted of a good amount of liquid courage, gossip, and trifles over inconsiderate neighbors—Annette and Noel being the prime candidates to talk about. Still, the neighborhood was a step up from the apartment they had in Queens but still not where Noel wanted to be. He had his eye on the Hamptons. Annette wished they were there already.

"Glad to do it," Annette continued. She forced her eyes to Ivan. "Any trick-or-treater still parading at this time of night and carrying such a big bag of candy has definitely earned the grand prize."

He stared at his diverse candy collection, wide-eyed and proud; when he looked up to Annette, his attention quickly redirected, catching sight of something beyond Annette, across the street. Little Ivan stood there confounded, jaw open, eyes wide as if he'd been caught with his hand in the cookie jar, complete deer-in-the-headlights type of stare. When he finally did meet Annette's gaze he looked like he'd seen a ghost. His eyes, his face, his whole body for that matter had gone stiff. Little Ivan stood there with his jaw open, not knowing what to say.

"What do we say, Ivan?" Of course, Annette knew Meredith couldn't allow a thank you to slip away. Not in her child. No way in hell's damnation would her child grow up ill-mannered.

But it did take him a few seconds to comply, standing there with that empty look on his face. Annette waited for the good manners to appear, feeling uneasy under the child's stare. "Thank you," he said but kept looking. His words dropped off his tongue like a concrete block dropped off a third-floor steel rail.

Not polite to stare, Annette thought as she started to feel…off. As if Ivan's eyes revealed some character flaw Annette would never dare speak of. She wanted the moment to end, and end quickly. Annette felt grimy, buggy even. She desperately wanted to shower and go to bed.

Are you taking this little vermin away now?

As if she heard Annette's thought Meredith reached her hand to Ivan's bag. "Thank you, Annette," she said, securing the pillowcase in her left arm and took Ivan's hand in hers.

"No problem," replied Annette, standing stiff watching Meredith and Scarecrow cross the street on their way home, walking with a spring in their step. She remained until they disappeared into the house across the street. Sam barked and barked, almost gnawing on the window. The night was done. Halloween was over.

She picked up the stool, still holding the salad bowl in her left hand, and walked up the drive to the front door. She set down the stool and salad bowl, lifted the top off her pumpkin, and blew out the candle. Sam was relentless as she did so.

"Oh, Sam, could you please just *shut up!*"

Now a gust of cold bitter wind raged across her skin, tensing the neck bones as if some icy cold hand wrapped around her neck and squeezed. Annette stood stiff, the hairs on the back of her neck erect. Her arms tensed, her entire body constricted, standing, waiting to go inside, her hand on the doorknob. She thought about turning around when she was hit with an empty sensation in the pit of her stomach, wrenching and grinding and twisting her innards. Now she couldn't turn around, difficult to move as if she were paralyzed, her body no longer receiving instructions from her mind.

Just go up and take a shower, she thought. It's nothing. Imagination is all it is. Nothing's there. See for yourself. Look back. Look over your shoulder. Nothing to see but the neighbors watching from the window across the street who will definitely have something to say about you during the next drunken gossip fest.

She elected not to look. Instead, she scurried inside, told Sam to be quiet when she placed the salad bowl on top of the stool and locked the door, including the dead bolt. Not that she had to. Most everyone in the neighborhood kept their doors unlocked, but tonight she needed to lock out the neighbors, be done with the past and move forward. Once she slid the dead bolt locked, Annette looked through the window beside the door.

A crack of thunder just about broke the sky. Her house shuddered. She could see the wind gathered strength, and yes, those leaves found their open concrete coffins, swirling on the sidewalk with more than a few caught in the wind's upheaval, circling the dead leaves into a large oval in front of her house.

Another loud roar of thunder, and Annette used all her strength to move away from the door. Sam sought refuge in some room out of sight, hiding. That damn watchdog feared the roll of thunder. She stood away from the front door, assessing the home, the chandelier and the still quiet in the house. More thunder, this time accompanied by a bolt of lightning that turned the night sky momentarily blue. Annette could see it through the hall that stretched to the back of the house lined with windows and a back door for easy access to the back yard designed for entertaining and a child's continuous use for play and optimal growth.

Not that I'm ever going to use it for that purpose.

The crystal chandelier trembled as the hand of thunder gripped the house.

Gonna be hard to sleep tonight, she thought and went up to shower. The approaching storm dulled from her ears once the water started running, and the shower felt good—doesn't it always? Getting off the muck and grime, cleansing the day's dark energy from the skin. She liked the shower hot—steaming even— and when she finished she opened the window to let out the steam and allow the cold air to calm her heated skin and heart. More thunder, and another bolt of lightning accompanied the roar. The rain had yet to arrive, although the wind stirred into a frenzy turning the air especially bitter.

That uneasy, unsettled sensation returned. Her first thought was that someone was in the house. Perhaps trifling around those neat little trinkets, those keepsakes she loved to…keep. Maybe they were still down there, admiring the David replica. Noel had wanted that statue so bad he could have tasted clay on his tongue. "That's me," he had said. "Gorgeous, brave, and Godly."

Annette was grateful for having met Alena, a high society sculptor—also an esteemed member of the Hamptons Country Club Annette had joined a few years ago and the hostess to many New York City social gatherings — who had directed Annette on where to secure the most prominent David replica. Annette laughed, sitting on the toilet bowl wrapped in a towel, beads of sweat and water on her upper lip, forehead and temples, remembering how Alena had offered the original (the one on display in Florence is always a replica). Alena had means to attain it, and Annette had no doubt she could. Women like Alena were a step above normal society, even above elite society (old money indeed).

And she laughed at herself. For being paranoid. For being anxious and silly. Absolutely silly with her rolling thoughts of sinister beings. *That's what I get for indulging in Poe and Lovecraft.*

She stood, and when she stepped towards the sink she caught a glimpse through the window. Across the street stood two trick-or-treaters. Two kids, one taller than the other, holding hands, looking and staring at Annette in her bath towel. Her chest constricted. Something was oddly peculiar about them, standing across the street under the sycamore tree with its branches bending under the force of wind, staring, looking up to the window, to Annette. Her body shivered under their dark gaze. Her stomach churned acid into the back of her throat.

The little one can't be more than four.

Something was very off about how these kids were dressed. She knew how children received hand me downs from their siblings or cousins — Annette had been a recipient of many hand me downs—but these were old, very old, from the 30's, during the Great Depression. Tattered and frayed with blue and white checkered print worn by both children. Maybe they were going for a Raggedy Anne and Andy duo? The little one was in a dress with really short hair for a girl, and the older child was in pants and a buttoned-down shirt—same patterns—although the shirt had been oddly buttoned. His hair, not short at all, dropped down below the ears and the back was long enough to grace the shoulders. No parent either.

Sam started barking.

The older one cupped his hand and whispered in the young child's ear. Whatever was said brought no response, the child remained still, standing and staring. Now thunder cracked against the night sky as a wallop of wind rushed through the window. Her body still, constricted, as if some demonic hand carried on the wind had wrapped around her body and squeezed. And then she saw black. The world turned dizzy as if drawn into a vortex.

When she came to she was sitting on the floor, back against the wall. Had she fallen? No, she would know if she had. She held her head in her hands and, as her vision returned, she saw blood on the towel. When she wiped her nose, there was blood on her fingers.

"My lord," she said, stood up and turned on the sink. The steam had dissipated from the mirror, and she surveyed her nose and the blood that now seemed to have stopped. She washed her hands, nose, and mouth.

Knock! Knock!

Annette snapped her head around, staring through the open bathroom door, into her bedroom to the door leading into the hall. The moment tense and quiet. Annette's shallow breath, cold puffs of vapor over her lips; chest constricted, tense, the beating of her heart like a flicker in her temples. She craned her neck; eyes searching into the hall, noticing the bedroom was dark.

I thought I left the light on.

"Is someone there?" she said, although in such a low whisper even if Noel had been in the bedroom he wouldn't have heard it. Unsettling fear choked her throat, swallowing her breath as if she could disappear if she kept her breathing calm and whoever was in her house wouldn't be able to see her. Then she remembered…Sam. If anyone was in the house or tried to break in, he'd be barking his head off.

"Sam!" she hollered, more out of relief than an anxious command. "Sam Sam. Come here, boy."

Another stiff moment as she waited. Annette pursed her lips and swallowed her breath. "Sam?" she murmured. Am I just playing the fool? she thought, remaining inside the hope that someone was not in her house.

Sam scuffled to the bathroom door.

"Oh, Sam," Annette said. "You scared the bejesus out of me."

Sam sat in front of the bathroom door, panting as if he'd run a few miles, a whining, fearful wheeze beneath his breath. His tongue dripped across his canine teeth.

Knock. Knock!

Sam whimpered, rolled in his tongue, and backed away from the bedroom door. Annette surveyed the room. Another trick-or-treater? Maybe, she thought, but at this late hour? Anything is possible. She looked in the mirror, stretched her nose to make sure all the blood was gone (it was), then took a glance through the open window. The street was empty although leaves were bustling in the wind being carried on its heels.

Thunder!

Lightning!

Strong wind getting stronger!

She closed the window and locked it, then pulled off her towel—wiping some dried blood from her chest with it—and tossed her nightgown over her shoulders followed by a thick velvety robe.

Knock. Knock. Knock. Knock. KNOCK!

Is this a joke, she thought and hurried to the hall, knotting the robe around her stomach as she stomped to the stairs when lightning and thunder rolled together. The lights went out, and Annette stood at the top of the stairs in darkness with her hand on the banister. The hair on the back of her neck stood erect, and she couldn't shake the feeling that someone was behind her. She saw a face flash in her mind of a man with white paint on his face. His eyes and mouth were smeared with black paint. And his eyes, black to the core, revealed there was no light in the body, only darkness.

Knock! Knock!

Maybe they need help? Was that her thought or the dark man in her vision? She didn't know.

The lights returned to illuminate the house.

Knock!

Knock, knock. More like a tapping this time. Or maybe a rapping. She couldn't remember which one. She held a fleeting thought to go to bed and hide under the covers until whoever was rapping on the front door would go away. *I don't care if you need help or were in a car accident. Don't care if you're bleeding to death and need hospital attention... go away. Just go away. Just...*

Rap Rap Rap.

Thought gone and now she was headed down the stairs, feeling like a clown for the thought she had. Not very nice, is it? To leave those in need to themselves? She approached the door, reached for the dead bolt, and paused. Her hand pulled away from the lock as if it had a mind all its own. Her left hand on the doorknob, her right hand found the middle of the door and gently rested on the thick wood. She stretched her neck to the window. Staring back were those kids, and Annette recoiled from the window. Her stomach churned.

Rap Rap.

She was about to scream but held her hand over her mouth instead. "Who is it?" she stuttered, a crack in her speech.

The voice that answered was monotone and matter of fact. She couldn't tell if it were boy or girl. "May we come in?"

"Why do you need to come in? Was there an accident? Do you need an ambulance?"

"May we come in?"

Pause. Brow furrowed. She pursed her lips and swallowed.

"Where are your parents? Aren't they with you?"

Another pause.

"They'll be here soon. May we come in?"

Annette nervously and slowly peeked through the window. As if this was anticipated, the little one was looking, staring, blank faced and...peculiar. Yes-the clothes were tattered, but what does that mean, their parents are poor? Probably trick-or-treating in the good neighborhood. But there was more not yet revealed. Their eyes, Annette thought. What's wrong with their eyes? The little one, boy or girl she wasn't sure although the dress definitely indicated girl, was mesmerized and blank faced. And the eyes. Yes, Annette could see it now. Her eyes were pitch black! No pupils, no iris, just jet, metallic bulging black eyeballs.

It was the older one who continued to speak through the door. "May we come in? Our parents will be here soon."

Annette noticed Sam wasn't barking. Noticed Sam wasn't anywhere close to Annette.

"May we come in?"

Thunder! Lightning! Annette's breath stuttered, constricted. She snapped her head around, looking through the hallway. Pitter-patter pelts of rain snapped against the back windows. Lightning illuminated an empty backyard.

There's no one there, no one out back. Am I going to leave needy children out in a rainstorm?

Then the little girl said, "Let us in!" Annette knew it came from the little one because the voice changed. Although still monotone there was a softness to it only little children carried.

The wind lifted into a furious frenzy. The rain fell hard now, showering the windows. Thunder. Lightning. Wind. Rain. Heavy rain.

"Can we come in?"

"Parents will be here soon."

"Let us in."

Annette caught sight of Sam at the top of the stairs. The retriever cowered in anticipation of Annette's next move. Now the storm strengthened with a swirling, squall filled wind that howled through the house. She gripped the dead bolt, and Sam whimpered and whined and rushed down the hall to the bedroom.

"It'll be all right," she said. "They're just kids."

2

November 1, 1951
New York City

This was indeed a big day for John Ashton. He was meeting with Captain Knowles for what John was supremely confident in assuming was his promotion. Detective Ashton, missing persons unit. There was no reason not to assume. A World War II veteran, John had been on Normandy Beach. And he put his time in, working the beat over the last few years and doing so with stellar recognition. He put in for the promotion (a detective's badge meant status—one day he'd be chief) a few months ago, and the timing couldn't be any more perfect. John's wife, Laura, was pregnant with their first; the extra money would be more than needed – babies cost a lot, according to his father. And then there was the recent collar. John and his partner, Frank Peterson, had apprehended a truck of stolen cigarettes that had been hijacked in Brooklyn about a week before John's heroic arrest. It was the first time he'd used his Smith and Wesson in the line of duty. Had to actually. When you're staring down the barrel of a gun you shoot back. That's what you do, no ifs, ands, or buts about it.

Frank Peterson was not as lucky. He'd taken a bullet while John was inquiring about the contents in the back of the truck. Frank passed away a few hours later. What had been a typical day had turned into a blood bath. The only person left standing was John, but the cigarettes were there and the truck that had been reported stolen a few days before. A good collar indeed.

Perhaps the collar propelled John to the top of the detective list. Or perhaps the accumulation of a decent flatfoot career capped with the cigarette collar brought the promotion. Didn't really matter on this fine November morning. He was alive and ready to do some good work in what John had great hope would become an incredible career.

"In my office at eight AM," as Knowles had instructed, would be no problem, John would be at the precinct well before eight, incapable of suppressing his excitement.

————————

"Congratulations, Ashton," said Captain Knowles the second John walked in his office. "You've been promoted to detective." He offered his hand, which John took, a smug smile plastered across Knowles' lips.

The situation wasn't as John had envisioned. Of course, the parade and his fellow flatfoots holding him on their shoulders was something he knew wasn't going to happen, but he did expect a bit more gratitude from the Captain, more celebratory than matter of fact as Knowles now projected. Considering how disheveled and worse for wear Knowles appeared, John surmised the Captain had indulged in one too many drinks the night before – possibly even before arriving to the precinct. The captain squirmed beneath his tweed suit, uncomfortable. Probably nursing a headache and wanting to get this over with as quickly as humanly possible. Although alcohol wasn't an indulgence for John, he knew more than half the department—maybe all of them—depended on the drink. It seemed a stiff scotch at the end of a shift (sometimes during) was as necessary as a sidearm. His dad drank, and John always noticed how the discipline was twice as bad when the old man had a few drinks in him. Shorter fuse too. So, in principle, he stayed away from the after shift drinks.

Even when Normandy returned full force— sometimes in the middle of the day—he dealt with the memories, the shaking hand and quivering full of fear lips by tapping his right hand on his left shoulder, telling himself over and over again: *Pull it together. Pull it together. Pull it together.* Tap tap. Tap tap. Tap tap.

"Thank you, sir. You won't be disappointed," John said with conviction—he'd practiced his response all morning.

"Take a seat," Knowles ordered. His jaw was tight; he looked like a man with a bad stomachache; his face constricted and John noticed how the Captain's skin under his right eye sagged, perhaps from years of tired abuse through alcohol, the eye rumbling like a nervous twitch. John thought then that Captain Knowles was headed home immediately after this meeting. John took his seat. He was hoping to receive his detective badge with the handshake, yet no such badge had been offered. Too, too, *too* many, he thought.

Captain Knowles sat too. There was a brief pause before Knowles said anything, during which John shifted in his seat, uneasy and antsy, as his stomach started to boil, twist into knots. He felt his face flush and turn hot. He could taste it like a tinge of metal on his tongue. He was about to receive his first assignment. Like a bloodhound on the scent of a hot trail, his anticipation brought him to the edge of his seat.

"Do you know district attorney Charles Xavier?"

Hearing that name formed goose bumps on John's arms. The hair on the back of his neck stood up. Of course he knew DA Xavier, his daughter had gone missing almost two years ago. The investigation was still ongoing. High profile case too. John's apt anticipation took a turn into pure one hundred percent excitement. Couldn't believe it really, his blue eyes gleamed with that same excitement and he did all he could to taper down that smug, way-too-happy smile. This *is* about a missing child. Mental check: learn to hide your excitement.

"Not personally but I have kept up on the investigation regarding his daughter. As much as I possible could with limited access and…"

"It's a dead end," Knowles interrupted him. Maybe he didn't like the excitement he saw in Ashton's face. Maybe he had no time for new recruits and their *let's save the world* attitude. Maybe he wanted to get this over with as quickly as possible. Still, his "dead end" declaration was disappointing. "I'm sure that child is calling someone else mommy and daddy right now or fertilizing daffodils. Either way, the politics in the situation is obviously paramount." Captain Knowles wrote something on a pad on his desk. Maybe something he had to remember for after this meeting, but the gesture infuriated John. *We're talking about a missing child. Could you be a bit more humane?* "We've exhausted all avenues over the last year. Came up empty and still empty. We normally would close this case but considering it's the DA, as a courtesy, it's still open." John listened, waiting, anticipating, eager for the assignment to be handed to him; he could feel it in his bones. "However, there is a new lead." Knowles looked up from his pad, his brown eyes stiff as if he was sizing up his new detective, looking for any sign that could break him. Knowles rolled his tongue inside his cheek and sat back, still holding his pen over the pad he'd scribbled on. "Have you ever heard of Alena Francon?"

The name did ring a bell, although John couldn't place a face with the name. "Sounds like high society," is what spat out of John's mouth.

The captain didn't laugh as John expected. He sat there, stiff and staring. His smile appeared a few seconds later. John thought then, *He doesn't like me, does he?*

"High society is just the tip of the iceberg with this one. Remember the ClairField Hotel?"

John did remember the ClairField. Who in New York didn't, especially after a fire ravaged and destroyed the hotel earlier in the year? The ClairField had been slated for demolition by the city, however the fire had taken care of all the demolition needed. All that remained of the once highly prestigious upper west side hotel were shards of brick and concrete.

"Of course," John replied. "Did she have something to do with the fire?"

"Officially, no. Officially hot coals left unattended by the destruction crew started the fire.

Unofficially, we have reason to believe she *is* the reason for the fire. A few firemen pulled her out, a bit delirious too. Kept going on and on about the children. Had a delirious story to go with it."

John crinkled his brow. "Story?"

Now Captain Knowles laughed, more like a chuckle of disbelief. His eyes were cast down, as if he'd found some bug on the floor. "Said the Golem had kidnapped and was holding captive a horde of children in the hotel."

To this John perked up. "Really?" and then a second later, "Did they find any remains?"

Captain shook his head, brushed his shirt off and sat forward. "None. We ceased the search after hearing her story." He laughed again. "She indicated this Golem was a statue of hers that came to life. Talk about a wild goose chase."

Knowles ran his palms across his face covering the wide yawn that stretched his jaw.

Ashton said, "Then why continue? If no bodies or traces of children were found? I assume she's been detained?"

Knowles nodded. "She's at Bellevue."

"Sounds about right where she belongs."

"Of course, but on Sunday an artistic rendering of how the DA's daughter would look now made the paper—an attempt to keep public eyes on any possible sighting of the girl."

"And Alena saw the picture and started hollering holy hell."

"That's what the crazies do," said Knowles. "Said she knew the girl and that she was part of this Golem's 'collection,' as she so adamantly put it.

Anyway, Bellevue psychiatrist called us and now…it's all on you, *detective*." First time someone other than himself used the term to describe him. "Go in there and interview her. Take her statement and follow up on any possible leads. I'm sure you'll find none, but we have to cross our i's and dot our t's now, don't we?"

Is he that hung over or did he make the mistake on purpose?

Knowles was still talking. "I'm sure you'll come up empty but at least we can tell the DA we followed through."

A pause as John wondered what to do. A second later he said, "I'm on it," and stood up as if he were sitting on a spring. He shook Captain Knowles hand. "I won't disappoint you, sir."

"I'm sure you won't," Knowles said. He caught Ashton before he opened the door. "Detective…"

John turned on his heels.

Knowles continued, "She's a bit…strong willed and according to the psychiatrist…a doctor…" he looked at his notepad, "Elliot, she's been trying to escape since she was admitted. She's taken out a few orderlies too. So, don't get your panties in a bunch over anything she says. Just take the report and follow up, got it?"

"Duly noted, sir. Consider it done." John smiled, turning to leave, his hand on the doorknob.

"Detective!" Knowles called again. John turned around as Knowles tossed him his badge. "You'll need this now. Truly earned, detective. Good work with the cigarette bust. If you want to go home before your interview and change into a suit, I'm ok with that."

John looked over the badge, moving his thumb over the shining gold that glimmered in his eyes. "Of course," he said, his voice a hush as he stared at his new badge.

Knowles held out the report on Alena Francon.

"Sir, thank you." He took the report.

On his turn out the door he was greeted with a congratulatory applause.

3

He did go home. Had a celebratory breakfast courtesy of Laura—ham, eggs, and buttered-to-the-max toast, changed into his tweed suit—brown and he only had two; he would have to buy another with his first pay increase—then took off toward Bellevue. He even donned his lucky fedora, although the black hat didn't match the brown tweed.

He'd been to Bellevue a few times over the last few years, mostly to admit the mentally deranged he'd found on sidewalks while walking the beat, although he had never actually gone *in* to Bellevue. Nope, drop 'em off and let the professionals handle it from there. He didn't know what to expect (having heard horror stories about the psychiatric ward) but gave it no more than a second's thought. It is a hospital after all, how bad could it be? He made his way in and directly to the reception desk where he flashed his new and shiny detective badge, a ticket to anything he wanted. He was a bit disappointed when the nurse who admitted him had no reaction other than "oh, ok," before directing him to the psych unit and handing John one of those fancy visitor badges to pin to his lapel.

"Go through the hall to the elevator...down one flight. When the doors open, you'll see the reception desk. But be careful because at this hour the patients are allowed to roam the hall. It's their daily exercise time."

John cocked his eyebrows. Exercise hour? He'd pictured rows and rows of padded rooms with individual patients in each room. How many were down there, he wondered.

"Dr. Elliot is on the ward. He'll get you all set up in an interview room."

————————

He'd looked over the report in between eggs and toast. What he'd forgotten to ask Captain Knowles was, why? Why the two stories? The official and unofficial. Why not book Alena for arson and be done with it? After reading the report he suspected the *why* had something to do with Alena's father. Although the man had passed on in 1944, he'd left a legacy in Manhattan that would live on for at least the next quarter of a century. He'd been friends with many police officers, the district attorney's office, and his philanthropic endeavors could be seen all over the city. Perhaps this respect for Mr. Francon had been stretched to his daughter and securing the family name, despite Alena's apparent mental break.

And it wasn't as if she was a continuous threat. Except to the orderlies of course. According to the report Alena was responsible for injuries to three orderlies, one of which had slipped into a coma. Alena smacked his head so hard against the concrete wall his skull cracked. *Inhuman strength resulting from an incessant delusional fear* is what the report indicated, signed by Dr. Elliot himself. That was their job though, John thought. It's what they signed up for and society was safer for it. Safer because an arsonist was in custody. The law worked in many ways; sometimes things aren't always black and white. There are many layers that need to be considered, including circumstance and there's more than one way to skin a cat, so to speak.

In addition to the report about the orderlies there wasn't much in the file other than a family history, Alena's original statement, and the attending officer's—one detective William Reilly—follow up report, which indicated a contradiction to Alena's claim of children held captive at the ClairField. As the elevator dropped to a stop, John made a mental note to speak with Detective Reilly.

―――――――

The room was large and open. A nurse's station—set behind a glass pane—was in the corner on his left. A single nurse behind the glass, her head down. A television sat on a table on the far right. Two couches, facing the television, bore burnt orange fabric, tattered and worn. His first note to himself: shouldn't that television be secured somehow? He thought about the report on Alena. If she's as violent as the report says maybe leaving a potentially threatening object at her disposal is a bad idea. In between the two couches was a round coffee table covered with magazines and newspapers.

The television was off. Basement windows lined the opposite wall where the sun brought natural light to the basement psych ward. Overhead lights cast a yellowish glow on the basic concrete walls and polished white floors. The room was filled with patients wearing the classic hospital gown. There were scores of patients, some sitting in various sporadic places, others standing, talking to themselves or talking to whatever delusion produced the strongest internal stimuli. Others paced the floor and still more paced so fast —looking over their shoulders and staying as far away from everyone else—John was sure they'd walk at least the equivalent of a few miles during *exercise hour*. John was also certain they weren't walking that fast for exercise. One of these runners kept biting his nails and spitting the little shards on the ground. John noticed a stream of blood trickling down the man's hand and wrist.

Another patient, directly across from the elevator, sat against the wall smacking the back of his head, although lightly it was consistent and on every sixth rock he smacked it hard, flexed his arms with wide hysterical eyes glaring into open space, then returned to his common endeavor. The one spitting his nails and trickling blood down his hand paused, looked at John with wild stiff and staring eyes. He thought the man was on the verge of running at him when an orderly stationed on a chair beside the elevator jumped off his seat and stared the man down.

"That's no way to treat a visitor, Shane," the orderly said. He had to be towering at six feet five inches and was definitely well over three hundred pounds. Shane gave up his examination, wedged his bloodied finger between his teeth, and held it there as he dipped into his run.

John held out his badge, "Detective Ashton," he said.

Maybe it was how Ashton's hands shook when holding his badge up, or maybe it was his youthful face that brought a smug smile from the orderly. John thought he must be in his forties; probably working here most of his life and would retire here having put in a life of service to the mentally ill. Or maybe he felt at home (he looked very comfortable).

"Alena?" he said, his voice thick and heavy. John thought he could use a shave.

"Yes. Can I speak with Dr. Elliot first?"

The orderly—DeShawn according to his ID badge—gave a quick shake of his head. "Doc's seeing patients right now. He should be done soon. I'll get you set up in one of the offices with Alena. She's been waiting for you all morning. Hasn't eaten a thing either so I'm glad you came in. I saved her some food. She needs to eat. It's better to eat with her medication. I'll tell Dr. Elliot you're here. He'll meet with you after."

Disappointing. John wanted to speak with Dr. Elliot prior to his interview with Alena to gauge the professional's opinion on Alena's claim. Unfortunately, that would need to wait. Just take the statement and follow up on any claims. Cross the i's, dot the t's, as Captain Knowles had said.

"Ok," John said and was about to ask DeShawn about Alena's current mental state when he noticed the female patient standing next to him.

"You're here for me, ain't ya?"

"Leave 'im be, Wanda," said Deshawn.

John recoiled from Wanda—she was a bit too close for comfort. Wanda couldn't be more than nineteen. Blonde hair that looked like she hadn't hit shampoo and water in more than a week, and blue eyes like an angel, but when John looked deeper he could see this angel held a knife behind her back. Her features were soft and youthful, as youthful as they could be until time stakes a claim on the face and years of stress take their toll. And John was sure she'd see more than her share of stress, considering where she's at now. The mentally ill don't get better, it's a lifetime disease, John thought. Her frail thin body seemed to disappear beneath the hospital gown. She couldn't be more than five feet tall either. She reached close to John, standing on her toes and whispered, "They have private rooms here. We can do it in there. My roommate won't mind. She's catatonic." And then her eyes lit up. "We can do it on top of her. Yes, oh that would be too, too much…fun."

John wondered if DeShawn was assessing his reaction to this offer or if he was perhaps enjoying the moment. Little mentally ill girl taking on the big detective.

"He's here for Alena. Leave the man alone."

About time, John thought.

"Alena?" she said. She had both hands on her head. "That whore." Wanda's voice changed. She screamed, "That fucking whore!" and the nurse looked up, assessed the situation then went back to her magazine, or maybe she was counting pills, John wasn't sure. The scream pierced John's right ear. He was sure she would pull her hair from her head but instead started walking at a rocking pace, her arms now crossed over her thin body, tears, cries, and whimpers behind the grimy hair now hiding her eyes.

"She'll be fine," DeShawn said. "First experience with the crazies?"

"Something like that, yeah."

DeShawn snapped and slapped his right fist into his left palm. Snap pop! "Pay them no mind, it's a daily struggle. C'mon, I'll get you set up."

————

DeShawn excused himself — he went to escort Alena to the room he'd brought John to. Not much of an office really. A small desk and two chairs — one on each side — in what John had sensed was a broom closet prior to becoming an office. White chipped paint turned yellow more than likely from the overhead lighting John surmised was depleting his mental capacity the longer he sat in the room. He opened his file, let it lay on the desk, took out his notebook and pen, then thought better of it and stuffed the pen back inside his breast pocket. DeShawn had said to be mindful of contraband. "She won't use it against you, but she'll hold onto it and try using it to escape and any poor orderly working the floor when she did try may find it wedged in his skull" were DeShawn's words of warning.

He fixed his hat which had dropped a little too much to his left when Wanda the screamer rattled his eardrum then heard the doorknob twist. John stood up. DeShawn was in the door; so big and large John had first thought his endeavor to gather Alena to the room had been a failure. Maybe she's reconsidering her story, John thought, but when DeShawn stepped into the room Alena was behind him, too small to be noticed behind DeShawn's large frame. Alena, short blonde pixie cut, fair and soft features resembling strength with a "don't mess with me" gaze of green eyes, stared judgmentally at Detective John Ashton. Her thin arms were crossed over an even thinner frame. And he had thought Wanda was thin. Alena was nearly invisible. She remained in the doorway, assessing, looking him over. John thought it was amazing how she looked nothing like the others. She was clean and pristine. She'd been here a year? How was she so well-groomed? Her hair was cleanly washed as if she had gone to the salon yesterday. Her nails were delicately painted with fresh nail polish, her skin had not one blemish, as if she was allowed her daily facial cleanser and cream. Even her arms looked soft and well taken care of. Her file stated Alena was thirty-two years old but she appeared no older than twenty. Her face was narrow, her thin lips sealed closed as she glared at him. Quite obvious to John that she was displeased.

"Captain Knowles sent *you*?" she said. Her voice was strong as if chiseled from stone with a slight hint of a Russian accent. His report indicated that although Alena was born in America, her Russian immigrant parents had crossed the ocean in their late twenties (with a boat load of money too). John surmised the slight twinge of accent had rubbed off on her otherwise American heritage. Quite common in New York's melting pot of blending foreign accents.

"That he did," John said. He offered his hand. "Detective Ashton."

She never so much as looked at his hand. Instead her eyes stared straight through him, and John's heart tightened in his chest.

"Did you make detective this morning?" Her snarl and disgusted stare coupled with this statement of knowing rattled the new detective.

Get some control, detective. Buck up for heaven's sake.

He noticed DeShawn wasn't helping. John cocked his eyebrows. Don't respond, he told himself. "Can we talk?" he managed to squeeze from his closing throat, gesturing to the seat opposite him.

"C'mon Alena, he's just taking a statement." *DeShawn, thanks for the help.*

Alena looked at DeShawn while still standing in the doorway, now leaning against the doorframe. Then turned back to John and shook her head displeasingly.

"Please," John said not knowing what else he could or should say.

Alena gave a quick shake of her head. "At least you have manners," she replied, dropped her arms and went to the offered chair, muttering Russian verbiage as she did so. John didn't speak Russian. He understood nothing she said.

"English, please," John said as he sat down. "We are in America." He was being tart and possibly a bit rude, but he despised it when people didn't speak English, especially in matters concerning the law. People plot your demise right in front of you without your knowledge. Better to speak just one language. Plus, he wanted Alena to know that he, Detective John Ashton (and yes I made detective this morning), was in control of this interview.

Alena stood with one hand on the back of the chair, once again gazing at him and shaking her head. "And aren't *you* rude," she shot back. "Your mother should have slapped that rude out of your mouth when you were a child."

"My mother," he mumbled.

"Yes, your mother." Alena's eyes were wide. "What would she say about her son's blatant disrespect?"

John raised his hands and shook his head. "What?"

Alena pursed her lips. "I refuse to answer questions from such a disrespectful American or anyone for that matter. You will apologize, or I leave." She waited, all the while her stare burned through him, and John cocked a nervous smile. DeShawn raised his eyebrows and widened his eyes. His arms folded across his chest. He gave a quick *let it go and don't push it*, shake of his head.

John sat back, thinking it was best for him to concede to Alena's desire.. "I'm truly sorry. No disrespect meant. As an officer I…"

"For the love of Pete, there's no need for an excuse, just an apology. Excuses turn apologies on their head."

Again, he raised his hands. "Ok," he said. "I apologize."

"Accepted," she said then uttered something beneath her breath, not English either; definitely Russian, and John noticed her accent was more prominent when she spoke her native language. He dipped and shook his head. *Let it go, John. Remember you are in a psych ward.* DeShawn's returning stare confirmed his thought as the right way to handle the blatant disregard. Alena took her seat.

He proceeded with caution, carefully selecting his words. "You reported to Dr. Elliot you'd seen the DA's daughter…" he studied the report, finding the DA's daughter's name. "Isabelle. She's been missing for the last eighteen months. She'd be four years old now." He looked up from his report and eyed Alena. "Can you elaborate?"

She was staring at his hat, John noticed.

"Alena?" He cocked his eyebrows returning Alena's stare. "Can you elaborate?"

Alena leaned back. "I saw her picture in the paper. Last Sunday. Ideal day for the article to run; Sunday papers always garner a larger circulation. I noticed her immediately. She'd been in my house since she disappeared. Strange as it is, I never added it up. Charles has been a frequent guest at the ClairField, even before he was the DA. He's been to several gatherings over the last few years. When his daughter went missing, he was devastated. But I never put it together until I saw her picture in the paper."

"In your house?"

"Yes, detective, in my house, and at the ClairField. Highest probability she had been there when the DA was there himself. Although in secret of course. Odd, isn't it? Sometimes the answers to our most dire circumstances are right under our noses."

John cocked his head. "Wait a minute, are you saying you took her?"

Alena rolled her eyes. "Detective, did you read my original statement?"

He looked at her, stone cold stare. "Of course," he said. He wanted to smile but held back. "You claim a person named Golem kidnapped children."

"Correct, detective."

"And this Golem…" now he did smile, "is one of your sculptures that came to life?" He cocked his eyebrows. "Do you see how we have difficulty believing your claim, Alena? Inanimate objects don't come to life."

"They do if you ask them to," Alena, her voice curt as if containing a finality to the claim.

He relaxed in his chair. Closed his eyes for a moment and took a breath. "But no one's ever seen this Golem, correct? Other than yourself."

"Many have seen him," she shot back.

John glanced at the report; a gesture meant to jog his memory of its contents. "People were interviewed," he said. "Not one person backed up your claim. In fact, not one person has come forward and admitted to knowing or having seen this…*Golem*."

"Well, detective…" she moved in her chair, leaning forward, closer to John. "He's very, very good at manipulation. It's his…gift. Charming too. And when you've got someone in the palm of your hand you can either set them free or squeeze and crush the life from their lungs. Most people choose freedom, even though said freedom is a continued illusion. They just bury themselves deeper and deeper inside a dark hole."

"So, everyone is lying?"

"Of course, they're lying. Their reputations are on the line. Considering…"

John's interest was piqued. "Considering?"

"Their participation."

He waited for more but received no further explanation. "In what?"

"Rituals, detective. The kind that could destroy reputations and brand prominent men heathens, even if they weren't aware of what they were participating in. Court of public opinion is the only court in session on a constant basis. Since McCarthy's speech everyone has been on edge, especially in this city. False claims can stretch to just about anyone nowadays. No proof required, now is there? Just an accusation. Fear has forced every prominent person in this city into the typical damage control response and it'll only get worse, considering McCarthy is on a hot, seek and destroy rampage.."

"I'm sure the DA would place his daughter's safety above his reputation, Alena. It is his daughter after all."

"Well, detective, perhaps the DA isn't as innocent as you perceive him to be."

"Meaning?"

"Meaning," she huffed. "You're on a fool's mission, detective. You really have no idea what you've gotten yourself into. Surrounded by devils you believe are angels. Be careful, detective. Be very careful indeed."

"Are you a communist, Alena?"

Her eyes widened. "How dare you! Because I am Russian? I reject communism. Communism was the reason my father left Russia; our family has no such ties to a Communist Russia."

He decided to return to the task at hand. Thought he'd gone too far, but communism made his blood boil and his first thought was that she was describing a communist gathering. He glanced back at the report. "Tell me more about the DA's daughter. Where do you think she is now?"

Her eyes were wide while staring at him, gritting her teeth, John could tell she was angry: at least she didn't ask for another apology. "Wherever Golem is, she is with him. If she is still alive. Golem likes to…indulge certain appetites. But I don't think so, not with that little one. Golem had taken a very special interest in her."

"Appetites," John repeated, paused to allow the word to sink in. Disturbing as the word was to him—especially when referring to children—he made a mental note and continued. "Your report indicated there were children in the ClairField when you burned it down…"

"Correct."

John eyed her. "But when the property was searched they uncovered nothing. Nothing more than burnt embers and desolation. No kids. No bones. Nothing. How do you account for this, considering your claim?"

"He was able to get them out before the hotel burned down. Or the policeman, what was his name?" She narrowed her eyes.

"Reilly," he answered.

"Correct, William Reilly. Perhaps he wasn't the right man for the job. Or perhaps he was the perfect man for the job—depending on who you're asking."

Now John sat back. "Are you suggesting Detective Reilly is part of some elaborate cover up?"

"Apparent conclusion, detective. If the children were in the hotel, and he was responsible for finding them and he didn't, what other conclusions can there be?"

John shot back, "That he didn't find anyone because there was no one to be found? Isn't that a possible conclusion?"

"Of course, for the ignorant and corrupt."

Or the sane. "Understood," he said clearing his throat. "Do you have any possible suggestions on where I should look to find the DA's daughter…or any child this Golem has kidnapped? According to your report, there were quite a few children involved."

"Go back to the hotel," she said. "Search through the desolation; there has to be something. Anything. I'm sure the remains are still there," she scoffed. "Takes this city forever and a day to get anything done. Then go to my home in the Hamptons. Search the basement."

"Is that where I can find this Golem person?"

She smiled. "I doubt he'll reveal himself, detective. You're not his type and he's gotten what he needs up to this point."

"Noted," he said then continued. "I'll be sure to be on my toes *just in case*."

"Are we finished?" she asked.

"For now."

"Good," Alena replied and stood, DeShawn behind her. He'd been so quiet, John could have easily forgotten he was there had he not been of such a large stature. He opened the door for Alena as John was skimming over his report. Follow up on any leads, the Captain had said. Which meant he was going to the hotel and the Hamptons. But then a thought crossed his mind that required further inquiry.

"Oh, wait. One more question, Alena, if you please."

She paused in the doorway. DeShawn beside her. Her eyes wide with anticipation.

"You admitted to burning down the hotel. If there were children in there, why did you do it knowing they would die in the fire?"

DeShawn seemed to brace himself, as if he had anticipated Alena attacking him.

"A soulless body is no life to live, detective. If you knew what I do, seen what I've seen, you'd understand. There were many revelations that night and all roads led to one conclusion."

"Which was?"

"Golem's demise was required."

"But he didn't die in the fire, right?"

"Unfortunately, he did not, *detective*. Nice hat by the way."

————————

That was strange, John thought as he waited for Dr. Elliot. He wrote a few notes, ClairField and Hamptons, thumbing through the file for the address. Made an additional note to speak with Detective Reilly, who worked the homicide department. Although John had come across multiple names and introductions as a police officer, Reilly rang a bell but he couldn't remember where he'd heard the name.

He was glad the interview did not last long. Being in this place made his skin crawl. Although sympathetic to the traps mental illness generated for the recipient, he was comforted they were here, in the hospital and not disturbing the good citizens of New York. The NYPD had a mountain of corruption to deal with on a daily basis; having to track down delusional, mentally ill claims was a waste of manpower and resources. He'd be happy once his investigation was over.

Follow up on any leads. Captain Knowles' order. John was confident he'd have this wrapped up quickly. Would have it completed today if he didn't have to go to the Hamptons - the long drive from Manhattan would take at least a few hours each way. He ran down his list of to do's: ClairField, Reilly, contact Hamptons PD (to inform them he'd be arriving in the morning— his report indicated the house was abandoned), speak with DA, write report, and submit report. And the last he wrote in all capital letters: RECEIVE NEXT ASSIGMENT.

Captain Knowles was accurate in his assessment. Alena was a wild goose chase. Although John sympathized with the DA's circumstance, Alena's story was completely off the scope of mental sanity. Inanimate objects did not come to life. That was it, beginning and end of story. Although he understood the necessity for investigation into all possible leads, some leads were strictly common sense. And Alena's claim was neither common nor did it make sense. He didn't take Alena as someone who sought attention, but he had a nagging intuition she was attempting to make a case to claim some sort of insanity. She confessed she burned down the hotel—although the deed was covered up and put to rest as fast as humanly possible, assuring Alena would not be charged with any such crime.

So why bring more attention to it? You got away with it. Everyone involved has buried the story. *Let it go.* Why tear off the bandage and open the wound back up? Mental illness. Delusional. That's why. Maybe the delusions have gotten the better of Alena Francon?

Is there any possibility she's telling the truth, even some insane version of the truth? Maybe she'd been so traumatized by what she did she created this story as an effort to defeat despair, guilt, and shame. Perhaps Golem is a statue and perhaps to save face she created the story to hide her deeds. But then where are the children? Maybe they're just a part of the delusion. Maybe she did kidnap Isabelle. Alena admitted to knowing the DA and that he had made many appearances at the ClairField. Maybe she just couldn't help herself. *And maybe the mental breakdown had been due for some time, caused by some stress I'm unaware of. I should have asked more questions. Next time, ask more questions. Perhaps Dr. Elliot will know.*

As if on cue, Dr. Elliot knocked and opened the door.

————————

"What are your thoughts, doctor? Your professional assessment on Alena's claim?" John had taken the seat on the opposite side of the desk. A gesture of respect for the doctor, whose appearance indicated he'd been locked in this psychiatric unit for most of his days. Assessing and treating. Treating and assessing. A cold almost lost stare in those eyes above a thick wrinkle that twitched above his cheek.

Dr. Elliot was short in stature, about five six, with glasses and thinning salt and pepper hair. He looked like he hadn't exercised over the last few decades and, judging by the spare tire around his waist, exercise wasn't on the doctor's to do list any time soon. He was wearing the typical white coat and his high quality, checkered blue-and-white shirt was pressed to perfection — lots of starch — and his necktie seemed too tight around his throat. The overhead light glinted off his glasses and, although the doctor paid no mind to it, the bulbous glimmer kept John's attention as the doctor provided his assessment, cigarette between his fingers.

"Have you had any experience with schizophrenia, detective?"

John shook his head, "Not at all." There was relief in the doctor's question as it seemed he was about to reference Alena's mental illness, which John assumed would shed light on her multiple and rather ridiculous claims. It also meant John had been correct in his previous assumption that this wild goose chase was indeed just that.

"There are several incidents in Alena's past that have to be considered concerning her delusions. Schizophrenia can be caused by a deep seated stress that manifests over time."

John gave a quick nod. "And Alena's? What happened to her?"

"Well, let's go over a quick chain of events. Alena was very close to her father. Being an only child of such a prominent family has its stress to begin with, and Alena did all she could to live up to her father's expectations. For a long time she did well, extremely well. Her philanthropic work with underprivileged children has been duly documented, including the introduction of the arts program for which she's had great success. Have you ever seen her work?"

Another shake of the head. "No."

"She's excellent. A true artist, that's for sure. Brilliant, really. But in hindsight, typical. Artists are often plagued with mental illness, genius too and Alena is no exception."

John wrote down: Genius. Artist. Skitsofrenia.

"Her first true break occurred after her father's passing. Keep in mind, detective, Alena's mother passed away when Alena was twelve years old and Alena assumed the role as caretaker to her father. After his passing…"

"How did he pass?"

Dr. Elliot paused. "Cancer." He cleared his throat. John wrote down: Dad Cancer. "Alena took over the family business. However, steady financial decline would be the ruin of Alena and the family business— the family had a large stake in the ClairField, among many other businesses and dealings. Alena's father loved the ClairField; it was his home and as dear to him as Alena herself. In late 1948, the hotel began to decline, and Alena did not have the resources necessary to turn the hotel around, back to the status and precedent the hotel held since its construction in 1804.. She couldn't afford the lease and when the city declared they were going to tear the hotel down and make a park, she cracked."

ClairField. Decline. Crack.

"And then there is the loss of the child."

John's ears perked up. "Child?"

Elliot nodded. "Indeed, detective." Dr. Elliot stared at John through those bulbous glasses. "Alena was deeply involved with a young man of old money, family prestige too. In 1947 Alena became pregnant, although out of wedlock. This pregnancy brought shame to both families."

"So, he left her?"

Elliot shook his head. "Not at all. He planned to marry Alena prior to the pregnancy becoming public knowledge. They were set to marry in July of that year…"

Dr. Elliot paused, took a last pull off his cigarette, then stamped it out in the ashtray he'd brought with him.

"Did they marry?"

"Never made it. In June Alena lost the baby. She was three months pregnant, and there were complications associated with the loss."

"Complications?"

Elliot cocked his eyebrows. "Alena is unable to have children."

NO Children. June 1947.

"So he left her?" John said. "No baby. No ability to have children. Prominent family. I'm sure they wanted to pass along the family prestige."

"Correct, detective. Correct. Which resulted in a mental breakdown. So, we have one, two, three breakdowns. First her father's passing, then the loss of the child resulting in an inability to have children, then the decline of the ClairField, her father's most prized possession. Add it all up, detective; common sense will lead to a mental breakdown in every way possible. Not to mention the stress. No husband. No family. And the finances were declining, losing all her father had worked to achieve."

"Makes sense," John said as he wrote down: One Two Three Breakdown, then sat straight dropping his pen on his pad. "So, tell me if I'm wrong, doctor. She concocts a delusion that her sculpture comes to life to fulfill her need for a man in her life and to have someone to blame because she's mentally trapped and can't get out of the hole she's in. Then she burns down the hotel because it's better if it burns than gets demo'd by the city, therefore saving a bit of face in the public and inner circles she's dealt with all her life. Kinda like, the hotel burned down and I'm not reopening it instead of, I squandered my dad's fortune and can't keep the doors open so the city took it from me. Is this accurate, doctor?"

"Exactly, detective. Right on point."

"Ok. But why do you think she's making this claim about the DA's daughter? In your professional opinion, do you believe she's capable of kidnapping?"

"Anything's possible, detective, when you're dealing with a diseased mind. Considering the trail toward her breakdown, I wouldn't be surprised."

"Which begs the question: what did she do with the child before the fire? Reports indicate no body was found at the hotel nor the Hamptons home."

"That, detective, is why you're here."

John pursed his lips and nodded. "What about her escape attempts? What has she reported are her reasons for escape?"

Dr. Elliot smiled. "It's quite common around here, detective. Patients are delusional and medications aren't always accurate. Sometimes they create an escalation in symptoms. Unfortunate as it is, getting the right medication is like hitting a bull's eye on the first try. It takes a few adjustments to get it right."

John noticed he did not answer his question. "Noted," John said. "But did she give a reason?"

"Of course, detective, there's always a reason. Most of my patients want to escape because they believe they are being held against their will, and there is nothing wrong with them. Of course, escaping from a mental institute is completely sane and rational." Dr. Elliot's eyes widened as he leaned closer to the desk.

"Is that what she said? Her reason?"

Dr. Elliot shook his head. "Alena reported wanting to escape because Golem was still out there. She said she'd seen him, in here," he gestured to the ceiling. "Allowed in by someone working with him. Someone under Golem's control."

John gave a quick *hmm* and a nod. "Who?" he asked.

Dr. Elliot met John's eyes.

"Me," he answered with a slight tilt of his head.

John smiled. "Must be difficult to treat a patient who doesn't trust you." Dr. Elliot was about to answer when John interrupted him with, "Who was the boyfriend? Or almost husband? I'd like to speak with him. Character reference so to speak."

"Unfortunately, Mr. Astor is no longer among the living."

John wrote: Astor Dead

4

Annette Flemming could not stop the thoughts raging through her mind. She sat with a drink in her hand—a stiff scotch—at the edge of the couch in the sitting room. The David replica watching patiently, perfectly placed in the room's corner. Annette returned the stare.

She was irritated like her skin was crawling and all she wanted to do was get up and go. But go where? Situations and circumstances aside, all personal connection had been lost over the last year, since Alena's unfortunate circumstance. Annette longed to be back at the ClairField with the high society elites. Couldn't believe she missed those drab and pretentious gatherings, since from the very beginning she couldn't stand to be around any of those judgmental pompous fools, but as all things do turn we can get used to just about anything, including social gatherings with elite and prominent New York bureaucrats. Alena had been one of the only fair, conscientious, and mindful people she'd been introduced to, even if she was only a mere acquaintance – Alena had her own very private circle of friends – Annette would love nothing more at this very moment to be away from her home, talking gossip with the elites. But all that changed when the ClairField was ravaged by fire, and Alena was committed under duress in an apparent mental break earlier this year. That was when the parties ceased as if a proverbial blanket had been ripped away and now there was nothing more than cold bones and skin. Now every thought that popped into her brain was escorted by irritation no matter what the content of those thoughts were.

She waited to hear from Noel; however, a cross-country phone call was often difficult to push through and she waited with bated breath for the phone to ring. Plus, he was in California where the sun had yet to rise and perhaps too early to attempt a phone call. Annette anticipated he would call sometime this evening after his meetings and dealings were completed for the day - and before he went to mix it up with the California socialites. Noel required Annette to be social with the prestigious New York elite. To be, in fact, the model of success and portray an appropriate façade with an applicable cause. All the other wives have causes, he'd told her. Pick one and let me know what you need. Also, it may be good to host benefits for the cause. You're such a gracious wife, Annette; people will take to you quickly. You're all heart. That's what Noel had said about her: you're all heart.

She took a sip of scotch as she saw herself as a hostess, much like Alena had been. Alena was the perfect hostess, graceful, elegant, beautiful and remarkable with a savvy wit that made prominent men adore her company. And her parties always boasted a guest list of New York's who's who. At one time or another anyone who was anyone had attended one of Alena's parties. That's what reputation allows for, a guest list as prominent as any English queen would be proud of. Annette had believed Alena was her ticket to prominence and as a grand hostess. Didn't matter that Annette was always quiet in Alena's presence, like a mouse surveying the scene for any possible predator cats, sometimes too frightened to venture out of the mouse hole. Annette attended many parties given by Alena, a few with Noel (and how she loved it when he was with her; he could hold a conversation with all Alena's guests), but mostly on her own—she always left early, even when Noel was her escort. She'd hoped Alena would have become a strong friend, but that hope had gone with the wind.

Further irritated, she took another sip as a cold November wind rattled the bay window. She glanced at the grandfather clock and noticed it was a few minutes after two. She wondered where Camilla was. Perhaps she'd gone shopping prior to coming to the house. She hoped so; the icebox was practically empty and Annette wanted the icebox packed before Noel returned home. She thought about cooking up a nice steak dinner for him served with baked potatoes and a fine red wine. A few bottles of wine would make the time absolutely splendid. And they could make love by the fireplace. With David watching, jealousy revealed in those clay eyes. But no children, she thought. Noel was adamant about this and they always used a condom, which brought no real pleasure other than a little more girth. Truly needed, Annette thought, thinking of Noel.

"What's wrong with me?" she whispered with a firm and angry tone and dropped her head, being sure to keep her eyes open. Open because every time she closed her eyes she saw black metallic eyes and a shudder would run through her bones. Metallic eyes like the eyes in the nightmare she'd had last night. She remembered glimpses, glimpses as real as the David statue in the corner. A child in the shape of a black spider clung to the ceiling in her bedroom, watching as she lay in bed. And in the dream she couldn't move, pinned to the mattress as someone outside the window kept chanting in a language she did not understand. She thought it could have been Latin but she wasn't sure.

She was, however, sure about the spider in the corner. A spider with a human head, a child's head with those black eyes and its teeth, children's teeth, like small pebbles, would chatter. Every few seconds they would chatter, stop, and then chatter again. Then there was the chanting outside the window. Unable to move, lying naked on the bed. The room illuminated by candles on top of tall black metal stands secured in each corner. A hand on her head, the palm and fingers small, the skin clammy, wiped beads of sweat off her brow because the room was piercingly hot, completely opposite to the cold winter winds clashing outside against the window as it was now. No, the room in her nightmare had been scolding hot, so it must have been a dream. Wasn't it, Annette?

Then a bell, like a cowbell, clunked and dinged in her ears. Continued chanting, chattering, sweaty palms, unable to move, hot sweaty naked burning skin and the clunking dinging bell. Annette finished her scotch, downed the rest of the drink in big gulps. Scotch streamed from the corners of her lips, down her chin, washing away the waking nightmare but leaving an echo, that damn clunking, dinging raging bell.

Annette jumped off the couch when someone knocked on the front door, and her glass dropped to the carpet. Heart and breath constricted as terror washed over her. She stood frozen, petrified, her breath caught in her chest, tense and constricting bones, her whole body tense. The silence in between each rap, tap, and knock lasted a lifetime while Annette stood in the sitting room, her thoughts wiped clear. All focus was on that door.

Again, the knock.

Annette was relieved when she heard Camilla's voice on the front stoop.

5

A car accident. That's how Astor died. He was found twisted in the front seat with his neck broke. The car wrapped around a tree on a dirt road just off the highway. This was according to Dr. Elliot and, of course, John made a note to check the consistency of the doctor's story. "Crows ate his eyes," the doctor had said. "Must have been a gruesome scene."

Was this a coincidence? Dead ex, kidnapped girl, arson. He suspected Alena should have been the target of many investigations but not one charge had ever been filed. He understood the way New York operated; favors and cover-ups were a part of law enforcement, but this situation seemed a bit deeper than the typical scheme. Perhaps the whitewash had implications into the department or politic rhetoric happening in the city. No one wanted a witch-hunt. McCarthyism was becoming a plague among politicians and high society New York elites. Alena had at least that much right, but the movement had yet to expand across the country, although, she seemed sure that it would. Considering Alena's Russian heritage, anyone implicated in a conspiracy or arrest would be required to make a statement and possibly even provide additional testimony in court. Perhaps this possibility alone stalled any filing of charges, to spare the innocent from blemishes on their reputation and to spare them the embarrassment of being accused of communist sympathy.

If this was the case, John knew he'd have a difficult time moving forward with any charge against Alena, even if he did prove Alena kidnapped (and possibly murdered) the DA's daughter. It could be the DA asked for the crime to be covered up. He could always be accused of giving up his daughter for favor of the communist party. *A personal sacrifice to show loyalty.* It was a stretch but not entirely impossible. People were afraid of the communist accusations being thrown around across the city. Fearful enough to tuck tail and hide, that was for sure.

See it from the DA's point of view. Your daughter's kidnapped and more than likely not among the living, why take the chance with destroying your career due to subjective ties with communism. Especially since the possible kidnapper and murderer were under lock and key. Why add more fuel to the fire? Should this assessment be accurate the DA would need to disclose how he knew Alena and perhaps these…rituals would be called into question.

What were these rituals? Alena was very specific there was no communism involved, so what *did* happen at these ceremonies?

These were the questions that rolled through his thoughts on his way to the ClairField.

————

There wasn't much to see or find for that matter. What had been the ClairField Hotel in West Harlem was no more. Nothing remained but a barren piece of land. No embers, no walls, nothing but shards of concrete and wood, now embedded in the ground within growing grass.

There's nothing here, John thought. He remembered hearing about the fire; it was in all the papers. There had even been a picture of the hotel, side by side, the first portrait was of the hotel in all its glory, bright and beautiful, the second was taken after the fire and revealed the torn desolation that ravaged through the hotel. In the time since the fire…since Alena burned the hotel down, the city must have removed the wreckage to pave the way to erecting a park.

He remarked, "Great view," as he stood in what had been the center of the hotel watching the sun descend behind the New Jersey skyline across the Hudson River. His breath frosted in the cold air. The wind off the Hudson combined with the same from the East River tore through him like an invisible knife with the purpose to freeze his bones. He noticed an eerie still quiet in the park. Perhaps, he thought, if I'm quiet enough the sounds of the past will rise from the ground and shed light on Alena's claims.

He'd seen more than his share of what he called the supernatural, although he kept such happenings under lock and key in his thoughts. Kept them to himself. It was where his insight came from and his intuition. His mother had had the gift, what she referred to as *seeing*. A concept that had taken John well into his teen years to comprehend or, rather, admit to. His father was not as open to this interpretation of the supernatural. The gift of seeing beyond plain human eyes, the *seeing* existed intuitively, displacing reality to a subjective experience of the heart.

And it manifested in his dreams. Most prominently since after the war when he officially closed off the *seeing* part of him. The ability to recognize ghosts and intuitive energies had no place in the war where he required reality, solidification of substance, and his eyes. See the enemy? Yes. Well, kill them. And do it swiftly. He required a gun and ammo, not mental psychic sensations to kill Nazis. And then the dreams started, about six months after he returned home. It was as if the seeing part of him was trying desperately to break free, to live and breathe and found its only way to remain alive, his dreams. The sleeping state where all defenses were at ease.

He remembered very little about his dreams. He always awakened with a scream – also in his head – constricted throat, his heart thumping and a cold sweat streaming from his forehead. In those moments he would attempt to remember the content of his dream. His mother, Edith, had always cautioned him to remember the meaning, the sensation, and the details, but when he wiped his forehead any remembrance dissipated, as if wiping off his forehead wiped the dreams clear.

Sometimes his hand would shake, something that was not in his control. He couldn't stop his hand from shaking. Shaking like it was now. He hadn't noticed it while watching the sun settling in for the night. His hand was shaking. Trembling as if the limb was attempting to flee.

"Stop it," he hollered watching as the sun's rays raced in between Jersey buildings to meet his eyes while night crawled awake over his shoulders in the east. *"STOP!"* He grabbed his shaking hand with his free left hand, pressing the limbs against his coat and his wrist jumped, the trembling jutted up his arm and his left hand followed it to his shoulder where the shaking ceased, returning to his hand. He considered this a personal defect. How could he shoot his gun with his hand trembling with a mind of its own? Historically reserved to those waking moments in between dreams and reality, now it was happening in a complete waking state of existence. And this event he had not anticipated.

He heard gunfire and bomb explosions. Heard screams from soldiers long gone, their essence scattered across Normandy Beach where they would haunt for eternity. Closed his eyes and he was back on the beach, scared to all mighty hell. His heart pounded so hard he felt it in his throat surfacing with acid on his tongue and his stomach churned. His head spun. He wiped his forehead with his left hand, hoping his memories would fade like those dreams had dissipated in midnight, but no such reprieve would come. John Ashton vomited on the remains of the ClairField Hotel. The sun was gone and night had taken control with an iron fist.

––––––––

His hand ceased shaking. Detective John Ashton, knees on the ground turning his suit pants wet and muddy, felt his head clear on the wings of a cold breeze. A situation he'd be sure to keep out of his report. Perhaps the release of acid-depleted eggs and toast stopped the shaking. Maybe I'm sick, he thought. Stomach bug, nothing to be concerned about. He stood up, stretching his back, and took in a deep, stuttered breath closing his eyes. With his head and thoughts clear, the sound that assaulted his ears came from somewhere far away. A child's scream. Multiple screams now. His head turned one way then another; sure he'd find someone.

Am I dreaming still?

No one was there. The screams kept coming. Louder. Like echoes across time driving a wedge through his brain. Where are they coming from? Where's the location? The beginning?

Now I'm gonna end up in the Bellevue basement. He saw pictures in his head – like the pop and crack of camera flashes – of children huddled together, their eyes wide with terror, somewhere in the darkness, locked in cages they could not escape. Saw little hands and fingers reaching through rustic moldy steel bars. Heard a roar like a lion closing in on its prey. And the children, all the children – so many in cages, so filled with fear their eyes wide, bodies trembling, whining cries and screams as horror approached – watching over the shoulder at a presence that equaled hell's pain and conviction in a bleak and dark future. And a life spent under the thumb of servitude.

John Ashton cupped his hands over his ears as if he could cease the screams. Now someone was walking. Walking outside the cages. John saw the oil lamp swaying gently by this person's side. Dull yellow light illuminated the children's eyes, the flame ingrained in their pupils. And then chanting, the voice deep and haunting….

AGIOS O BAPHOMET! AGIOS O BAPHOMET!

And the children's screams subsided. Their breathing calm, standing still, frozen like statues as the lamp was raised

AGIOS O BAPHOMET!

Their eyes followed the light as whoever was holding the lamp floated across the cages.

AGIOS O BAPHOMET! AGIOS O BAPHOMET!

In the background a single sound could be heard; of a raging goat baa, baa, baa. The children watching, their eyes turning.

AGIOS O BAPHOMET! BAA BAA! AGIOS O BAPHOMET!

The goat's call grew louder. The children's eyes turning, circling, hypnotized by the unwavering light. John's skull twisted as if a knife had been stabbed in his brain. He held his temples…pain wrenched across his face.

AGIOS O BAPHOMET!

BAA. BAA.

A cowbell now erupted. Baa. Baa. Cowbell. Cowbell.

AGIOS O BAPHOMET!

John's eyes closed trying to ward off the pain in his skull. But he could see the children, standing unprotected, watching, unmoving. Saw the whites of their eyes turn to cold black steel.

AGIOS O BAPHOMET!

Cowbell and *BAA* subsided as the scene twisted, spiraling into the children's black eyes. And the reflection in those eyes, behind the flame, at first smeared and clouded now came into focus. The hand that held the lamp masculine, thick and strong with olive skin, jutted up into a dark cloak. The hood a dark peak that silhouetted the face within.

The lips moved, chanting, *AGIOS O BAPHOMET!*

John saw his face beneath that hood. Saw his eyes as black as the children's he stared into. Heard the thick slow beat of his heart beneath a quick shallow breath. His skin burning and the twisting, tightening of his brain like a wet rag being rung dry. His eyes wet and that acidic slither tainted the back of his throat. His hands reached beneath his fedora, gripping and tugging his hair. The hat flew off, absconded by the wind.

He couldn't remove the picture of himself in that dark cloak, now a stain on the back of his eyes. The lips now a plastered toothless evil grin.

AGIOS O BAPHOMET!

Now an echo rattling between his ears.

AGIOS O BAPHOMET!

He wiped his nose and found blood on his trembling hand.

6

John Ashton returned home, poured a stiff scotch from the bottle he'd purchased on his way home. Drank it down quickly. Poured another and took a seat at his kitchen table. Laura was sleeping, and he did all he could to not disturb her. He even closed the bedroom door as softly as possible upon entrance into their one bedroom Harlem apartment. He took another pull of scotch trying to numb his thoughts. Now he understood why Knowles drank. It's all one can do to stifle the screams echoing in the mind. To silence the past and smear the constant horrific images from consciousness.

Those kids. *His* face behind the candle's flame, reflected in the children's eyes. The chanting. The BAA, BAA signaled by cowbell clunk. Screams hypnotized into silence. And the smell. That moldy damp basement clung inside his nostrils and refused to be blown away.

Go away, he thought. Get your stuff and go. Perhaps Captain Knowles was correct with his warning to not allow Alena inside his head. Rational thought concluded she'd dropped this cellar seed in his consciousness. The alternative would include a belief in something otherworldly and supernatural and an admission that he possessed an ability beyond basic instinct. He shook his head, staring into the glass he held close to his mouth. As if his answers resided within the brown liquid.

People don't come to life through statues, he told himself, as if he needed reassurance for the irrational thought process of a crazy woman. John emptied his glass down his gullet, snarled and bared his teeth. Stress deepened his eyes. He heard his father's voice telling him: There's no place in today's society for mesmerism and irrational thought. Such things only lead to hell. They can break the mind. Best to dismiss them as the devil's work. Keep your wits about you, son.

His father, a career postman and fighter pilot during the First World War, was tough and rough around the edges. He paid no mind to the irrational or to things that went bump in the night. The wind is just the wind. Not a scream from the past. Getting caught up in such temptations is a distraction from everyday responsibilities. It's a careless hobby. Women can indulge in such things, not men. Men cannot be careless; we must be rational. We must live in this world and not engage in some half concocted indulgence of useless tools. His father would always scold his mother for encouraging his *seeing* behavior.

Don't fill his mind with that poison.

Poison. He called it poison.

John filled his glass, felt the tears forming in his eyes, thinking about his mother. He swished some scotch in his mouth, swallowed and bared his teeth again, fighting with all his power to hold back his tears.

She died when he was sixteen; a victim to a cops and robbers shoot out in Hells Kitchen. A similar situation had John declared a hero and boosted his career. No citizen had died on his watch. None ever will if he could help it. Find the DA's daughter. Find her and all will be right in the world. Perhaps the screams and tears would stop then. Perhaps….Laura?

She shuffled into the kitchen from the bedroom. Tired eyes and a yawn, her right hand holding her back as if supporting that baby bump. John immediately smiled.

"Home late," she said in that soft tired tone. She went to him and kissed him.

"First assignment," he said.

She stretched her sleepy eyes noticing the bottle and glass. "Scotch?" she said and gave him an inquisitive stare.

John shrugged, "Missing kids," he said. "Helps soothe the anger."

She smiled and kissed him again.

"I'm sorry I woke you."

Laura went to the cupboard where she kept an ashtray, lighter, and a pack of Stripes. "Wasn't you," she said. "I never heard you come in." She placed her tobacco indulgences on the table including a pamphlet that bore an advertisement for a special liniment. The picture on the pamphlet featured a woman with a broad smile, happy that the liniment had relieved the woman's pain. Laura pulled a cigarette from the soft pack, her eyes, still tired, stared at her husband.

"Is your nose bleeding?"

John wiped his nose. Crusted blood fell off his fingertips. He laughed. What had he looked like to the clerk who sold him the bottle of scotch? Now he realized why the clerk had looked at him so strangely.

"Nose bleed," he said. "Probably the cold weather." John was reserved, sitting at the table with his wife. He hoped she could wipe away the screams and jarring thoughts ravaging through his mind.

Laura tugged on her cigarette. A slight cough escaped from her smoke filled throat. She blew out the smoke, "Your hat?" she said. "Did you lose it or leave it at the precinct?"

His frustration mounted; he wasn't enjoying the inquiry. "Wind took it," he said, abrupt and curt. Then, "How was your day?" wanting to change the subject.

She obliged, "Good," she said. "Back hurts and all I do is sleep." She took another drag of tobacco.

John pointed to the pamphlet. "Maybe you need some of that."

Laura first gave an unknowing stare then remembered the pamphlet she'd brought over. Her eyes lit up as she blew out her smoke. "That's right. Can I buy a few bottles? It really helps." She stretched her back against the chair. "My back throbs all day." She rubbed her belly, cigarette still burning between her fingers. "Baby girl here's sitting on my spine."

John cocked his brow. "You mean baby boy," he said. The thought of having a boy brought his smile back.

"Maybe," she said and smiled. "If you're lucky."

Lucky, John thought and glimpsed Laura's soft pack. He despised cigarette smoke. Hated the stink and smell but he understood the need for relaxation. Plus Laura's doctor had warned her against quitting when pregnant. The sudden cessation of tobacco can cause hysteria and is not good for mother or child, the doctor had said. They both heeded the good doctor's advice.

Laura looked at him as if she waited on a response. "So?" she said.

John shrugged.

"Can I purchase a few bottles?" she said pointing to the pamphlet.

John then remembered her desired question.

"How do you know it works?"

"Salesman was here today," she said taking a pull off her cigarette, exhaling smoke through her nose. "Nice man," she added. "Gave me a small sample bottle and the pain went away…quickly too. I told him to come back in a few days. Told him I had to ask my husband first."

"That was kind of you." Laura would normally purchase what she needed without consent. John rarely ever made an argument. He trusted his wife. Believed in her ability to do what was right.

"I'm a kind wife," she said, then, "So?"

John looked down, staring at the pamphlet with the cartoonish woman drawn to appear as if all was normal in normal land. Laura sucked in another wallop of smoke. His eyes returned a stiff gaze. "Sure," he said. "We can afford that now." And why not? What was he working for anyway, why go after a promotion if you weren't going to provide better for your wife who took care of you?

"Thank you," she said, her voice simple and soft, stamping out the cigarette, blowing smoke over her lips. She ran both hands through the thick bed of dark hair. Her eyes seemed to fall ever the more tired. "I'm going back to sleep." Laura stood up, stretching her back and minding the close to six-month baby bump as she did. She went to John. "Don't stay up too late," she said, leaning over to kiss him then shuffled across the tiny kitchen towards the bedroom door. "And please don't leave the light on. Wakes me up every time."

"Ok," John said, his voice soft, almost a whisper. Watching his wife with that thick stomach housing his child brought a sense of well-being. All was right in the world as long as he had his wife. And then he said, "Laura." She turned to him, both hands now holding the lower part of her back. "Why did you wake up?"

"Oh." She ran her left hand through her hair. "Bad dreams," she said. "Strange though." She shook her head. "It was about your hat."

———————

He woke up in a dizzy. Another pesky nightmare he couldn't remember. And he was glad he couldn't, the dream dissipated from consciousness on the moment of his first waking breath. Perhaps that scotch business does work. Laura stirred beside him. Uttered something about her back then drifted off to sleep. John wiped the sweat off his brow. His flannel pajamas clung to sweaty skin. He sat up, glanced at the clock on the bedside table. Three-thirty-three. The second hand ticking away seconds.

He thought of going back to sleep but knew he'd never make a return to sleep town. And then there was the possibility the nightmares would return and without liquid numbness to whitewash the surrealism associated with a sleeping state he didn't want to take a chance. Instead he rifled himself out of bed, went to the kitchen to make coffee then walked quietly and softly into the bathroom. Shit, shave, and shower in that order. Took out his second suit – *and I really hope I don't have another episode, I can't risk getting this suit all muddied up* – and dressed himself to perfection. He missed his hat. He'd waited for years to be able to don his fedora, replacing the classically worn flatfoot cap with his prize possession. He'd purchased the fedora when he was stationed in Great Britain during the war. John Ashton loved his fedora. Ironic, isn't it, he thought. Waiting so long for the privilege to wear his hat only to lose the precious garment his first day as a detective.

Probably floating down the Hudson at this very moment. I'll buy another soon enough. Get one I can wear with any color suit I buy too. He enjoyed looking sharp, something he and his father had in common. But his mother was the fedora lover. She'd always said it made a man look prestigious. He had purchased his fedora with his mother on his mind, right before his battalion was shipped off to Germany. That had been in January 1944; a few months later he'd be on Normandy Beach, and over a year later the war would end, John Ashton returned home, and the fedora would wait. Wait for him to make detective. And then…gone. Gone with the wind, literally.

Didn't last more than a day, he thought. John shook his head then pulled his tie to his throat. Waited a second then loosened the knot a bit. He drank his coffee at the kitchen table. Black and hot. The apartment seemed to sway with the wind outside his window. *Winter is definitely here.* That Halloween rainstorm not only drenched the city it dropped cold air on us like the B29 Superfortress dropped the atomic bomb.

He finished his coffee, rinsed his cup in the sink and made sure to unplug the coffee maker before he opened the door to leave. His eyes widened when he saw his hat on the floor.

7

He walked proudly with his fedora in his hands – *it's windy today, I'll limit my chances for a repeat of yesterday's loss.* A note had accompanied his precious fedora, penned by some stranger, a Good Samaritan who'd found his hat scuttling across the empty lot in West Harlem. Laura had penned their address inside his hat – maybe *she* has the ability to *see* – which must have curbed the stranger's thought of good fortune, coming across such a good find. There's still some good people left in the world now isn't there, detective John Ashton?

The note was simple – My children found your hat in the park, Mr. Ashton. We wanted to return it to you, as a gift. Such a prestigious hat should remain with its rightful owner. No signature was included; if there had been John would find the Good Samaritans and thank them appropriately. Would have brought the children a reward. Perhaps a box of Charleston Chews or tootsie rolls. But no signature meant a dead issue.

When he arrived at the precinct, he contacted the Hamptons police department to inform them he'd be arriving late morning or early afternoon. Afterward he put in for a requisition vehicle, then climbed the stairs to the fourth floor to the homicide department to speak with Detective Reilly, the detective who'd first investigated the ClairField arson. John had more than a few questions for the detective. Namely, why the cover up? And of course, did you find anything that could lead to the DA's daughter? Anything at all.

John had no care for the cover up, a more than common practice in the police department. Understanding the politics involved and the need to maintain an appropriate level of integrity in the public eye, sometimes it was better to keep certain true elements concerning life's sinister motives out of public consciousness. No one wanted a public outcry and fiasco on their hands. There was enough going on in the country already and there was no need to tip the boat. Or sink it for that matter. It was a little after six in the morning when he arrived. John hadn't expected too many detectives at such an early hour, but he was sure he could learn Reilly's whereabouts and possible schedule; even leave a message with his inquiry to speak with the detective. The homicide unit was barren; only two detectives were on the floor. One at his desk, the other by the coffee maker, filling his mug.

"What can I do for ya?" the detective at the desk inquired. Definitely Italian this guy, John thought. Dark hair, olive skin, thick mustache and dark eyes that greeted John with that inquisitive stare common with policemen.

John introduced himself, provided his credentials. "Little young to be a detective. Wait a second," the detective, one Fredo Balamini, said waving his finger at John. "You're the flatfoot that nabbed the cargo heist. Made detective on that bust, did you? Good work, rookie."

John offered his thank you while Fredo lit a cigarette. "What brings you up here?"

"Detective Reilly," John replied. "I'm working a missing children's case, and he may have information necessary for my investigation."

"Oh," Fredo leaned back; his wood chair creaked beneath his weight, blowing smoke over his lips. "Which investigation?"

"The ClairField arson." John noticed his head began to hurt. The first sign of a coming headache. Or perhaps he was getting sick; considering the weather, he would not be surprised.

"Gotcha, rookie." Fredo winked at him, took a pull off his cig and bared his teeth; something John assumed was a smile, exhaling through his nose. Fredo sat forward, flicked his ash in the tray on his desk.

"Do you know when he comes in or where I can find him?" John asked.

Fredo stared at him through narrow eyes. "How much money you got?"

John cocked his eyebrows. "Come again?"

Fredo flicked his cig again. "Because unless you've got enough money for a plane ticket to California, you won't be speaking with Reilly today."

"California?"

"Yep." He wedged the cig between his lips. "Reilly retired six months ago. Took his stuff and went out to LA. Probably to be a movie star," he laughed. "Everyone's got delusions of grandeur these days; why would he be any different?"

"Retired? Didn't know he was old school."

Fredo shook his head. "Not really. Said he came into an inheritance and took off. I'd have done the same. This weather's only good for two things, making you old real fast and making you crazy."

John's inquisitive mind went to work: Arson cover up, inheritance, retirement, California. Not out of the question to presume Detective Reilly had made out with quite a bit of cash on hand in a classic New York cover up. Of course, this was merely speculation; on the surface the official story would have to do.

"You can see the file if you want," said Fredo. "Maybe you'll find what you're looking for without the L.A. plane ticket."

John agreed to take the file, an event he could have done without although its inevitability would have surfaced whether he talked with Reilly or not. It took Fredo the better part of the hour to find the file – the file room was colossal with rows of boxes on shelves stretched to the beginning of the century- and John's head felt like a cantaloupe that dropped to the floor; dented, bruised and jumbled. Fredo handed him the file.

"You ok?" Fredo asked. "You're looking awfully pale."

"Just a headache."

"Well, this job'll definitely do it." Fredo said, then added, "Get used to 'em, rookie. Nice hat by the way."

————————

The file was practically empty. Only paper in it was Reilly's report indicating having been alerted of an arson murder by Alena. Children had died in the fire she admitted was started by her own hand. Reported he'd performed a thorough search of the hotel remains and concluded there was nothing to report. There were no children in the fire. No bones were found, no remains. Nothing! The woman – that being Alena – was off her rocker; committed to Bellevue for treatment of psychosis and schizophrenia. Also included in Reilly's report was his interview with Dr. Elliot, whose assessment of Alena described her close ties with the hotel (her final break from reality). Perhaps she attempted to save the hotel from burning, accounting for Alena's presence during the fire and this psychological break from reality resulted in the outlandish story. The report also indicated the fire department determined the fire was started by hot coals – used by the demolition crew to warm their hands – that were left unattended.

Hence, the fire department's conclusion coupled with Dr. Elliot's psychiatric assessment and the resulting property investigation where no remains were found, all led to one conclusion: Case closed. Nothing more to report. Six months later Detective William Reilly was retired and living the high life in sunny California. A fact that did not sit well with Detective John Ashton. Understanding Alena's father's philanthropic lifestyle and relationships with the multitudes of New York's high society hags, those in charge did what was necessary to not bring shame to the family name; on the surface it was a reasonable excuse for the cover up, but did not sit well, not at this moment, with Detective Ashton. Not after Alena had talked about rituals – the kind that could destroy reputations and brand prominent men heathens were her exact words - Ashton wrote them down verbatim. John had a burning thought that there was more, much more to the cover up than protecting a philanthropist's dying name.

High society was afraid of Alena and what she knew about them. Perhaps these rituals were merely strange in their content – perhaps a little more than that – but nothing as sinister as communism. Alena was quite adamant on her stance against a communistic society. Nevertheless, there were rituals that high society had engaged in and, with the rise of McCarthy, any reputation could be ruined with a simple claim. *And then there is this Golem.* And Alena was as adamant about the statue coming to life, as she was her communist rejection.

Ashton thought, do I have to entertain the idea that Alena is telling the truth about the statue? Inanimate objects do not come to life; so, this claim was accurately assessed by Dr. Elliot as the construct of a schizophrenic mind. And if this is accurate, Alena's additional claims are all called into question, and all falls apart, leading to one conclusion: Alena *is* off her rocker.

Follow up on any claims, that's what Knowles told him and to Ashton this order did not appear to indicate an elaborate cover up. It meant all leads would result in the same off her rocker conclusion. Simple logic, John thought. Simple enough at least. Finish the investigation, submit your report and receive your next assignment.

John checked the time: a few minutes after eight. The DA's office would be open or at least close to it. He decided to speak with the DA prior to driving to the Hamptons, which he was sure would be a complete waste of time. With a bit of luck he'd have his report on the Captain's desk tomorrow morning. And on his way to receiving his next assignment.

When he stepped onto the street on his way to the DA's office, John Ashton's dull headache turned his stomach the moment the ever so slight winter wind blew against his brow. He secured his fedora with his right hand, squeezing his prestigious hat over his forehead to protect against further sickness brought on by the cold. Thoughts of Reilly in the warm California sun helped to take his mind off his aching head and stomach.

––––––––

"Detective John Ashton," John introduced himself to the DA.

DA Xavier gripped John's offered had. "Pleasure to meet you, detective."

Xavier offered him a seat, which John took, taking out his notebook and pen as he did so.

"Can I offer you some coffee?" Xavier said then added, "Or tea? You look a little under the weather."

John shook his head, "I'm good, thank you."

"To each his own," Xavier replied. He sat behind his desk, a large English style desk. His chair was old wood mahogany with brown leather. Xavier crossed his legs as he regarded John, fixed his silk tie, readying himself for the interview. He was reserved from what John surmised, not like a man whose daughter was missing. Then again perhaps the DA had accepted the worst possible conclusion concerning his daughter. She had been missing for quite some time at this point. Of course there is the hope that never fades for parents who've lost a child. Until the inevitable was discovered – that she was indeed never coming home – that hope would always remain. Remain enough to follow up on any new leads, even if they did derive from the mind of a mental patient.

John flipped through his notes. The DA waited patiently. John noticed his stare was nervous, his eyes skipped from one side to the other, as if he was mulling over something more important than what detective Ashton could uncover. The wind howled outside the DA's window that overlooked downtown Manhattan, the Brooklyn Bridge a prominent feature outside the window.

"Alena Francon," Ashton began, clearing his throat. "She reported knowing you and your wife….is this accurate?"

The DA smiled and, although a thin, smug and sad smile, John thought it inappropriate, considering. He uncrossed his legs, pushed his chair closer to his desk, took up the pack of cigarettes, pulled one out and lit up, offering John one for himself which John provided the appropriate, "No…thank you."

"Not entirely accurate," the DA said. "Of course I've met her…a few times." He leaned sideways in the chair, facing the window. Took a puff from his cigarette, exhaling feverishly. The smoke hovered above the DA's head. "But never more than a handshake and a few kind words."

Ashton looked up from his notebook. "Ever engage in any…rituals at the ClairField?"

"Rituals?" The very word seemed to unnerve the DA. His voice shuddered when he said the word and John noticed he swallowed hard down his throat.

"Yes, rituals, Mr. Xavier. Alena indicated engaging in rituals…" he flipped through his notebook, "'The kind that can destroy reputations.'" He looked up, eyes roaming over the DA, ascertaining, inquiring, studying, detecting.

Xavier returned the gaze, as if he too was studying the detective. He answered simply with, "No, detective." A nervous twitch in his right eye.

John replied, "Sorry, Mr. Xavier. Understand it's my duty to exhaust all claims."

"Of course, detective. I wouldn't expect any less."

John returned to his notebook. "Tell me, Mr. Xavier, about the day your daughter went missing. How did it happen? What were the circumstances?"

Xavier inhaled, paused, then blew smoke over his lips. "I was here that day with my staff, assessing current and new cases when my wife called…frantic. She had taken Isabelle to a midtown street festival. My wife loves festivals…." John waited patiently for him to continue. Xavier flicked ashes into his marble ashtray. "She said she'd been admiring crafts and jewelry…that the stroller was unattended for a few seconds, maybe a minute, and when she went to leave, noticed the stroller was light, too light for a child to be in the seat. The baby was gone." John anticipated tears from Xavier but none came. Or he didn't allow them to come. Men don't show their emotions; it's a sign of weakness. "We haven't seen Isabelle since." Xavier turned to John. "That was almost two years ago, detective. Two years of loss, pain, and heartache."

John thought of Laura then, thought of the baby. His stomach turned septic. His headache dropped acid into his gut. He locked eyes with Xavier's dark pupils. Stared into them.

"You ok, detective? Your nose is bleeding."

John snapped his hand to his nose. Felt the wet blood above his lip. Xavier took a handkerchief from his suit pocket handing it to John.

"So sorry, sir," John said, wiping his nose and mouth. "Must be the cold weather." He wiped until his appearance was clean.

"No concern, detective," Xavier replied. He took up a small trashcan from the side of his desk and held it for John to deposit the bloodied handkerchief.

"Thank you," John said and dropped the bloodied rag.

Xavier placed the trashcan back beside the desk. "What other questions do you have, Mr. Ashton?"

John was embarrassed; felt his face turn a flushed and cold blotchy red. He tipped his hat back and noticed he was sweating. His hands trembled, nervous. He cleared his throat and continued. "Alena," he said. "I interviewed her yesterday and she claims that after seeing your daughter's picture in Sunday's edition, she recognized the child immediately. Said a person named, Golem…" John kept the statue part out of the conversation, "had taken Isabelle. Said Isabelle has been living with her and Golem since her disappearance but didn't put two and two together until she saw the article." He looked back at the DA, whose cigarette had been burned close to non-existence. Big long drags, John thought. The cherry seemed to strengthen on its own, streaming a thin line of gray smoke that rose to the DA's inquiring eyes.

"Question, detective?" Xavier said.

"Two actually. What are your thoughts on her claim? And what initiated the story appearing in the paper? After all this time, why now?"

"Noted, detective." Xavier stamped out his cigarette. He leaned back in his chair, holding his right forefinger to his temple as he leaned against his knuckles. "Alena is a brilliant artist, but like most artists, especially those with a creative genius, crazy as a loon," he said, paused then continued. "She was always gracious, but all have known for a very long time there was a sickness there. A devilish thought that seems to have ultimately consumed her. Honestly, detective, neither my wife nor I believe a word she has said. Although I have requested the manner be looked into; obviously, detective, that is why you're here. There is a rational and logical stream of consciousness where perhaps, in her insanity, she did take Isabelle. Anything is possible."

"If you don't ask the answer is always no, correct?"

"Exactly, detective," he pointed at John. "Exactly."

John gave a quick nod and a tight-lipped acknowledging grin.

"And the second question?" asked Xavier, then, "The article?" John nodded and the DA continued. "My wife," he began. "Her state of mind has been…" He tilted his head side to side. "Fragile. Very fragile since this happened. She requested the article be written. Do you have children, detective?"

John shook his head. "Not yet but soon," he replied then added after clearing his throat, "My wife is pregnant with our first."

"Ahh, I see." Xavier stared out the window. He seemed to be lost in thought. "I've always believed parenting begins the moment we discover we're having a little one of our own." He sat forward, turned in his chair, his hands now folded together on the desk. He cleared his throat. "This situation has been all too difficult to bear, Mr. Ashton. The memory of our daughter…the way she was, the joy she brought us, lives with us every minute of every day. Included with it are our fears and thoughts…one can't help thinking of the horrors she may have endured." He was staring at John with sullen and stiff eyes, void of life and sparkle. "May you never have to endure the heartache and loss of a child, Mr. Ashton. I'd never wish such a circumstance on anyone. The thought is too difficult to even fathom."

Ashton sympathized with the DA's suffering; it dropped his heart to his stomach. He forced his eyes away from Xavier's, understanding that if he continued to be captivated by the saddened depths and despair those eyes contained he'd become lost in fury and rage. And a man who does not have control of his emotions, one who gives in to blind hate, makes a lousy detective. Lousy person for that matter, because it leads to suffering, suffering on all sides of the hate coin. And John Ashton knew what he required was a clear head to do this job right, with a logical and rational mind, not emotion. Pity the man who wears his heart on his sleeve, John thought. He gathered his wits, pursed his lips, and swallowed the frog creeping in his throat.

"I'll do all I can to find your daughter, Mr. Xavier."

The DA gave a short nod, his lips curled in a frown. "I know you will, detective. My wife and I are grateful for your efforts." Xavier sighed and his eyes were blinking when he said, "Any other questions, detective?" in a solemn, soft voice.

John was uncomfortable in the DA's presence. Felt small and continued to shrink, breaking his concentration on the task at hand, nervous, as if he'd been scolded by his father. He flipped through his notes, not seeing them, just flipping, rifling through his memory for a question when it came to him. He looked up. "Golem," he said.

The DA shook his head, his eyelids fluttered. "Come again?"

John straightened his back. "During any of your visits with Alena and at the ClairField, did you ever came across or were introduced to a man by the name of Golem?"

"Golem?" the DA repeated as if he used the name attempting to recall the person. He moved his head back and forth. "I can't say that I've ever met a man by that name. I think I'd remember if I had. That is not a common name. Who is he?"

John widened his eyes. "Alena…" he said, "She reported this Golem character was a frequent guest at the ClairField. Also stated she'd taken Golem as a lover…" moved his head and body back and forth. "Under…*strenuous* circumstances."

"Understood," said the DA, adding, "I've never even heard of such a person, detective. But you never know with Alena. She's very…*eccentric*, for lack of a better word."

"Indeed," John agreed. He flipped his notebook closed.

Xavier took a cigarette from his pack. His voice seemed shaky, but who could blame him after recounting his daughter's disappearance. "Any other questions, detective?"

John paused a moment, looking over the DA whose eyes were downtrodden, as if he were following a thought to fruition. "Not at this time."

Xavier lit his cig. "Good," he said, standing, offering his hand, lit cig transferred to his left. John stood with him, taking his hand. "Where does your investigation lead now?"

"The Hamptons," John said. "To Alena's home and a thorough search of the property. I'll keep you informed." John stuffed his notebook inside his inside breast pocket. "If I have further questions, I'll be in touch and, if you think of anything more, you can reach me through the precinct."

Xavier escorted John to the door. "Thank you, detective. As I said previously, we don't expect any large revelation from Alena's claim, but we do keep up hope."

"Of course," John replied. Xavier opened the door for him.

Xavier added as John moved through the door, "Hope, detective, is all we have right now."

8

At the same time Detective Ashton was arguing with his fellow officers over not receiving a vehicle acquisition – "Sorry, rookie, if you want a vehicle you'll have to put in a request at least three days in advance" – Annette Flemming was arguing with her golden retriever, Sam. The dog was curled up in her closet, whining and gagging. The dog had been throwing up for the better part of the last twenty-four hours; he appeared lethargic and wouldn't eat a thing, not even the human food Annette offered him. Sam crawled into the closet earlier this morning and refused to come out. Annette tried all she could to coax the retriever from the closet, but with no luck.

Naturally she was concerned over the vomiting and included symptoms. What's gotten into him? Annette thought. She'd gone over the events of the last few days, at first thinking that Sam had gotten into a bag of left over Halloween candy, but she was able to string together a blurred recollection that she gave all the candy bars to little Ivan so she dismissed that possibility. Perhaps the weather, she thought; the rainstorm on Halloween night had brought winter on its heels.

"C'mon Sam, c'mon," she patted her legs, sitting cross-legged on the carpet outside the closet. All she received were more whines and one bark in between those whines. She wished her husband, Noel, were with her. Annette always felt safe with Noel. Camilla, the help her husband had hired was downstairs scrubbing the kitchen floor–a typical day for Camilla– while singing along to Nat King Cole playing over the radio in Noel's study. Perhaps Annette would feel better if there were children in the house – someone to pass the time with, someone to feel safe with. Someone more like Annette. But the Flemmings had no plan for children, not in this house or any future house for that matter. No children, husband away – again – and it all added up to one eternal aspect that Annette could not get used to: loneliness. Sam had always been her rock, her companion to pass those lonely hours and days and now it seemed he was throwing in the towel, refusing to come out and obviously sick as a dog.

Noel had called the previous afternoon, informing Annette his business was taking him from Los Angeles to Chicago. He would not be home for at least another week. Bad news for Annette; she wanted her husband. The house seemed strange since Halloween, as if the house itself had grown weary of the Flemming's presence and wanted them out. Perhaps Sam felt this too, resulting in his latest obscure behavior and sickness. Although there was good news; Noel had contacted a Long Island realtor who informed him there was a home for sale in the Hamptons – Noel's prize status, at least in his own mind. With a little luck, Noel had said, his business in Chicago would pay for the house.

Sam whimpered, and Annette could hear his breathing was heavy, his chest heaving as his heart hammered.

"C'mon Sam," Annette tapped her legs again, her voice desperate in spite of her will to project playfully for Sam to come away from the dark closet. Her eyes filled with frustrated tears she wiped clear. "Please, Sam, come out of there."

"Perhaps a doctor for Sam," said Camilla, now standing in the bedroom door. Her voice carried a thick South American accent.

Annette had been growing weary of Camilla. Her presence irritated Annette, and her suggestion fueled the irritation. Annette wanted to be left alone, not catered to in a small house she could clearly maintain on her own. Annette rolled her eyes. I don't need advice, she thought. I'll take care of Sam on my own. This thought process surprised even Annette; she'd historically been appreciative of Camilla's contribution, but today that accent annoyed her, like twisting a knife in her ears.

"It is good to give back," Noel had said. "To provide employment to the underprivileged and those who were dependent on policy with no desire for building the American dream. Take what you're given philosophy and be grateful for it; I've given you employment and a small income."

Although Annette knew this was old school philosophy, it continued to reign dominant even today. Sooner or later, policy always changed, for whose benefit would be the question.

"No, Camilla, he just needs some water and food," Annette said.

"Si, signora," Camilla answered. "Should I bring a water dish for Sam?"

"Please, Camilla, that would be great," said Annette then returned to coaxing Sam from the closet, now lying on his side in a panting fever. "Oh, Sam," she said. Perhaps a doctor is best, she thought, but neither Annette nor Camilla had the ability to drive so far out on the Island, which meant they would need to take a train. Annette hated trains; being so close to other people made her skin crawl. No need, she thought, he'll be fine, he just needs water and food. Dogs get sick just like people do, let him flush it out with a good bowl of water. Annette sighed and gave up her coaxing efforts. Just for now, she thought. If Sam isn't better within a few hours she would take the train. She went to the stairs where Camilla, dish of water in hand, was returning.

"Thank you, Camilla," Annette said allowing Camilla to pass on her way to the master bedroom.

"No problems, Mrs. Flemming," said Camilla.

Annette watched as Camilla made her way down the hall into her bedroom. "Master Sam," she said. "Water for you." Annette watched amazed as Sam hobbled from the closet to Camilla's carefully placed bowl.

"Not on the carpet," Annette said as Sam started to lap his tongue into the bowl.

Camilla looked at Annette feverishly. "It's ok, I clean," she told Annette then returned her eyes to Sam's lapping. "Water for you, Master Sam."

Annette watched Sam drink as if he'd been riding in a desert, and water was the dog's only reprieve, watched as water splashed and splattered on the carpet. Annette shook her head, her jaw tight taking the stairs down where she stopped abruptly, looking over her home. Theirs was the only house with two floors in the neighborhood, a fact she'd welcomed with pride, considering the neighbors and their untrustworthy treatment Annette experienced the day they moved in. People always have something to say, she thought then. She'd been immediately put off by the neighbors. At least she had a husband who went out and made something of himself and wasn't looking for handouts like everyone else. She couldn't wait to get out of the neighborhood. Even more she couldn't wait for the moving truck to be outside their house, for the For Sale sign to be erected on their lawn.

She pictured herself telling their neighbors they were moving to the Hamptons. *Talk about that during your Friday afternoon social gatherings. I'm sure I'll see you again when my automobile requires a tune up.*

"I've become bitter," she whispered and noticed her hands were shaking. She went to the sitting room in the front of the house where the radio now projected French horns and a saxophone melody. She picked up her latest reading venture: Ayn Rand's *The Fountainhead*, for which a growing contempt for Howard Roark kept her reading. Not her usual type of read but Annette wanted a break from Lovecraft and Poe. Especially after last night's nightmare which portrayed Annette with an iron fist – literal iron fist – hammering away at the heads of children. She'd seen her face, constricted and trembling, her eyes wide, dark and mad, enjoying every time the hammer crushed the children's skulls.

Alena had recommended *The Fountainhead* years ago. Poor Alena, Annette thought holding the book on her lap. Succumbing to illness and hysteria. Some were weak minded, others had the will of a bull to put their heads down and go for it, giving up on their pursuit the moment they stumbled. Still more just closed their eyes and wished for good to happen. And the few, like her husband, went out and made it happen. Alena had proven the latter, weak, and fragile.

Annette had been subjected to talks by the infamous Ayn Rand when Alena brought the author to the ClairField for a speaking engagement years ago, when Annette had first met Alena. Although the concept Mrs. Rand spoke of seemed reasonable, Annette was not entirely sold on the idea. Some people need their hands held, their minds are inferior, and what a tap on societal resources they were. It was best to keep them in the dark. They don't know what's good for them anyway, so little do they know and so little can they comprehend for that matter. Rand's objectivistic philosophy was a fad and nothing more, Noel had told her. It'll never gain steam. Why would anyone who's worked their fingers to the bone need to be responsible for others? Plus it rejects the existence of God. It's blasphemy.

Now that Alena was committed to Bellevue, there was nothing more to argue. See how such thought processes create a crack in the mind? Annette looked down at the book. Her eyes moved across the page, one word to a sentence, paragraph and beyond. Why continue, she thought, and slammed the cover shut, her right foot crossed over her left knee bobbing in a nervous twitch. She took a deep breath, held her head in her right palm, looking over the room and the replica statue of David Alena had given her. Sitting there now with knowledge of a Hampton's home she wished she'd agreed with Alena for the real statue of David. What a remarkable gift that would be, story too for that matter as the real David would be a conversation piece all her life. All who entered her home would remark on the statue, and her good fortune for securing it. She dropped the book on the coffee table then sat forward a moment while staring at David. He looked so honorable and noble, calm and courageous. She stood up; arms folded together and walked closer to the replica.

Now Camilla started hollering, "Mrs. Flemming, Mrs. Flemming, it's Master Sam...please come...please," in that accent that drove Annette wild with rage.

Annette rushed to the stairs whispering under her breath, "Can't do anything right," on her hurried way up, and "What is it, Camilla?" while she trampled down the hall.

"It's Master Sam," Camilla called. "He's bleeding."

"Bleeding?" Annette repeated and hurried to the door. Camilla was holding a limp Sam in her arms. The water dish was spilled over into what looked like clumps of red vomit and bile. Camilla had tears in her eyes. She must have been hit with a wallop of bloody vomit because she had blood and bile smeared on her arms and pretty little yellow dress.

"Mrs. Annette," Camilla said to her, looking at Annette through a wall of tears. "He no breathing."

She wanted Camilla to stop crying. *Why is she crying? It's not her dog.* Annette tilted her head, taking in the scene of vomit, water, limp dog, and a bloodied tearful Camilla. Annette thought, she's probably more concerned she'll lose her job than what happened to Sam. Frustration mounting, her carpet was more than likely ruined. *It'll have to be replaced before we sell.* She moved her head back and forth, arms now crossed across her stomach, gritting her teeth.

Camilla screamed, "What do we do?"

Annette's eyes jolted to the window. She wondered if her neighbors could hear Camilla's screams and she was not pleased.

"Stop it, Camilla," Annette said in a constricted angry tone. Camilla looked up at her, let out another whimpering cry, which she attempted to stifle. Eyeing Annette she was able to calm herself. Her breathing, at first in a fury, now started to subside to normalcy. Annette took in the scene, shook her head and went to the window where she observed there was no one on the street. She turned back to Camilla, who used all her might to calm herself down.

"What do we do?" Camilla said as calm as possible. Her voice reflected a feebleness that further irritated Annette.

Now Annette was contemplating a simple solution. Sure she was furious over Camilla's apparent outburst and with every held back whimper she wanted to dismiss her immediately and get her out of her house, forever banished for being a true annoyance, especially under duress. Annette shook her head when the thought surfaced. *If I banish her I'll have to bury this dog myself.* She drew in a deep breath. *Sam is dead*, she thought. *What do you do with the dead? You bury them.* Of course, Annette wasn't digging the grave.

Annette went to Camilla, knelt down on the carpet – away from the blood, vomit, bile and spilled water – and put her hands on Camilla's shoulders. "It's ok," Annette said. "Go to the garage," she said. "Get the shovel. We'll need to bury him in the backyard."

Camilla sniffled. "We'll give him a burial and say some prayers." Annette smiled. "Ok?"

"Si, Mrs. Annette."

After all what else could they do? What could Annette do? It was better to keep Camilla on her side than send her packing.

————————

"Ashton!" Captain Knowles practically hollered his name interrupting John's argument with his fellow officer over the vehicle he required for his Hamptons investigation. If he had no vehicle, he'd have to take the train, prolonging his trip by at least a few hours. Everyone in the precinct stopped and took interest in the Captain's possible scolding of the new detective.

John stood at attention. "Yes, Captain?"

Knowles' shoulders seemed to ease up. "Your girl's off her rocker," he said.

"My girl?" John repeated. "Laura?"

Captain shook his head. "Not your wife, rookie. Alena, the one you interviewed yesterday. Dr. Elliot called this morning, said Alena's gone completely out of her mind since your little visit yesterday. Tried to escape last night and refuses to talk to anyone but you. Tell me, rookie, why would that be?"

John's jaw hung open. "I've no idea," he said. "All I did was take her statement. Now I'm following up on her claims. That's what you said, isn't it?"

Captain moved his head back and forth. "Rookie crap," he said. "Get down there and talk to Elliot. Alena, too, if you have to."

John stepped forward. "I've got all I need from her, Captain." His voice was low like a feeble child being scolded by abusive parents.

His response elicited a stern, don't defy me stare from Knowles. John raised his hands before Knowles could respond. "Ok," he said. "I'll go."

Captain Knowles looked him over; eyeing John suspiciously then disapprovingly shook his head. "Clean yourself up, boy," he said. Ashton remembered the dried blood crusted inside his nostrils. "Have some dignity, for Christ sake."

9

Alena paced back and forth in the office John Ashton was provided, this one even smaller than the first. His arms crossed over his chest as he sat, watching Alena basically sprinting from one side of the office to the other.

"He was here...I can't believe it..."

Detective Ashton had no idea why he was in the room with her; he's not a medical professional like Dr. Elliot; what could he possible provide to calm Alena down? Nonetheless Dr. Elliot had insisted John talk to her. "She won't speak with anyone but you, detective. She's very adamant about it. And after last night's events, my staff could use a reprieve from her exploits." Alena had been caught attempting to break one of the basement windows. The orderly on duty had taken a few fists to the nose – he was now at home, nursing his bruised ego. "Just try to get her to calm down and talk with us."

John's first thought was to suggest Dr. Elliot provide the necessary intravenous cocktail and put her in bed for the day. Problem solved, but he dismissed the suggestion, not wanting to overstep any possible boundary. As far as John was concerned his dealing with Alena Francon was over; he'd received all the necessary information his investigation required and he had to go out to the Hamptons—now by train no doubt—and his frustration was mounting. How do you calm someone who's clearly out of their mind? Dr.

Elliot suggested listening. That was all just *listen*. Let her get out what's eating her alive and all will be fine. She'll retreat to her room and carry on as usual. Dr. Elliot had also suggested an alternative procedure that according to Dr. Elliot "is becoming exceedingly necessary should Alena continue such violent behavior towards staff."

And again, John shrugged. "You're the doctor, not me," which had no impact on curbing Dr. Elliot's insistence that John speak with Alena. Now he was in a room with an apparent insane person and John wondered what he'd do if Alena tried punching *him* in the face. He would not take kindly to such an event.

Just listen, he told himself. And get out of here as quickly as possible.

"Calm down Alena," John said. "Take a seat. Tell me what you need to tell me."

Alena eyed John, grabbed the back of the chair and just about flung it against the back wall had she not dropped it down hard against the floor. Flustered, John sat back, thinking this conversation may have ended right then and there. Alena dropped onto the seat, scratched the legs against the ground when she jutted closer to the table that separated the two occupants then ran her hands through her hair, patting her cheeks afterward as if she had to wake herself up. John's eyes were wide, his nose curled in disbelief over Alena's mental state. He sat back and tipped his hat further back on his head. Alena blurted Russian rambling in rapid succession.

"Alena," John said, "English, please."

Alena seemed to calm down instantaneously as if whatever had been eating away in her mind was suddenly wiped clear from the eyes. Her shoulders eased, and the bones in her face appeared to relax although her eyes carried a darkness to them, staring at John. No, John thought, staring *through* me. He wondered if she could tell there was a tinge of unease and uncertainty behind his eyes.

She stared at John for a long while, always looking straight into his eyes as if she were surveying and studying the edges of his pupils, looking deep into each iris, searching for something. *A sign of life, maybe. I've no idea.* He cocked his eyebrows, waiting for Alena to finish her inspection and begin to speak.

Her voice was soft although stern when she said, "Did you sleep well last night, detective?"

John shook his head. "I don't see how that's relevant, Miss. Francon."

Alena ran her hands through her hair as if she needed to reset her position. John quiet, waiting, anticipating, his right hand shaking. Ashton hid the trembling hand beneath the table on his lap, dreading what she would say next. Yes, there was a nightmare, although he had no recollection of the contents of the dream; he'd had nightmares off and on since the war.

Just listen. John heard Dr. Elliot's voice. *Just listen.*

Alena appeared to be running through multiple scenarios; her eyes kept jutting from one side to the other as if with each new thought her eyes skipped. John was becoming increasingly impatient. His eyes wide as he shook his head, frustrated. He sighed, breathed hoarse as his nostrils flared. "Alena…"

She put her hand up to stop him from continuing. "Please," she said. "There's so much I need to tell you, I'm not sure where to begin."

John tightened his jaw with a subtle and slow nod. "Why don't you begin with what happened last night? That's why you asked me to come, isn't it?"

Alena's eyes widened as if she'd forgotten this vital piece of information. "That's only the end of it," she said. "There's more you need to know. Everything. You need to know it all."

"Know all of what?" John snapped. *I don't have time for this.*

She slumped forward as if John Ashton's tone was cause for alarm. As if she'd already lost whatever game she was playing. He waited. Silence. She had that look in her eye again. John did not like that stare. Not at all. It made his skin crawl.

"Listen," John said and stood. "I don't have time for this." He took a step to the door. "Talk with Dr. Elliot," he said, his hand on the doorknob.

"He's coming for you, detective." Alena's tone harsh and subtle. John froze, and looked back. Alena was watching him. Although her body had not moved, her eyes were fixated on him. A single tear formed in her right eye, welled over the eyelash and ran across her cheek. "That's why you need to hear this. All of it."

He shook his head. *Did she just threaten me?* He wanted to pull out his model 10 .38 special and put a bullet in her head right then and there. No orderly would object to him doing so, that was for sure. Although the moment this thought raged within him, the sad and petrified stare in Alena's eyes told him to sit down and listen. Just listen, remember. He sat back down, sitting stiff like a statue. His bones and muscles tense.

"Well," he said and crossed his arms. "What story do you have to tell me, Alena?"

She forced down a swallow, her throat moved as if she struggled to do so. Then took an unnaturally long and deep breath when her eyes closed then opened with an exhale that revealed a deep and dark sadness behind them. "I have to tell you, detective." Another swallow, this one delivered with more ease than the first. Shallow breath. Her lips trembled, her voice cracked when she said, "The story of Golem."

Part II

Alena Francon
10

Manhattan
June 1947

Alena Francon lost her mother to tuberculosis when she was twelve years old. After her mother's death—before which Alena had cared for her ailing mother, assisting with pounds on the back to wrench the pieces of lungs wedged in her throat—Alena took on a dual role as daughter and care taker to her father, Fredek. A role for which she had been exceedingly qualified; Alena possessed a natural ability for compassion, understanding and encouragement. And this gentle although tough and savvy exterior transferred to her ability to entertain and welcome guests to the ClairField, the prestigious hotel and restaurant Fredek had secured on lease from the city. In fact, it had been Alena who recommended the restaurant provide cuisines suitable for and affordable to all residents of New York. Some—some being Fredek's many high society associates—had dismissed the idea to welcome the underprivileged to dine within the prestige associated with the ClairField. They were ultimately proven wrong. Alena's concept not only saved the

ClairField—and Fredek's investment—it brought new life to the hotel.

Fredek Francon brought his family – and his riches - to New York after the First World War, where he prospered in a multitude of business ventures including—as secretly as it had been kept—bootlegging and gambling. Despite his pristine reputation among politicians, he'd kept his gambling racket open after prohibition until his untimely death from brain cancer in 1944. Alena, a young and ambitious artist of twenty-four, had cared for her father whom she loved dearly and, in spite of a large family remaining in Russia (whom Alena had never met), when Fredek Francon's battle was over and done, Alena had experienced something she'd never thought was possible: loneliness.

Perhaps it was this loneliness that ultimately brought William Astor into her life. Not long after Alena had gracefully and tearfully provided a final goodbye to her father, William Astor walked into her life, filling the void and sorrow the past kept hidden in a box. Yet William Astor was not—according to Alena's social circle—the perfect match for Alena. The two were complete opposites, butting heads on a multitude of issues, and most specifically on the issue of philanthropy. William believed the art of philanthropy was to provide fuel to reputation while Alena believed philanthropy to be a duty any and all with privilege should provide out of pure delight and pleasure. Alena was a compassionate and elegant hostess, William a cold and cynical pessimist whose only thought was how society could benefit him most and which future venture would provide the maximum capital to add to the ever-growing family prestige. William also had the reputation to indulge too much in the drink—there had been several occasions when the family had to retrieve a rather drunk and ultimately degenerate William Astor from the country club his family attended.

Nevertheless, the couple gathered together a guest list of the highest social caliber to social gatherings hosted at the ClairField—mostly, this guest list appeared after the dinner crowd completed their cheap meal. In April 1947 Alena and William learned of Alena's pregnancy—a delightful event kept out of the public eye. A child out of wedlock would not be hailed in 1947 but would be seen with the utmost sneers, judgments and jeers, and there was the suggestion made by William to abort the pregnancy. A suggestion that resulted in countless arguments. Alena wanted the baby, wanted a child of her own; those natural caretaker instincts galloped into overdrive with the simple thought that a child was growing inside her.

After much reluctance and continued argument by William, he agreed that if this baby is coming, they needed to marry, and do it soon. They could always inform the public the child had been conceived on their wedding night. Their wedding was scheduled for late June. An event that would never occur. Although the fairy tale wedding approached with the gracious glamor associated with American royalty, less than a week before the planned wedding, Alena's condition would prove ultimately to twist and spiral toward a fate never conceived by Alena. And this demise, this twisted spiral into hell's fury all started with a drink prepared with the closest precision and the most dutiful eye from the most desperate of people. Seven days before the wedding, Alena would meet the gypsy woman.

––––––––

Maleva Ouspenska would prove to be the catalyst that altered Alena's fate. Mid-June arrived with a hint of summer off the heels of spring, and Greenwich Village was hosting a street festival in honor of the Beat Generation counter culture that held fast to the village. The energy was freedom, love, and intellectual sovereignty through artistic expression. Alena felt right at home in a place where societal rank and class systems were impenetrable in this small corner of the world. She was able to drop the façade and be herself, if for even one afternoon. Her friends, Jacqueline (or Jackie), Crystal, and Hanna—also Alena's would-be bridesmaids—were not as open to the movement, calling it silly and desperate and, of course, immoral.

They referred to the movement as a typical fad— brought on through a fog of reefer madness—that would lose momentum once the "kids grow up and need to care for themselves and families. Then they'll scatter, scurry, and run to the nearest suit and beg for a career." Such judgment always brought the same reaction; Alena's rolling eyes and often embarrassment, especially when the bridesmaids would sneer and snicker at the locals. She knew they did not want to be in the Village, but she kept pushing to continue. She wanted to buy a fabulous piece of art or jewelry finely crafted by one of the "locals." They purchased not one item with the excuse that any item bought here and produced by such weary hands would never find a mantle, table, or wall in their homes. High art to them was fashioned by those of high quality and social status. "We have the Mona Lisa, why bother with the miniscule color representations of a dying generation?"

She wanted to run from them. Or keep them in the Village as long as possible, tie them in, and never allow them to leave. Maybe then they'd conform and accept the counter culture. Sometimes you have to beat stupid out of people for them to wise up. Most often there's no getting through to hardheaded stubborn judgments. People only see what they want to see and put on blinders when discussing alternative possibilities as if they shouldn't be bothered with someone else's opinion. When you're part of the elite, all the answers reside in what you have. The more you have the more you know and those who have nothing know nothing.

Alena was fed up within the first hour—plus morning sickness seemed to have a mind of its own, never reserved solely to morning—her growing irritation ramped into overdrive when they came upon the goat.

"Who keeps a goat in New York City?" Laughter and giddy sneers from the bridesmaids.

"It's the village," Jackie said with laughter in her voice, "Maybe it's to sacrifice when the sun goes down."

Crystal yanked the rope tied around the goat's snout. "Black goat. Black goat," she said. The goat returned with a baa baa and kicked its hind legs eliciting further laughter. Alena was not pleased.

Neither was Maleva for that matter. Maleva Ouspenska tore out of her shop. Hanging bells on the door burst into jingles and caught Alena's attention.

"You leave him alone," she hollered in a thick Polish accent. Her bony finger raised, scolding the bridesmaids who stepped back from Maleva's protest. Scowls replaced their laughter. "He's good boy." Maleva turned her attention to the goat, petting the animal's head and chin. The goat gave a sympathetic baa as if the animal said thank you, acknowledging Maleva's protective behavior.

The bridesmaids glared at Maleva. Alena's eyes narrowed. She stepped closer to Maleva.

"*Pozhaluysta, prosti ikh, oni nevezhestvenny*," said Alena to Maleva who turned to Alena, her hand still on the goat's chin. (Please forgive them they are ignorant.)

Maleva studied Alena. Looked her up and down. Her gaze stopped when her eyes met Alena's. "*Nevezhestvo ne opravdyvayet zhestokosti*," she shot back. (Ignorance is not an excuse for cruelty.)

Alena paused, looking over her bridesmaids and their narrow stares. They could have the gypsy's shop closed down Monday morning if they wanted to. It was that simple, a phone call to the Mayor by way of their fathers or significant others and this gypsy woman was out on the street, goat in tow. Alena wanted the situation diffused as quickly as possible. She returned her gaze to Maleva. "Agreed," she said and gave a quick acknowledging nod.

Maleva maintained her study of Alena, assessing and scrutinizing as Alena forced a sincere comforting stare in return, allowing the assessment in an effort to prove all was right in the world-or, at least in this particular situation. Alena's eyes then caught sight of Maleva's and Alena's eyes now narrowed, intrigued.

Both of Maleva's eyes were a charming crystal blue, although her right eye shared the blue with a deep black on the top right corner of the iris. Sectoral heterocrhomia, Alena thought. When one iris has shades of a separate color. This abnormality provided Maleva with a depth of character that elicited a mysterious and enigmatic response. Possibly it was a part of the show — the sign in the shop's narrow window read "Palm Reading" — that Maleva relied on to engage her customers. Those beautiful crystal blue eyes captured the customer and welcomed further inquiry. Further inquiry resulting in a tilt of the head accompanied with a studious gaze that lead to the tiny compartmentalized black of her eye. As the blue was welcoming and inviting, the black drew you in and captured your attention as if the black were a trap door; once you locked in on it, you fell through in a blinding mesmerized state of trance. A trap door in the back of the eye.

And that's when she got you. To shell out more of that hard-earned cash.

The goat's baa, not once but twice, broke the ladies' concentration. Alena noticed Maleva now looked at Alena's stomach.

"You…" she said, her voice soft, sympathetic, and as she cocked her head her gaze moved from Alena's stomach to her eyes. "Need reading?"

Alena covered her stomach with her hand and forearm. She knows, Alena thought. Not even the bridesmaids knew.

———————

It was necessary to maintain secrecy. William and his family required for the pregnancy to remain a secret to protect the family reputation against all outside influences. As a result, Alena jumped at the chance for a palm reading, shushing the bridesmaids when their protests reached a fevered pitch. Alena promised the bridesmaids she'd meet them at the ClairField for a late lunch—honestly the best possible way she could get rid of them. Alena's interest was piqued with Maleva's ability to know she was pregnant. How could she know? At three months pregnant Alena had barely started to show and even what did show was manifested in a slight fattening of the stomach, which Alena had explained away as a stress response to planning an on the spot wedding. Not the best excuse but it did work. The bridesmaids had their mothers to help with all the preparations needed to plan a wedding, or any event for that matter. Alena had no one. Of course, William's mother helped her along, as much as Alena would allow. Truthfully, Alena secretly despised William's mother and all the prejudices and judgments behind each and every decision the woman made.

William's mother had said to Alena, "Don't feature lilies, they are out of season", and William's grandmother would scoff at having such a flower featured at her grandson's wedding. "Don't have a buffet, it signals a poor vocation. Can we have the ClairField prepare a finer menu?" Of course Alena succumbed to the requests—demands rather—

although reluctantly. In the end she wanted her wedding to happen without a hitch, and she wanted the event to pass without revealing the pregnancy. With only a week until the wedding, she couldn't have a palm reader giving up her secret so she jumped at the palm reading offer to shut down the situation, believing if she hadn't, Maleva would have continued her inquiry and allowed the proverbial cat out of the bag.

Maleva's store was small, tiny even, allowing for a small table with the expected crystal ball on top, three chairs (Alena guessed she read the palms of couples), and shelves on the side and back wall where a door led to a back room. The door consistently drifted open and closed, leaving a few inches between open and closed. Alena surmised there was another door in the very back of the shop that was open ushering in a wind that continuously rifled against the shop's back door. She strained to see what was behind the door but all she could see was black darkness. Hair on the nape of her neck cringed across her skin; her eyes wide, staring, breath constricted and her heart skipped a beat. Something eerie about that room. Alena had thought someone was in the back room, watching and listening. Possibly another goat or friend or family member? She couldn't help that her attention was drawn to the darkness every time the door gently flapped open then closed again.

She attempted to distract herself from that eerie feeling by looking over the many trinkets, crystals, beads, incense, and candles displayed on the shelves, while Maleva sat at the table, lit a cigarette, and prepared for her customer. Maybe it was Maleva's eyes roaming over Alena that brought that eerie sensation. Perhaps all of the above contributed to the same resulting in Alena's nervous disposition. She locked in on a small wooden statue of a gypsy woman with a crystal ball featured on her lap.

"You like?" Maleva said. "For protection," she added. "Gitana is the gypsy who protects."

The statue woman featured a fair and trusting face, solemn and soft. The door flapped closed with a slight brush of wood against wood, then creaked back open.

Alena forced a smile, sensing Maleva was in tune with Alena's nervous demeanor, as if Maleva could see straight through her. The goat gave a baa baa.

"Does he always do that?" asked Alena.

"Of course," Maleva said. "He is goat."

Alena dropped her shoulders. "Of course," she said and turned to Maleva. Although she'd released the tension with an obvious inquiry, that tension returned when she took in Maleva's gaze. Cigarette smoke framed her countenance, and Alena's eyes stared at Maleva through the haze. Alena's stomach twisted with a sharp pain and that damned morning sickness slithered into her throat.

"Sit," Maleva said, motioning to the chair opposite her. The door creaked open and cold wind rushed into the shop. She thought she heard the clunking of a cowbell.

Alena gathered herself and went to the seat. "How does this work?" she asked, taking her seat as a wallop of smoke circled her head. She coughed into her fist, a dry hacking cough that brought tears to her eyes forcing Alena to clear her throat as if something had been wedged in her windpipe.

Maleva seemed to not care about this raging smoke-filled room she'd put together for her customers. She puffed again, smoke slithering into her lungs, then billowing over yellow teeth and then she exhaled through her nose. She stamped out the cigarette.

"Your hands, please," she said, cupping her hands across the table on opposite sides of the crystal ball.

Alena froze. The door creaked closed with a light soft thud against the doorframe then opened again, catching Alena's attention. Whatever was behind that door filled her heart with fear and terror. Her eyes searched through the door crack, looking for something, or someone behind the door, in the room, watching and listening. She had a rising thought that the room breathed on its own; that the wind was its breath and the door its lungs, holding its bated breath in apt anticipation.

"It's ok, we are alone."

Can she read my mind too?

Maleva moved her head back and forth. "We are safe here, no intruders are welcomed."

The door creaked closed. Alena's hands trembled when she placed them within Maleva's. The gypsy's hands were cold. The skin like crepe paper, thin but rough like sandpaper with long fingers and nails gnawed down to the nub.

The goat baa'd as the door creaked open. And those eyes, Maleva's eyes, the blue seemed to gleam with a glint of crystal light. And then the trap door.

Alena attempted not to look. She tried to turn her eyes away but the black drew her in.

"You've endured great tragedy." Maleva's voice, her attention fixed on Alena's left hand. "Have you lost those who are closest to you?" Her voice more matter of fact than probing.

Alena cleared her throat. "My parents," she said.

"You were caretaker, yes?"

Alena's hands shook. "For my mother." Her body and bones tense as if the subject was too taboo, too painful to delve into. As if she could hide the pain and memories, close up her heart and shut the door on her thoughts.

Maleva's eyes moved from the palm to Alena's eyes. Slight and brief, as if she felt the constriction. Alena pursed her lips and forced a nervous smile that screamed, "Don't go there." Felt her face flush and grow cold as beads of sweat formed on her upper lip and her stomach turned uneasy, gurgling acid to the back of her throat. Maleva returned to the palm.

"Yes, when you were very young. She was sick?"

"Tuberculosis."

Maleva turned her head, eyeing the palm lines, following them with her eyes. "Your father, too. You took care of him. For long time. Being caretaker is natural for you." She pointed at Alena with her left forefinger. "It is purpose."

Alena gave a quick nod, although Maleva's attention was maintained on the palm that she studied with apt intrigue. Another baa outside the shop and the door creaked closed. Alena's skin hot, stomach acid now slithered to the back of her teeth. Her hand shook again, and Maleva tightened her grip to steady the hand. Alena winced.

"You are very loving person. You care for others more deeply than yourself."

Maleva's eyes widened as she ran her hands up Alena's forearm, her thumbs pressing against flesh and cartilage through to the bone, then back down to the wrist where her fingertips brushed across the palm. Alena cocked her brow. Is this a part of the show? She wanted to throw up, to vomit without restriction. Her lips quivered, wanting this reading to end as soon as possible. Needing the reading to end so she could throw up.

Now Maleva took Alena's right wrist, touching the palm with her fingertips. Alena noticed the bones in her left hand ached.

"Two children," Maleva said and she leaned back in her chair pulling Alena's wrist further across the table. "You will be responsible for two."

To this Alena perked up, despite the gnawing sickness. "Boy or girl?"

"Both," said Maleva.

Alena dropped her head satisfied with this response.

"No married," Maleva said.

Alena was unsure if this response was a question or statement. She said, "Next Saturday."

Maleva looked at her, inquisitive, skeptical as if she knew something Alena did not.

"Our wedding is next Saturday. We haven't told anyone that I'm expecting. We decided to wait until after our honeymoon."

To this statement Maleva's lips curled into a smile as if she possessed a revelation she did not wish to share with Alena. Alena shuddered under the shadow of that knowing grin and noticed how Maleva's eyes changed, as if something devious tried to force itself from a heart filled with locked chambers.

Maleva cocked then bowed her head. "Congratulations," she said. "You hide pregnancy from ignorant friends?" She released Alena's wrist and Alena immediately pressed her hand to her stomach.

"Of course," she said. "They are my friends but there would be judgments, and my fiancé's family will not allow the news to be made public. Not yet anyway."

Maleva moved her head back and forth. "No good," she said. "No good for baby. Brings bad energy to baby's health, pretending baby does not exist. In gypsy life pregnancy is celebrated, husband or not."

The statement hurt yet she felt small under Maleva's stare. Alena thought, don't judge me and thought of defending herself and her way of life although she agreed with the gypsy. When she'd first discovered her pregnancy she wanted to tell everyone, especially her friends. It was a time for celebration. Maleva was accurate in this regard, yet societal norms had to be adhered to. Alena understood this, too, and being judged for her decision boiled her blood. Her face turned red with compounded blood pressure. She said, "We're not gypsies. We live in a community of judgments. Everyone waiting for the next scandal so they can have something new to talk about." She needed to defend her friends and their way of life, and

Maleva seemed to take offense to the comment, her brow curled into a scowl.

"Perhaps gypsy life is best for you," said Maleva.

Alena laughed, a simple abrupt laugh filled with immediate regret. Maleva's eyes narrowed as Alena cleared her throat. "I'm not suited for such a life. That would be a drastic change."

"Change is good," Maleva said and then her eyes widened. "Change comes to you if like or not."

Alena shuddered at this last comment. The baa followed by the door creak and soft thud. Her head spinning, over stimulated and heated. "What does that mean?" she thought, too afraid to ask. She crossed her arms over her stomach and her spine twisted, stiff and painful. Maleva tipped her head, glaring at Alena. Her eyes seemed to shimmer, to circle and spiral as Alena wrestled with the thought to delve into the trap door. Instead, she avoided the black compartment fixed to Maleva's right eye, the skin beneath the eye thick as if a vein swelled beneath. She thought she heard voices swirling in the darkness, in a room behind the trap door, speaking soft yet rapid, incoherent, perhaps chanting, ushering in darkness with depths of despair. Images of ghouls, goblins, and demons standing, with black eyes staring, glaring, and chanting and lapping tongues across serrated teeth and purple chapped and cracked and bleeding lips in an endless sea of darkness where hate, terror and suffering reigned over the sea like a god of despair and wretchedness, twisting hatred in the emptiness where a heart should be. And when she moved back to take in the full view of that dark room she saw that the sea continued for what seemed an eternity.

Alena's eyes were wide, the room started spinning, circling. She could hear a continuous alarm like a dull ringing between her ears.

Maleva's lips moved. Her voice a lifetime away. Alena tried to read those lips. Her heart racing as if her body were aware of a threat her mind had yet to discover. Her head heavy, her neck stiff, and when she tried to move her head refused to move, restricted as acid tore into the back of her teeth and her throat swelled as if the windpipe was being squeezed and air was required.

And then the drop, as if she returned to her body with a heavy thud. Her eyes rolled, and she threw up on that crystal ball. Her head, sweaty and heavy, flopped side to side as her body fell back. Maleva caught her before she hit the floor.

"My dear," Maleva said, cradling Alena.

That buzzing and ringing softened. Behind it a loud clunking like a cowbell furiously clanking.

In unison with a continuous baa.

Alena fell through the trap door. And darkness followed.

11

She awakened with a heavy gasping inhale. Alena had been placed on a cot, which she surmised was in the shop's back room. Sweat beaded her face and forehead. And she felt sick, her stomach wrenched, and her head weary. Maleva, her back to Alena, stirring a pot on a small half stove on the far end of the room.

"You sick," Maleva said continuing to keep her back to Alena. Daylight struggled to find its way into the room through the room's single window that had either been painted black or was covered in soot from years of neglect, giving a dark soft glow to the room that could not have been any larger than six feet by five feet.

She remembered vomiting. Remembered passing out in Maleva's arms.

Whatever Maleva was concocting she mixed frantically as if the recipe called for furious mixing or she was hurried due to a lack of time. "I'm making a tonic. It'll help with the sickness." Her voice was different, hoarse, but somehow high pitched as if there was a snicker behind the thickness. "Old gypsy remedy," she said pouring the liquid into a small cup. The scent was God-awful; it turned Alena's stomach into a wrenching, grinding twist of boiling acid. Alena draped her legs over the side of the cot. The cement floor was cold to her bare feet. She wondered where her shoes were. She held her head in her left hand, her right hand across her stomach.

"Always safe..." Maleva said forcing the cup into Alena's left hand. "For those with child."

The dark liquid steamed from the cup. Alena turned her nose away.

"Drink," Maleva said. "You will be better soon."

I want to go home, Alena thought. To lie down in her own bed, beneath the sheets and nurse herself back to health. To comfort her baby.

"Drink," Maleva repeated forcing Alena's hand—and cup—to her lips. "You have fever."

She was hot, burning even, her head seemed to weigh a thousand pounds, difficult to hold up, and she was fighting off the need to flop back down on the cot and stay. Alena wanted her own bed, not this decrepit cot in this small dark back room. Not with the gypsy woman. Away from the darkness to the comfort and light of the ClairField where she'd always felt strong and delighted.

"Drink," Maleva said. "Drink and feel better."

Alena stared into the cup through wet, narrow eyes. Steam rose from the cup and circled her head, as if the steam forced her head down and her lips to the brim. The thought of her mother passed through her mind. She'd always possessed an aggressive demeanor. If her mother were here now she'd be telling Maleva exactly where to stick her cup. But she wasn't here. Alena was alone. Alone with the exception of Maleva, standing and hovering like a brick wall, guarding against Alena's escape.

Or attempting to stay Alena's eyes from the goat in the corner sitting on its hind legs wrapped and shaded in darkness. The room buzzed with waves of unrelenting continuous vibrations. A slight humming beneath the buzz as Alena's eyes rolled behind limp eyelids then resurfaced on the goat. Its chin raised high and proud, the goat watched Alena through the corner of its black eyes as if anticipating Alena's response. No baa, only silence, and Alena noticed a cowbell tied around the goat's neck. She thought the goat smiled but dismissed the notion. Maleva brought the goat inside when Alena passed out. Why wouldn't she, after the bridesmaids' taunts? Of course she would demand the goat come inside.

She could never remember drinking, but she knew she did. She remembered the taste, like drinking liquid dirt and the pain that followed. Like acid depleting her insides. Remembered hearing Maleva say, "Good girl. Good girl," as she took the cup from Alena's hand. And how Maleva changed then as if somehow she'd become lighter and younger as if the stress of old age was torn from her thoughts.

Maleva escorted Alena through the shop where sunset beamed through the windows with a gold tint that drove the beat generation into a frenzied cycle of cheer and high energy.

Sunset, Alena thought. How long have I been here? She remembered telling the bridesmaids she'd meet them for a late lunch and now evening was ushered across the city. She couldn't recollect the last few hours. Had she been sleeping the entire time? She stood at the door, almost afraid to leave and venture through the street festival. She thought they'd pass judgment, thinking she was some fall-down high society drunk.

"A gift for you," Maleva said, standing behind her.

Alena turned and Maleva was holding that small statue, the gypsy statue she'd said provided protection.

"Will you take it?" Maleva again, her eyes staring. Alena thought she looked younger.

Will she ever let me leave? Alena thought. She took the statue. And Maleva smiled, her head bowed. "Manners, my dear," Maleva said and for a brief moment Alena was confused. A perplexed gaze on her countenance. "For the statue," Maleva said. "A gift."

Alena looked at the statue in her hand and those beady little eyes that watched her. She wanted to smash the statue and run; to curse Maleva for whatever had taken place in this shop; for whatever atrocities Maleva had subjected her to while unconscious. Alena's skin crawled. Felt that stinging pain in her stomach.

"Thank you," Alena said in a soft hush.

Again, a smile from Maleva and Alena noticed how white her teeth now were as the memory of Maleva's yellow grin passed through her thoughts. Alena squeezed the statue.

"You go," Maleva said. She opened the door for Alena.

"Go," she repeated. "And may the gods be with you."

————————

But God was nowhere to be found. Alena did make it back to the ClairField; how she could never be certain. The moment she breathed clean air her body wrenched as if whatever concoction Maleva dredged up kicked into overdrive with the addition of clean air.

She'd managed to enter the ClairField before the evening rush where she was brought to her living quarters—the top floor – with the aide of the ClairField personnel.

"Sick," she told them. "So sick."

She felt as if she were drifting, floating across the ClairField's extravagant dining hall, being carried by staff to her bedroom where her bed waited. Once there she caught a quick glimpse of her reflection, or what she thought should be her reflection. Instead, Maleva (the old Maleva) reflected her eyes at Alena, although the blue was gone replaced by all black eyes and a sinister grin pinned across her lips. As if Maleva were in the room, watching.

Alena turned from the mirror, and noticed she held the Gitana statue in her palm, the same statue that bounced against the plush bedroom carpet when Alena dropped on the bed in a weary state of hallucinatory fever drenched in sweat. The room was buzzing and thumping with a vibrating heat. As she drifted off to sleep, in the distance she heard the baa.

She heard the baa in her dream where she awakened on that damned cot, and the clunking of that cowbell accompanied the baa. Saw through narrowed eyes the goat in the corner, drenched in darkness, white teeth gleaming, wide mad eyes, staring. Her shoulders pinned to the cot unable to move, naked. Sweat ran down her throat. The room was red hot with waves of heat. The goat now standing, a woman's body, lapping its tongue across its lips. Alena's arms now stretched above her head. She felt hands tighten around her wrists. Maleva, she thought. Flashes of light, gritting teeth, pain in her abdomen. The goat in the corner, now a masculine form as pain tore from Alena's groin, rattling her skull with a wince and shudder. The cowbell clunking furious, the baa, baa, baa, ferocious.

Out of body now.

Staring.

Quiet.

Seeing herself on the cot, her body moved up and down, up and down.

Up and down, the rhythm continuous.

Saw her eyes, lost, wide, coated black. Watching, she dipped closer to her own eyes. Her reflection revealed the head of the goat, staring, grinning.

And Maleva's voice kept repeating, "*AGIOS O BAPHOMET!*" as the clunking cowbell rang even louder.

Heat erupted in her stomach, turned burning like poison. Saw herself, drift into sleep.

Now awakened with a hand on her head, she was lying in her own bed and Bill was beside her, his face grave with concern.

"Alena," he said. She knew he was hollering as if he was screaming for her to hear him, although his voice seemed a mile away. "You're bleeding," he said. "You're going to the hospital. The blood is bad. There's so much of it."

Her head flopped sideways. Saw the gypsy statue on the floor before her eyelids closed.

"Alena!" Bill's voice. "Alena PLEASE! There's so much blood…There's so much blood!"

———————

"The wedding has been cancelled." That's what the guests were told followed by an apology for inconvenience. No reason was provided leaving the guests to speculate over the possibilities. A direct order from Bill's mother who was concerned with the prominent guest list's ability to discover the truth. They could have cited medical reasons but such a claim may have induced further inquiry and talk within the social circle, which did include many doctors who would no doubt inquire further and more than likely under the guise they offered help in such areas. People loved to flap their gums about other people's tragedies and misfortunes and always came under the premise of friendship to hide ulterior motives. Pointing fingers is always easier than looking in the mirror, or talking about ideas on how to fix any particular situation. The rarity in life was someone who placed their own interests below the needs of another, a common—and rather unfortunate—human characteristic Alena had come to know all too well.

Alena had been admitted to the hospital under an assumed name, Clara Fields, as told to hospital staff that evening by Bill himself. Assuming an identity for medical reasons was common practice, and Bill–although distraught and losing his mind (he couldn't get the blood images out of his head)–acted instinctively when hospital staff required personal information. Although the attending doctor bore a familiar face, he was easily hushed when handed a thick envelope a day later along with a promise he would handle all concerns related to the family, providing Bill with updates on Alena's condition twice daily–in this way Bill would not have to be seen at the hospital with the exception of quick visits during off hours. The plan was to discharge Alena to her home in the Hamptons as soon as she stabilized.

But the bleeding continued. And the patient was incoherent as if a coma had taken over, except she wasn't in a coma, just sleeping with brief periods when her eyes would open, she'd say something under her breath and sometimes even scream, then drifted back to sleep. Doctors could not stop the bleeding and surgery was required — which had been caused by a ruptured ovarian cyst.

Ten days later, Alena awakened in her home in the Hamptons. She was surrounded by Bill and the house staff who were informed of the cyst and the surgery required to stop the bleeding, but not the pregnancy and subsequent miscarriage. She awakened, and she knew immediately. She felt empty and hollow, torn and twisted. The tears came quickly.

Bill sat beside her, brushing the hair from her tear filled eyes. "Welcome back," he said. "You gave us a big scare for a while." Alena noticed how his hand shook.

She didn't need to be told although she wanted to hear the words in case the morphine had altered her perception and instincts. She mouthed the words "the baby" as if whispering might provide shelter from the truth.

His eyes told her the truth. Those sad and downtrodden blue eyes revealed the heartache he felt. Bill moved his head back and forth with an expression stained with sadness. Perhaps, she thought, he too had difficulty saying the truth out loud.

"What happened?" she said.

He turned away from her. "Doctor Myer will be here soon," he said. "He'll explain what happened better than I and what had to be done."

"What had to be done?" she thought. She slammed her hand against the mattress to draw his attention. "Tell me," she demanded.

Bill pursed his lips forcing a swallow down a narrow throat. "It was a ruptured cyst," he said. "They had to perform surgery to stop the bleeding."

But there was more and Alena knew it. She wanted to know everything and she wanted him to tell her, not some doctor she'd never heard of.

"And?"

He turned away again. "There were complications that resulted in…" His words caught in his throat, Bill shook his head, gritting his teeth.

Alena rolled her eyes, frustrated and growing angry. "Resulting in what?"

"Infertility," he said, his voice soft, caring, sympathetic. Now he met her eyes with his. "Alena, you can no longer have children."

12

A week later was Bill's last visit. He'd been compassionate and supportive, although Alena could tell there was something more to his reserved mental state than the loss of an unborn child. He used the words *you* and *I* and not *we*.

You've been through a lot.

You need to move forward.

You can never have children.

No, Mr. Astor, WE *can never have children.*

Distant, that's the word Alena used when she confronted him. "You're so distant. Please tell me what you're thinking." As always, the compassionate Alena placed his needs above her own. She wanted him to feel comfortable. To talk and express himself; whatever it was: anger, loss, thoughts that circled around arriving at a conclusion where he felt cheated by life or by God—as she did.

Also, shifting her focus to Bill brought a reprieve from the sadness. Focus on someone else, she thought. If it's pain you feel, be compassionate. If it's anger you feel spread joy. And then there was the fear—the fear that he would not be moving forward with Alena. So, if it's fear you're experiencing, be confident, that's what Alena told herself in those early morning hours when the pain caused by the surgery awakened her to the silence of the Hamptons mansion. No Bill sleeping next to her. Only silence carried on the ocean waves outside her bedroom where she'd sit for hours watching as the dark sea glimmered with the first sprinkles of gold in anticipation for the rising sun.

Some days Bill never came. Other days only for a brief period of time and as the weeks went by those brief periods became even shorter. And then the letter arrived and Alena had no use for it. She knew what was written in that letter. He was gone, and she was sure he blamed his family legacy. Astors require offspring. They require the fortune be reserved under the thumb of the family namesake.

She placed the unopened letter on the fireplace mantle where she could glance over at it as a reminder that when the chips are down those who don't care will scatter and those who do care are all that matter. Although Alena's bridesmaids had also scattered, she knew they'd at least come back, when she resurfaced in the limelight with so much more to share.

Once Alena placed that letter on her mantle a switch had been turned. Bury the past. Kill it if you have to but be done with it. Be the cause, don't stay in the effect; create something new. She started drawing again. A medium that served multiple purposes allowing the expression of pain and suffering to drain from her mind and body with every thin line drawn. Plus, her recovery—yes it took a while for the stitches and pain in her stomach to heal—hindered her ability to paint while standing for considerable hours. Even the passion of sculpting may have proven to be a bit too strenuous.

And the wine helped—she hated morphine-those red grapes brought the pain to a dull discomfort. She'd draw for hours, mostly of memories when she and Bill would take walks together, although every drawing featured Bill with some defect, either with mad hypnotizing eyes or some deformity anyone perusing the drawing would need to search for to find.

Sometimes she'd stain the drawing with drops of wine, right over Bill's bleeding heart.

She'd take phone calls from the ClairField staff who always seemed to be in a frenzy over the continuously thinning guest list. And they were losing employees daily to which Alena would shrug while offering no condolence. *Let them go. Let them all go!* The ClairField was quickly becoming a ghost, no longer holding the prestige it once had. Let it burn, Alena thought. Let it all burn. The hotel that had brought so much joy now stood as a testament and reminder of the past, whatever its fate she had no such concern for. In the end all things go away; people, places and things, there is no exception to this rule of constant change.

Not one thing held any sort of meaning or substance any longer except her art and she planned on making a comeback with an art exhibit. Perhaps, she thought, I'll shut down the ClairField and re-open with a new art show. Although such an event would require a mainstay, a work of art as dazzling as the ClairField. Something all people would marvel over. To show everyone that Alena Francon maintained dignity and revelry even in the face of adversity. "What could it be?" she thought. Certainly not drawings clearly revealing what was behind the mask of a jaded female. No, she would require a structure that exuded temperament, prestige, and man's ability to become God. To be worshipped with its sizzle and detail.

Marble, she thought. I need a large block of marble. To chip away at and create something remarkable. A piece of my heart given freely which can never be given back.

The marble arrived in mid-August.

The ClairField closed in early September.

Alena became a recluse. She'd even dismissed the help; those who'd tended the Francon mansion since she was a child. Alena Francon wanted no distractions. No help, no friends, no romantic entanglements. She wanted to create, to be alone with her thoughts and reinvigorated muse. The loud clunking bell that raged on in the distance with every thought and every chip of marble, seemed to grow louder with every obsessed detail she would spend days cultivating. She dismissed the bell to simplicity. To Alena, the bell represented a comeback and the signal that something larger than herself loomed off the horizon like those glittering bulbs of twilight sparkling across the sea. Alena Francon was sure her sun would be rising soon enough.

And that clunking bell would prove to toll for her.

––––––––

In mid-October Alena received her first visitor, the first human face she'd seen since dismissing the housing staff two months earlier. Crystal arrived in late afternoon. She'd met friends—Alena's friends—for lunch at the Hamptons Country Club, an event where the conversation had addressed Alena and her well-being. No one had seen or heard from Alena—their phone calls and inquires had gone unanswered when news of the break up with Bill Astor was all anyone could talk about—which to them was not completely unheard of. Alena often spent months out of the limelight when she was working on a new project. As friends they respected her request for privacy. As socialites, now that public opinion had waned with the rise of the most recent scandal—the Bronx district attorney had been caught taking bribes from the Italian mafia—making an effort to reach out to a lost friend (and hopefully reinstitute events at the ClairField) was in everyone's best interest. Plus, this inner circle of friends never did have a chance to receive Alena's story. She had shut out everyone, remaining silent since the hospital. Now it was time to start poking around and see what Alena was up to.

————

Alena—chisel and hammer in hand—heard the car engine motor up the long driveway. She'd gone out the day before to secure a few needed supplies and never so much as thought twice about closing the gate—she expected no one. Now she wished she had. She was in the zone since early morning, sensing, feeling, allowing the mind to go where it needed, drinking coffee while listening to the waves crash on the shore on the heels of autumn's wind and all too happy the summer heat was no more than a thing of the past. Autumn brought with it a renewed sense of creativity, and she looked forward to the coming winter. The change in seasons always ushered in a creative flow, and creativity was in full bloom; Alena's statue had taken on a life of its own. Most days Alena was fascinated over the progress she'd made with the statue and often wondered if she was creating it or if somehow the statue was driving her hand (and her mind) willing itself to come to life. To be the picture-perfect model of all a man should be—quiet, reserved, poignant, driven and gorgeous.

Alena's first thought—once she realized Crystal was behind the wheel—was to hide, to not answer the door. But that would do no more than send out smoke signals and sooner more than later everyone and their mother would be knocking on her door. Perhaps a few reporters, too. As she watched the car hum to a stop, she noticed how the foliage was overgrown— dismissing everyone meant *everyone*, gardener included—and knew this would be Crystal's first comment. Alena rolled her eyes and shook her head, tightening her jaw. She turned to the marble, the thick block chiseled to perfection giving the head an appearance of a body rising from the depths of solitude, despair and bondage as if it were climbing out from the underworld into the light.

She dropped the chisel and hammer on the couch, and hurried across the room, gathering the sheets she'd laid on the floor to capture those remnants of marble chiseled and chipped from the slab— climbing the ladder set beside the statue that when completed would be over seven feet tall, a three feet high base where the man was bowing or pleading, perhaps to God or maybe to Alena, his left hand held out, palm up, as if offering his life or begging to be freed, eyes steady, face solemn, should he stand he'd be close to seven feet tall - and tossed the sheets over the statue being sure not to leave any part of it for Crystal to see. She wasn't ready to share her love with the world. Wanted, no needed, the statue to remain solely in her embrace.

Crystal blocked the sunlight from streaming through the front doors and knocked twice. Alena climbed down the ladder but not before she dipped her forehead to the statue, her eyes closed as if protecting the sanctity the statue possessed, offering an apology for the intrusion. Again, the knock came, and as Alena went to open the wide double French doors, she ran her hands through her hair, which, although short, she was more than certain appeared raggedy since bathing had gone by the way side over the last few days. She planned to take a bath this evening. When creative juices were flowing, bathing may prove to wipe clear the flow she was in. Only regret, she thought, she should have brushed her teeth.

She opened the door, and Crystal's expression was both leery and concerned. After the typical greetings and explanation for the visit—obviously, Alena thought you're on a fishing expedition – Alena fixed a pot of tea which she served outside, using the excuse that the weather was fabulous, although to Alena she was protecting her statue, attempting to ward off any chance Crystal would make an inquiry on the large and covered monstrosity that now took up most of the sitting room.

Small talk started the conversation. How are the ladies? What's the latest news? What have you been doing? What is being served at the country club—she always despised their menu. All the while Alena waited for the ball to drop. For Crystal to ask about Bill and what had happened. Some dirt is too good to not inquire about, Alena knew, but what she received from Crystal came as a surprise.

"Why did you call off the wedding?" Crystal asked.

Alena's brow furrowed, eyes narrow. "Come again?"

"The wedding," Crystal repeated. "You know that wedding that was supposed to happen in June? *Your* wedding. The one that would have changed your name to Alena Astor?"

"Oh, that wedding," Alena said, and she automatically touched her stomach but snapped the hand up quickly, nervous, she shrugged and gripped her tea cup, holding the cup close to her lips. "Didn't seem to be that important when the time came." Alena could see the envelope, still unopened and still on the mantle above the fireplace and she had a fleeting thought that she should have opened it for the simplest reason she wouldn't be blindsided as she just was with questions on the matter. And then she thought with a small gesture moving her head side to side, Son of a bitch, you told everyone I called it off. You're a true coward, Bill Astor.

Crystal's eyes widened. She curled her lips and Alena hoped she would let it go. Leave it alone. Kill the past remember? It doesn't exist unless you feed into it.

"Besides," Alena offered, "I'm much happier not having to pretend happiness in the realms of Astor."

To this Crystal forced a smile. "You've always been independent, Alena, so we weren't surprised." She sat forward, close to the wrought iron table, opened her handbag and took out a cigarette. "Could have called one of us though. Reading the wedding was cancelled in the paper made us all feel like outsiders. And then the rumors." She lit her smoke, took a deep drag, and exhaled. "At least Bill offered the explanation before the rumors turned into something that spawned two heads." She smiled and sat back, eyes gazing over the sea.

They sat in silence for a while; Alena allowing those angered thoughts regarding Bill Astor to be caught by the wind and brushed out to sea. It was Crystal who broke the silence.

"For a while, we all thought the gypsy woman had something to do with it." She flicked the ash from her cigarette.

Total blank. At first Alena thought she heard Crystal wrong; she had no recollection of the gypsy woman, or her time spent in bondage in that small back room. What she did sense was the speed of her heart, which kicked up more than a few paces and followed with a constricted throat. A painful sensation in her navel, as if something were inside her stomach attempting to break free.

"What was with that goat?" Crystal laughed but Alena had no response.

She tried to remember the goat, or any recollection of a goat. Her thoughts kept spiraling into darkness, a void where no memories existed as if someone had wiped the incident clear, leaving no remnants, no trail leading to that sinister event. She felt like she'd grown old and weary, unable to recollect, sitting with Crystal, staring out at the ocean waves but not seeing them. Alena receded within, trapped by a memory that evaded every instinct as if the tragedy wished not to be revealed, like a child not wanting to be found, hiding somewhere in a dark closet, as quiet as a mouse. Disappearing into the folds where light could never be revealed.

And in those black hidden folds there was the bell. The clunking, jumping, thumping, thick impression loudly rapping somewhere beyond the sea, so close she thought she could reach out and touch it only to find that her fingers remained inches away. No amount of stretching or jumping could capture it. It may as well have been on another planet.

"Alena," said Crystal, her voice faded, far away, as if it called to Alena from a distant memory. "Are you there, Alena?" Crystal sat up studying Alena, the sudden movement registered in Alena's stare. She blinked rapidly, her eyelids flapping like the wings of a butterfly, and saw Crystal, her thick blonde locks forced by the wind to stretch and reach behind her. Alena for the first time since Crystal arrived noticed how she wore the latest new look: a fashionable plaid dress with rounded shoulders, a shapely bust line and closely-defined waistline leading to the billowing skirt hanging below the calves.

Alena smiled nervously, a slight tremble in her lips. "Love the new look," she said, her voice monotone as if the previous conversation had removed all emotion.

Crystal tipped her head, staring at Alena with a confused gaze, cigarette burning low between her fingers. A slight shake of the head. "Thank you." Alena thought it was kind of Crystal to play along in the change of subject. Or had she not caught that? The way she was staring made Alena nervous, as if Crystal was privy to Alena's lost memories and inability to remember. Crystal took a final drag off the cigarette then stamped it out in the marble ashtray. Alena watched as the wind circled the ashes, the cigarette glowed in the wind and the ashes drifted away.

Marble, Alena thought, and a smile graced her lips. She thought of the statue. He will need a name. I have to come up with a name. She saw his head, traced over every perfectly smooth and precisely accurate edge. When she saw the eyes, it was as if he were looking directly at her. No, through her. Admiring Alena in the same manner as she admired him.

Alena closed her eyes drawing in a deep inhale content with her statue. Opened her eyes and said, "How are the girls?"

"Good," replied Crystal. "Everyone is good. Concerned about you and your silence but we do understand. Major decisions and all…and it looks like you're in one of your creative phases. Will you be gracing the world with more masterpieces? Perhaps when the ClairField is reopened?"

Now Alena got it. The world was bored and required a central point to usher in the new look with entertainment and reasons to get all dolled up, while parading in a thicket of who's who and glamour. Alena eased back, gave a slight nod as a thin smile slithered across her lips. "I believe you will all be very happy. There's nothing more grand than a new look and new beginnings." She met Crystal's sky blue eyes with hers.

"Excellent," Crystal said then announced she had to leave.

Alena escorted Crystal to the front door where the ladies said good-bye with a hug and kiss on both cheeks and a promise for Alena to meet Crystal and the girls sometime soon, before the holidays were in full bloom, at the country club to reconnect to which Alena half-heartedly agreed. Only if my work is complete, she thought.

"What's under the sheets?" Crystal asked gesturing to the large figure in the middle of the room.

Alena looked over her shoulder at the hidden statue; her hidden statue. And he was waiting, calling her, wanting to feel the small of her hands crafting those miraculous edges. To awaken him and give him the life only she could provide.

"Oh," she said, "that's my new man."

13

Once she closed the door Alena watched as Crystal's car putted down the driveway before tearing the sheets off the statue. She stood unmoving for a long while. Looking, studying, delving deep into the creative muse and deriving from it the required meticulous nature to set her man apart from all other artistic expression. The hair, she thought. He should have beautiful flowing locks of thick hair. The kind of hair that, when out of place, would fall across his dark and mesmerizing eyes.

And it will be all mine. To brush from his eyes with a gentle finger.

Alena took the hammer and chisel into her hands, and stood a moment longer studying him. Him? What is his name? she thought. Got to have a name.

She heard a muffled voice, either in the back of her mind (maybe in that fold she couldn't access) or carried on the wind ushered in from the sea. Alena made no attempt to clarify the voice; she knew it waited, waited for her to finish her work.

The statue was the perfect host for Alena's mission, unmoving and unwavering, guiding her hand so that every part of him was perfect. Alena believed both she and statue were in this together. He drove her hand, and she conceded to his desire.

She approached him with a cautious and gentle step. "Ok," she said to him. "Man to be named later, when we are finished, send your name to me. Send your name and your manifestation will be complete."

Thoughts of Bill Astor's letter, of the gypsy woman, and the goat had dissipated. She thought and dreamt of nothing other than the statue. She'd even begun to say good-bye when she went out for supplies, food, and of course, more wine, and good-night before retiring for the day.

————

She completed the statue after midnight on December twenty-sixth. He became more than she had imagined, delicate yet strong, courageous although compassionate, a leader who captured the pain of his people on his shoulders, and in his eyes.

Completed and marveled over, yet his manifestation brought Alena a sense of loneliness. She'd obsessed over him for so long that, now that he was complete, she experienced loss. And she wanted more from him. "I love you," she told him, standing with a bottle of wine in one hand, a glass in the other, sipping slowly as she had been most of the day. Now the wee hours of early morning (three AM) brought silence. And with the silence, the air changed with a sting of winter cold.

She'd lit a fire, which burned relentlessly, casting shadows on the walls. The crackling, popping wood received a breath of air from the chimney, raging the fire into a fury. Windows, buffeted by the outside wind, seemed to be on the verge of splintering, cracking, and caving with shards of glass blown across the sitting room.

She took a sip of wine, held the acidic liquid on her tongue before swallowing. Her eyes, dry and wide, gleamed admiration and frustration.

"Tell me your name," she whispered. His eyes were brought alive by the flames that didn't reflect off the marble, but were *captured* by it, swallowed by his soul. She wanted to lie in his arms, to fold herself in his embrace. To take that hand in hers, the hand that stretched toward her, palm up, as if he summoned her to him. *Take my hand. Give yourself to my embrace. Kiss my eyes, my forehead, my lips. Declare your love for me. An undying, forever love, and I will protect and keep you always. Neither sickness nor tragedy will ever befall you. The world will appear beautiful, always.*

She went to him and for a brief moment she thought he moved. That he was watching her, anticipating her every movement, willing her to him. Both glass and bottle dropped from her hands. The glass shattered. Bottle clanged against the marble tile then rolled to a stop; wine gurgled from the open bottleneck. Alena heard neither. She stepped on the stool beside the base, never turning her eyes from his. She placed her hand in his and as she stepped up it was as if his hand had helped her.

Her lips were shaking when she said, "I dream of you. Every night. I close my eyes and you're there. When I wake, you are still there." She leaned her head in his palm, gazing into those fiery eyes. "Wake up," she said. "Please wake up. For me. For love and for beauty. Let me look on you with admiration and wonder." Shadows flickered across the statue, providing an appearance of slight subtle movements. Her eyes, wide and staring, wanting to will life into the statue as a single tear fell from her right eye. Alena caught inside the pain from the past, as if the devil's hand captured sadness and squeezed it into her heart. Tears now in both eyes, she lifted her head from his hand, Alena's fingertips gently caressing the palm lines she'd created. And the tears fell into his palm.

"I gave you a long life," she referred to the palm lines she crafted then looked at him. "You should be grateful." Alena wiped the tears off his palm. Brushed those wet hands across the smock she wore then wiped her eyes as she sniffled. And she laughed. Laughed at herself. At the ridiculous wish that this statue would respond. That she *wanted* the statue to spring to life. To take her in his embrace and never let go. She glanced at his eyes hoping he would turn those flames in her direction. "No?" she said then shook her head turning away, her eyes roaming. To the floor, to the ceiling, to the walls and fireplace, avoiding his eyes because she knew he would not look at her, and she hated him for it. This statue, born from the depths of her soul, was already gone. Had already abandoned and betrayed her, refusing to manifest her wish and desire.

Alena took the bottle off the floor by the neck and walked with grace to the fireplace. The crackling fire devoured its wood prey as she watched the statue reflected in the Victorian mirror above the mantle, hoping and praying that he would move now that she wasn't in front of him. Paying no mind to the sweat, soot, and marble dust disturbed by smeared tears on her face. Her greasy hair seemed like marble in the way the hair matted within thick gobs across the forehead and down the back of her neck. She set the bottle on the mantle and her eyes fell on the letter, still sealed. In front of the letter was the gypsy statue, and she looked on it with a puzzled stare as if she'd never laid eyes on the gypsy before.

For protection. She heard these words as if they came from the dark recesses of her mind. Something that had been locked away but now peeked its head through a crack in the door and requested entrance to Alena's thoughts. To survey if the coast was clear and all was safe before revealing itself.

She took up the statue and, as if a trap door had opened, the memories flooded into conscious thought. Alena saw the gypsy woman, the palm reading, and the goat. Remembered how sick she'd gotten, the hospital, and the aftermath. Her stomach wrenched with a stinging pain, acid gurgled in the back of her throat. She tightened her grip on the statue. Her hand was trembling, lips quivering, and the memories drove into consciousness. But she did not believe them. Did not believe that any such circumstances had taken place. Alena questioned her sanity as she stood by the fire glaring at the statue trembling within a shaking grip. She heard Crystal's voice. "We thought the gypsy woman had something to do with it."

"Did I hear her right?" Alena thought. She turned to her statue as if believing he would offer an answer. "Is it even real?" she hollered. How did this gypsy figurine find the fireplace mantle? The memory surfaced, being handed the small gypsy statue by Maleva. Then she saw the gypsy statuette on the carpet before losing consciousness so many months prior. Those tender gypsy eyes staring, unmoving, as Alena's eyes closed.

It all seemed like a dream. Like drifting within a waking trance with no understanding where reality began, and the dream concluded. *Had this statue been on the mantle all these months? How could I not have noticed it before today?* Because she never looked or gave so much as a glance at the mantle, diverting her eyes from the letter every time she stoked the fire. But she was certain the figurine was not on the mantle earlier that day and without a doubt was not present when she'd added wood to the fire a few hours ago. And she could not be certain about the memories either, no matter how real they now seemed. Or Crystal's declaration. She could be using false information to fill in the gaps in her memory, attempting to make sense of this new revelation.

"Did you…" her voice trailed off glaring at *her* statue, her new man unmoving with the exception of the shadows that animated his resonating bones. Her stomach twisted, acid gagged her throat. She dropped to her knees and vomited, feeling the goat inside her. A lingering sensation eliciting pressure in her abdomen.

"Can't be," she pleaded. "None of this is possible." She cried, tears streaming from her eyes, down those thin cheeks, pooled on the jawline where they hung briefly before falling in small drips to the floor. She coughed and gagged as the fire's heat burned her skin.

Her body shook. She gazed at the gypsy in her hand, clenching the statue. "You took everything from me." Lips quivering. She squeezed the statue. "EVERYTHING!" Her face constricted squeezing with angered rage. The gypsy cracked in her hand, slicing through her palm as she squeezed even more. Blood dripping in streams escaped between her fingers. Her fist was trembling and when she opened her hand, small crushed porcelain pieces fell to the floor. Remaining in her palm was the statue's backside and she could now see the evil eye staring at her. An eye had been painted on the inside.

For protection.

That's what Maleva had said. The gypsy statue meant protection for whomever it was given to. *The only protection I needed was from you.* She let the remains drop from her palm and she sat on her legs, cradling the bloodied hand.

"My God!" she cried holding the trembling blood streaming hand close to her chest as she rocked back and forth. "I've completely lost it." Her body jerked. Alena's legs flopped from beneath her and she sat now on her backside, holding her wrist watching and staring as the blood kept coming. Bleed to death, she thought. For all I care.

Life is a cruel trick that God gets off on playing.

And hope is nothing more than a delusion.

She raised her head, her eyes to the back of her skull. She saw the goat. Heard that clunking bell as the beast mounted the cot. The thought disgusted every inch of her skin, tainted every thought, and constricted every muscle.

She felt Maleva's hands on her wrists.

Alena stood.

She heard the bell. Heard the baa.

Alena went to the statue, *her* statue.

She saw the goat snicker. Her lips trembled.

Alena was gazing at the statue with no ability to see the statue.

She heard Maleva chanting, *AGIOS O BAPHOMET!*

Alena held her clenched fist high over her head, squeezing the blood into droplets that fell from her palm.

AGIOS O BAPHOMET!

"You come to me," she said, her voice gripped with anger. "You come or I will be no more." Blood dropped on the base—*"DO YOU UNDERSTAND ME?"*—streaming down the base where the thick liquid pooled to where the marble protruded from the smoothness like an overhang for the floor. Alena scowled at the statue, whose eyes raged with fire. She dropped her fist. "Hear me," she whispered. But the statue remained silent, unmoving and unwavering.

"You're all I have," she said, her head now bowed staring at the blood droplets cascading down the marble as if the stone was slashed by bloodied talons.

Now, outside, snow arrived with a relentless fury that turned night into a blanket of white reflected by the moon. The fury pelted the windows like white hail.

Alena shook her head. She walked away, to her room to attempt to find some form of peace within sleep. A rest that took her willingly and quickly. Should she have stayed to watch the furious falling blankets of white she would have seen how her blood was absorbed into the marble. She would have known he was arriving. She would have witnessed a transformation that could only be born from the depths of agony.

14

Alena was awakened by a painful groan that reached into the depths of sleep to arouse those dry eyes.

She dismissed the groan; relating the noise to the nightmare she was sure had captured most of her slumber. Although she had no recollection of any nightmare, nonetheless, where else would such a groan come from? "Maybe it was mine?" she thought. Now she was awake, lying in bed staring mindless through the windows where sheets of white fell in thick curtains from an icy gray and overcast sky. She would love the chance to return to sleep no matter what nightmare waited her arrival. She was overwhelmingly tired. The last few months of constant labor, obsessive work that allowed little sleep, had caught up with her. And the bedroom was dark. The blizzard blocked the sun from shining through the windows. Perfect weather to spend the day in bed and sleep. But her mind was turning over on itself. Thoughts of the gypsy woman, Bill Astor, and loss of the unborn gripped her heart and squeezed.

She heard another groan, followed by what sounded like constricted coughing. Alena shot up in bed. Her first thought was that her statue had fulfilled her wish, although she dismissed the notion the moment it occurred. Statues don't come to life no matter how powerful—and deranged—the creator may be. Wind howled outside the window forcing those sheets of snow against the glass as if the weather were jealous, pleading to be allowed inside. Just the wind, she thought. Playing mind tricks. She pulled the sheets to her throat, leaning on the headboard. The house was cold, and Alena was sure the fire had gone out. Judging by the raging storm outside her window the fire was not only out it was piled high with snow.

She thought about freezing to death. How long would it take for her to be found? Who would come to check on her? Crystal? Alena hadn't seen or heard from Crystal since her last visit. And the others? So-called friends who never so much as offered a helping hand. If the task were left to them it would be spring before they found her rotting corpse. Not that it would matter to her in the least, she would be dead and off some place where the dead mingled and congregated. She thought of her parents. She thought of the unborn child, snatched from her womb as if God were a sadist.

She thought of being with them, in death, spiraled from this hell into the light.

Now she heard a scream. Howling screeches filled the house as if they came from someone who was dying and trying, fighting to remain, within the woes living delivered. Because what waited on the other side of living was an eternity of terror. Perhaps it is the dead, forcing their will into this world with a declaration that the pain accompanied by living follows with a vengeance after death.

"A–L-L-E-E-E-E-N-N-A-A-A-A!"

She assumed it was the dead, calling her to them, or she had indeed lost the ability for sane and rational thought; the storm plays tricks with the mind when the recipient is encased in a lonely endeavor.

"A–L-L-E-E-E-E-N-N-A-A-A-A!"

The voice again, this time followed by hacking, pleading for a helping hand. And Alena froze. The voice was coming from downstairs, and she thought then that the house produced an intruder. But an intruder who knew her name? Perhaps a friend had been caught in the storm and now required her help, her mansion being the closest possible location to receive that help. Maybe they were downstairs and dying, too wounded to climb the stairs and find her.

"A–L-L-E-E-E-E-N-N-A-A-A-A. H-H-E-E-L-L-L-P M-M-E-E-E."

"Go away," she whispered. Eyes filled with tears. "Please, go away." She pursed her lips, constricted her throat and forced a swallow.

"I'M-HERE-FOR-YOU-U-U-U-U."

No, the voice wasn't in her head. And definitely not a product of the howling storm. There was someone in the house with her. Someone who needed help. Someone in pain. Should she not go they would die. From the way the voice carried pain, whomever was down those stairs, would certainly die. She was terrified but slipped off the bed all the same. If they are in pain, they are wounded and, if they are wounded, they are less than a threat. But they could be playing. Putting on a façade to get her down stairs. *Easy prey.* A weapon was required. Something to smash over their heads should they make even the slightest gesture towards impropriety. She grabbed a letter opener off the side table by the bed. Good enough to plunge into someone's gut—or throat—if needed.

"A–L-L-E-E-E-E-N-N-A-A-A-A!"

The groan was louder now. The house shook from its vibration. Now armed with her weapon, Alena cautiously went into the hallway, peeking from the stairs down, hoping to see this person. See the condition they were in. Whoever it was, they were not on the bottom of the stairs. They must be in the sitting room, maybe waiting, sitting by the snow filled fireplace. Maybe sipping her wine and gurgling her name with it before swallowing. She stretched her neck peering down the stairs. She could see the bottom of her statue, no more. The house was dark concealing any possibility of seeing shadows that would alert her to their location.

"*A–L-L-E-E-N-N-A-A!*"

This time the voice was so loud, Alena was sure it reached the pinnacle of heaven—and the bowels of hell. She took the first step. Then the other. The sitting room opened wider with every step down. It was on the fourth step that she saw it. No, saw him. Her statue no longer kneeled in a forever frozen posture calling for her. He was alive, lying on the floor beside the base, coughing and hacking. Shaking, constricting and trembling.

And Alena dropped her weapon.

———————

She was afraid. Deathly afraid. He hadn't seen her. Not yet anyway. And she thought she should run back to her room and hide. Or get in the car and go, drive all the way to California if she had to, whatever needed to happen to forget this…her…it…him…thing—lying sick and painfully groaning on the floor.

Alena thought of her mother then, in her last days and how her body wrenched and twisted, gasping for a breath of air to draw into those depleted lungs. The same as this monster was doing now, gasping for breath. Funny how both dying and birthing reflected the other. From the first breath to the last. The only difference was that the former brought with it the compounded pain the in-between had accumulated.

"A-L-L-E-E-E-N-N-A-A-A-A!"

It started huffing. She could see his body jumping. Leaping for what she assumed was air. Air to bring life into his body. He reached those trembling marble arms high over his head, his fingers curled as if to grab at something. Anything to hold onto. So much pain, Alena could feel it, feel his pain in her rapidly beating heart and choking throat that swelled with a tearful lump she thought would choke the life from her. Now she felt his pain. Behind this pain was fear. Fear of the unknown; terrified by the present confusion and existence.

Am I dreaming? Surely, I must be. Inanimate objects do not come to life. This isn't a horror novel, and I'm no mad scientist. What power do I have to cause such a thing to happen? I am not God, nor do I want to be.

Now he started flailing, his body wrenching, twisting and Alena could hear his bones tighten and constrict. She covered her ears when his scream just about tore the roof off.

"A-L-L-E-E-E-E-N-N-A-A-A-A. *PLEASE!*"

His body rose then fell. His chest jumped then fell back down. He coughed and gagged as if life were already choking the air from his lungs. His chest just about leapt to the ceiling and his body moved. Moved closer to her, toward the stairs and Alena could see how his skin was drenched with sweat. His body shimmered, from his head to his toes like some magical force slithered down the marble body this *thing* was trying to break free from, turning the stone into flesh, blood, bones, veins and organs. Another flailing wrought with pain and his neck turned. Alena heard the crackling popping tendons, cartilage and bones.

Now she could see his eyes. Those emerald irises held sparkles of fiery orange as if the fire had laid a permanent mark on his soul. Alena experienced shame in that moment. Her creation had found her, locked eyes on her and what those eyes said was help. *Help me, please.*

————

His flailing calmed, and the pain seemed to dissipate when Alena approached as if her presence meant the end to his pain. His hand reached for her and she hesitatingly took it. His body was cold; the marble reflected the temperature in the house. And the hand was thick, solid, and smooth. Another shiver ran down his body and his hand turned soft within hers, more flesh than marble.

He was staring at her, his eyes pleading for help and behind those eyes Alena sensed fear. Unknowing, frightened, and scared-to-death-compounded fear.

His throat bucked and constricted as if he was trying to speak but the words were caught in his throat. "Help me," he said and now that he wasn't screaming his voice was soft and gentle.

She gazed at him with wide innocent eyes. "How?" she asked in a soft, gentle, pleading, whisper. His body constricted, his head flopped to the side, and

Alena could see he was struggling to breathe. That shimmer again and when he returned his eyes to look upon her his hair—the hair she'd spent weeks perfecting—flopped across his eyes. He was attempting to speak, trying with all his strength to force the words across his lips. Those sad frightened eyes pleaded with her from beneath the veil of hair. She removed the hair from his eyes with a brush of her finger, still holding his hand with her free hand. She turned her head to the side, staring at him, looking into his eyes. Her lips tight across her mouth with a warming smile as she looked on him adoringly, lovingly.

"Breathe…" he said but was interrupted by a wrenching pain that had to come from inside his chest, his body cringed as his chest heaved, suspended in the air before he dropped down with a thud and the back of his head thrashed against the floor. He pursed his lips and forced a dry swallow down his throat. Now gazing at Alena his body settled, and she could feel how the tension, and the pain, eased from his body as if the simple sight of her brought a release from the terror he was going through. "Put your lips to mine," he said. His eyelids narrowed but his eyes continued to reflect that pleading adoring stare. "Breathe life into my lungs."

And then he ceased moving. His hand fell limp in hers and his eyes turned stiff with the look of the dead. No more flailing. No longer jumping. And the thought passed through Alena, a knowing that should she not place her lips to his and breathe into his lungs he would not continue this manifestation. He would return to be the statue she'd created. This was her only chance. And whatever was coming, whatever life was waiting over the horizon, after the storm cleared, either with him or without diverged two separate paths. The first, the path she had been on, the lonely meaningless life that existed in that cold bedroom waiting for her upstairs. Or to share that bed with what she had created. This was her chance to make a choice that was not derived from God's plan, but from hers.

She leaned in close, staring into those stiff fiery green eyes, placed her lips to his soft and delicate mouth, and forced her breath down into his lungs, blowing as strong as the blizzard outside, emptying all her breath, all the air from her lungs into his. She watched as his eyes shimmered and were brought to life.

15

He was like a child. He slept through most of the day and into the night, in between a few hours of waking that consisted mostly of painful groans—if he were a child these would have been cries for food, diaper changes, and general requirements to have his needs met including if he were too cold or too hot. Alena watched him as he slept, in her bed in her room. And how she was able to walk him upstairs was something she surmised could only be a miracle.

He was still not completely human, not even after the breath she'd provided him. His feet were still marble and that shimmer continued, although the event had become less and less frequent. Perhaps, Alena thought, whatever magic existed in providing her statue with life required time to complete the manifestation. And she speculated what was happening within his body. Was this shimmer creating organs, blood, and veins? Would he become an actual man, or would he be plagued to walk the earth with marble shoes all his life? And what about rational, logical thought? Would he become intelligent like a child educated in the ways of the world is given to abstract thought? Or would he continue, forever grunting and only capable of producing her name or simple words? She was sure his language would progress, considering he did call to her. He knew her name. He knew how to ask for help. He knew he was here for her.

Once they arrived in her bedroom—Alena was sure the venture up the stairs had taken more than an hour—he flopped down on the bed on his back and fell into a deep immediate sleep. His head continued to dampen, and Alena wondered where the sweat was coming from. His body was also hot to the touch, burning hot as if he'd been born in the fire, which had become a permanent part of what lie beneath the marble exterior. Considering the house was freezing cold—Alena's breath spewed frost—she wasn't sure how he was sweating or how to cool him down.

She had a passing thought to bring him outside, into the blizzard that relentlessly dropped sheets of snow. Should he not be able to cool down under the throes of a winter storm, what other options would there be? Perhaps his temperature would cool once the shimmer passed through for the final time. Maybe then he will feel the cold sting winter brought. Alena sat in front of the bed on a red velvet chair she gathered from one of the twelve rooms on the second floor. She bundled herself in winter sweaters, socks, and thermals and put on a pair of gloves—her fingertips weren't cold; they were frozen numb.

When he stirred, she stirred and when he groaned, she would stand, as if she could receive a better view of any possibility he was choking, requiring a slam on his back or to reach into his mouth and pull out whatever could possibly be choking him. She noticed how his face grimaced and winced, even while he slept, as if wherever he came from tried desperately—and forcefully—to not allow him to leave.

Maybe he's lost between two worlds, she thought. Like a new born baby, in between this life and the last. Inside two dimensions at the same time and only pain, or rather the awareness of pain could drive that consciousness head first into this life.

He shook and convulsed, sometimes his chest leapt off the bed so high she thought he would spring up chest first and stand on the bed. And he kept sweating. As if every pore seeped sweat from within, looking to escape what stirred beneath the surface. She had an inclination—during one time when the body flopped from side to side and his arm lifted high then raged down hard, slamming the mattress—that he was fighting to break free as if the darkness from where he came was fighting to keep him.

Alena kept her eyes on the storm. There had been no previous reports of a blizzard—only flurries were predicted. She wondered if the storm had something to do with him. Maybe he was carried on the heels of the storm, brought from another world to this one, and the storm was relentless. Electricity was out so Alena lit candles when the sun retreated from the storm, no longer attempting to shine light on the day. Judging by the amount of snow already on the ground, she surmised they would be snowed in for the next few days. Alone. Alone with her statue.

He started gagging again. His eyes were closed, so she went to him with a towel to wipe the sweat off his forehead. She noticed his breathing was labored. "Is he fighting?" she thought. "Fighting to stay alive? Fighting to come to life?" She noticed his flesh, how his skin was turning pink and when she touched his skin it felt real, no longer the stiff, smooth marble he had been an hour prior, now living flesh and that marble surface receded beneath the skin allowing a faint whisper to reveal what he had been. He is changing. Becoming human, but would he ever truly be human? Capable of human thought and human interaction? Would he have dreams of his own, not the dreams she had for him but real, tried and true dreams with the ambition to make them real? And what about emotions? Will he feel fear? Hate? Love? Joy? For the moment he was no more than a child, vulnerable and in need of help. Does this not mean he will become as we all are, navigating through the storm of life?

Now the double doors leading to the balcony rattled in their frame, then pressed and were pulled by the howling wind. The doors burst open and in rushed the snow. Alena went to the doors, battling the elements to force them closed. She thought the wind demanded to stay, the sheer force of it she thought would toss her over had her conviction not been so strong. She latched and locked the door, then placed a chair in front of it.

When she looked back, he was watching her.

————————

He was gagging as if being strangled, his eyes bulged, his head jumped up and down.

Is he choking? She ran to him and then froze. What could she do? She looked on him not knowing how to help, hoping he'd be able to direct—and verbalize—his needs. His head lifted off the bed. His throat swelled like a balloon.

"Tell me," she said. "Tell me how to help you?"

He reached his hand out and she took it. The same hand that had been thick marble less than a day before was now warm to the touch, and rough like a day laborer whose hands had seen their share of hard labor. The same hand she'd created, extended and welcoming, reached out now in the same way to Alena. She wondered if she had made him too large. His hand was the size of a baseball glove that fit perfectly within her two hands. And strong. He gripped both her hands when his throat swelled and she thought her bones were going to snap.

His eyes revealed pain-filled fear. Maybe, she thought, he's as unaware with what is happening to him as I am. Maybe he doesn't have all the answers. And maybe he has no idea how he had come to life no more than any human philosophical thought could prove how we all arrived here. Those eyes…it's all in the eyes. Those orange sparkles looked on Alena with a plea for help. They revealed how helpless and dependent he truly was.

His lips moved, attempting to force words from his throat, to express his needs…to help her help him.

"Wa-t-er," he whispered.

"Water?" she repeated, and he gave a quick nod.

She ran downstairs, passed the sitting room where he'd come alive, now covered in marble dust. It was so bitter cold her nose and ears stung. She could hear him, choking and gagging. Her hands shook when she gathered his cup of water, taking it upstairs quickly. Alena held the back of his head to help him reach his lips to the cup. He sipped slowly in between heavy breaths, then flopped back down. She wiped his brow again. His eyes stared at her in adoration.

Alena had so many questions. So many had rifled through conscious thought while she watched him sleep, but now her mind was a blank with one exception. Passing the remnant statue had brought back the memory from the night before. "Your name?" she'd asked. "Tell me your name."

His lips moved open then closed several times. Alena moved closer to him, the look in her eyes conveying that she waited for him to verbalize his needs. Maybe more water, she thought. Maybe he needs food.

"G-G-G-G-Golem," he said.

"Come again?" Her eyes widened with a confused stare.

Then he smiled. He *actually* smiled. It was a thin, toothless smile, but his eyes lit up. "My name is Golem."

The blizzard, which had been falling all day with no sign of ever letting up, kicked up a nasty wind that Alena had thought would take the house away and like Dorothy, be transplanted to Oz. *Maybe I am in Oz.* She turned to the balcony door, noticed the chair was holding in place, then returned her gaze to him. His eyes were heavy, and she knew he'd be returning to slumber — or to wherever he had been born, waiting for this moment. Waiting for Alena to help him escape.

"Golem," she repeated and although his eyes were drifting, he managed to nod acknowledging she heard him correctly. His eyes rolled behind narrow eyelids. His body eased beneath her, falling limp. "Where are you going?" she whispered, not to him but to herself.

His eyelids closed, although his mouth still moved as if he were chanting silently. Perhaps he was attempting to force a sound over those moving lips.

And before sleep overcame him, Alena heard him whisper, "Xibalba."

Again, that confused stare. *What the hell is Shibalba?*

16

At some point in the early morning Alena herself succumbed to sleep. She'd lain down on the chaise lounge in her bedroom. After hours of watching him sleep, she was sure it was safe to catch a few winks. She was exhausted and had no idea what to expect in the coming days. Would she have to feed him? Would he need more water? Would he need to use the bathroom? Odd questions suitable for an equally odd situation.

The snow had started to let up. The howling wind now a simple whistle and the sheets of snow had turned to a flurry. Alena looked at him with one last check before closing her eyes. He continued to stir but even that—like the storm—had lessened. She mouthed his name, "Golem," as if to reassure herself of the correct pronunciation.

She was at peace the moment she fell asleep. Drifting off to her own subconscious, she thought perhaps he would be there to greet her. Maybe he could share her dreams as well. She thought she'd heard him—or someone, although she tried to open her eyes but to no avail. She believed she was sleeping. But am I sleeping or awake?

She was drifting, drifting backward, leaving him behind, falling asleep.

"Sleep now," this voice whispered. A thick finger brushed the hair from her eyes. "Sleep peacefully and dream of beautiful things."

————————

She awakened without a stir or jolt. Her eyes simply opened returning from the depths that sleep had brought. She was curled in a ball on the lounge chair with her head turned in to the back of the chair. Her eyes opened and were staring at the red and white pattern that featured daisies made bright by the welcoming warmth of daylight.

She wanted this moment. To lie quietly as if life had not changed and all remained as it was before the gypsy. Alena checked her ring finger to verify there was no ring on that finger. If there were, she'd have known it was all a dream—a nightmare—complete with tragedy and loss of sanity. But there was no ring on that finger. No newborn baby wailing for a diaper change, and certainly no husband preparing for a day of business meetings and to-dos.

The nightmare was real. As real as the floral pattern. Alena held back her tears, refusing to allow herself to cry. She'd wasted too many tears already and they were useless. Nothing changes without action, she thought. And how she did act. Considering there was some sort of—whatever—sleeping in her bed. Who came from…

She couldn't place the word that evaded her like a criminal hiding the truth. Instead, she stretched her bones then flopped her feet to the floor. The balcony was covered with snow more than four feet high, and the sun's reflection turned the day even brighter. Now she felt heat and warmth. The house was warm. And the smell of coffee found her nostrils.

He was not in bed any longer. The thought came again—that it had all been a dream—but who then had made coffee? Who stoked the fire to warm the house? Had to be him, this Golem, her Golem, born from her hands, her mind, her soul, and her blood. Yes, she was sure her blood was required to bring him out of the marble shell. Her breath, like God's breath, turned his body real.

She had questions. Many questions, although she wasn't sure if he even knew the answers. Perhaps he was as in the dark as she was. Truly there's only one way to find out, so Alena stood, ran her hand through her hair, and went downstairs.

————————

He wasn't in the house, which possessed an eerie quiet that clung to the air as if the supernatural were watching with wide eyes hidden beneath the folds of time.

Golem, or someone, had created a fire that burned with a soft crackling. Also, there was firewood piled high to the right of the fireplace, and the house was clean. The marble shards and dust had been removed. The tile sparkled. Even the kitchen was immaculate. The dishes cleaned and put away, the bottles of wine—too many to count—gone. The house smelled like lemon-scented spring. She noticed a fresh pot of coffee was waiting for her with an empty mug set to the right of the coffee maker.

"Hello," she said then noticed how the sun shone through the house as if cleanliness had brought renewed and reinvigorated life. And she felt good. For the first time in a long while she felt like herself again, as if all the pain from the past had dissipated and appeared trivial now that confidence and a sense of freedom replaced her agony.

Is this what happiness feels like? Or content? Alena wasn't sure which one, nevertheless she felt good and that emotion was all that mattered.

"Hello!" Her voice raised and she couldn't help but to smile. She was energized. Excited to be alive like a teenager who has the world on a string with an undying sense of immortality. She left the kitchen and went through the dining room, noticing how the long English-style table was polished to a shine. Even the chairs were gleaming. It was as if the last six months were erased. The house was reinvigorated with life the same as it always had been before tragedy reared its ugly head into her world.

The back wall in the dining room was all glass doors and windows that led to the outside balcony complete with a red stone floor, a pool (covered for the winter), and furniture—Italian imports—with steps that led down into the sand. The ocean was a short walk through the white sand. On a summer day the view was breathtaking with sparkles of light that gleamed off the sea captured on the heels of the wind and deposited across the balcony. When Alena was a child she would sit in this very room wishing for spring and summer to arrive but now she saw the mounds and piles of snow that covered the balcony, furniture, pool (with the exception of a shoveled straight and narrow path,) and down to ten feet before the tide, in a different light. It was peaceful and calm.

Alena stepped closer to the double doors. She saw him then, out on the beach, his back to her, his arms stretched, palms up, and his head raised to the sun. She recognized he was wearing her father's clothes, although the pants and jacket were a bit too small (the pants a few inches above his ankles, the jacket a few inches above his wrists). She could see how the sun shone on him, as if the bright and soft yellow glow encapsulated him in light. He was tall, she could see that even from this distance, concluding he must be close to six feet five inches (her father had been six feet two). She noticed how his hair was kept in perfect thick strands brushed back from his eyes with a single out of place strand (the one she'd fallen in love with) blowing gently.

She stood by the door watching him. That childhood sense of wonder sparkled in her eyes. On the back of a chair at the head of the table were Alena's jacket, leather gloves and winter hat. Her boots placed neatly beside the chair. Alena dressed and went to meet her creation.

17

The cold air bit into the skin gnawing on the bone. Alena held her excitement, walking cautiously across the ice-laden patio, her heart racing. He tucked his arms across his solar plexus as if shielding himself from the cold, and Alena wondered if he was aware of her approach. She took the steps down into the sand, using the handrail to help sturdy her decent. Ocean waves, gentle like a child brushing their fingertips across a painting with eyes of wonder, tagged the shore then retreated back into itself.

She noticed how his body tensed, as if retreating like the ocean waves, when she came up behind him. "What do I say?" she thought. "How do I begin?" She wanted to see through his eyes, to know and understand his thoughts. Alena hoped he was all she had dreamed of and more. Hoped she was all he needed, all he would ever want, without cause for leave or folly. Would he be like a child to her, receiving a mother's undying and devoted love, even after he retreats into the world? Or would he be a love and lover, always devoted and forever enthralled by those little intricacies that make Alena unique? Would he grow old like she undoubtedly will, or will he be forever young without a care for the dying?

And then there were the other questions. Would he remember where he came from? Could he recollect what existence permitted him before he took the statue? Do any of us remember the realm of pre-birth? Did he possess the answers to life after death and the in-between?   Had he talked with God? Had he been judged? Did he exist inside paradise?

Whatever the questions she hoped there were answers.

"Your presence is soothing."

Alena stopped within an arm's reach. His voice was soft, carried on the wings of an accent she ascribed European or Middle Eastern.

"Exciting too, I can sense the jump of your heart."

He raised his face to the sun, and she could see there was a small smile on his lips, his eyes closed under its warmth, breathing deeply as if drawing in the calm wintery stillness.

"My lady," he said. His smile contained the excitement she felt. Or was that trepidation that he marveled at? He closed his eyes and bowed. When he opened his eyes, Alena could see how those fiery sparkles brushed across emerald jewels. "I am honored," he whispered.

Every question Alena had pondered escaped her thoughts as a half-smile graced her lips. And as if he recognized her forgetfulness he said, "Do you know how I've come to be?" as if he was asking God. And his eyes changed, no longer containing the confidence held a moment ago. Now desperation, an infinitesimal confusion coupled with childish wonder, stared back at her.

After a long pause Alena said, "I was hoping you would have that answer."

He cocked his head as if he was pondering her words. Isn't God supposed to have answers? His gaze drifted as if he'd heard someone speaking and looked to address them.

"What do you remember?" she asked. "Do you have any recollection at all?"

"Feelings," he responded. "Emotions. Nothing more. No recollections or memories. Nothing before. An awareness of…love that drew me in. Followed by pain. Lots of pain." He looked off to the sea. "And then awareness. I woke up in your bed as if…as if I'd always been there. I understood what was required then. Heat from a fire. Cleanliness. Warmth." He laughed. "Hunger. Thirst." He turned to her. "Desire. Watching you sleep. You must have been very tired," he said. "All you did was sleep. For three days now you've slept."

Alena looked down. "I'm sorry. I should have…"

He shook his head. "No," he said, "I am grateful for your return."

She looked back at him. His gaze was soft and gentle like a dependent who required someone to guide and direct and for the first time Alena understood what it meant to be responsible for another; to hold their future in the palm of your hand with a chance to pass on a piece of her heart, and to give love freely and without regret.

She looked at him. Truly looked at him. His skin was like porcelain; smooth to perfection and soft like a child with that slight marble tint sunken beneath the skin. His hair, perfectly combed, thick, dark locks plastered behind his ears. She wondered what he looked like underneath the tight fitted suit he wore. His hands were large, like gloves made from stone that commanded the strength of a warrior.

She met his eyes. They contained depths into another world, an ancient understanding of all things past, present, and future but with an innocence to this world, this time, that he did not understand yet wished for, yearning to learn all there was to know. She turned away, not wanting to become lost in those eyes, for she thought she might never return. She turned to the ocean with its glimmers of sunlight reflecting in her eyes, and she could feel him, knowing his eyes watched her. She felt his stare. There were more questions, of course. So many more, although they seemed trivial now, yet she knew all answers would surface in time. For now, there were preparations to be made.

"Well," she said and turned to him. "We can't have you walking around with ill-fitted clothes." Her eyes narrow, scrunched from the sunlight.

He cocked his head inquisitively. A thin smile curled in the corner of his mouth.

"Seems we need to get you some clothes that fit."

18

March 1948

Alena searched through her home. She'd awakened in mid-day to nothing more than silence. Even the soft push of ocean waves was lost to her ears—one can grow so used to things they are rarely ever again noticed. She'd called for him after a few minutes where she observed the silence, hoping to hear a rustling or clanging below only to receive quiet in return, as if he'd gone and nothing more had remained of him. She dressed and went downstairs.

This wasn't the first time she'd awakened under such circumstances. Golem was strange like that; he often disappeared, taking refuge in one of the multitudes of empty rooms in the home. And he never answered her calls or inquiries, always citing his dire need to explore, fixated with knowledge to the point that Alena's pleas did not find his ears.

"Golem," she called, more of a formality than a plea. She knew he would not answer, a behavior she found innocent and playful on the first few occurrences, however increasingly irritating it had become, like a teenager who mutes their parents' list of chores. Nonetheless, Alena overlooked his behavior, believing his compounded protestations.

He was not in the sitting room or the kitchen, where she'd hoped he would be. Looking for more to do and discover, Golem had learned the culinary art, taking to the craft quickly, serving his hostess with a gracious and exiting mannerism, although he did not eat. Alena had not seen him indulge in food or drink, no matter how exquisite the meal or wine was.

She looked through the bay window. The car was in the same spot from the night before. He was in the house—somewhere. Perhaps on the beach, she thought and went to the back of the house, to the dining room. Her eyes roaming over the cold sand, first right then left but he was not there either and she shook her head, her shoulders tight, disappointed and growing frustrated. A week after his arrival, it had taken Alena more than an hour's time to find him and when she did, he was sitting, in the dark no less, wearing a stare that curled the blood in Alena's veins.

"Are you ok?" she'd asked him. His response came after she received a pair of eyes revealing irritation over the question. "I am fine, Alena. You don't have to follow me everywhere."

Most of the time everything between them was like a dream come true but he did possess a natural irritation.

She had purchased a wardrobe for him. Gave him all he needed and asked for and she understood he wanted more. He wanted to explore, to meet people, talk with people, not just Alena - but like a mother protecting a sick child she forbade it. "Not now," she'd tell him. "People will ask questions and what am I to tell them?" A simple question with one answer: *lie*.

Alena knew she couldn't keep him all her years hiding like a disgraced family secret, like a hunchback kept hidden from existence. She knew it would never take, nor last long enough, considering he was, in fact, like a child and had a child's hunger for exploration, wonder and discovery. She understood his youthful cheer; it wasn't that long ago when she held that same fever, a passion for life, for creating, for ideas, for discussion and for change. An incessant need to take on the world and change it—although, as Alena held in private thought, if you count the world's population for anyone above the age of eighteen, you'd find that such a passion is misdirected, and more often than not, slams the dreamer on their ass and sends them tuck-tailed and begging to join the establishment, considering nothing in this world seems to ever get any better or change, like a constant cycle spinning over and over again with the same result. Nothing truly matters except living.

She took one last long survey of the beach. No sign of him, not even below the brush as she could see. She shook her head, "Damn, Golem," and turned around.

He was standing at the far end of the room, watching her, wearing a distorted and confused stare.

"Golem," she said, her voice curt, annoyed. "Did you hear me call you?" Now she noticed he was holding a thin, white towel, streaked with red blotches as he wiped his hands. Her eyes narrowed. "Are you ok?" she said.

He looked up from the towel, "Yes, my lady," and raised his right hand, "Paint," he said. "Just paint." He bowed his head, seemingly embarrassed. "I'm afraid there's only one artist in the family." He laughed. "I didn't do so good."

She couldn't help but smile back. "I'll teach you," she said. "If you want." He seemed distant today.

Alena wondered when his plea for outside entertainment would surface.

He shook his head. "No, I'll stick with cooking. For now, at least."

"Where did you get the paint, I…"

"In the cellar," he said. "I found them in a box hidden in a corner. It's huge down there, one could definitely get lost." He tossed the towel on the table when they were interrupted by a humming car engine headed up the drive.

His eyes turned delighted. "They're here," he said.

"Come again?"

Golem cowered under her grimace. "Don't be mad," he said. "I…I called and invited them."

The car was coming closer.

"Invited who?"

"Your friends, the bridesmaids…at least that's how they were identified in your phone book. Crystal, she's the one I called."

She moved her head back and forth. "Why would you do that? And without asking me first."

"Please!" he said. "I grow so bored staying in the house all the time. I need more company. More excitement."

"Am I not enough?" She hated letting those words slip. She sounded desperate.

"Of course you are," he said and the look in his eyes - one of pity and remorse - confirmed his response. "But you sleep so much, and I, I don't sleep at all."

Whoever was driving wailed on the horn. The car stopped.

Alena rolled her eyes. "Can't believe this."

"I'm sorry," he said.

"What did you tell them? Who did you say you were?"

The car doors opened.

Alena's heart jumped.

"I told them I was…"

She scrunched her face and raised her shoulders. "Well?"

Now he smiled, ear to ear. "The butler."

Alena shook her head. "I can't believe this. The butler. And they believed you? I can't see that happening."

"Well, I told them I thought it was best for you to meet with old friends. That you were thinking of reopening the ClairField and wanted to talk about it."

"You what?" her voice hit a fever high pitch. "I told you I wasn't doing that. I told you to leave it alone." She'd taken him to the ClairField a few weeks after his arrival. He fell in love with it instantly and had been begging Alena to reopen the hotel ever since.

"Alena, please."

A knock on the door and Alena could hear the bridesmaids, giddy and loud outside the front door. She rushed past Golem.

"I seriously can't believe you did this." She didn't look at him. She walked through the foyer, checked herself in the mirror, running her hands through her hair.

"It'll be fine," he said. "I promise."

She looked at him through the corner of her eyes. "I'll deal with you later," she scolded.

He stiffened and raised his chin, that smug smile brought out his eyes.

"Our first fight," he said. "Kinda cute, isn't it?"

And she smiled, too. She shook her head, "Don't patronize me."

She just about melted under the weight of his stare.

"It'll be fine, believe me."

She stomped to the front door. Again, a knock followed by the girl's calling, "Alena, we're here. We brought an exquisite Bordeaux. A few actually!"

"For both of us!" Golem hollered after her.

Alena flailed her arms. "We really have to figure out how you can sleep."

She was close to the door. The girls continuing to call her name. She had to admit their return to her home felt good. Comfortable.

"I don't see the need for sleep," she heard him say. At the time she never made heads or tails about it, as if his voice was not meant to be heard by the ears but instead, were dropped into her thoughts as if he did not verbalize them aloud but had thought them to himself. "While the world is sleeping, we have time to plan....

And reap."

She shook it off, slipping into the socialite skin as quickly as flipping a switch.

19

Golem brought wine glasses to the sitting room and uncorked two bottles, pouring the wine for the ladies. Alena made small talk over current events as Golem excused himself. "I'm afraid I dropped some paint that requires my attention. When I'm finished, I'll bring the pate' I've been slaving over all day." Alena thought he excused himself so she could speak with them privately about the new butler.

She could sense he was becoming restless, never going out, never allowed to socialize. She knew he was growing eager, in more ways than one. And she'd caught their eyes looking him over. She did not like it. Crystal was the main offender. She knew she had to tell them, if, at the very least, to stake her claim and ward off any further inquiries.

Like clockwork, it was Crystal who first addressed the issue of the new butler.

"Tell me, Alena," Crystal began, "What is with your new butler? Does he satisfy every little request you give him?" She laughed and the others followed suit, Alena included.

Hanna chimed in "If he's for hire, Alena, I've got more than a few chores I'm sure he can accommodate. Of course, only when Steven is away."

Although she managed to maintain the socialite façade — old habits do indeed die-hard — Alena was burning up inside. Resentments began to take hold, her body quivered, and her jaw tight.

"How is your husband?" said Alena.

Hanna rolled her eyes. "That Steven," she said. "Started new businesses and took on a new partner. Some Noel person." She sipped her wine. "He's ok. His wife on the other hand…" she shook her head. "That woman's got a stick up her ass. So conservative, you'd think Jesus Christ was holding her hand and scolding every little move she made. The woman's so uptight she looks like she's fending off the devil in every waking moment. She'll come around though. Don't we all? Just takes a push in the right direction. In the meantime, I've got to play the role of the happy content wife." She sipped her wine again. "You know how it is."

They all did know, all except Alena.

"Maybe someday," Alena said, her voice a whisper. Hanna's words hung in the air and the ladies paused as if considering where the conversation was going. The bridesmaids shared glances with stiff eyes.

It was Jackie who turned the conversation. "He's not a butler is he, Alena?"

Alena moved her head back and forth, "Not at all," she said looking at the area where she had built her statue, now empty and wiped away, cleaned of any remnants and remembrances of existence. Her statue was in the cellar, cleaning up paint.

"Told you she was building her own man," Crystal said. "We all do. Seems to be the lot we ladies have in life. Build the man up. They'd be peddling snake oil if it weren't for us."

Alena looked peculiar at Crystal. She'd forgotten having told Crystal about the statue during her last visit. That's my new man, she'd said. Crystal noticed the perplexed look and reminded Alena about the conversation.

"What happened to it?" Crystal asked. "It was a statue, wasn't it?"

Alena sipped her wine; the dry acrid taste blossomed on her tongue. "It was but I had to scrap the project," she said.

"Weren't feeling it?" Jackie said.

Alena responded, "Not at all," her voice a hush as she thought of Golem and the events that transpired.

"How Shakespearian," Crystal said. "Building a statue of a man and then he shows up to whisk your heart away."

Again, that peculiar stare from Alena.

"Oh, c'mon Alena, it's quite obvious you're smitten with him. Judging by the way you were watching us watching him I do believe you could be in love with him."

"Good thing, too," Jackie said. "Considering Bill's gone off the deep end. Seems you dodged a bullet with that one."

"What do you mean?" Alena asked.

The bridesmaids paused looking each other over.

"He's succumbed to the drink," Crystal said. "You really need to get out more, Alena, or at least pick up a newspaper. Bill's been in the headlines lately."

"For what reason?"

"A drunken bar brawl in Hell's Kitchen," Crystal said. "He just about stabbed a man to death. His mother publicly shamed him for the incident. Seems they are keeping him under lock and key until the trial.

Holed up in that extravagant beach house not too far from here."

"They'll offer a plea," Hanna said. "He'll be fine. A year or so in hiding and he'll be back out there again. Running the family fortune into the ground."

Alena felt a stab in her heart. A stab that once punctured brought relief as if the piercing proverbial knife killed off the painful memory, twisted it and turned that resentment into freedom. She actually felt pity for Bill, if only briefly.

Alena sipped her wine, pursing her lips as she swallowed. "Unfortunate," she said.

Hanna said, "But satisfactory isn't it? Considering you made the right decision calling off the wedding. You came away like royalty on that one, Alena."

No response from Alena. She sipped her wine thinking of her former love.

"Well, Alena, can we have a more formal introduction on the new man?" Crystal said. "Set the man free, Alena. There's no reason he has to pretend being a butler and slaving over pate' all day while we sit here sipping a fine Bordeaux and he's cleaning up paint in the dungeon."

"Cellar, not dungeon," said Alena.

Crystal rolled her eyes. "What's the difference?"

Alena cocked her head. "True."

Hanna and Jackie requested his presence as well. Jackie said, "Bring him up, Alena. Let's get the inquisition over with." Of course, as Alena's closest friends, they had to give their stamp of approval.

"Ok, ok," Alena said. "I'll get him, but please be kind and patient. He's a bit on the shy side and doesn't have experience with…social New York gatherings."

"Don't worry, Alena, we'll break him in the right way," Hanna said.

Alena placed her wine glass on the side table by the Victorian couch, ran her hands through her hair, and went into the foyer. She was stopped when Crystal asked, "What's his name, Alena? Or do we just call him the butler?"

The girls laughed and Alena stiffened. Eyes roaming. They waited for Alena's answer. She hadn't expected the bridesmaids to be in her home and she hadn't given even a second thought to his name. Such an odd name as it was. She cursed herself for not giving him a different name; something more in line with trending modern society as she stood paused hoping a new name would drip off her tongue. Yet none did.

"Golem," she said. "His name is Golem."

————

She couldn't remember the last time she was in the cellar. Has to be at least a decade, she thought. The entrance was through the kitchen, although a separate entrance was outside the house, locked most of the time.

The kitchen was in shambles. Pots, dishes, bowls, and food scattered across shelves and counters. And the smell was God-awful. The stench wrenched her stomach and turned acid in the back of her mouth. She wasn't a fan of pate' but this was a bit different, more like rotting maggot infested meat than chicken liver. The thick stank seemed to hover in the kitchen like a storm cloud and Alena wondered how long it would take to clear the stink.

She opened the cellar door and the smell followed, pooling down the steps and she noticed the smell was ever the more prominent in the cellar. A thick blackness enveloped the bottom step. "Golem," Alena called but it appeared as if the darkness stole her voice, forcing her words back up the steps with a shuddered echo.

The door creaked moving on its own as if it, too, felt the echo. She listened hoping to hear Golem but the cellar was quiet and undisturbed. She thought perhaps he'd gone out the back, cleaning the paint he'd spilled. She took the first step and it creaked beneath her weight. The air turned cold, nipping her skin with a grip like strong icy fingers.

"Golem," she said again, her voice a cracked whisper. She held the wood banister, took steps two, three, four, and five then dipped her head down, hoping she'd have to go no further. Hoping she'd see him but only darkness greeted her. She took the last step, and her bare feet melted into the cool dirt floor.

The cellar was as large and open as the house. Although the house allowed for sunlight with its many windows and glass doors, the cellar held no such admittance of light. Alena hugged her arms to ward off the cold. In front of her was the light bulb fastened to the ceiling (about seven feet high), with a string hanging below Alena's chin. She tugged the string and the bulb flickered on.

Golem was standing in front of her just beyond the light bulb. How did I not see him? Alena thought, startled by his close presence. He seemed hurried as if shaken by Alena's inquiry.

"You scared me," she said. "What're you doing? Are you ok?" She looked from one side to the next, as if expecting someone or something to come out of the darkness.

"I'm good," he said, his voice hurried as if catching his breath.

She locked in on his eyes, noticing how those fiery speckles appeared to have grown, masking the emerald iris.

He ran his hands through his hair. "How's it going up there?"

"Good," she said then admitted, "They know you're not the butler."

"Thank God," he said, his voice rushed with relief. "I wasn't sure how long I could keep up the charade." He looked up the stairs. "Where are they?"

Alena forced a swallow. "Waiting for you to join us."

"Perfect," he said and yanked the bottom of his suit jacket, which had been scrunched a moment ago, straightening his shoulders and standing tall. "How do I look?"

He seems nervous, Alena thought. Of course he is, who wouldn't be nervous, especially a statue who came to life no more than three months ago? She noticed that thick strand of hair fell across his eyes. She brushed it back.

"Perfect," she said. She met his eyes with her own and she felt small beneath him, crawling under his gaze, hoping he couldn't see through her because then he would know, he would know how jealous she was in that moment. *They're going to love you, but you are mine.* She did not want him to go up those stairs. She wanted them to stay in this stink and cold infested cellar until the bridesmaids got the picture and took leave from her—no, *their* house.

"Shall we?" he said, offering his hand, which she hesitatingly took, Alena's tiny hand disappearing within his as he led her to the stairs.

"How can you see without the light on?" Alena asked. Golem led the way not letting go of her hand. The steps buckled under his weight. She was sure they would crack and splinter and he would fall.

"I see better in the dark," he said as she followed him. "I guess I'm used to it."

Alena looked over her shoulder and cringed. She thought she saw something crawling in the darkness, out of the light's reach.

———————

Golem was sweet, charming, funny and exciting. Alena watched him with a certain amount of awe. It was as if he had been practicing for this moment, rehearsing and planning his performance. He was different in front of the bridesmaids than he was in her presence. With Alena he was shy and innocent like a child and with a child's ferocity for knowledge, wonder, and understanding, but now it seemed he matured with the grace and charm of an accomplished aristocrat.

Every word, every retort, every simple gesture perfectly planned to woo over Alena's friends. To be accepted by the social circle Alena had been born into. She had to admit this newfound confidence was not only intriguing it was erotic. He filled their wine glasses—Alena's too—although he did not drink one drop, never allowing an empty glass in his presence.

"He's fabulous," Crystal whispered to Alena after Golem excused himself to gather another bottle of wine. The others confirmed this statement. They were all indeed enthralled by him.

He returned and uncorked the wine, the room now quiet, watching him— the center of their attention—as he poured and filled their glasses.

"Tell us, Golem," said Hanna, "Where is it that you are from? I sense an Eastern European quality."

Golem filled Crystal's glass. Alena caught her friend's devouring stare as she leaned back on the couch. She saw how Crystal shook her head as if shaking off the wine-infused euphoria, stretching her back to sit up—like a lady—on the couch. Golem placed the close-to-empty bottle on the side table.

Alena hadn't thought about this question, although in that moment she cursed herself for not having an already planned response.

"Yes, Golem," said Jackie, "Please tell us where you hail from? What country or city are we indebted to for your company?"

Golem laughed as he eyed Alena with a slight nervous twitch revealed in his pupils. She saw that innocence retreat like a child hiding in the closet from the monster in their bedroom; afraid to open the door out of fear the devil will rush in.

His voice cracked when he answered—continuing to stand over Alena, his eyes never leaving hers.

"A place of immense suffering," he began and ran his hand through his hair as if such an action had become a nervous twitch. "A place so distant—so far off in the universe—no light ever shines bright enough to reach. A horrid darkness with levels of pain, each one more excruciating than the other." Alena offered her hand and he took it in his. Alena saw Hanna place her hand to her heart. Jackie sat up, on the edge of her seat, and Crystal seemed to freeze.

"A heinous realm where torture is the norm and all who are condemned to live in such hell long to breathe and escape. To be able to gather as much suffering—tenfold to personal experience-as a gift to the darkness, with the hope that these gifts will suffice and satisfy the king. An effort in exchange for freedom." He squeezed Alena's hand. "I hope to never return."

His eyes returned then. Alena believed she saw those fiery sparkles rage into fury. He released her hand and turned to the ladies brushing his hand through his hair once again. Alena was captivated; she knew this was not a part of his performance. For the first time today, she thought this revelation was the absolute truth.

He laughed and remarked, "Also known as New Jersey," and they all laughed with him. "I'll get the pate'. I'm confident you will love it." He looked at one then the other, addressing all the ladies in attendance. He excused himself and went to the kitchen.

Hanna sat on the edge of her seat, leaning into the room and whispered, "He's not really from Jersey, is he?"

"Of course not, New Jersey has yet to produce a man of such fine and distinguished quality," said Crystal.

Jackie said, "Alena, truly a great find."

"He's eastern European like you said," Alena responded. There's no possibility they will believe he is from anywhere in this country, she thought. European is the best possible story. Then to Jackie, "Thank you."

The ladies seemed to stiffen now that he was out of the room; Alena caught their wondering eyes and the tension that tightened in the room. He returned with a tray of pate' and artisan crackers. He served the ladies, providing a plate for each with three crackers, each with a fair amount of pate' spread evenly. They all provided their assessment.

"So unique."

"Grand texture too. Truly exquisite."

"The best I've had to date."

"You're a culinary genius, Golem. What kind of pate' is this made from?"

Alena caught the small grin he tried to hide.

"Chef's secret," he replied, an answer they all accepted.

What is *in the pate'?* Alena had no recollection that he went to the store. Although she had been sleeping more so over the last few months—and of course he did not sleep—so he could have gone out at any time and she simply did not notice. Golem poured more wine—now their fifth bottle.

"Tell us, Golem, now that Alena has enlightened us with your true European heritage," said Jackie and Alena caught Golem's eyes as if to tell him her declaration was the best possible and to just go with it. "What are your thoughts on our grand America? Surely it must be a splendid respite from war torn Europe."

"I find it remarkable," he began taking a seat beside Alena, watching with what Alena would recall an air of delight as the ladies drank and nipped at their pate' crackers. "A country completely open for anyone's gain, considering..." He paused as if he caught himself and wished not to continue.

"Considering?" Crystal said, who had been mostly quiet since the pate' had arrived.

Golem stiffened, and Alena felt his heart jump. "Well." He moved his head right then left and Alena was sure he was stalling, coming up with a lie to explain his statement. Or maybe the truth he thought was too difficult to tell. He cleared his throat. "Where I come from, America is for the taking. Any country born by men of a particular worship and conviction, birthed for the purpose of handing off the hearts and dreams of its citizens under the guise of grandeur delusions as an exchange for power, is certainly up for grabs for those permitted to walk the line between hate and corruption. Everyone teeming for the same purpose, to have what is promised, to be content with what they have, or to...take what they believe is rightfully theirs, although with a certain amount of unholy restraints required. Pay to play type of republic. Keep all under the thumb by placing a carrot they will never eat as a distraction to real power. I love this country, the opportunities are immense."

Alena wondered if any of the ladies had actually heard what he said, or if they had tuned out—possibly because of the wine—only hearing the last of his declaration.

"And so do we," Jackie said.

Crystal moved to the edge of the couch, holding her glass high. "To America," she said.

Glasses lifted, "To America!" And they sipped from their crystal goblets. All but Golem who, with a clever tongue, changed the conversation to the ClairField and its potential reopening, a conversation Alena had attempted to avoid. Although she often wondered what would happen to Golem, and what place in history would he take in this world? It seemed opening the ClairField would provide him with purpose—any culinary expert would undoubtedly thrive under those lights. And he can be gracious, charming and the perfect host as was made obvious during this gathering. After much coaxing, pleading and pressure, Alena agreed to reopen on the Fourth of July and would do so in the grandest fashion with Golem at the helm and leading the way.

She believed it was what he was born to do.

20

Perhaps it was the wine —always easy to blame. Or maybe it was the way Golem presented himself in front of the bridesmaids. Even more maybe it was the gestures, simple gestures like when Crystal's eyes revealed admiration and desire. That stare that made Alena cringe with jealousy. It could have been when Hanna talked of her desire, "When Steven isn't home, of course." Or perhaps it was all the flirtatious gestures the ladies, her friends, showed to Golem, as if he were for the taking.

Or fear that he did not desire her as she wished and would take any of the bridesmaids to bed without a moment's pause or thought in between. Whatever the reason, once the ladies climbed into the car and putted down the drive—albeit laughing and scurrying, the car swerving—Alena's desire reached a fever pitch. She wanted him—for the first time in three months she wanted him in her bed, not in the guest room or toiling with paint in the basement.

Ever more, she wanted him to want her, to choose her over all others, and to consummate their bond in the sweetest of gestures. She felt it, this need, this want and desire, writhe in her bones, blood, and veins. So, she went to him after the ladies found their way through the gate, in the kitchen, cleaning the pate' dishes and half eaten crackers.

———————

She approached with soft delicate steps, coming up behind him, and thought she heard him laughing. Laughing to himself as he scraped off pate' into the garbage. He must have glimpsed her in the corner of his eye because he backed up quickly against the sink.

"Alena?"

She reached in, stood on her toes, and kissed him. His body froze, his lips stiff. Yet she could feel his enhanced response.

"He doesn't understand," she thought. "Does he even know about such things?" She ran her hand down from his chest to his pants. Obviously, his body knows. I'll show him.

"I'll be gentle," she whispered leaning her head to his chest. "I'll show you what to do." She lifted her head, her dreamy eyes caught his and she cringed. There was fire and resentment in his eyes. A scowl plastered on his face. A stare wrought with disgust. She felt that stab in her heart again and her blood turned cold.

"What is wrong?" she said. "Do you not want me?"

His voice carried angry tremors. "This isn't you wanting me, Alena. This is you afraid of those flirtatious stares your friends sent to me. This is jealously not desire."

Alena stepped back. Folded her arms across her stomach and returned his angry stare. "How dare you talk to me in such a way?"

"I talk truth, Alena. Tell me I'm wrong, and I'll carry you to bed in the same moment."

She froze, unbelievingly froze. Yes, he was correct. There is jealously behind her actions, although this jealously was second to her want and desire. She'd thought about it on more than an often occasion. She even dreamed of sharing her bed with him.

"You want me all to yourself," he said. "That's why I had to coax you into the ClairField." He ran his hands through his hair. "If it were up to you, you'd keep me here," he moved his head to the right and left. "In this place like a dirty secret. Only now that the secret is out has your desire reached a fever pitch. Don't fool me into thinking it is the opposite."

She felt his anger, like a wave of heat, seep into her skin. Her jaw tight, grinding her teeth.

"This morning you treated me like a child, now you wish to take a man to your bed." He moved his head back and forth. "No. I refuse to be treated in such a way."

She slapped him. Slapped him hard and she thought she broke her hand. His face still carried the strength and solidification of marble stone. An action she immediately regretted; the fire that raged in his eyes leapt at her. She thought he could strangle her to death in this very moment.

"How dare you," she said nursing her hand with tears in her eyes.

Golem sighed reaching his hand to hers. "Is it broken?" he said. "Let me see."

She pulled her hand away, remembering the cut on this very hand. The one that dripped blood, her blood, onto the statue. "You were born from this hand," she whispered. Her eyes turned to his. "Born from my blood." Tears streamed across flushed cheeks.

"Molded from my hand. Brought to life by my very heart."

He appeared to retreat, his eyes looking to the floor then back to meet her stare. He pursed his lips and swallowed. "I know," he said. "And for that I am forever bound to you. Forever yours until the day you release me to another."

Her mouth agape, she moved her head back and forth, perplexed. "You disgust me. Leave," she said.

He stepped toward her. "Let me see your hand."

She turned away, tucking her right hand under her left arm.

"Alena, let me see your hand," he demanded. "I can fix it."

She hated him. Wanting him gone from her sight. "Just go," she whispered.

"Alena, please."

"Just go, get out of here. I don't want to see you right now." Her stomach twisted, her heart drenched with anger.

"Alena…"

"LEAVE!" she screamed.

He stepped back. "Where do you want me to go?"

Alena shook her head. Her hand throbbed, the blood rushing to the wound turned her face pale and she felt sick, on the verge of vomiting.

"Go to the cellar," she told him. "Seems you prefer the cover of darkness over the light of my heart."

He stood over her, unwavering. "Alena," he said. He moved to her. Wrapped his arm across her shoulder and she cringed. "Alena, please."

She shuddered, swiped his arm away from her shoulder and screamed, "Gooooo!"

Golem held up his hands. "Ok. Ok," he said. He went to the cellar door but turned back. "You are my love, Alena. I do want you to know that. You are my lady, and there is nothing I wouldn't do for you."

Alena shook; her entire body shook, watching as he closed the door behind him. She heard his footsteps descend. Her eyes filled with tears, nervously twitching, taking in the kitchen and the plates on the table and next to the sink. The stink of pate' writhed in her nostrils. Her stomach turned. She vomited in the garbage, dropping to her knees. Eyes wet with tears. In the garbage, twirling in red and gray vomit were maggots slithering and curling.

She threw up again.

21

She couldn't sleep, no matter how she tried, listening as attentively as possible to what Golem was doing in the cellar. On the couch, sipping wine to the point where her vision fogged with tears and her head ballooned with heavy drunken weight.

There isn't anything I wouldn't do for you.

His words kept looping through her thoughts.

I am forever bound to you.

Forever yours until the day you release me to another.

"What does that mean?" she thought. "Does he look on me as a child does his mother? Is that why he stayed my hand? Denied his intimacy? Refused to share my bed?"

Alena held her cup in her left hand, nursing the broken hand in close proximity to her stomach. The hand had swelled to a ghastly large size and shook by her side, the pain immense although numbed with wine.

Does he believe me to be like a mother? Someone who will hand him over on his wedding day like a father releases his daughter to the groom?

Her head flopped from one side to the other, eyelids closing and her stomach twisting with the acidity of red wine bubbling into the back of her throat. Now the house quaked beneath her accompanied by a large growl, or what she surmised was a growl.

Now whispers found her ears. Whispers in the dark, in the shadows cast by the few lamplights she'd switched on when the sun retreated with the close of day. Faint, incoherent whispers were rambling and sometimes laughing, although often scurried across the room, right to left and back again. She thought she saw someone through the foyer where she could see the head seat at the end of the dining table, sitting and watching. Watching her. This person bathed in darkness and sat so still their silhouette was only revealed with the passing of a bird or some nightly creature, perhaps a bat, outside the patio doors, fly through the moon's reflection.

She blamed the wine. Told herself she was thinking too hard about her father. Alena's intoxicated eyes alighted to seeing him conjuring his ghost into his favorite seat. Her father's ghost sat by the table, staring at Alena before bending his head as his ghost dissipated. Gone!

And the growl? The boiler in the cellar. Gurgling and belching. Simple reasons to explain the unexplained.

And where was Golem? Still in the basement like a good scolded child. Sent to his room by his mother and hasn't made even so much as a peep since she banished him. Of course, she heard him scurry, quiet like a mouse in the cellar. What was he doing down there? Painting? Had he left the house, finding refuge down by the shore to think? She thought of joining him, heading down into the cellar to speak openly. To apologize for the slap and scold. "Maybe then I can sleep," she thought. Put this day to bed and begin new with the dawn.

Alena stood, her legs wobbly. Her head spun, and she sloshed into the kitchen. Again, she heard those whispers, arriving in her ears with such ferocity and speed it was impossible to make any coherent sense out of them. They seemed to nip at and breathe on her ears. She felt warmth on the back of her neck like warm breath. Subtle low laughing now like a hiding child on the verge of discovery, unable to contain themselves.

She walked past the dishes and crackers and pate', not thinking, not wanting to even entertain the thought that maggots were delving into whatever meat Golem had used. She went to the cellar door, stood there a few moments wobbling and thinking. A surge of vomit nipped at the back of her throat; she swallowed it down.

"Golem," she said but the word came out as a whisper, more like a plea for help. She cleared her throat forcing his name over her lips with a profound conviction. "GOLEM!" She wavered but caught herself from falling back; her left hand seized the doorframe to steady herself.

The whispers ceased.

She closed her eyes in an attempt to ward off the spinning but she forced her eyelids open. Her vision smeared the door and kitchen and she leaned her head against the doorframe. She thought she saw someone standing in the kitchen but when she forced her eyes to focus there was no one.

Alena shook her head attempting to wake herself. She pushed off the doorframe and raised her hand, which jerked painfully. Alena winced and drew the hand to her stomach. She banged on the door with her left hand.

"Golem, please," she pleaded, receiving no answer. Alena ran her left hand through her hair. "Ok," she said. "Ok." She grabbed the doorknob and pulled the door open, awkwardly shuffling to the left to push the door all the way open. To her surprise there was now a wall in the doorframe. Panic struck her heart.

He put this wall here. He's locked me out.

She had no recollection of hammering or hearing any sort of fumbling or construction. Alena reached her hand to the wall, pushing on it. No budge only solid wall.

She slammed the wall with her left hand. "Golem," she called. "This is what you do? Lock me out?" She balled her left hand into a fist and hammered on the wall. "Golem," she yelled. "Let me down there this instant. This is my home not yours. I refuse for you to lock me out of my cellar."

Be careful, Alena. You don't want to break your only good hand.

Did she tell herself this? She wasn't sure. The declaration seemed to have come from the dining room, distant although profound.

Alena stepped back from the wall. Now an engine hummed. A car. Someone was coming up the driveway. Alena looked through the kitchen window. Her eyes scrunched by approaching headlights. There was indeed someone coming to her home. At this late hour?

She steadied herself, widening her eyes, attempting to clear the blurred drunken vision. A sudden fear gripped her heart. She didn't understand why, but in that moment, she was afraid for whoever was headed up her driveway.

Bill Astor was drunk. Incoherently, raging drunk. Watching through the window, Alena thought he'd drive his car through the front door, instead it jerked violently then jolted to a violent stop. A moment later, Bill emerged from the car, stumbled to the ground — flask in his hand — then forced himself to his feet using the car door as leverage.

"Alena," he called; his back bent, head flopped back then forward. His fedora dropped off his head, absconded by a gust of wind and scuttled across the drive.

A sobering moment for Alena, seeing him like that, drunk off his rocker. The bridesmaids. Alena thought of them. Where did they go after leaving today? Probably to the country club to continue their festivities with wine and social interaction, she was sure of it; rambling and foaming at the mouth about Alena's new man.

Word of this new union must have made its way to Bill's ears. Why else would he be here?

"A-L-L-E-E-E-N-A!" he hollered. She noticed his face was flushed with pale red blotches revealed by the glow of the silvery full moon.

She brushed her hands through her hair and the broken hand, numb and swollen, cringed and constricted, pain welling up her arm. She felt like she was floating, traipsing across a cotton sky. The house seemed to belch at that moment; accompanied by a strong wind that erupted from the front door clearing every corner in the house as if its purpose was to cleanse the house. And then silence. Silence like the still quiet after a party when all guests have gone, leaving nothing and no one, not a sound or peep. Simply quiet.

And where is Golem, in the cellar or down by the shore? Did he hear Bill's hollering? The engine putting over the drive and the sudden loud jerk caused by Bill's slam on the brake. Was he listening to Bill's angry hollering? Waiting for Alena's reaction?

She was afraid for Bill and for Golem. What would these two men say to each other? What would happen to them should one confront the other? Bill screamed again, so loud she believed the neighbors, hundreds of yards away, could hear his scream.

She went to the front door, turned on the porch light, and opened the door. Bill Astor was standing in front of her. *How did he make it to the door? He was still standing by the car a moment ago.*

"Insolent bitch," he gurgled and slapped her across the cheek. The force of his hand propelled her already unsteady gait to the floor. She smacked the back of her head against the marble and her vision blurred. Her face stung, her head swelled with pain.

Bill walked into the house with heavy feet. She was in shock. Bill Astor had never so much as laid a hand on her. In all the years she'd known him he was always sophisticated. Always treated her with respect. This is not him, she thought. This is a different person.

Alena forced herself to her knees, then pushed herself up. Anger boiled her blood. She caught a glimpse, out of the corner of her eye, of someone standing in the dining room by the patio doors. A dark silhouette, but with eyes like fire. She felt strong then, her jaw tight. Bill stood in the foyer, his head moving side to side surveying the room, and the house.

"Where is he, Alena?" Bill said. "This man you've been harboring for so long. Keeping him here like a dirty secret all this time."

Had he gone mad? What follies did the bridesmaids tell him? What stories had they conjured?

"What are you talking about?" she said, her voice steady and angry.

Bill turned to her. "You know exactly what I'm talking about. Keeping secretes FROM ME!" His voice raged with fire. And that look on his face; bones constricted, snarling at Alena although it was his eyes she focused on. His eyes were mad. Raging mad. And black, metallic black. She saw no white, no pupil, no iris, only black as if a gateway to the dark reaches of hell had found its way to his eyes.

This isn't Bill, she thought. This is the devil himself.

"Lie to me?" he raged. He reached for her. Gripped her arms with hands like iron. She thought her bones were going to snap in half.

"Get off of me," she screamed twisting her arms to break his grip, but she couldn't shake him off.

"I despise the ground you walk on." He slapped her again. Alena's teeth cut her lip, which swelled instantly.

She didn't know how, maybe it was the adrenaline, but Alena balled her broken hand and punched him square in the face. Bill reeled back. Blood jutted from his nose.

"How dare you hit me?"

Bill held his hands in front of his face looking at the blood he'd wiped from his broken nose. Alena registered the glint in his eyes as if an ocean wave rushed from one side to the other. A scowl of confusion glinted in his eyes, as if recognizing what was happening and not knowing *how* it was happening. But his confusion lasted mere seconds. Alena saw his body constrict as if some massive dark hand wrapped around his body and squeezed. His body shuddered and twitched. And his eyes snarled at her. She could see her reflection in those black eyes. Saw how her face turned to pure fear, knowing what was coming. Her jaw open wide and Bill Astor jumped on her, taking her throat in those ironclad hands.

Alena's eyes bulged from their sockets. His grip so inhumanly strong, she thought he crushed her larynx. Alena slapped his hand, raked his arms with her nails that drew deep into his flesh, drawing blood. Yet he squeezed even more. She raked his face, her thumbs finding his eyes; those black eyes, forcing her thumbs in but this only angered him more. He shook her body, lifted her off the ground by her throat. Her feet and legs kicked and wailed against him but still his strength, fueled with angered rage, tightened ever more around her throat.

And then the thought came. The plea. *Golem, please help me!*

Bill was hit with a force equal to a battering ram that threw him against the front door. Alena's head snapped back, dropped with a heavy thud to the floor where she began gasping for air. In the corner of her eye, while she begged for air to return to her lungs, she saw Golem. Saw Bill Astor collect himself after the blunt force of Golem's push. She saw Bill's eyes, no longer black, return to those blue dreams she'd once admired.

Heard Bill declare, "You," in a hushed sinister voice.

Alena flopped on her ass, sitting, holding her throat, and forcing air into her lungs while gaping and gasping.

"Wretched devil," Bill hollered and rushed at Golem, his fist crashed against Golem's cheek. He returned another blow with his left fist. Then another. And another. Golem fell back, his large body slammed to the floor, and Bill was on top of him throwing fist after fist. Golem never moved, not defending himself, allowing this onslaught to continue. "I'll kill you," Bill hollered and squeezed Golem's throat.

Now Alena heard Golem's plea. Dropped in her mind like a stone dropped into water. Help *me*, Alena!

She saw Bill's relentless grip. Saw Golem's eyes, like those of a fearful child, staring at her and bulging from his skull. Her head spun and she thought she saw eyes, so many pairs of eyes looking down on them from the ceiling.

"I'll kill you." Bill shook Golem's throat, his head flopping back and forth, smacking the marble floor.

Alena heard Golem gurgle. Heard his plea in her mind.

"Stop it," she said. More like a whisper. She forced herself to her feet. "You're killing him," she said as she jumped on Bill's back wrapping her arms around him, forcing his grip loose. Her arms now draped around Bill's throat, clutching the air from his lungs.

Bill stood. He sent an elbow into Alena's gut, and she lost her grip. Bill twisted around, his open hand cut across Alena's temple, and she stumbled to the floor, smacked the side of her head which bounced on the marble.

She thought of dying then. So much pain. Her head, her hand, her lips, her face. Her heart and soul. Thought she wanted nothing of life after this moment. Whatever the outcome it will be too much to bear. Death was better than living with the memory of this moment.

And then Golem rose. A black figure in the grim lamplight. Bill turned to see him and his eyes widened. Wide with fear. Golem was quick, lightning quick, on top of Bill before he could even flinch, pounding his face. Alena heard Bill's cheekbones crack and crush under Golem's heavy fist. His eye sockets splintered his eyeballs. Alena saw blood drip from those eyes, his face sunken.

She saw Golem's eyes, strained with madness. Seething and foaming at the mouth. Striking with a killing force. And with his final blow, Alena heard Bill's neck crack, the bones snapped and severed from his spine. His eyes turned black, not the metallic black like before, but black like death.

Bill Astor was dead.

And Golem dropped on his backside, holding his hands, those bloody murderous hands, trembling in front of him. He breathed hoarse, his lips trembling, his eyes found Alena and he scuttled to her.

"My lady," he said taking Alena into his arms. "Are you ok?" His embrace was warm, comforting.

And Alena grew stiff with fear.

The dead eyes of Bill Astor twitched. His body jerked as if the devil had come to claim his soul.

22

"We should call the police."

Alena had wrestled away from Golem's embrace. Now she held Bill's cold body in her arms, brushing her hand through his hair. Tears in her eyes looking down on what she knew was Bill Astor although his wounds made him unrecognizable, his forehead swollen like a balloon and his face, crushed under Golem's hand, bruised and bloody, sank into his skin. His teeth were broken, what remained were either sharp jagged morsels or completely gone.

"And tell them what, Alena?" Golem sat on the couch, covered by shadows, his right hand, elbow on the couch arm, held his head, thumb close to the jawline, forefinger by his temple. "He came here to kill you. And me too. He was in a rage. A fit of madness. Whatever has happened to this man he is wrought with guilt. There's no telling where this drunken madness would have led."

Alena cried; a tearful whine escaped shuddering lips. She cradled Bill Astor's head against her chest and kissed his cold, bloodied lips.

"You've wished for this," Golem said. "I know you have. You've thought many times about his untimely death. And you called for me to do it. You asked for my help because he was mad with rage and strangling the life from your throat. What are we to do? Tell me, Alena, should we call the police? What will you tell them? That your statue took his life?"

She couldn't think. Between grief and fear, panic and pain, every sensation, every thought tumbled, one on top of the other.

"They'll lock you up should you say such things, Alena. And look at your neck, your face; the police would arrest you for murder. Self-defense or not, Alena, I'm sure Bill Astor's mother would use all her power to make sure you never see the light of day again. No, this situation is better dealt with in other ways. He tried to kill you and me, and that was his purpose…coming here so late at night, to kill us both. We defended ourselves, Alena, there is no reason to complicate the simplicity of this situation by involving the police."

He shifted on the couch, leaning forward. His hands held in front of him, fingertips touching. Alena was hysterical; crying, shuddering, heart racing, whining, and cradling the dead as if she could bring him back to life with tears. Golem turned his head. He sprang off the couch, held his hands behind his back, pacing the floor. Head held down and thinking. He stopped then, in front of the David statue, the real one Alena was so proud to have in her home. His head twisted to the right, looking, studying, thinking, admiring. Golem ran his hand through his hair as if he were looking in a mirror. After a moment he turned on his heels, addressing Alena.

"I've got it," he said. "A simple solution to our most dire situation."

A car accident. That was Golem's solution. Bill Astor was stark raving drunk after all, and Golem surmised he had been drinking somewhere close to Alena's home, which would obviously contain witnesses to his lunacy. Golem required Alena's help, carrying the body to the car. She tried not to look at Bill Astor, tried to see him not as Bill but as the lifeless body he now was.

And she had to drive. Had to drive right into a tree just off the highway. Then help Golem squeeze Bill Astor's body into the driver's seat, leaning his head to the steering wheel. "They'll believe he broke his neck upon impact. His wounds explained by the blunt force the accident caused." Golem made sure to include the flask, Bill Astor's flask, tossing it into the car.

And then the walk home. The long walk home in the darkness. Neither said a word. Alena, wide-eyed, unable to elicit even a simple thought. Her eyes revealed her heart was locked in a nightmare, hoping that once she awakened to the morning light all would be normal. Her legs ached, her throat burned, her head swelled and throbbed. Striking pain raged from one temple to the other. And she was sick, having thrown up three times on the walk back.

The house was quiet. Too quiet. Alena went to the kitchen, poured a glass of water and drank, gulping down the water, which streamed down the corners of her mouth. Her hand was trembling. Golem was behind her. His presence brought fear into her heart, her body tense.

"What did we do?" she whispered.

Golem answered, "We protected ourselves. Protected ourselves from a raging drunken loon. There is no need for the guilt you feel. He would have killed you, Alena, that is for sure and then we would both be..."

She waited then turned to him. "Be what?"

Golem turned his eyes to meet Alena. The fire was gone from his eyes, which now contained a black pitch where no light could penetrate.

"Be what?" she hollered. "Why is my life so important to you when it is clear you want nothing to do with me?"

He stepped toward her, moving his head back and forth. "How wrong you are, my lady. I owe all to you; that is for sure. Your heart, your devotion, your life, that is how I remain here. Without you I am doomed to the dark fire that waits in hell." His expression changed, no longer chiseled strength but vulnerable and soft. "Is that what you wish for me? To be swallowed by darkness? Crushed by iniquity? Forced to spend eternity under the most unimaginable torture? Is this what you brought me to life for? To send me back? And why? Because I've defended you. Stopped a madman from taking your life. Is that how you repay my devotion?"

"You didn't have to kill him," she said. "You could have..."

"Who knows what could have happened? Above all things, this is true...had I not intervened it would be your body under discovery and inquiry, and Bill Astor arrested for your murder. Just as you gave me life, I have returned the favor. It's painful being reborn, isn't it?" He turned to the floor, his eyes wide and staring. "I know how it feels." When he raised his head a single black tear stretched from his right eye down to the corner of his mouth.

She had no sympathy for him, her heart jumped, her jaw tight.

Alena cleared her throat. Her voice low. "You said today that you are bound to me until I give you to another; how is that so?"

"The torch must pass, or I return to darkness. That is the rule and the price of rebirth."

"How is the alternate selected?"

"I do not know. The presentation comes without my knowledge."

She sensed he was lying.

"But I do know that once the torch is passed beauty comes to she who passes it."

"And if it's not passed?"

Golems face scrunched. "Nothing good for either. Nothing short of withered compounded torture."

She shook her head. "You go from one lady to the next. Like a parasite, destroying all in your path." She looked at him, her eyes burning into his heart. "We are even, Golem. As far as I am concerned there is nothing that binds me to you. Nothing at all. You bring no reciprocation, no joy, no laughter."

He approached quickly halting a foot away, snarling. "I killed for you, Alena, never forget that. For you, for your life…what other man has ever done such a thing for you? What man ever would?"

She stood erect, stiff, not wavering. "Consider us even then. I will do no more for you." She thrust past him, wanting nothing more than to go to bed and put this day behind her.

"No, Alena," he said. She stopped in the doorway. Golem turned to her. He laughed beneath his breath. "Need I remind you, Alena, of what has taken place here tonight? Do you really believe I will not provide information to the police? Perhaps an anonymous phone call, no, better yet, to the newspapers. You'll be ruined, and Mrs. Astor will certainly have a field day with you. I'm sure her attorneys would have their way with you too. Think about it. Think about living on the street, better yet, a jail cell. Do you think you'd last more than a minute in prison, Alena? You and those well buffed and manicured nails and your plucked and precise eyebrows. Think of that, Alena. Think of living as an old woman in the streets." He shook his head. "No need for such things, Alena. No need at all. What binds you to me now, Alena, is our crime. Our dastardly dirty cover up. Think of your father's legacy, Alena. Think of his good name being dragged through the mud of public opinion, forever tarnished in the eyes of history. All he's ever worked for gone. Do you really believe your friends would defend you?" He laughed. "Such a scandal would be the talk of their circle for years to come. Truly you have no friends, Alena. Except for me, and I can bring all your dreams back to you. All your love and desire."

"What is it you want?" She could hear the desperation in her voice.

He grinned. "Spoken like the true daughter of a tyrant." He stood tall, stretching his shoulders, raising his chin. "Allow me to take over the ClairField. That is all. Introduce me to all whom you know. They're all corrupt souls to begin with what do you care what will become of them? You, above all, know their minds and their hearts. Give me the ClairField, and I will be gone."

"Fine," she declared. "Once the ClairField is reopened, once I've introduced you to all, I want you gone. Do you understand me? I want you gone from my life."

"Of course," he whispered, a snaking scowl across his lips.

Her eyes narrowed. She said nothing. Provided no response. Instead she went to her room and crawled into bed, crying beneath the covers, thinking of Bill Astor's body being found. Thinking of the scandal that would erupt from his condition.

Would the police believe it was a car accident that did that to his face? Only time would tell.

————

She awakened with a stinging pinch to her vein. Golem was sitting beside her on the bed.

"For your pain," he said, holding a syringe.

Alena tried to move, to stop him but her shoulders wouldn't follow her thought. She was pinned to the mattress as if some phantom were holding her down. And Golem's strength, his grip on her wrist was iron clad.

"Don't…" she said but then Golem injected the brown liquid floating in the syringe into her arm.

"The physical *and* the mental," whispered Golem. Alena's eyelids fluttered furiously then stopped abruptly. She felt as if she was not in her body, every sensation numbed as if she sank into a small room of darkness that allowed no presence of thought, emotion, or bodily sensation. Only existence, however meek and feeble it was.

Her eyes floated from left to right then to the middle and down. She saw Golem, his eyes fixed on something over her shoulders as he gave a quick nod and the bed moved beneath Alena as her shoulders were released. And then darkness found her and pulled her in.

23

July 4ᵗʰ 1948
The ClairField Reopens

It was midday when Alena drove from Long Island to the ClairField. Her new dress–bought for the occasion–hung from the back window. She thought over the very prominent guest list for the hundredth time. Golem had insisted on inviting everyone and anyone for the reopening.

"This will be the grandest opening in ClairField history," he'd said while addressing the new staff during last month's staff meeting, a claim Alena had scoffed at.

Alena's one and only responsibility was assembling the guest list, a task she'd delivered with supreme execution. The guest list doted a who's who of New York elite. Artists, actors, politicians including New York's mayor, the district attorney, and several senators, topped her list, and of course, Manhattan's crème de le crème of high society. Over six hundred were on the guest list and most, if not all, she was sure would attend.

The event was sure to set Golem apart in the eyes of high society. Even film producers from California had flown to New York to attend. Golem had displayed interest in California, *a unique inquiry* she'd thought at the time. She wished he would go there once he received the recognition he was seeking. She wanted him gone. The last few months were a blur, memories were faded and steeped in darkness, and Alena was inclined to believe Golem was poisoning her—those memories of needles and brown concoctions always just out of mind's reach. Although there was no proof of the events—surely a needle would leave a mark, wouldn't it—Alena was certain they were happening.

And then there were the noises in the cellar. The scuffling and scuttling, pitter-patters on the ceiling profoundly heard in the sitting room. And those growls that shook the foundation. Golem spent all his time in the cellar during the infrequent visits when he actually came to the Hamptons. Most of his time was spent at the ClairField, dictating needs and preparations and of course the dinner menu, for which Golem had taken the lead, providing the appropriate recipes for a menu he'd termed, "the finest and most exquisite cuisine any and all of our guests will ever have the satisfaction to indulge in."

Alena thought of the maggots she'd seen in the pate'. A memory she could not shake, turning her stomach every time the thought slipped into her mind.

She turned onto Riverside Drive from 123rd Street and headed south. The ClairField stood prominently in view with its elegance and grace and, just as she had since childhood, her eyes went to the third floor, where she had spent most of her youthful years. The view of the Hudson always elicited a still calmness; no matter what the weather or time of year, she found refuge and solace in the panoramic view from the third floor. Her thought went to Golem and she cringed. Surely he'd taken the floor to himself and more than likely *all* the floors—Golem did not plan on opening the rooms for rent unless a guest became too inebriated to find their way home. He'd even allowed a few staff members in need of housing to stay in those rooms on the condition of: one, anonymity (no one was to speak of the rooms nor that they stayed there), and two, providing around the clock care for the ClairField.

Alena turned onto the long crescent shaped cobblestone driveway and was met by a valet who arrived on cue to open the door for her.

"My lady," the man said as he opened the door.

"Fredo, thank you," she told him. Fredo offered his hand, which she graciously took.

"Miss. Alena, it's good to see you. Would you like for me to carry your dress for you?"

Alena told him no, although Fredo did open the back door, gently handling the dress, and passed it to her.

"Thank you, Fredo. You are so kind." She handed him a c-note. "Keep everyone happy tonight, please."

Fredo swiftly took the hundred-dollar bill. "Of course, my lady. Say no more. Beautiful day we're having. Seems the weather showed up for the reopening. Such a clear sky too, the fireworks display will be the best anyone has ever seen."

She offered a smile for his enthusiasm, taking her dress, which she draped across her shoulder.

"Do you know where Golem is?" she asked.

"Mr. G? Last I knew he was in the basement, finalizing preparations."

"Preparations?" Alena was not informed of any preparations for the basement. Although she was not surprised in the least, Golem seemed to prefer underground living.

Fredo regarded Alena with a confused expression. His voice cracked, "Yes, my lady. For the men tonight. Mr. G is expecting a most unruly game. The construction is in its finality. Well, half of it at least. The half Mr. G wants for the game."

"Game? What game?" she thought.

Alena had become privy to the happenings in the ClairField basement mere weeks before her father's death. During prohibition the basement served as a watering hole, a speakeasy where drums of rum, vodka, and whiskey were prepared. The basement was also reserved for gambling, with poker and blackjack tables scattered across the basement. In its heyday the ClairField was known for its big games, but how Golem became privy to this information she was not sure. It seemed he was reinstating the game, a decision she was not fond of, not in the least.

She was not pleased.

————————

She searched for him in between staff working through chaos, running hurriedly back and forth across the ballroom, dining room, the outside garden (which Alena had gotten lost in when she was eight), and of course the kitchen. None had seen him.

She went to the basement and, sure as anything, Fredo was accurate. Poker and blackjack tables occupied the floor, and Golem had made preparations.

The floor was now cherry wood where concrete had been, velvet couches were set strategically around the room, giving any occupant the ability to watch whatever game was being played. The walls were painted with a lush taupe color and the ceiling, normally nine feet high, was now eight feet and painted with a replica of the Sistine Chapel. Dealers were setting up their tables, and waiters and waitresses were being provided instruction by an older female Alena had never seen before.

Equally strange, everyone in the basement paused when Alena arrived. The room turned quiet. The older lady met Alena's eyes.

"Miss. Alena," she said, more like alerting staff to Alena's presence than an actual greeting. "You look ravishing. That dress you are holding will do your beauty no justice. It would be impossible." And she smiled. Grinned actually. Alena cocked her head.

There was something familiar about that grin.

She continued, "How is everything in your world?"

Equally strange. Alena said, "Do you know where Golem is?" Her voice cracked. Alena cleared her throat. That stare, those eyes, the unsteady shift of energy in the room as if something had dropped and caught everyone's attention, brought a scowl to Alena's eyes, confused.

And then that grin again. "I do not," answered the woman. A second later she continued, "Perhaps in the rooms upstairs. I do recall seeing him make his retreat to the rooms not too long ago."

Alena rolled her tongue inside her cheek. A stabbing pain in her stomach curled her lips. Her breath constricted under the woman's heavy gaze, uncomfortable, skin crawling.

The woman bent her head. Her eye contact was relentless, but Alena couldn't place her. She knew she'd seen this woman before, and she did not like the fear-riddled sensation that pushed down on her, as if the woman's presence slithered with disease.

"Is that all?" the woman said. "Is there something more we can do for you?"

Alena had the inclination the woman was waiting for Alena to leave before continuing to address the staff who sat wearily and waiting.

"No," Alena said. She went to leave but looked back quickly. Eyes narrowed, the woman still watching. Alena cleared her throat. "Thank you," Alena offered, ascending the stairs to the ballroom and towards the staircase that stretched right and left opening the second floor in grand fashion.

A tickle on the nape of her neck, Alena's shoulders cringed. The woman's face flashed in Alena's thoughts and her spine constricted. She paused with her foot on the first step. Goosebumps across her arms tightened the skin. Slowly she turned her head.

Is she watching me?

Alena clenched her jaw, gnashed her teeth, as she looked behind her but the woman was not there, only staff walking hurriedly across the ballroom.

"I must be losing my mind." Alena bounced up the stairs; hand on the banister, shaking her head. Climbed to the second staircase and as she made her way up the stairs something familiar glimpsed in the corner of her eye. She turned to the first floor and froze, jaw open, eyes wide. Her father was standing on the ballroom floor, watching her. Alena's eyes narrowed. A sad, although fearful stare plastered across his face, dark fear sank within dark eyes. He stood perfectly still and erect like a statue, his brow furrowed as if in a forever state of fear, watching Alena as a waiter hurried across the floor, moving through him. And her father disappeared. Alena's eyelids blinked, eyes fell downtrodden with a lost stare.

"Where are you?" she thought while moving her head around, searching, finding nothing other than painful memories.

I can't wait for this night to be over.

24

The third floor consisted of four rooms—more like lavish penthouse apartments—with views facing north, south, east and west. Alena had lived in these rooms as a child and knew every crevice and inch of wall and carpet. She went to the room facing the Hudson, overlooking the garden below. Stopped in the door, looking over the room with a satisfied nod, her eyes roaming over the furniture, pristine carpet, spotless windows and bright clean drapes. Golem had done well; a month ago spider webs were strewn across the ceiling and walls, and dust caked every piece of furniture. Now, the room sparkled with newfound life, polished to a rich and glossy shine.

She placed her dress on the bed before going to the window. The Hudson was calm today, still and quiet like a blanket of water without a wave or squall. In the garden, staff hustled back and forth, preparing for the guests to arrive.

Alena sympathized with the staff, working their fingers to the bone, and preparing for the reopening with a sense of pride and belonging for being a part of an event larger than themselves. The ClairField's rich history solidified the Inn as a staple in New York's antiquity, and she was sure the staff felt a degree of belonging and connection to this history with plans and thoughts to continue its growth and revival. She knew several staff members left good jobs to work at the ClairField.

Unfortunate, she thought, rolling her tongue inside her mouth. Once Golem was gone, she had no plan to continue. The city had plans to turn the area into a park, and for this decision she carried both relief and regret. Regret that the prominent and historic inn would be no more, its history wiped off the map. She was sure should such an event happen the ClairField would be forgotten in time. Relief that there would be no other to take over the inn after her tenure had expired. Alena couldn't bear the thought of another ruling over its domain.

What did all of this mean? Those new staff members would need to find new employment, their passions and invigoration crushed by her hand. "Cause and effect," she thought.

Alena sighed, bowed, and shook her head. "Forgive me," she whispered when the hairs on the nape of her neck stood up, and a chilling quiver raced down her spine.

She thought she heard a whimper, as if someone muffled a scream or tears. Alena looked over the room. All was quiet, although with so many staff members, perhaps a few had come to the third floor for a reprieve. Maybe she was not alone.

"Someone there?" she called.

She heard rustling as if someone had moved. She was certain the sound came from the large walk-in closet.

"Come out of there immediately," she said, her arms folded.

Quiet, not a sound nor peep. She pursed her lips, face scrunched. *Maybe I'm wrong?* But she had to be sure. She went to the closet, held her hand on the doorknob, and stopped. Another whimper. She put her ear to the door. Someone was indeed in the closet and this person, whomever it was, was crying, holding back tears to ward off their discovery.

She opened the door just a crack but the closet was bathed in darkness. Another whimper as daylight crept into the closet when Alena opened the door further. First she saw tattered shoes, thin legs, and a thin torso with loose fitted and worn clothes. The boy's eyes were downtrodden, his head in his hands. He sniffled and, when he raised his head, a teardrop raced down his cheek. His hair was long—at first Alena thought it was a girl—matted and greasy. Soot and grime stained his skin and he looked at Alena with wide, bright, blue eyes filled with tears.

"My God," Alena blurted. "Are you ok?"

The boy did not respond. He turned his head and Alena noticed he was shaking, no, trembling, as his bottom lip quivered. She noticed how his tears streamed down his face parting the dirt.

"Ok, okay." Alena held her hands up as if to calm the situation. Her voice soft and comforting when she asked, "How did you get in here?" He took his head in his hands then pulled his shaking hands away, clasping his left into his right as he turned his head away from her.

What to do? Her eyes narrowed. She saw how he swallowed his cries, his throat jutted up then down with a stuttered breath as if stifling his tears. Alena dropped to her knees and forced a thin gentle smile.

"My name's Alena," she told him. "I'm the owner of the ClairField, so, I promise you're not in any trouble." He shook his head, and rolled his eyes. "Don't believe me?" He shot his eyes to her, wide and skeptical, untrusting. Alena looked away then caught his stare. "Well, since I can't with good conscience leave you here, how about you come with me to the kitchen? You look hungry; let's at least get you some food." And she smiled, smiled wide with a trusting undeniable comfort. And as he looked at her, Alena noticed his shoulders slacked.

"Are you hungry?" She nodded and smiled again offering her hand. "C'mon." She gestured to the hall. "Food sounds good, doesn't it?"

The boy nodded and took Alena's hand. She brought him to the kitchen where she fixed the boy a plate of food. He looked at Alena before eating as if asking for permission. "Go ahead," she said. "It's for you."

No reluctance with the food. He started to devour the meal with his hands when Alena showed him the fork and spoon, which he used as if he'd never set eyes on utensils.

Alena smiled, hoping he would feel comfortable in her presence. Quite obvious the boy was destitute and had been through more than his share of trials and tribulations.

"Do you have a name?" she asked, her voice soft, caring.

He stopped eating, holding his fork loose between his fingers. His voice was cracked and garbled, as if his throat was covered with the same soot that clung to his soft cheeks. "Jonah," he said, keeping his eyes down.

"Jonah," Alena repeated. "How long have you been hiding?"

Jonah looked at her, almost cowering under her stare. No response came.

"Do you remember?"

Jonah shook his head.

Alena bit her lip. "Your parents," she said. "Where are they? Do they know where you are?"

"Gone," Jonah said. Alena cocked her head, looking inquisitively. The boy continued, "They died a long time ago."

Alena closed her eyes, bent her head. She thought of her parents.

"Are you going to call the police?"

Alena looked at him. "Why would I?"

"People always call the police, and then I have to go back." He paused. "I don't wanna go back."

Alena cocked her brow, eyes wide. "Go back where?"

He placed his fork on the plate, gentle. His body shuddered and Alena could sense how his heart trembled in his chest. He placed his cuffed hands on his lap. "To the orphanage," he said and then whispered, inching closer to her, "Bad things happen there."

"Oh." She was on the verge of pressing but decided it was best not to go there. Alena had heard about the orphanage and the numerous atrocities that went on within its walls. There was no reason for such an inquiry; it was quite obvious he'd been through enough.

"Do you work here?" Jonah asked.

"Something like that," Alena said, and Jonah smiled, his teeth like pebbles yellowed from neglect. Her heart sank. "How old are you?"

"Nine," he said.

"Nine," Alena repeated. "Do you have any other family you can stay with?"

Jonah shook his head. "All are gone." Then after a pause, "I have no one."

She could see his eyes fill with tears.

"It's ok," she said. "It's going to be ok."

She had to lie to him. Every conclusion regarding this situation led to only one road: Jonah would have to return to the orphanage, although she wasn't sure if the lie was meant for him *or* for her. Perhaps both, she thought. Little did it matter though, because Alena knew she had to contact law enforcement. And do so quickly. The time was drawing close, guests would begin arriving soon and she still had to prepare.

That phone call would need to happen soon, very soon.

——————

"You said it would be ok."

That's what Jonah said to Alena when the police officer escorted him to the patrol car. His voice was soft, his blue eyes sad and defeated.

"It will be," she told him, another apparent lie. Alena followed them to the car. The officer opened the door for Jonah and he took his seat after a moment's pause. The officer closed the door, walked to the driver's side. Jonah did not look at her, his eyes downtrodden.

"Thank you, Miss. Francon," said the officer. He tipped his hat then took his seat. Alena watched as the officer said something to Jonah who never so much as gave the officer a look in spite of a response. A second later the car moved forward, rounding the cobblestone drive back onto Riverside Drive.

Alena watched as they disappeared. Her eyes drifted to the red sky as dusk crept over the city, the sun was setting beyond the Hudson River. The air was hot and sticky, and sweat glistened on her brow. Alena stood with arms folded across her chest.

What did I just do? She knew where Jonah was headed, understood how afraid he was. *Bad things happen there.* His words surged through consciousness like a jab to her stomach. *What else could I do?*

"You ok, my lady?" Fredo, he was standing behind her having witnessed the event.

Alena said nothing, offering nothing more than a thin smile.

Fredo gave a quick nod. "Understood." Alena's eyes downtrodden. "He will be fine, Miss. Francon. I grew up in the same orphanage. Little to say for it, but he will be fine."

Alena nodded. "Thank you, Fredo."

Fredo pursed his lips. "Best to get ready now," he said. "Guests will be arriving soon, and what will they say when the grandest hostess is not here to greet them?"

"I know," she said. "I know."

She caught Golem then, in the window on the third floor, watching. Watching her, she was sure. He waved then shrugged. He could still be sweet sometimes.

Everyone has their moments.

25

By the time Alena presented herself, the ClairField had already welcomed more than half its guests. Golem played the perfect host, wrapped perfectly in a tuxedo that carried the slightest hint of the darkest purple; so slight the shade was barely recognized. His hair, those thick dark strands perfectly placed. And something new; a red cane, dark blood red burgundy wood crafted with so many symbols any inquiring mind would require more than a day's conversation to learn about them – to Alena they bore the reflection of agonized souls. His charming confidence won over every roaming eye and, in fact, he'd become the center of attention, this new elegant host riding the coattails of his mistress—as the guests referred to Alena. They regarded him as Alena's perfect complement, considering she'd dodged the turmoil and catastrophe the Astor family had been coping with.

Alena had remained on the top of the stairs, watching Golem receiving their guests, listening to the chatter and small talk, while staff members took questions and special orders and the live music filled the Inn with a symphony meant to keep all calm and content.

Alena was always proud to see the ClairField bursting with life; these events fulfilled the Inn's purpose. If a purpose could be assigned to places, she thought. She had to admit, she felt good. Golem had done right by the ClairField, reinstituting class and prestige to the landmark inn. Although there was something different about this night, both different and familiar, she was not able to put a finger to it.

Perhaps it was the absence of her father. She could see him now, greeting guests upon arrival as she took the stairs. Talking with the many politicians and high society socialites who so often frequented the ClairField. And she could hear his voice as if his presence remained, engraved within the folds of time never to be erased as long as the ClairField remained.

Now Golem had taken his role. From what she could hear as she approached the receiving line, doing a fine job at it, too. *Maybe I've been too harsh on him*, she thought and caught Golem's eye. He was greeting Mr. and Mrs. Myer, charming Mrs. Myer with his gracious smile and bold conversation.

"There she is," Alena heard him say. He offered his hand, which she took. "Absolutely ravishing," he said. Then to the Myers, "Isn't she breathtaking?"

Alena wore a pink satin evening gown, long white gloves, and diamond hairclip barrettes.

"Always the definition of true class," said Mayor Myer. He greeted Alena with a kiss on the cheek, something his new wife seemed to not like with her narrow eyes. She was much younger than the mayor; even Alena was her senior.

"Bill," Alena said. "Timeless magazine treated you very well. Wonderful article for a wonderful mayor." Bill had been featured on the cover of the June issue.

He held Alena's hands. "I'm sorry to hear about Mr. Astor. Give my condolences to his mother, please." He kissed her cheek again.

"I will," Alena said. No reason to correct New York's standing mayor on the social and romantic conversations of one Alena Francon, she thought.

"I see you've found a most suitable replacement," Myer said, referencing Golem. "I'll have to watch his career with great interest."

Golem's eyes narrowed. "It would be an honor." And then he smiled, his lips never parting, the corner of his mouth curled to the right.

"Of course, come to my office, there are many issues we can learn about together."

"Indeed." A glint waved in Golem's eyes and Alena's body tightened. Something about Golem's eyes did not sit well with her. Even the mayor appeared to tense.

"Well," said Myer. "Congratulations on the reopening. I trust the city's investment has been received with the care this great city righteously deserves."

"Undeniably." Although the word was delivered instinctively, Alena understood this connection with the Mayor provided Golem with the credibility he longed for and was undoubtedly rehearsed by Golem.

She wished to take it back but there was no having it. This credibility she then understood was Golem's underhanded purpose. The Myers departed to their table and Alena surveyed the line of guests snaking through the ballroom. In line waited a number of guests so uniquely prominent, anyone who ever had plans for world domination would just have to show their face and take over. The guests had arrived under Alena's invitation but they were here for Golem, handed to him on a silver platter with the name Francon engraved on it.

Meeting Golem's eyes with her own she understood what was different. The façade had changed. No longer did her father's presence claim the ClairField; she'd given the Inn to Golem, regretfully too. Whatever plans he had for it, Alena was certain those plans would end in catastrophe. The air too was different, the energy that wafted and wailed through the Inn, to every room, every crevice, every misshapen blemish, contained a piece of him, of Golem. She could smell his skin on the walls.

She wanted to run, squirming and uncomfortable beneath her dress, while greeting her guests with small kisses and fake smiles. She knew that Golem heard her thoughts, knew what conclusion she had come to. She watched him as he greeted person after person, couple after couple, and all were taken by him. Undoubtedly, Golem will be the new talk of the town come morning.

Her stomach turned.

She thought of Bill Astor, his face crushed by Golem's hand.

Saw her father wearing an expression that echoed disappointment.

Thought of Jonah. *Bad things happen there.*

Not just there, Jonah. *Everywhere!*

She had to throw up.

————

To Alena the evening was like death by a thousand cuts. In every turn of events, every person she talked to something new was revealed. She was suffocating through the event as if she were drowning, her stomach churning in a continuous knot. When she finally was able to breathe, she did so on the third floor, her mind swarmed with the little tidbits discovered over the evening, and from the lips of her friends. She thought of each one, each discovery. Alena had not been informed that Hanna's new friend's husband, Noel, had been hired by Golem to provide the ClairField with a facelift, especially the basement which she was sure would be the evening's greatest success, considering the loud and obnoxious hollers, cheers, and jeers coming from the basement all through the evening.

Hanna introduced Alena to Annette and Noel Flemming. Noel had sought Alena's approval on the facelift. Startled, Alena provided the appropriate response, praising his company's work. She'd provided Golem with a list of three companies to provide the service, companies she'd worked with for years. Companies her father had approved of. Apparently, Golem did not agree with her assessment.

And then there were new guests. An extra hundred or so people she'd never seen before. Alena did not approve of this new guest list, although she'd always been the person to welcome anyone and everyone. They arrived late, very late, attendants for the after party for which Alena had no knowledge of. Personal invitations to the after party were sent by Golem himself, however, Alena had learned the invitations were made in her name, signed by Alena Francon as an exclusive social gathering.

"Yet another manipulation," she thought. "Not only am I playing hostess, now I'm handing out personal endorsements."

Now a boom erupted outside. Alena snapped her head around. The fireworks display had begun. Hundreds of onlookers gathered in the garden. The OOOOH's and AAAAH's swallowed by loud bangs and sparkling fizzles. A dark sky ignited with a swarm of color.

She surveyed the crowd below, looking for Golem. She had questions and wanted answers although she'd been unable to locate him throughout the evening once their host and hostess charade had ended.

He was not among the crowd.

"Where are you, Golem?" Alena thought, grinding her teeth. "Where are you hiding?"

"Not hiding, my lady," said Golem, his voice, soft, gentle but with an edge behind it that screamed terror. Alena snapped around. Golem stood in the door. "Preparing."

The bedroom went dark when Golem turned off the light. He stepped into the room. Alena's jaw constricted, her bottom lip quivering. Instinctively she stepped back and hit the window.

"Preparing for what?" she whispered, although she knew the answer. Felt it in her gut.

Golem never looked at her, not directly. He was quiet, methodical, and almost compassionate. He closed the door with a soft push, shutting out the hallway light. Those bursts of color sparkling over the Hudson reflected inside the room.

"Alena," he said. "You know full well what is happening here, but you choose not to see it. Rather disappointing, I must say. I've never had one like you before; most of my ladies welcome these things I do. But you, Alena…you are truly special, perhaps a step above on the moral code. Although I must say that you have posed quite the challenge for me to continue my work and that is something you know I will never allow to be displaced or discontinued. No, Alena…"

He was in front of her in a flash as if his form molded into the darkness, manipulating it to allow him to move as if he were the wind. A second ago he was standing by the door, now he gripped her wrist.

"Somehow we're just going to have to find a way to respect each other's purpose."

He twisted her arm, and she screamed in pain. Outside, the fireworks erupted swallowing her screams.

She tried to move away, twisted her arm attempting to free her wrist from his hand. "Time to take your medicine, Alena. For tonight's entertainment, you'll have to be front and center, no more sitting on the sidelines. I've protected you enough up until this point; now you have to play your part."

"Get off me!" she hollered, trying to pull her arm free, her eyes wide. "I said get off ME!"

"Come on, Alena, let's play nice now." And he laughed, a sneering conniving snicker.

She bit his hand, sank her teeth into flesh and bone, not marble stone. And blood. She could taste his blood on her tongue. Golem flinched and held his hand. Lifted his wound to eye level, the blood streaming down his hand.

"Blood," he said, smiling. "My blood." He dropped his hand, head turned to the side. "Seems surreal, doesn't it?"

Alena stepped back. More fireworks exploded outside, and bright fizzling lights reflected in Golem's eyes. Alena ran to the door.

"Come now, Alena, you know what waits behind the door."

Without hesitation, Alena gripped the doorknob, thrust the door open, and froze. What stood in the door was surreal; translucent although Alena could see the outline where this beast ended and the real world began. And then its eyes gleamed, red like blood. She stepped back. Mouth agape. This translucent beast growled, drew in Alena's constricted breath, and stepped into the room.

"*AGIOS O BAPHOMET!*" declared Golem.

Alena stepped back, slow, fearful, as the beast slithered towards her. Her legs pressed against the bed, and she dropped on her back to the mattress. Golem, she was sure it was him, gripped her wrists stretching her arms over her head.

She tried to scream. Wanted to scream. Every instinct told her to holler, scream for her life but no words manifested. She was paralyzed, unable to move or speak.

"*AGIOS O BAPHOMET!*"

The beast was on top of her; she could feel the bed buckle although she felt no weight on her person.

"Stay still now, my lady, this will be over soon." Golem gritted his teeth.

The beast, its head dipped toward her, opening wide its translucent mouth, and Alena could see how the hall light and fireworks burst within it. She was immobile, unable to move, scream or flail. She was staring into its eyes, black to the core, as its lips touched Alena's. Her mouth was on fire, open and wide. The beast came into her mouth. Her throat swelled to an unimaginable size, swallowing this beast down into her gut as she jerked, twitched, and shuddered. Like a snake slithering within, Alena's skin protruded, circling down her throat, across her chest, ribs and stomach, then down her legs and feet and her eyes, her eyes turning black, she knew it, could feel it, saw herself out of body as her eyes filled with black death.

She felt Golem release her wrists and she sat up looking over the room. Seeing perfectly, even in the dark, black corners, she could see everything with a heightened vision. And she could hear. Hear the mice and rats in the attic pounding across the floor. Heard the chatter and conversation in the garden.

"Are you in, Baphomet?" Golem asked. She turned to see him standing tall beside the bed, bathed in darkness and hall light that turned his skin gray.

"Yes," Alena breathed. She felt her mouth move, although the voice, her voice seemed far, far away as if she spoke from the hall or steps. As if it was not Alena who spoke, but something or someone else. Alena now a passenger in her own body.

Golem bowed, dropped to one knee, his head down.

The fireworks outside were now popping and fizzling with a grand finale. Alena felt her body move as she touched Golem's head and noticed how her hands looked different, now long fingers with jagged nails and scaly grey skin. She went to the window, eyes wide looking over the Hudson. Golem stood; she felt him rise. Actually felt him lift off the ground to his feet as if the air between them provided the knowledge, brought to her in the folds between them.

Alena's stomach wrenched. She sensed hunger and thirst crawl into her throat.

And then that voice again, her voice with a slight edge, a sinister rasp cusped on the edge of her words.

"Where are the children?"

26

She was suffocating, struggling to breathe, existing inside her own mind like a passenger, a passive observer with no control, and no influence on her bodily movements. She could hear breathing, hoarse, profound breathing, thumping in her ears. Darkness was everywhere, the only light directly ahead like viewing the outside world with blinders on, tunnel vision. Behind her there was only darkness. No end, no beginning. She heard movement like pounding and scattering packs of wolves. And then howling in the distance, huffing and heavy breathing, moaning, painful, torturous, wrenching screams. Far away but inside her mind.

Accompanied with the darkness, howls, and cries, was a sense of security. Comfort within the perils of timeless darkness.

Golem escorted Alena to the basement, passing any possible wandering eyes; the games continued as they had before. The people moved in slow motion, never offering even so much as a glance in their direction. Except for one, the woman Alena had conversed with earlier. She stood within the hollering, gaming crowd. Golem looked on her, gave a quick nod with closed eyes, Alena's hand in his.

The gypsy woman, Alena was certain she was looking at the gypsy. She could see it now, in her eyes, the trap door, although she was younger than she had been in the store, as if she'd turned back time by decades. Alena noticed she was on the verge of tears.

Golem moved with Alena. She thought she was floating, her limbs moving without a thought through a dark hall. This is what Noel had mentioned, the back of the basement. And the air turned cold, freezing cold. Golem released her hand, taking from his pocket a large round silver keychain with a single key that he slipped into the door in front of them.

Alena felt her heart race, not sure if it was excitement or trepidation that caused the thick beat to escalate. The door opened with a suctioned pop.

"Have all preparations been made?" Alena asked.

Golem stepped through the door. "All has gone as planned," he said. "All have consumed flesh and blood."

The room glowed with a red tint. Eleven cages lined the room on the left, open space on the right. Each cage was no more than six feet long and two feet across – enough room to lie down and sleep - reaching to the ceiling seven feet above.

Whimpers held back, cries and fearful scurries came from those cages, all bathed in darkness despite the red tint overhead. Golem closed and locked the door behind them, his movements smooth and calculated. He leaned against the door. Alena arched her head back, seeing him.

"They wait for you, Baphomet," he said. "Please, choose your desire."

Alena turned to the cages, walked to them, felt her hand run across the steel. Inside each cage was a child, some no more than four but none more than ten years old.

Alena felt herself grin. "Delightful," she said. "How did you retrieve so many so quickly?"

"The orphanage," Golem breathed. "They came willingly, of course. So, so easy it was; they came like hungry dogs to a steak dinner."

Alena pursed her lips, tightened her jaw.

"Please, my lady, can you help us?" asked a voice in the cage behind Alena, the voice soft although strong.

Alena turned to the seven-year-old girl who pressed her forehead to the steel fence. Soft blue eyes gazing at Alena. The girl's face covered in soot, matted blonde hair. Alena bent down eye to eye with her.

"Of course," Alena said. "That is why I am here."

The girl paused, staring at Alena, sizing her up.

"Why are your eyes like that?" The girl was trembling, Alena could see.

"Don't be afraid, my dear. Not of me, not ever. I only wish to help you…can you believe me? That I am here to help you?"

The girl pursed her lips then swallowed. She gave a quick nod. The other children softly and quietly stood, watching, their eyes sad, confused, defeated. Listening and observing. Alena could hear their shallow breathing and the restricted beat of little hearts.

"Good," Alena said, shaking her head and smiling. "I only need for you to do something for me. Is that ok? Can you help me too? We all need help in this world, do we not? Will you help me—?"

"Sophia," said the girl. "My name is Sophia."

Alena felt the grin on her lips. "Such a beautiful name. Tell me, Sophia, what are your dreams?"

Sophia hesitated. "Dreams are not real," she said. "Not for us, not ever for us."

"Oh, my darling, so, so not true. Dreams are for everyone."

She heard Golem snicker over her shoulder. Sophia looked at him but Alena's hand covered the view, returning Sophia's eyes to her.

"Tell me, Sophia, do you wish for riches? Fame? Power? Do you wish to come away from this cage and be free?"

Sophia nodded, those blue eyes sad and downtrodden.

"Oh, wonderful. Absolutely wonderful, Sophia." Alena felt hunger turn her stomach and wrench into her throat. She licked her lips with a slight movement of the tongue. "I can do that for you, Sophia. I can make all your dreams come true."

"Are you a fairy godmother?"

"Oh, yes, Sophia. That I am and I have all your dreams and wishes right here..." Alena held out her hand, palm up, for Sophia to see. "In the palm of my hand." Light emitted from her palm, sparkling red and blue light as if she held a crystal that reflected the rainbow. Sophia's eyes glowed.

"You *are* a fairy godmother."

"Of course, Sophia. I wouldn't lie to you. Not to a child. Not ever. But can you please do something for me first? Before I give you such beautiful presents. Do I have your permission? Can you give that to me, your agreement? Like a sacred pact between two people.

You do for me, and I do for you. Will you allow this, Sophia?"

Sophia looked left then right, seeing the other kids with unknowing stares. She turned those blue eyes to Alena and nodded. "Yes," she said. "Yes, I will."

"Oh, wonderful. So brave, Sophia. So, so brave." Alena stood and looked at Golem, who went to the cage, key in hand. He unlocked the cage and the door creaked when he opened it. Sophia ran into Alena's arms, looking at Golem through the corner of her eyes, fearful. Alena ran her fingers through Sophia's hair.

"My dear," Alena said. "Come with me, we must prepare. Time moves fast, and we must move faster." She took Sophia by the hand, led her to a second door tucked in the corner.

"Where are we going?" Sophia's voice soft with a tinge of excitement, relief.

"To prepare, Sophia. We must make you look like a princess. Isn't that wonderful? To be dressed like a princess? That way all who see you will know..." Alena turned to Sophia as Golem now unlocked this second door, pushing it open for them to enter, a long dark hallway led the way. "They will know you are a princess."

Golem stood in the door, watching. "The corridor leads to the third floor," he said but Alena and Sophia never looked back, they moved, hand in hand, down the corridor.

"I'll begin the ceremony," Golem hollered, his voice bounced off the stone walls. "All will bow. All will pay homage to you, dear Baphomet."

––––––––––

She bathed and dressed Sophia in a white dress—what had once been Alena's—brushed her hair and applied makeup. Sophia was the perfect picture of a porcelain doll when Alena finished. They stood in front of a long Victorian mirror, Alena behind Sophia, hands on her shoulders. A princess and a queen, standing together.

"I've never had such a pretty dress before," said Sophia when the ClairField vibrated, the sound coming from the ballroom, as if someone had banged a crystal bowl or xylophone. Five loud dings in all and the vibration shook the foundation before writhing up the walls to the third floor. Alena felt the vibration in her chest and bones. The sensation was sweet like ecstasy. Her mouth was agape, black eyes wide. Sophia shook with fear as she saw Alena in the mirror, Alena's hands squeezing her shoulders and pulling her close.

"It has begun," said Alena in that new raspy voice, not her voice, but she felt her lips move.

Sophia stretched her neck looking over her shoulder to Alena. "What?" she said, her voice cracked. "What has begun?"

Alena's head drifted, seemed to pivot on a swivel, the vibration writhing and rattling inside her skull. Her eyes closed with a deep inhale then opened to Sophia. Those black eyes absorbed the lamplight, drawing the light in to dissipate the yellow glow. Alena hooked Sophia's chin with her fingertips.

"The ball," she told Sophia. "Certainly a princess must attend a ball in her honor."

"For me?" said Sophia with a slight bounce as a smile crossed her lips.

Alena closed her eyes with a quick bow. "Of course, my lady. All for you." She offered her hand. "Come," she said. "Take my hand and I will escort you to the ball."

Sophia stood a moment, surveying Alena's hand before she folded hers within Alena's palm. Alena's lips parted with a devilish grin. She led Sophia into the hall, to the stairs.

Sophia said, "You really are a fairy godmother."

27

"Why are their eyes like that?" asked Sophia.

"It's the blood," Alena responded. They stood at the top of the steps, hand in hand. The scent of sulfur came from the ballroom below where the after party attendees stood, all eyes on Alena and Sophia, all black eyes that is. The attendees stood erect, heads held high, eyes wide with anticipation. They stood single file in rows and columns, nine in each row, eleven columns in all. At the bottom of the stairs a red carpet split the columns, leading to Golem who held a chain in his hands. Attached to the chain was a bell, a clunking cowbell.

Behind Golem was a marble slab, not large enough for an adult to stretch their limbs across, although a child may find comfort on the smooth marble stone.

It was Golem who initiated the chanting, addressing Alena, "*AGIOS O BAPHOMET!*"

The attendees repeated the same.

Sophia cringed against Alena's arm, hiding her eyes.

"What blood?" Sophia screeched. "This doesn't look like a ball."

Alena forced Sophia to release her arm, taking Sophia's hand with such force Sophia's bones just about snapped. And when Sophia's mouth opened with a scream and holler, she caught Alena's eyes and the finger she pressed to her lips. *Shhhh!* And then that devilish grin erupted on her lips.

"All in time, my princess," Alena said. "All answers in time. Good things come to those who wait."

Alena's eyes glimmered as if something lived inside those eyes.

Sophia screamed, tried to pull away from Alena's grip only to be hushed quickly when Alena dropped her free hand to Sophia's lips. "Shush now," Alena said. "After tonight, my lady, you will find no cause for screams."

She led Sophia down the steps to the red carpet.

AGIOS O BAPHOMET!

The attendees followed them as they walked the carpet to the marble slab.

AGIOS O BAPHOMET!

Golem, bell and chain still in hand, bowed.

"The children are the future," said Golem. He set the bell down, lifted Sophia by the waist, placing her upon the slab. "And the future is ours." He kissed Sophia's forehead then gently forced her to lie down. His hand, so strong and gentle. Sophia, confused, stared at Golem's wide mad eyes. She shook with fear, her lower lip quivering.

"It's ok," Golem whispered. His head cocked when he said, "We all must go through pain to taste freedom." He offered Sophia a caring toothless smile. "When the pain is over, Sophia, you will be my most prized possession." He turned to the ceiling, his eyes roaming left then right then back to Sophia. Fire raged in his pupils. "No more orphanage, Sophia. After this night you will have all your heart desires. Unlimited power with the snap of your fingers."

AGIOS O BAPHOMET!

Alena looked on the attendees. The chanting ceased.

"All who do not follow will meet their doom." Her eyes darted from one attendee to the other. None stirred, all looked on Alena with apt focus. Inside Alena saw her friends, people she'd known all her life, friends of her father, the bridesmaids and acquaintances she'd smothered with kindness all those years as the ClairField's hostess positioned within the new guests like stones swallowed in an ocean. A passive observer in her own body, like living in a waking nightmare with no control.

"The children are the future," she said. "And the future is ours."

Golem brushed the hair from his eyes as he leaned over Sophia, those fiery pupils wavered and crackled. Sophia's body relaxed as Golem touched his lips to hers, forcing his breath down her throat.

———————

"I remember the fireworks," said Alena. "The rest is…" She tried to think, tried to remember but the thoughts kept cycling. Rapid-fire successive recollections—the guest list, her friends, and the fireworks—with a flash every now and then of the ceremony, although these memories were gone quickly, rushed across her thoughts like watching a film on fast forward. A single frame among thousands.

She gripped her head in her hands, sitting on the edge of the bed on the ClairField's third floor. Golem was in the bathroom, listening to her speak, door opened, apparently washing his hands with the sink turned on high. Tears pricked her eyes as she breathed heavily, trying to makes sense of her memories.

"Probably just stress, Alena," Golem said from the bathroom.

She didn't hear him. "Why can't I remember the past three days?"

"I told you before, you've been sleeping. More than likely you're sick from all the stress."

She stood abruptly. "I don't believe you," she hollered. "You're doing something to me, I know it. I feel it."

"C'mon, Alena. What can I possibly be doing to you that you're not aware of?"

"If I knew, we wouldn't be having this conversation."

Golem turned off the sink then stood in the door. "You're mad," he told her. "Absolutely raving mad."

"*LIAR!*" she screamed then started pacing the room. Pounding footsteps across the carpet.

"Look at you," observed Golem. Then with a passionate voice, "You've cracked, Alena. Ever since Bill Astor you haven't been the same."

She stopped pacing. "Bill?" she said as if to herself. "You killed him. My Bill. My poor, poor Bill."

"No Alena," Golem said. "*WE* killed Bill Astor."

Alena's lips quivered. She thought she saw a grin on Golem's lips. He walked to her.

"And not without cause. He would have killed you...and me, if we hadn't fought back."

He took her hands in his.

Golem said, "We are in this together. Bound together by blood." He moved his head side to side.

His eyes narrowed. "I will carry you, my lady. You need not be concerned with anything regarding Bill Astor. This I promise until my dying day."

She was captivated by his eyes, mesmerized, hypnotized. Her hands in his so smooth and...like skin not marble. She regarded his hands and the healing wound on his right hand. From the wound protruded small black hairs. She ran her thumb over them, smooth like silk.

"What's this?" she said. "You," she met his eyes. "Turning human? Flesh and bone?" Her eyes narrowed.

Golem pulled his hand free and stepped away holding his right hand to his chest. "It is inevitable," he told her. "In time I will turn..." He turned away.

"How?" she said. "How is that possible?"

He shrugged, his stare, she thought, captured by fear. "I don't know how, Alena. I am only aware of certain things."

"Like what?"

"Borrowed time," he told her. "Aren't we all on borrowed time? Where *your* flesh will grow wrinkled and gray with age, mine will...Mine will meet a fate I do not wish to discuss." He dropped his hands. "I will return to the ether as shall you. Our physical form is simply a borrowed vessel in our time here. No one makes it out alive."

"I thought you would live forever." She did think these thoughts although now — with this new revelation — he appeared more...human.

Golem shrugged. "Depends on point of view. But our bodies cannot last forever. They just aren't built that way. We all require new lives and new bodies."

"How do you know this?" She was intrigued. When Golem was first born she had so many questions. Wanted so many answers. "What is beyond death?"

He stiffened with a snarl. "I know nothing of that. Do you? What do you remember before you were born, Alena? Nothing, correct? Only a void of existence. Well, there you have it then. The void awaits you. It waits for all of us."

She shook her head. "You're lying," she said. "You know more than you tell. Why? I want to know why?"

"Foolish woman. Be careful, Alena, you know what happens to curious kittens."

She snarled at him. "Damn you," she said. "Damn your existence for whatever it is you are here for." She moved her head back and forth. "Not on my watch. This will be no more." She went to leave, trampling to the door.

"Alena, come now…I wouldn't do that if I were you."

The moment she reached the door, her body was flung back. She crashed on the bed. Something in her brain, like a heavy dark hand, reached into her skull and tossed her back pinning her to the mattress. A growl then erupted. Not in the room or from the outside but in her head.

"Leave me," she screamed. "Leave me be!" She tried to get up, her body flailing and jutting from one side to the other. Tears fell from her eyes.

Golem shook his head. "Let her go," he said. "She needs time to think. To think about what matters most. She needs purpose. Some project of caring to feed that bleeding heart."

She continued to flail. Continued to feel the hand holding her down.

"Release her!" Golem hollered.

She felt the release. And as quickly as it happened she darted out the door. Heavy breath as she tore down the steps to the ballroom where she stopped running and halted, spinning around. She heard voices and laughter accompanied with painful screams and pleasurable moans. Behind it clunking bells and vibrating crystals. The scent of sulfur. Her stomach turned, and she thought she would vomit right then and there when all she wanted to do was run, get out and go. Breathe air, fresh air. Alena bolted from the ballroom, and out the front door.

She knew Golem was watching from the bedroom, she could feel his eyes on her. Heard his thoughts, his words dropped into her mind.

Nowhere to go, Alena. Nowhere to run! All alone, Miss. Alena.

She ran across the drive.

Your father gone. Mother too. And Bill Astor is no more.

Through the garden. Tears in her eyes.

No more friends, Alena. They never were!

To the Hudson until she could run no more.

Nowhere to run, Alena. Your time has come.

Her heart raced in her chest. Alena heaved bile from the back of her throat and dropped to her knees on the grass. She started to wail and cry.

All Alone, Alena. But worry no more. I have a gift for you, Alena. A wonderful surprise.

28

There was someone in Alena's head. She felt the presence as sure as she felt the grass beneath her skin. How else could she have been dropped onto the bed like that? Golem was nowhere close, and she didn't feel hands on her skin, she felt them in her mind.

And then there were the voices. Soft, incoherent whispers miles away.

Alena wiped off her tears. She hadn't moved in hours, sitting by the Hudson, trembling as she held her knees. She felt numb, that's the best way to describe it. Numb to the core. Numb to the bone. Thoughts and recollections raced through conscious thought so fast they might as well have not existed, unable to focus on any one thought before the image was catapulted to another corner of her mind. Hiding from view in plain sight in fear of being discovered.

It was twilight now, and the air turned hot and sticky as sweat beaded off her skin. Across the Hudson, carried on the brink of day, thunder roared on the heels of lightning bursts. Storm clouds raged in the distance, dark gray turned velvety purple with the coming dawn over her shoulder.

She'd spent the time attempting to find that corner, to seek and secure those elusive thoughts, but to no avail. Every time she came even remotely close it was as if that hand reached out to grab and hide the thought once again, playing some supernatural game of hide and seek. Hiding the truth.

Lightning pumped in the storm clouds. Silvery blue thumps claiming the cloud as their own. And then thunder, so loud her bones rattled.

"Looks like a grand storm to usher in a new day," said Golem. Alena tensed under his voice.

She heard the crunch of dead leaves under his boot. Felt his presence coming closer. She turned away from him. Shook her head, gritted her teeth.

His voice was soft, caring. She despised every ounce of his being, turning her head further with every step he took to see her. He bent down, took a grip of dead leaves in his hand. "Funny, isn't it? What was once beautiful and fresh…is now gray and dead." He dropped the leaves then brushed off his hands. "Some have longer lives than others, but all do pass."

She didn't want to, but she turned to him. With his elbows on his knees, he surveyed the lightning flashes. Alena's eyes were wide and staring. She hated him, she told herself, but there was a connection she couldn't shake. As if she were drawn to him, tied to his heart by some invisible string she could never clip. Maybe it's *my* heart in there, she thought. Maybe it's my blood that rages in his veins.

"You've been out here a long time," he said, not breaking his intake of the storm. Not looking at her. "Come up with any answers to those questions you so desperately seek?"

She pursed her lips, swallowed hard. "You said you would leave once the opening was over."

He sighed, rolled his eyes, and then breathed deeply. "I did say that, didn't I?"

"Yes, you did. You promised." Her voice desperate and dry. "Keep your promise. Go to California and leave me be."

"I can't do that, Alena."

"Why not?" she shot back.

"I don't make the rules, Alena. I just play by them." He picked up a rock from the earth, stood up, and tossed it into the river.

She could feel his anger. Feel it in her bones.

"Who does then?"

Golem shrugged. He whispered, "Couldn't tell you."

She turned away, and shook her head. Felt a lump in her throat but fought off the tears. Don't cry in front of him, she thought. *Don't give him the satisfaction.*

"Are you the devil?" she asked, her voice cracked.

He laughed. "No more than you are. Or any human being for that matter. Words like the devil, Satan, evil... semantics to explain what we fear the most. Think about it, Alena. To the fly the spider is the devil, or evil or whatever you choose to name it. But if that same spider chose not to eat the fly, well, then he would be a merciful god." He shook his head, stuffed his hands into his pockets. "To some, you are the devil, Alena. Look at the poor and starving who stare at you with your glamour and fame, your mansions and fancy clothes. To the poor, it's the devil's work."

Lightning now, followed closely by thunder as the clouds crept over the Hudson.

"No, Alena. I like to set people free. Everyone deserves to live the way that you do, Alena. Everyone deserves to be free."

Her eyes narrowed. "As long as they obey your every order."

She expected that conniving grin. Thought it was about to arrive but he pulled it in, and his face turned to stone. "Give and take, Alena. There's always give and take with every balance."

Alena grinded her teeth, her jaw tense. "I hate you," she told him. "You've stolen all I hold dear."

"Hate," he said, his eyes gleaming. "Such a strong word coming from the person who is responsible for my existence. You must hate yourself then too, Alena."

She turned away, her hands and lips trembling.

"That's ok, Alena, but let's give some balance to that hate of yours." He bent his head to the right then left as if he searched to find her eyes. "I have a gift for you, Alena. A great surprise. Something to make your time with me more…purposeful."

She turned to him, and met her eyes with his. "I trust nothing you say."

Golem bent his head. Took a deep breath. "Understood," he said. "I'll just tell them you refused to come."

He walked away.

Them, she thought. The rain began to fall. Light sheets of rain, soft and cool.

"At least have enough sense to get out of the rain, Alena," Golem called.

Lightning flickered three times; white silvery lightning striking in some unknown existence. Thunder on top of it, forcing the wind to strengthen and with it, the rain, the hard rain was on its way. Those dark clouds drifting overhead, over Alena's shoulder, on top of the ClairField, destroying the coming light, like a black spot on the sun.

And Alena felt that supernatural hand clench inside her heart.

––––––––––

"I've kept them in here. They are waiting."

"Them?"

Golem led Alena to the locked cellar door. Key in hand, he waited before unlocking the door.

"Yes, Alena, *them*." He did not make eye contact but there was that grin. Alena felt it although his face was like stone; she felt that grin wrench in her throat. Golem unlocked the door. "This is where the more tender part of our story begins."

Relief, even if only briefly. *Tender*?

The basement was dark. Golem lifted a candelabra off the wall at the top of the stairs. The wicks lit on their own. Her body tensed, and she caught Golem's grin. The candles' flames reflected in his pupils.

"Follow me, my lady." He offered his hand.

She could see his wound had healed although those small hairs were still present.

"As you wish," he said then took the first step into the basement.

Alena could hear scuffling in the cellar, and the creak of the stairs as Golem descended. She waited at the top, bent her head, attempting to see what was waiting.

"Come now, sit down as I said before," said Golem once he reached the cellar, turning on the lights and fitting the candelabra on the wall. Golem looked up to Alena. "They're waiting," he said then disappeared into the room.

She paused, looked back into the ballroom. She pursed her lips as she heard breathing between her ears. Anticipatory breathing, she thought. *The more tender part of our story.* She heard Golem's voice. She looked at her shaking hands then took the first step down, then the next, bending her head to see what was waiting, or coming; thinking something would jump at her from the shadows. Another step and now she did see. Golem was standing proud beside a blackjack table. Two children sat at the table, on opposite sides. She recognized the boy immediately as Jonah. The girl she did not recognize. Blonde hair and the biggest blue eyes she'd ever seen gazed back at her. She was sure the girl was trembling.

"Fair Alena…" Golem said and he wore a proud visage standing erect over the children. "You've already met Jonah, yes?"

Jonah's eyes were downtrodden although he forced himself to look at Alena. His eyes were dark and frightened. Alena nodded, confused with what was happening.

"And this is Sophia," he said stretching his hand as a pseudo introduction. "I don't believe you've met. Correct, Sophia?"

Sophia's eyes searched over Alena. She seemed absolutely frightened in Alena's presence. Where Jonah was disheveled, dirty and emaciated, Sophia was clean, pristine, and well nourished.

Alena shook her head then looked at Golem. "Why are they here?"

"Purpose, Alena. Purpose."

"These children need to go back to the orphanage."

Sophia started tapping the felt on the table, rolling her fingertips in anticipation. Sophia looked at Golem then Jonah then Alena whose eyes narrowed taking in Sophia's nervous gaze.

Something about those eyes, Alena thought. *I've seen them before.*

"Come now, Alena, you know how devious and cruel the orphanage is. Why, Jonah provided the explanation earlier. How could we allow this boy's demise when we are able to offer him convenience, riches, and opportunity he will never have without us? You've wanted to save life, Alena, to do good by those less fortunate; here is your chance. To make something…beautiful from our union."

Alena shook her head. "There are rules and procedures for such things, Golem. This is kidnapping. Maybe you can't comprehend such a thing." She turned to the children. They were quiet, so very quiet. "I apologize to both of you, but I must contact law enforcement."

They both turned to Golem who did not take his eyes off Alena.

"Perhaps there are things that you are not aware of, Alena." Golem said, his voice stiff. "If you send them back, Alena, they will return." He bent his head trying to lift Alena's eyes to his. "And perhaps next time I will not be so kind in this tender family moment. The children stay, Alena. They belong to you now."

"Not a chance. Not under my roof and definitely not under my watch." She turned to leave.

"ALENA!" Golem's voice. "You don't really believe you'll be leaving here so soon, do you? You know what happened last time you tried to run."

He was right; Alena felt that hand in the center of her brain, tightening its grip. Felt that string pull in her stomach as if Golem were tugging on it. She stretched her neck turning ever so slightly to look over her shoulder. Golem was over Sophia with a fistful of her hair. He yanked her head back as a squeal escaped Sophia's throat.

"I will offer you a moment to reflect on current circumstances, Alena, but only briefly, I don't have time for your inconsolable bleeding heart and righteous claims." He was pulling Sophia's thick locks, forcing her chin up. She was staring at Alena through the corner of her eyes, a pleading stare for help. Her jaw tight and tense, frightened. "Such a fine throat isn't it. So tender and soft." Golem's eyes watched Alena, his free hand on Sophia's throat. "This one is ripe for the taking. Isn't she sweet?"

"You wouldn't?" Alena, her face turned into a scowl.

Golem grinned. "Come now, Alena, search your feelings. Do you not know that I will do what is necessary?" He stood tall still with a fistful of Sophia's hair, tightening his grip. "Should you walk out that door, Alena…should you contact law enforcement as you so put it a moment ago, these two children will meet a most dire fate. This I promise."

Alena caught Sophia's stare. Her eyes reflected depths to an unknown universe; one filled with fear. Her body shivered and shuddered. She started to cry.

Golem threw Sophia towards Alena. She landed on her hands and knees next to Alena's feet. "Go, child," scolded Golem. "Go to your mother!"

Alena bent down. "It's ok," she said.

Sophia jumped into Alena's arms. "Don't let him hurt us," she pleaded, her body shaking.

"Perhaps it's the boy then," Golem said as he trounced over to Jonah. "Maybe it is this one that's stolen your heart?" He took Jonah's forehead in both hands, forcing his head back, for his eyes to look at Golem, his hands tense around Jonah's head, squeezing. "I can cut this one into tiny pieces and serve him for dinner." He lifted Jonah off the chair by his head. Jonah's feet dangled and kicked in the air as he screamed and whimpered beneath Golem's hands. "Shush now," Golem scolded. "I'll have no signs of weaknesses from either of you."

"Let him go!" Alena said rising to her feet.

"Why, Alena? This one will be better off dead, sucking the marrow of society all his life. Some lives are better off dispersed."

"I said let go of *him. NOW!*"

Golem turned those fiery eyes on Alena, Jonah whining and wriggling in his grasp. He dropped Jonah to the chair with a thud, then gripped the nape of Jonah's neck forcing his head to the table. Golem grinned at Alena. Cries came from Jonah beneath Golem's grip.

"Tell me, Alena, what good could this young lad do? Who will he be, where will he turn? He has no one, Alena, even you are rejecting him."

"You bastard!" Alena cringed beneath Golem's stare.

"At least this one has use," he gestured to Sophia then tossed Jonah back against the wall. Alena ran to him, bent down in front of him. Jonah's eyes filled with tears.

Golem brushed off his hands. "Ok, Alena, we will do it your way. I'll bring them to the orphanage. Let them get abused with no chance in life."

"You ok?" Alena asked Jonah. He was on the verge of tears, holding them back to show face. "Come, let me help you." Alena took Jonah's hands, standing together; Jonah then clung to her waist. Alena looked at Golem, one hand on his hip the other in front of his waist.

Sophia walked up to him. Reached her tiny hand to his thick fingers.

Golem looked down on her, taking her hand. "Oh, my lady, it seems Alena has determined your worth is nothing. You must go!"

Sophia turned her eyes to Alena. "Please don't send us to the orphanage. It's not fair."

"Please don't," said Jonah. He looked up to Alena. "They do bad things there."

Not just there, Jonah. Everywhere!

"Please!" said Sophia, her voice soft.

Golem was watching Alena, waiting. He bent his head. Alena could sense that grin beneath his lips.

"Talk to the head mistress," Jonah said. "Darlene McGovern. She'll let us stay here; I know she will."

Golem's eyes delighted. "What a wonderful idea, Jonah. Seems he may be useful after all. What do you think, Alena? We can all go and talk to McGovern."

"Please, Miss. Alena," Jonah said.

"Come now, Alena, you are awfully quiet."
Sophia said in a monotone voice, "Please!"
Alena tensed when she caught Sophia's eyes.
Like a trap door in the back of the eye.

She felt that string jerk. Heard the breathing between her ears and felt that hand grip the center of her brain and pull.

29

It was nightfall when they went to visit Mrs. McGovern. She lived in a large two-bedroom apartment on the Lower East Side with her husband, James McGovern, and their eight-year-old son, Charles. Both Mr. and Mrs. McGovern were social workers only able to afford the apartment as a result of rent control, having inherited the residence from James' mother after her unfortunate passing.

Golem sent the children to the door first with clear instructions to gain access to the home. Alena remained by Golem's side in the hall and out of sight from the McGovern's front door; Golem continuously tapping his red cane across the wood floor as he paced back and forth, lost in thought.

Something's different, she thought. On their way over Alena's stomach and brain squirmed, as if something inside wriggled with anticipation. *Hearts and souls! Energy! Offering and sacrifice. Feed the monster and it will return with gifts.* Those thoughts appeared in her mind as if they'd arrived through an unknown source. And then the squeeze in her brain, turning the outside world into a blur.

She'd prepared (at least in her mind) what she would say once in front of Mrs. McGovern. She hoped the woman would be rational, taking the children back to the orphanage. And then there was the Golem issue, which she feared would not be dismissed as easily as she'd hoped.

If I could just have a day to think and prepare, she thought. That cloudy sensation and forgetfulness stayed with her, unable to shake clear these ailments. And then there was the larger issue, the loss of control. Alena no longer believed she was in complete control of her thoughts and actions, riding like a co-pilot into the storm.

The same as she experienced now, following Golem down the hall to the apartment, his cane tapping the floor with every step.

Tap…tap…tap…

Jonah opened the door.

Tap…tap…tap…

"We've secured them," he told Golem.

Golem stepped in. "Magnificent, Jonah. I knew there was use for you."

Alena remained in the door when Golem moved into the apartment. She saw Mr. and Mrs. McGovern on the floor in the living room, lying back to back, their wrists and ankles bound independently. Gags forced down their throats. Mrs. McGovern stared at Alena. Her eyes stiff with fear that grew large when she saw Alena.

Mrs. McGovern screamed through her gag. There were tears in her eyes.

"Where is Sophia?" Golem asked Jonah, their backs to Alena, standing over the McGoverns. Golem tapped his cane over their heads, forced the end against Mr. McGovern's temple.

"With the boy," Jonah said, his voice monotone.

As if on cue to verify Jonah's statement, a high-pitched squeal rang through the apartment, and the McGoverns returned with their own muffled screeches, breathing heavy through tears, and struggling to be free.

Golem stretched his neck looking over the ceiling. His narrow eyes then found Alena, still in the door.

"Having trouble, are you?" he said.

Alena felt that grip in her brain tighten.

"Not with this one; tell me it can't be true."

She felt herself float into the room. The front door closed with a heavy thud. Her eyes darted from left to right and she caught a glimpse of herself in a wall mirror. Her eyes were black, all black. Golem bowed to her.

"Take your rightful seat," said Golem. "We will begin soon." He then looked down on the McGoverns. "I don't anticipate this will take long. Mrs. McGovern is quite anxious to see us leave, I'm sure." Then to Jonah. "Bring Sophia first."

Jonah nodded as Alena took a seat in front of the McGoverns. He went to the room to fetch Sophia. Golem stood over the McGoverns, waiting, then looked at Alena. She felt herself bow as if she gave permission for Golem to begin. He returned the bow. His body seemed to relax, and he turned his gaze to Darlene who glared at him through petrified tearful eyes. Golem grinned as he circled around to Mr. McGovern; his eyes were closed, although tears streamed down his face to the wooden floor. His body shivered as his gag muffled his prayer for redemption. Golem bent down, hovering above James, cane in both hands. He reached his finger to James' forehead, wiping sweat off his skin. He licked his finger, and his body shuddered.

"Nothing better than the sweet taste of fear." Golem flipped James onto his back and tapped his forehead. "James," he said. James was crying, his eyes closed. Golem shook his head. "James, this could be over very soon. Really, there's no need for such evil things to occur. That's not why we are here, although we do take pleasure in our work." Golem looked down the hall and grinned then returned to James. He shook his head and tapped James' forehead. "Open your eyes, James," he said. Again, a moment later, "Look at me, James." He slapped James and his eyes nervously and reluctantly opened.

Alena felt a laugh escape her lips.

"Good boy, James. Good boy. I want you to see this. I want you to see what's coming." Golem bent his head closer to James. "Do not close them again, understood? If you do, I'll cut off your eyelids to make sure they stay open. I'm not here to play games and this will be over quickly. I will ask you a question, James, and based on your answer there will be either one of two effects. Blink if you understand."

James did as instructed.

"Good. Good, James." Golem took a deep breath, gnashing his teeth. "What we desire, James, is energy. The ether. One way or another after this night we will have yours, James. Same with Darlene, and of course that little pride and joy you've both spawned. Although we try to avoid doing this by force." Golem stressed the word force. "There's a bit of chaos associated with the forceful execution of the ether. Although we'll take it, but we've always understood that a lawful accord to give the ether freely has a stronger and more profound effect. A...cleaner form of the ether is a more accurate description. Are you following me so far, James?"

Although James did not respond, Golem proceeded.

"So, my question to you is twofold. First, do you offer your ether to us, in the name of Baphomet? To give over freely your life's energy and blood for us to do with as we please? That's the first part, James. For part two, we request for you to prove yourself to us. To prove your undying devotion to Baphomet with the sacrifice of your son?" James jolted attempting to free himself, struggling and grunting. "James. James!" Golem said. "Allow me to finish. Perhaps the verbiage I'm using is what's causing your dismay. By *sacrifice* I only refer to your son's ether, his soul, which is still under your thumb. An appropriate offering to the larger cause." Again, James wriggled and grunted. His body flopping on the floor like a fish out of water. Golem laughed. "Oh James, James, I can see you're a man of depth and recognition." He looked over the room with a smug stare as if sarcasm ran through his thoughts. "Something in return you say? Hmm, of course, James. Of course we provide greatness in return. Fame, riches, health, prestige. Honor. Think of all the good you can do. All you have to do is pledge your loyalty to Baphomet and in that moment, we will be here no more. This will all end instantly." Golem snapped his fingers, his eyes now burrowing into James' soul.

James settled down, staring at Golem. He was crying.

Golem looked at Alena then back to James. "What is it you're holding onto? Some better notion of the unknown you have no basis of fact even exists? I offer you everything, James. Give us what we want, Mr. McGovern."

James' eyes turned red with anger as he shook his head no, then leaned his head against his wife's back.

Jesus, help us. I'm sorry, Darlene. James' voice in Alena's head.

"Sorry, James, that would be the wrong answer."

Golem stood up, looked to the ceiling then stepped away from James. *Tap.* Alena felt her head shift, looking to the hall where Sophia was clinging to the ceiling, her eyes black, her teeth jagged, sharp, jutting across her lips. Where hands and feet should be were tentacles. *Click, click, click* across the ceiling.

"Come, Sophia," said Golem. "Time to eat." Golem turned, standing by the large bay window as Sophia clambered across the ceiling. Darlene wailed beneath her gag and James' eyes widened seeing Sophia over him. One final attempt by James to free himself in a hurried fearful rush as Sophia dropped down on top of him, her tentacle piercing his abdomen. James screamed under his gag. Blood jutted from his sternum, sprouting into the room like a fountain as his scream changed, now gurgling on his blood. Alena heard herself laugh. Felt it in her throat. Knew she was smiling, garnering satisfaction over the scene before her.

Sophia tore into James, tearing that tentacle across his torso. His skin split open igniting a river of blood as his body jerked and jutted up and back down with every slow inching of her tentacle. Sophia snarled, her wide eyes mesmerized, infatuated with the pain she brought. Alena experienced Sophia's satisfaction as if it were her own. Golem's too. Sensed an uncanny marble of personal gratification writhe from her stomach to her throat.

"Go ahead, Sophia," said Golem, his voice soft. "Eat his heart."

Sophia plunged her tentacle into James' torso, his body wriggling and convulsing. Further up she went, beneath the ribs into his chest where she squeezed and snarled, lapping her tongue across her lips. James' flailing ceased. Eyes fell cold and stiff, and Sophia ripped out his heart. Now Darlene's wailing cries rose into the room. Her eyes clamped shut. Sophia sniffed the heart as if it were a ripened piece of fruit. Her body quivered before she devoured the organ, her porcelain skin now stained with crimson chunks of organ with blood brushed on her cheeks like paint coated on a canvas.

When she finished, after she swallowed the last remains of the heart, the room seemed to drop. Everyone in the room was silent with the exception of Darlene. Her cries had turned soft. Golem dropped his head, took a deep breath as Sophia went to Alena, squatting beside her like a dog by its master. Alena ran her hand over Sophia's head, brushing the hair from her eyes.

"Good devil," Alena said. "Good girl."

Golem was watching them. He turned around, surveying the dead eyes of James McGovern, the pool of blood beneath him spreading wide across the wood. Golem moved his cane and foot before the blood could touch him. He shook his head then sighed. Darlene's cries were now whimpers. Golem looked down the hall. "Bring the boy," he ordered Jonah who had been witnessing the events from down the hall, standing in front of a closed bedroom door. "The boy is next," he announced in a raised voice as if he were addressing a large audience, eliciting defiance from Darlene with grunts and muffled declarations as she struggled to free herself, watching as Jonah led Charles down the hall, hand in hand.

Golem put up his left hand and Jonah stopped walking. Charles, his wide eyes wet with tears, his bottom lip curled and quivering as if he were on the brink of wailing.

"Sophia, darling," Golem said. "Can you please pick up Mrs. McGovern and seat her appropriately on the couch?"

Sophia clambered on all fours. In a swift rush she gripped Darlene's tied wrists and dragged her to the couch opposite Alena where she picked her up and deposited Darlene on the couch, remaining on all fours in front of Darlene's legs.

"Don't move, Darlene," Golem said. "The girl is still hungry." He then motioned to Jonah to bring the boy. "Come, Charles, stand by your father…or what remains of him."

Charles attempted to run but Jonah's grip was iron clad. He dragged Charles to the center of the room, standing him beside his father then stood behind the boy, holding Charles' arms behind his back. Charles took one look at the dead remains lying by his feet then looked at his mother, his bones tense with fright and fear. His lips trembling.

"Oh look," Golem said pointing his cane at Charles. "The boy is trembling." *Tap.* He turned to

Alena, a toothless grin graced his countenance. "How wonderful." He laughed as his eyes darted towards Darlene, his grin wiped clean from his lips, staring, his features stiff as if they'd returned to marble stone, his teeth gritted and his jaw clenched. Closed his eyes and breathed before he opened his eyes to Darlene then craned his head up, looking over the room, shaking his head, as if disappointment captured his heart before he addressed Darlene. "I grow frustrated sometimes," he began. "I offer so much, so much to deliver your life from servitude. I'm hoping that you, Darlene, will be a bit more open to my offering than this rotting corpse." Golem pointed his cane at the dead body. Darlene looked at her husband then back to Golem. "Look at him, Darlene, do you see anything enlightened about him?" He used the cane to push the dead face to the side, allowing Darlene a clear view of her husband's dead eyes. "Did you sense his soul lifting to heaven?" Golem twisted his head, his neck popped and cracked. "See his eyes, Darlene, how black and stale they are. No life left in this heart of hearts. No light." Darlene had tears streaming down her face, soaking the gag in her mouth.

"Now look at your boy, Darlene. There, don't you see the life in those eyes?" Charles shuddered. "How quickly do you believe it will take us to tear the light from *his* eyes? My, I can drive my fist through his chest and pull out his heart in an instant. Allow you to watch while the light fades into darkness." Golem went to Charles, being sure to step over the pool of blood. He gripped Charles' jaw then ran his finger across the boy's cheek. "So soft," Golem said. "So pure. Life has only begun for this boy. There's so much he can do. So much good in this world." Golem turned to Darlene. "And he can do it all, all those dreams will come true." He turned back to Charles, placed his hand on the boy's head. "He will have the power to do great and beautiful things. None will be able to stop him." He gripped a handful of Charles' hair pulling him off the floor. "Or it all ends tonight." Charles screamed and wriggled in Golem's grasp.

"Mommy!" Charles hollered.

Darlene jumped off the couch, stopped by Sophia's growl.

"There's only one question, Darlene. Do you give yourself to Baphomet?"

Darlene hesitated.

"I grow impatient." He dropped Charles to his feet, gripped his throat in his massive hand and squeezed, the boy's mouth open wide, his tongue jutted across his lips, eyes bulging, strangling and shuddering. "What's that you say?" Golem said to none in particular. "Cut out his throat and lap the blood off with my tongue?" Charles screamed a choked garble.

Golem looked at Darlene. "Your answer, Mrs. McGovern."

Darlene's stiff eyes traipsed over her son. She paused briefly then Darlene nodded, yes.

"Ah, someone has finally come to their senses." Golem thrust Charles to the ground, on top of his father and he scurried away from the dead corpse in a hurried rush of fear. His hands sliding across blood, his left hand slipped into the open wound that seemed to catch Charles' hand. In the boy's hurried frenzy he yanked his arm away. Fragmented intestines pulled away with it. Charles dropped back, scurried on his hands and feet into Golem's legs. Startled, he looked up at Golem.

"No worries, Charles, you'll see much worse in your lifetime."

Charles' bottom lip quivered. His eyes, wide with fear, welled with tears. He looked at his mother; sitting tied and gagged, her eyes lost looking over her boy. Golem crouched beside him, and Charles cringed.

"All is well, young one. Do you see Jonah behind you? He's a little older than you...like a big brother. I see the two of you having so much fun in this life." He ran his finger across Charles' forehead then held his chin. "I see a mighty appetite in this boy." He glowered into Charles' eyes. "But there is something missing. Let us begin again." Golem grinned as he stood up. He looked at Alena, or what was Alena's body sitting and observing. He bowed with a quick nod then turned to Darlene who shuddered in her seat.

"Mrs. McGovern," he said, his index finger raised. "Obviously we could never take you for your word. Who's to say that once we leave you won't contact law enforcement...which will certainly place our little ruse here on high alert."

Darlene muffled something incoherent beneath her gag.

Golem continued, "So..." he bent his head as if searching for the correct verbiage or registering with Darlene her understanding. "Our ritual will now begin. Simple really, that it is. Please rise, Mrs. McGovern."

Darlene's eyes grew wide, she looked at her restraints.

"Oh, those. Sophia."

Sophia's tentacles cut through her restraints.

"Please keep in mind, Mrs. McGovern, scream once, and I'll have Jonah eat your son's throat." He smiled as Darlene pulled the gag from her mouth and stood, slow and cautious around Sophia who never took her eyes off Darlene. Golem stepped to her. Darlene was trembling, breathing hoarse with a whining cry in her throat she would not dare to allow to escape. Golem brushed her hair behind her ear, Darlene's lips quivering; she turned her eyes to the floor, opposite from where her husband's dead bleeding body lay. "Much better," he told her then smiled as if attempting to calm her, forcing her eyes to look at him. "It's the fear, Mrs. McGovern. That fearful energy, the ether of polarized negativity, we swallow it whole…like food, it brings us strength. The more we indulge the stronger we become. Like evolution, our home grows with it, widens." He looked up to the ceiling, seeing through the ceiling, moving his head from left to right. "Dark energy across the universe, destroying all light in its path. One day," he said returning his gaze to her. "We will have all the universe bathed in darkness. And all will bend to our will." He put his hand on Darlene's stomach. "You have that darkness inside you Darlene, as everyone does. It will grow now, consume all in your path. Give you strength you could not imagine. Do you feel it, sense it, in your home now? The filthy, fearful energy created on this night, right here where we all stand. Like a stain on a carpet, this is a stain on the air, invisible as it may be, only those who look with wide eyes can see it but all can feel it. Do you?"

Darlene was calm now, looking over the room. "Yes," she said in a hushed whisper.

Golem smiled. He raised Darlene's arms. "Give yourself to Baphomet," he said moving behind Darlene. "Go to Baphomet. Kneel before Baphomet." He tore Darlene's clothes off, standing her naked in the room then brushed her hair behind her back. "Go, Darlene. Kneel and stare into the eyes of Xibalba."

Both Jonah and Sophia began chanting.

AGIOS O BAPHOMET!

Darlene walked to Alena, paying no mind to Charles who watched as she shivered with fear.

"Mom?" he said.

"Shush, Charles," Golem said. "Shush."

AGIOS O BAPHOMET!

Darlene's eyes stared into Alena's. Alena raised her hand and Darlene kneeled in front of her.

AGIOS O BAPHOMET!

Darlene's eyes were captivated by Alena. Alena- a passive observer numb to the happening outside her own body–looked on in terror from a dark prison in the corner of her mind, immobile, incapable of controlling her body, her mind, her self; alone and petrified. Inside this wretched prison of darkness, Alena witnessed energy, like electricity, spark like lightning from Alena's right pupil to Darlene's left eye. The passive observer Alena watched as that spark sank into Darlene's eye, slithered inside her brain and squeezed before spiraling inside her body, captivated every vein, every organ, every bone, and then jutted from her skin, circling around Darlene, wrapping itself around her, capturing and lifting her energy that peeled off her skin like wrapping paper off a present, becoming part of that electrical pulse from Alena's eye, and reversed direction with a quick pull back before the ether raced into Alena's eye, then past the eye.

Alena watched from within as this energy flew past her towards a dark void over her shoulder to what should have been the back of Alena's skull, but instead an eternal dark void existed and this electrical current raced towards the void and, like witnessing an electric storm in the universe, this spark found a home. An electric storm raged in the distance, so far away, so far off, and Darlene's ethereal electrical lightning joined with this electrical storm far out in the universe, arriving at what Alena could now see was dark energy, a gel like planet that shimmered with darkness. Alena heard screams, cries and anguish in the storm. She heard Darlene cry out, scream in terror when her ether joined with the storm in an eternity of fear. Sparks of white, blue, indigo, and violet raged with fury, igniting that black-gelled planet with thumps of color. Then that spark raced back toward Alena on the opposite side from where it came, different now, with an essence of pure evil, racing towards Alena, racing towards her eyes, coming full circle. What once was electric blue now was dark and that current that had escaped from the electrical storm now reached from Alena's left eye to Darlene's right pupil. Alena watched, on edge, waiting, seeing Darlene, feeling, sensing, knowing the change had come. Darlene's eyes returned Alena's gaze but with a slight difference.

There was now a trap door in the back of her eye.

Alena felt herself smile.

AGIOS O BAPHOMET!

Darlene fell back, shuddering, twisting, and convulsing.

"There we go," Golem said. "Take it in, Darlene. Don't fight. It is wonderful, is it not? A window for all of Xibalba to see through."

AGIOS O BAPHOMET!

When Darlene ceased flapping, her body calmed. She no longer appeared disheveled, no longer blemished. No more tears in her eyes nor across her skin. She appeared beautiful. More beautiful than she could have ever wished for.

"Rise, Darlene. Bow to Baphomet. Thank Baphomet for the gift you have received."

Darlene looked at Golem then back to Alena. She kneeled and bowed. "Thank you, Baphomet," she said.

Alena's hand was on Darlene's head. Alena felt the voice in her throat, that resonating raspy voice, "Do you give all to me?"

"Yes," Darlene answered.

"Do you worship the darkness?"

"Yes!"

"Do you give your life to me and in return accept my gifts openly and freely?"

"Yes!"

Alena felt that smile on her lips.

"Do you offer me the soul of your child in exchange for these precious gifts?"

"Yes! Of course!"

Charles jumped. He'd been standing quietly; his jaw hung open, eyes wide with a stare that revealed disbelief.

Golem breathed, "Ah, innocence. Simply the purest corruption we can ask for."

Alena reached her finger toward Charles. That voice again from her throat, over her lips.

"Come," Alena said, "Come, Charles. Bow before me."

30

March 24th 1951

I've lost my mind!

Alena sat in front of a vanity mirror in her room in the ClairField, her hands trembling as they so often have over the past few years since the reopening. Her heart fluttered, now a common occurrence. The reflection was not her own, although she could see the remains of years past, youthful purpose and praise existed somewhere beneath the worn paper-thin skin reflected in the mirror. Her jaw always tight, the nerves either tense or broken. Her once golden, shining locks now thin and gray. Drawn, wrinkled and blemished skin, liver spots like chicken pox blotted her forehead down to the jaw line.

The voices—always the voices day in and day out—developed in the center of her mind, ballooning to the point where she would swear her skull would crack and split in two. Those migraines brought out the worst erratic behavior, cussing like no woman should ever speak. Not a woman with the prestige behind a prominent family name. And definitely not a woman of God!

She'd come to the point where even the smallest of tasks brought on that nasty disposition, requiring every ounce of strength she could garner to complete the task. And her children treated her with no respect, nasty and degrading remarks spewed from their mouths so often she held no control over them. Week after week, after party leading to another after party, she had no reprieve, always having to ready herself and never, not once, enjoying the moment. Constantly concerned with the next moment—her past seemed to belong to another life, not hers but rather memories belonging to someone else, or a past life.

She opened her foundation with trembling hands. Truly mindless behavior that required no real energy or thought to complete the task; simply dip the brush into the foundation and apply to the skin. Only her hands were trembling, as they did on every occasion. She so often sat in front of the vanity taking so many hours to complete tasks that years ago had taken no time at all. And she avoided eye contact. Avoided looking into her own eyes. What once had been the deepest of blues now contained that black spot in the corner of her right eye. A trap door to another dimension. And this dimension was complete with fear, pain, anguish, and, of course, darkness. She'd done that before, fell into her own trap door, and could not remember the few hours after. Maybe it was days not hours; she couldn't string those thoughts together. The timeline of events was lost, the last three plus years like a burning streak smeared across her mind. She feared her own eyes. Petrified by the trap door.

Today was the same result, a simple task taking an eternity to complete.

"You don't need it," the voice said. "Your natural beauty is breathtaking."

Lies, she thought. Her focus was on the skin. Liver spots are not beauty marks.

Sometimes it's easier to give in and give up.

Alena breathed deeply, turning her eyes to the floor. A blank stare, flat affect. The chanting running across her thoughts like a string pulling her into darkness.

AGIOS O BAPHOMET!

Clunking cowbell beneath the chanting.

AGIOS O BAPHOMET!

Burning skin. Unable to speak.

AGIOS O BAPHOMET!

Hard to breathe. Choking on constricted thoughts.

AGIOS O BAPHOMET!

"Are you ok, my lady?" that woman, the one from the casino basement, said. She'd become a staple at the ClairField, occupying a room on the second floor, although she had been as elusive to Alena as the incoherent whispers beneath the chanting, where the screams and anguish hid like children from lightning and thunder.

Alena's head was heavy as if an anvil existed between the temples. Pressure behind the eyes. Her head shook as she lifted her eyes to see the woman, Maleva, in the doorway. Alena opened her mouth to speak but couldn't find the voice.

She'd grown young, Maleva had. Alena remembered when she'd first encountered Maleva in the casino basement and how she'd appeared old, older than she was now. Now she resembled a teenager, definitely no more than twenty. She wore a concerned expression. Alena didn't appreciate the pity her eyes offered.

"Let me help you," said Maleva.

Alena was trembling. Her hands touched her head then shook. She laid them on her lap.

Maleva took up a second chair by the bed, brought it over to the vanity desk. Alena looked away, embarrassed by her need for help. She looked to the mirror—avoiding her eyes—as Maleva sat beside her.

"Let's see what I can do," Maleva said. Even her voice carried a youthful tone. "Come," she continued, "Turn to me."

Alena turned hesitantly, her eyes turned down. Her jaw was tight with the slightest tremors just below the bottom lip. Maleva applied foundation, soft strokes across the cheeks.

"Excited for tonight's presentation?" Maleva said.

Alena tensed. She went to answer but no words came.

"It's ok," Maleva said. "You can tell me."

"I don't know these people," whispered Alena. "I'm not sure if we should be holding the ceremonies any longer."

Less than a year prior the city had shut down the ClairField to the public, citing noise violations after numerous complaints. Although Golem had maintained the dignity of the after-party guest list as private, invitation only gatherings, no longer was the general public allowed to enter the prestigious inn.

Maleva paused and Alena felt those eyes roaming over her, taking in Alena and the nervous demeanor.

"Golem's taken care of it." Maleva forced a quick smile. "You've seen the mayor and DA at the gatherings. There's no cause for concern."

After the city shut down the ClairField, Golem released all staff and the ClairField began its decent into decay and neglect. Dust gathered on the furniture, the garden was overgrown, difficult to find the path through to the Hudson, and the paint even seemed to be dissipating off the walls.

Alena did not respond. Maleva applied the brush halfheartedly.

"Your friends still come, don't they? I see them at every presentation."

The bridesmaids, Alena's friends, hadn't missed one presentation since the reopening. Alena nodded. "They do," she whispered. She felt Maleva's eyes on her, with what Alena surmised was a sliver of pity behind that stare. Alena's stomach rumbled sour and distasteful, like an acidic belch that rose into her chest.

Maleva continued, "Tonight's presentation will be historic. Golem's opened the door to everyone. So many people he'd never thought of before. All deserve the same opportunity, don't you agree?"

No response, Alena heard Maleva's declaration although her words seemed to slip away, into a void. Maleva paused then continued with the foundation working effortlessly and quickly, applying makeup after. Alena maintained silence.

She was listening to the chanting, the low breathing she knew wasn't coming from her lungs or throat. Beneath the breathing were the five gongs, vibrations Alena could feel in her heart. She jumped in her seat when the fifth vibration rang in her chest.

Alena pursed her lips, swallowing her breath then exhaled as if she were out of air.

"Should I apply eye liner?" Maleva asked.

"No, no," Alena said, she grabbed the eyeliner, holding it tight between her fingers. "I'll do it," she said avoiding Maleva's stare.

Maleva forced a smile. "Ok," she said. "Need help with the wig?" she asked.

Alena shook her head, no. "I…I can do it."

"Very well then," continued Maleva. "Best to get dressed now. Guests will be arriving soon."

Alena nodded, then slipped off the chair shuffling to the closet. She knew Maleva was watching her. When Alena turned on the closet light she walked in, waiting for Maleva to leave. Alena's hand shook; gliding over the many dresses she had to choose from but keeping Maleva in the corner of her eye. Watching as she scurried to the bed, noticing how her head was drawn to the ceiling. Alena, sensing Maleva may come into the closet, turned her back.

She never liked Maleva. Not that she could remember Maleva ever crossing or scolding her, but it was her presence, something Alena could never put her finger on. Alena closed her eyes when a slight wind graced the nape of her neck. A cool although warming wind. Alena's eyes fluttered beneath her eyelids.

When she looked over her shoulder, Maleva was gone.

31

The talisman was hanging on a silver chain from the vanity mirror. Alena stared at it, confused, so odd that it was there when it hadn't been moments ago. "Where could it have come from?" she thought while fitting the blonde wig over her head with shaking hands.

The talisman was no larger than a silver dollar. Featured on the circumference was a raised sixteen-spoke wheel, all made from silver although the talisman had no shine to it. Alena surmised the necklace must be centuries old.

She heard a snarling growl erupt in her mind, as if something had been awakened suddenly and made haste towards Alena. She reached for the wheel, her arm heavy, fingers curled toward her palm. Heard pounding, rushing footsteps, hurried in anticipation. Her body shook, sweat on her skin as her jaw and lips trembled. The wheel seemed to elude her touch. Or maybe it was she who feared the wheel. When her hand was a mere inch from the talisman it moved on its own accord like two similarly polarized magnets retracting. Alena pulled her hand away.

Again the trampling, heavy quick footsteps as if someone large were trampling in hurried frenzy to catch her hand.

Her heart fluttered, walloped into her throat. With every heavy thud her bones shook. She heard a door creak open behind her eyes blurring her vision as the room faded around her. Heavy breathing now quickly constricted, as if the world held its breath.

For protection!

Alena heard this voice arrive as a whisper between her ears. The voice soft, feminine, concerned. Her right hand swelled and ballooned, her right eye began to tear, and the right corner of her mouth twitched. Thick liquid, not tears but an ocean of saline in her left eye.

Now the ClairField resonated with an electric vibration as if someone had used a gavel on a xylophone. One vibration, two, three.

She reached her left hand to the necklace and gripped the silver in her palm.

Fourth vibration.

Alena's left eye shot open. Wind howled into the room driving the curtains with a fierce stiffness into the room. The bed sheets tore off the bed. The closet door slammed shut. The wind kept coming. The vanity mirror started shaking. Alena caught her reflection, bent her head, and stared at herself inquisitively. Her right eye was metallic black, her left eye blue, although a black ring slithered around the pupil. Her body trembled as the vanity desk was thrust by the wind, crashing into pieces when it slammed into the wall.

Alena sat, center room, shaking. Her left hand started to burn. Stuttered breathing, constricted heartbeat. Sweat smeared her makeup.

The fifth vibration dissipated, resonating in her bones.

She dropped the necklace, felt herself rise.

Something's different, she thought.

She heard her lungs breathing heavy although she experienced no sensation. Her mouth was on fire although she experienced no burn. She saw eyes in all corners in the room, in every place where shadow existed. She had no fear of them, their beady red eyes watching, glaring.

She experienced immense strength in her bones; a profound awareness accompanied by an ability to destroy. Alena's feet were moving, seemed like floating, into the hall toward the stairs and she attempted to stop the motion. Focused on stopping her feet with no success.

A ghoulish laugh erupted in her mind. She could sense she was smiling. What disturbed Alena the most was the distinct familiar sensation.

She'd been here before, although this time was different than the others. Alena held her breath, not the breath from her lungs but the proverbial breath of energy, spirit.

Alena was beginning to remember, memories on the brink toward revelation. And those eyes in the darkness grew tiny sharp fangs that glowed white within the shadows. They seemed to jump on top of each other like excited children hoping for a celebrity glimpse.

When she arrived at the second floor staircase, she could see all the people standing, stiff and waiting, staring those dark black eyes in her direction.

AGIOS O BAPHOMET!

The chanting began. Golem at the back, standing erect and proud, his sharp teeth gleaming in the light below the chandelier, a crystal goblet in his right hand, filled with blood.

Inside Alena was petrified.

Felt her hand rise to her lips with a hand that was not her own, although it had to be, she felt it move. The hand that touched her lips was dark gray, wrinkled. The fingers were long with nails filed to sharp points.

AGIOS O BAPHOMET!

She descended, one step, two, then three. Witnessing those red eyes everywhere, some on the shoulders of her guests. The new guests in line with the old, her friends, the bridesmaids standing prominently beside their husbands. All with black eyes except for these minions or devils or whatever, they clung to the guests' shoulders, whispering in their ears.

Children were also in attendance.

Alena recognized them all.

AGIOS O BAPHOMET!

For protection!

That soft whisper like warm breath on the nape of her neck. She thought of the necklace. Wished she had it now.

And Alena shook with fear.

32

"What did you see?" asked John Ashton. He'd been quiet during most of Alena's story, always scrutinizing—in his mind at least—all the fine details. His detective instincts surmised the story was a confession, no matter how insane the narrator was. He wanted Alena to finish the story so he could receive all information necessary to put Alena in prison forever. The way John saw it; Alena was digging her grave deeper with every passing word.

Alena, slumped in her chair, eyes staring lost at the floor, did not offer a response.

"Alena?" said Ashton and Alena at last returned his gaze. "What did you see?"

She pursed her lips, swallowed her breath. Sweat beaded above her lip.

"Hell," she whispered. "And all its devils and dastardly deeds."

John cocked his head, intrigued. "And you claim to remember not one incident? Not one death as you so described?"

Alena's voice was soft, low. "I remembered nothing. Not until the night of the 24th, after I was given the necklace, was I able to see. To harbor and understand those memories." She was on the verge of crying, sucking back her tears. Her eyes wide, stiff and staring, blank expression across her face. "It wasn't me inside my body. Wasn't me who did all those…things."

John moved his head back and forth. He scratched his elbow, then scratched his forehead. "Where were you then?" he asked. "If you weren't in your body, where were you? Do you have any memories of that?"

Alena stretched her back, her neck. Her hands trembling, lips quivering. She pursed her lips, swallowed her inhale. "Pain," she responded. "Like being wrapped inside of pain. Every bone, every muscle, every organ subjected to excruciating, unrelenting suffering." Tears welled in her eyes, creeping slow down her skin. She allowed them to fall, caressing down her face to the jawline. "The most unimaginable pain tearing a hole in your soul, leaving nothing other than darkness, agony. This is what Xibalba is, unrelenting, unimaginable, torturous energy."

John gnawed his lip, thinking. "What's with the eye? The trap door? What is it? Explain, please?"

Alena cleared her throat. "Hard to describe, really."

John raised his eyebrows. "Try," he said.

Alena nodded, thinking. After a short pause she said, "Television"

"Come again?"

"Think of a television. Let's say there's two TV's, one here in this room with us and one in California in a room with two other people. Picture the ability for us to see them and for them to see us with the capability to communicate to each other. Each television would need a camera and microphone to record us and them."

"Not logical but understood."

Alena wiped the tears from her eyes. Sniffled. "The black eye is like this camera. It allows the devils access to this world. To influence and communicate to the host their desires. They require a sound frequency, a vibration to enter this world. The frequency needs to be in both places at the same time, well coordinated too. This is because of the force field…" She stopped abruptly, as if catching herself.

John's eyes narrowed. He paused, thinking. "Force field?"

She shook her head. "Yes, an invisible electric field around the planet like radio or television waves we can't see that blocks conscious thought from leaving and arriving."

John grunted. Wanted to call bull shit but kept it to himself. "So, if this force field exists, how can they get here?"

Alena tucked her chin to her chest, staring at the floor. "They were given permission."

"Permission?" His body shook, unbelievingly so. "By whom? God?"

"Us," she said and sat up. "I know you have inquiries, detective, but allow me to finish. Your questions will be answered within the story."

He pushed back in his chair, pushed his hat off his forehead then folded his arms across his chest.

"Continue," he said. "Unless it's too painful, of course."

Alena shook her head. "I need to tell the story. I want you to know it."

As all murderers do, thought Ashton.

He gave a slight nod, welcoming the end to Alena's story.

————————

Golem stood among his guests. He was dressed in a tight tuxedo with a dark purple tint, his jagged teeth gleaming under the lights, his eyes black but filled with flickering flames, fire, electricity. Skin so perfectly white, the deep-seated marble tone smooth like porcelain, his hair perfectly groomed, that strand, thick locks by his right eye. His right hand wrapped tightly, the bandage snaking up his arm, disappearing beneath his shirt and jacket, his precious cane in hand. Alena sat beside him as he stood over her, voyeurs among their standing guests, watching, listening. The ballroom was filled with harmony; entertainment had become a part of all festivities. The singing voice was soulful, harmonious, graceful. Her voice like silk, as she rendered a symphonic Faust, *The Jewel Song*.

It seemed as if she sang to Golem alone, her eyes never moving from him as he walked to her, the song completed. Applause from the guests.

"You are the jewel, my lady," said Golem, graciously offering his hand.

She accepted his gesture; cautiously taking the three steps down from the stage, lifting her purple dress off the ground as she did so, her skin like black velvet, smooth and glowing.

Golem escorted the singer to the center of the room, the guests parting on cue then returning to their designated sacred spaces.

Where this singer came from Alena had never been told, although she knew. Knew everything about this woman the moment she laid eyes on her. She was invited to sing, her heart, her soul, her essence cried out to Alena, wishing entrance into the sacred circle. Alena felt herself smile. Tasted this woman's metallic blood on her tongue. Felt the moist delicate flower between her legs and Alena's body shuddered with ecstasy, her own body tingling, every inch, every atom writhing with anticipatory pleasure.

The sensation more than the pleasure of inflicting pain, it was sensual, giving itself over to Alena willingly and freely.

Golem released her hand, standing center ballroom among their minions. Alena watched as Jonah provided tiny goblets to all participants. Their eyes never left the singer, taking their glasses as smoothly as though the glasses were already in their hands. Golem was the last to receive a goblet. He bowed to Jonah who then took his rightful place by his side.

Alena saw Sophia, standing on the third step across from where Alena sat, eye to eye. She saw Charlie beside Darlene, their eyes dark as pitch, darker than any foul witch. The room was so quiet and still she could hear how the air folded in on itself, like a held breath constricted in the lungs.

Golem addressed his people.

"My blood is your life," he said. "AGIOS O BAPHOMET!"

Those in attendance raised their glasses, repeated the same as Golem sliced into his wrist with the sharp nail from his right hand. Alena noticed how thick black hairs protruded from his left wrist. He dripped his blood into his goblet. Alena watched as all the goblets also filled with blood, ceased at the halfway mark. Golem raised his goblet as did all in unison.

AGIOS O BAPHOMET!

The others repeated the same then drank from their goblets, just a sip. No more. The singer stood unwavering, her chin raised high. Golem then addressed his people, walking among them as though gliding, weaving within them like a snake surrounding prey, goblet in one hand, cane in the other, tapping across the floor as he walked.

"Power and control are necessary," he began. "The human race, those who are like a lump on the foot of humanity, must be subjugated, for they are no better than a roach scurrying through our garbage." He stopped abruptly, looked left then right, and then continued. "But unlike the roach, these...things hold the power; should they break free of the chains placed on them, we shall be no more. They scratch and claw for what we possess, never knowing it is already in their grasp. All they have to do is clamp down, and declare that it is theirs." His eyes raged with fire as he snarled revealing those jagged teeth. "Keep them at an arm's length. For the human who has awakened is our greatest threat. Instead, allow them to depend on our offerings...our kind and compassionate procession to maintain the veil that covers their eyes. When they've come to depend on us, always reaching for the next tiny morsel, content with the scraps we provide, they allow our grip to tighten...around their thin throats. Trust not the human who is aware, for he sees inside our nightmare. Knows the fear we thrive on. Such is our greatest enemy."

He came to the singer, looking over her, her locking eyes with him. And Golem grinned before returning to his people.

"But our circle does not pretend to be foolish nor prejudice to the sweet essence of all who fear…" he snapped his head toward the singer. "Those who wish entrance to our circle will always be met with open arms. We know no limitations of the soul. We accept all hearts willing to swallow the essence of our being. For those who threaten us are better accepted as allies than enemies, should they desire the essence of our social power."

He stepped to the singer, standing a few feet from her.

"We accept all applications," he said, and the people laughed with Golem. His expression then turned dire, his eyes on the singer seemed to bear down on her. Alena felt her heart shudder. Golem lifted his glass. "Do you accept Baphomet?"

"Freely," she answered, her voice a hush of strength and willingness, confidence.

"Hmm," Golem said. He stepped forward one step. "Disrobe," he ordered.

The singer hesitated.

"Should we eat your heart instead?"

"No, master Golem," she said then began to disrobe. Jonah was there by her side, she handed him her dress, her brassiere, her panties. Such smooth tantalizing skin gleamed beneath the light. And Alena's heart tightened. Her mouth salivating, her mind on fire. Golem approached the singer, holding his cup.

"Do you offer your blood, Niyah? Your soul? Your heart and essence? The etheric energy of your being?"

"Freely," she breathed, a slight stutter in her throat.

"And what do you offer in return?" Golem asked, then gestured to his people. "What shall we receive for this honor we bestow on you?"

"My soul," Niyah said. "My heart." Golem snickered, leering at Niyah. "My undying loyalty." Golem's eyebrows cocked. "My life if necessary. Whatever you wish I will do."

"You voice is sweet," he declared then grinned. Golem stepped closer, mere inches from her. "Be not afraid, my lady. You are the jewel you sang of." He bent his head; his eyes flickered with thick flames. "Your right hand, please."

The singer lifted her arm, palm up. Jonah took Golem's cane and goblet before Golem turned to Niyah, took her wrist and sank his nail into the vein. The singer winced as Jonah placed the cup beneath her arm and Golem drew her blood into his cup, mixing with his own. All the cups filled with her blood. Alena felt herself rise, towering over the others. Felt a growl in her throat that was not her own. Golem lifted the cup to the singer's lips.

"Drink, Niyah," he ordered, holding the cup to her.

Niyah bowed as she took the goblet, her purple lips drank from the cup then offered it to Golem who, after receiving the cup, raised it above his head.

"The blood is the life." His toast was received and all drank with him.

"The blood is the life," the guests repeated.

Alena watched as Sophia weaved through the crowd receiving the goblets, replacing them in a lead lined wooden box.

Alena glided closer, coming up behind Niyah. Alena could feel the erection between her legs, thick and pulsating. The sensation stiffened into her stomach, her heart, her throat. Alena wanted Niyah; she could taste her skin's sweetness on her lips. The scent of lavender wafting off Niyah's skin salivated Alena's tongue.

Golem handed his goblet to Sophia. She placed it inside the box then shared eyes with Golem who held her chin in his hand as if an approval to Sophia's service. Niyah shivered when Golem turned to her. He stepped closer, mere inches from Niyah's eyes. Reached his hand to Niyah's smooth skin, caressing her cheek with the back of his hand. The room so quiet all that was heard was shallow breathing from the guests.

Niyah's eyes held steadfast, her body tense. Golem's hand caressed her neck, her shoulder. His fingers softly moved down her chest and his eyes seemed lost in her skin, seeing through her breasts to the heart that beat with a walloping thrust.

He took her chin in his hand, touched his forefinger to those purple painted lips igniting a half smile from Niyah. Golem then lifted her arms, gentle, taking her wrists in his hands and, crossing her arms, left over right as he twisted her body to meet Alena.

Niyah's eyes widened as the air constricted in her throat, a breath that seemed to rip the air from the room, causing constricted heartbeats from the guests. Golem held Niyah against his body, her head below his chin. She fit perfectly in his embrace.

He whispered, "Just one more step, my lady. Just a little pain to make all things beautiful." Niyah shook with fear, her skin fluttered. She turned her eyes from Alena. "Be not afraid, my love. All will come to you now, all you've dreamed, all you've longed for. But you must look, my lady. You must…give yourself over to us." Golem set his eyes on Alena; those fiery red-rimmed eyes glowed from within his pale complexion. His grin bared those sharp teeth.

Alena could feel the hardened erection pulse with warmth between her legs, swelling thick with ecstatic pleasure. She felt her mouth open as if taking Niyah's flesh between her teeth.

"Look now, my love," Golem said. "The future waits no more."

The guests began chanting, *AGIOS O BAPHOMET!*

A soft whine escaped Niyah's throat as she turned to meet Alena's eyes. At first Niyah's eyes were narrow as if she attempted to not look, to not stare, but those eyes quickly widened, turned stiff, staring, finding the trap door and fell in.

AGIOS O BAPHOMET!

Niyah screamed, her voice shot through the ClairField as her body shuddered. Two huffing breaths as if her lungs begged for air followed with a shriek that caught the attention of every wild animal within a few hundred feet from the ClairField.

AGIOS O BAPHOMET!

And her eyes, the black oil slithered across her pupils, continuing its spiral then panning across the whites of her eyes until all was black, metallic black.

AGIOS O BAPHOMET!

Alena felt her own body release then as Niyah dropped to the floor, exhausted, mesmerized, eyes wide and staring. Golem stared at Alena, a snicker and snarl plastered on his countenance. She felt her lips part into a smile, and Golem closed his eyes and gave a slow bow. A growl erupted from Alena's throat. She lifted her arms as Jonah and Sophia gracefully removed her gown.

AGIOS O BAPHOMET!

Alena could feel a pulsating unnerving sensation writhing through her body. She looked on Niyah whose slow heavy breathing filled the ClairField. Alena had never experienced such wanting and desire, the sensation tore through every atom in her skin, peaking her nipples and hardening the erection between her legs. Alena now could see the animal erection, thick and large, pulsating with tantalizing elation. Alena delicately went to her knees in front of Niyah whose huffing breath ceased when she looked at Alena crawling over her.

AGIOS O BAPHOMET!

Niyah touched Alena's face, soft fingers caressed Alena's lips, and Alena moved over Niyah, pinning her back to the floor. Niyah caressed Alena's breasts, reached her hand to Alena's neck and throat then to the back of her neck, pulling Alena closer. Alena penetrating Niyah as a groan and sucked back breath choked Niyah's throat. And Alena experienced bliss unlike any she'd ever experienced. Niyah writhed beneath her, short huffing pleasurable screams.

AGIOS O BAPHOMET!

Alena thrust faster, harder into Niyah feeling the tip of her erection tingle with a tantalizing explosive sensation as she tore into Niyah's neck drawing the sweet blood fragrance down her throat.

AGIOS O BAPHOMET!

She touched her tongue to Niyah's skin, her breasts, nipping at her skin with Alena's long protruding teeth as her jaw tightened and she thrust harder, pounding Niyah whose moans rose high above the ClairField into the dark night, gracing the moon with the knowledge of pleasure.

AGIOS O BAPHOMET!

Alena's muscles constricted, tensed to the point of near explosion. The bones in her neck swelled as a growl erupted in her throat and she thrust faster, violently, in a mad frenzy to erupt and eject, the animal erection swelling with pulsating fury.

AGIOS O BAPHOMET!

The guests approached them, now a circle around Alena and Niyah. Golem's eyes wide and mad.

The thick droned scream erupted from Alena's throat as she ejaculated, slapping skin in a hurried fury as Alena snarled and turned her head to the ceiling with one final push, a force that could crumble the moon, and she pushed further, holding her erection inside Niyah whose arms flailed to her side, her head flopped left than right.

Niyah opened her dark eyes, her heart fluttering fast like the wings of a frightened butterfly.

"AGIOS O BAPHOMET!" exalted Niyah.

Golem offered his hand to Alena, hoisted her to her feet as Niyah continued to writhe and move on the floor. Alena looked over the guests. She saw her friends, the bridesmaids, gazing at her as if she were a god, their eyes black to the core, their husbands' mouths wide. It seemed that everyone in the room was seething with the same pleasure. Alena, a trapped witness to this evil, looked out to the ghost of her father standing outside the circle, a stare of fear and disappointment in his eyes. The minions with their red eyes snickered and laughed.

And Alena's heart constricted. *What have I become?* The thought raged in her mind. And she heard herself laugh, a dark, sinister demonic snicker.

AGIOS O BAPHOMET!

33

The guests chanted as Niyah lifted off the ground in one smooth gesture, standing on her feet. Her eyes mad, her mouth open wide. Alena stretched her arms and the guests dropped to their knees forming a large circle around the ballroom, all bowing to Alena.

AGIOS O BAPHOMET!

Golem, holding a chain in his hands, attached to a cowbell, swinging. Clunking! Ringing! He weaved through the guests like a python wraps around its prey, sleek and audacious. Expressionless. Those fiery pupils now dark pins that never deterred from Alena.

AGIOS O BAPHOMET!

The minions were dancing and laughing. Red beady eyes gleamed in the shadows. Now the scent of sulfur filtered into the room. Sophia and Jonah, outside the circle, one left the other right, carrying similar chains, attached to a silver-plated censer billowing the sulfuric smoke. They circled the guests, Sophia clockwise, Jonah counter clockwise.

And then the whimpering cries of a baby.

AGIOS O BAPHOMET!

Golem snaked his way to Alena, his clunking bell calmed by his hand as the chanting ceased. More newborn cries and Golem's eyes flickered with flames, his stare burning through Alena.

He sees me, Alena knew. Just as she had become aware of her possession, by the flickering light of

Golem's eyes Alena understood he knew she was aware.

He did not look pleased.

Sophia and Jonah, having completed their circle, gathered his bell, bowed and moved to the side, standing erect. Golem cocked his head to the right, glaring. And the baby began to wail. Maleva slithered through the guests. In her arms a newborn wrapped in blankets, now wailing and crying, as if the child had become aware of its fate. Helpless to this consequence, all the child could do in self-defense was wail.

Maleva handed the baby to Alena. "An offering from Niyah," said Maleva fitting the baby into Alena's embrace.

Those long, dark talons, bony fingers and sharp nails took up the child whose eyes widened and whose body slithered and constricted in Alena's arms. She could imagine what this baby saw. Could the baby even see? How old was this child? Where had the baby come from? Certainly Niyah could not have given birth in this hour, or even within the last few days. Torn from the womb or abandoned at birth, leaving the baby's fate to this evil procession?

All in attendance dropped their heads with a bow. All except Golem who looked on with apt anticipation as Alena's fingers traced over the baby's forehead. The baby jolted in her arms as if attempting to run. Alena gripped the baby tight against her chest.

"Are you not pleased, Baphomet?" said Golem and the guests shuddered.

Alena snapped her head to him. She could feel herself now, inside her body, staying her hand and nails from igniting a river of blood down the baby's torso. She could taste the baby's anticipated blood in her mouth and it was sweet. Delectable.

Over Golem's shoulder the ghost of her father looked on with an expression that bore pure disgust. He captivated Alena's stare.

Golem glanced back at the ghost, then returned to Alena.

"There are many ghosts now," Golem said. "Here at the ClairField." And he smiled, that evil half-cocked crooked grin. "They have no discourse here other than to offer remembrance of things long gone."

The baby squirmed, wailing and crying against Alena. She felt her arms tighten with unholy strength, squeezing the baby in her embrace.

Eat the heart of fear!

The thought surfaced from within as Alena's eyes floated, eyelids fluttered. Baphomet was inside begging to be free.

"Yes," the voice hushed. "The heart of fear. Devour the child and feel free!"

Her throat constricted, salivating in the back of her throat, an overwhelming thirst stronger than a dying man in the desert. Now she experienced heat, burning inside her heart that billowed inside her chest. Waves of heat pouring from every pore in her skin.

Jonah and Sophia shared perplexed stares. Golem did not notice them; he was transfixed on Alena whose throat swelled like a balloon. She turned away, breaking Golem's stare; her father's ghost dissipated. Her body shook, fighting to be free. She heard herself scream, crying out loud in the darkness.

And Golem grinned.

Alena's talons tore into smooth skin and soft bone. The cries erupted, wailing, filling the ClairField, abruptly ceased. Warm blood rushed across Alena's arm.

––––––––

Alena saw the talisman, once she retreated. Retreated back into darkness where the orgasmic shuddering of ingested innocence could not touch her tongue, the passive observer choosing to delve deeper, further from catastrophe. The twelve spoke wheel circling in her mind's eye.

Alena saw nothing of the outside world, shivering in the darkness. She wanted no part in what was happening, even as she felt her stomach fill and the sweet metallic taste of blood on her lips, tongue and throat she refused to open her eyes. Although she wanted to. She wanted nothing more than to see, instead she reveled in fear like a child cowering in the closet petrified of the monster in their room.

She stayed in that dark room until she felt the rush of leaving; Baphomet had returned to Xibalba. And Alena was depleted as if life was torn from her bones in reckless abandon.

Her eyes drifted open, witnessing dawn's twilight creeping outside her window. Then sleep, overwhelming exhaustion. She heard Golem's voice before she was overtaken by sleep.

We must prepare!

Mesmerize her.

34

Alena's eyes snapped open. Sunlight bathed the room. Light beams raged battle with shadows.

Something's different was Alena's first thought. Normally waking from slumber carried a weight to it. Over the last few years Alena had always awakened tired, depleted, as if sleeping brought no rest but now she felt strong, youthful.

And her wit had returned. Raging brain synapses sparked like a transistor radio receiving profound signals from otherworldly invisible resources. She now began to remember, recollecting the xylophone vibrations. One, two, three...four, five. She saw herself with Golem, Jonah and Sophia, in a basement, although she did not recognize this part of the cellar; it was new and smelled of mildew and brick after a powerful sun shower.

And there were children, locked inside cages, dirty and covered in bodily oil. In this memory the Alena who stared at the children did so with an immense appetite, loving every minute the children cowered in shadowy corners. She understood the children were a gift from Golem, Jonah, and Sophia. Understood the plan for these children; either a preparatory meal or an eternity of servitude. All in honor of Alena, Baphomet's host.

"This is ludicrous," Alena told herself. *Just a dream.* Although she knew differently. In her heart she knew this was the reality her situation had embraced.

"Do not convince yourself..." said Maleva, "The dreams are not true." She sat on a chair in the corner, those last rays of sunlight like beams from a flashlight steadfast in front of her eyes.

Alena sat up on the first word. Maleva stared through the sunlight, her countenance betrayed the light, holding firm in shadow. Even so, she appeared young with soft skin, and thick blonde locks. But the blue eyes carried the wisdom of age not youth. Nervousness twitched in those pupils and Alena noticed Maleva's hands—folded in her lap—were trembling.

Alena sensed nervous energy raging with nonconformity.

"How can it be?" asked Alena. "Such actions are not of this world."

No response. Alena noticed how Maleva's jaw tightened when she turned her eyes away. Maleva jumped out of her seat and Alena cringed as Maleva stomped to the window. Her eyes narrowed by the sun, lost in contemplation.

"Are you ok?" Alena asked.

Maleva gestured toward Alena, moving her head to the side although she did not respond verbally. She returned her gaze to the sun.

"We do not have much time," said Maleva.

"Time? Time for what?"

"They'll be returning soon," she said. "Golem, Jonah..." Maleva cleared her throat. "Sophia. Do you have the talisman?" Maleva asked. "The one with the spoke wheel, made from silver?"

Alena, eyes downtrodden, saw the talisman in her thoughts.

"Around your neck," Maleva said.

Alena gazed at Maleva, confused. She drew her left hand to her neck, feeling the silver chain on her skin. The spoke wheel she pulled from her nightgown. Alena's mouth now open. Her fingers smoothed over the silver.

How did she know?

"Because I placed it around your neck," said Maleva, as if she heard Alena's thought.

Alena turned her gaze towards Maleva, still standing in the window with her back to Alena. She asked, "Why?"

"For protection," Maleva snapped. "This is my fault, all my fault." Maleva sighed, her breath stuttering over her lips. "Because I wasn't strong enough when we first met. I only wanted the pain to stop." She bent her head, eyes downtrodden. "The unrelenting anguish." Alena watched as a tear fell beside Maleva's foot. "Torture. I still hear the screams. I don't believe they will ever leave. I only wish that, with what I do now, maybe God will forgive me."

Maleva turned to Alena.

"What did you do?" asked Alena.

"Come," said Maleva. "I must show you."

"Where?"

"Away from here." Maleva nervously looked around the room. "There are eyes and ears everywhere."

————————

They returned to the shop where Alena had first met the gypsy woman; although Alena could not recollect the shop or Maleva, there was a presence all too familiar.

The windows carried no life, blacked out with paint. Maleva produced a key and opened the front door when the stale stench of dust and mildew, rank decay as if something had died inside, wafted into the street. Alena cringed, and covered her nose and mouth. Maleva did not produce the same reaction.

"Do you remember now?" said Maleva holding the door open.

Alena shook her head no, although she recognized the street; it carried a weight to it like a foreboding pressure pushing down on her shoulders, and her heart. She saw and recognized the bridesmaids, in the street, laughing, and behind the laughter, subtle goat baas, and a clunking cowbell. All a distant memory the mind attempted to capture.

And the gypsy woman, standing in the street, old, depleted, wrinkled and angry. Alena saw the gypsy woman's blue eyes, the same blue eyes as Maleva.

How could this be possible? Time doesn't move backward. The gypsy woman if not dead by now would certainly be on the brink of death.

"You *will* begin to see," said Maleva. "But be privy to your thoughts, Alena, they are meant to betray."

For the first time Alena recognized Maleva's thick Polish accent. Her eyes narrowed, lost in memory, seeing the gypsy woman, hearing her voice. There was something about her eyes Alena could not put her finger on.

"We must go inside, even here, on the street there are eyes and ears and we must be prudent with time."

Alena moved her head left then right scanning the mostly barren street. "Why?" she asked.

"Because they are watching…and listening." Maleva locked eyes with Alena. "They will not be pleased. The window of opportunity closes quickly."

Alena tensed. A cold chill rushed down her spine, tensing her back.

"Come," said Maleva. She walked through the door which Alena caught before the hinges snapped the door shut.

The shop was dark and Alena's hands shook, her heart pounding in her chest. She touched the talisman around her neck and turned towards the sky as twilight faded into darkness. A thought then dropped into consciousness, *All will change tonight.*

"All has changed," Alena whispered then stepped into the shop as she prayed silently for the sun to return.

Nothing in the shop had changed since Alena's last visit except for layers of dust, cobwebs in every corner and the smell, stale and putrid burned the nostrils and choked the throat with rising acid to the back of her tongue. The shop was dark, *no electricity* Alena assumed as Maleva lit a candle on the small table in the shop's center.

"Close the door," ordered Maleva.

The stink continued to swell in Alena's throat. She looked at the open door, covering her nose and mouth with her hand, then shot a stare at Maleva like a child in protest.

"There are far worse smells in hell. Close the door." Maleva's stare unwavering, her body tense. Alena did close the door. "Lock it, please." Alena obeyed. Maleva looked through the window, searching the street through the few unpainted strips on the window, her eyes nervously darting from left to right. She closed her eyes then and her body shuddered. "We must begin," Maleva said opening her eyes. She went to the table. "Please, sit. Time is running out. I have no doubt they will be here in time, if not very soon. Take the talisman from your neck and hold it in your hand. You will need it. You will need it from now on."

Alena breathed deeply. She took the talisman from around her neck, holding the silver circle in her palm as she took her seat.

Maleva's eyes were tense, nervous. "Do not look into my eyes, only to the silver."

Alena shook her head, "Why?"

"Because the eye is a trap. It will take you to Xibalba."

"Shibalba?"

Maleva paused. "Is there not anything you remember?" she asked, a sense of desperation in her voice. "Hold tight to the silver, close your eyes, try to remember. Try to remember what happened in this very shop, in this room." She constricted, and swallowed her breath. "In the back room," she breathed.

Alena looked at her hand, and squeezed the talisman when the memory dropped like an anvil in her mind. She saw herself on the street in daylight, the bridesmaids laughing at a goat and the gypsy woman.

Saw how she had entered the shop under false pretenses for a clairvoyant reading.

The goat baa.

The clunking bell.

A dark room, drinking a concoction that tasted like salty dirt.

Her body jumped. She turned to Maleva, studied her face as Maleva closed her eyes to allow the viewing.

How can it be? Alena's thought connected Maleva to the older gypsy woman.

"Your intuition is correct, it is me," said Maleva. Then, after she pursed her lips and swallowed the lump in her throat, "It was me who allowed this to happen. Who brought Golem to you."

Now something dropped on the roof with a loud thump that caught their attention.

Maleva, continuing to study the ceiling, broke the silence. Her jaw tight. "If only we had more time," she said. "But evil travels fast when threatened." She turned her eyes to Alena. "You must never let go of the talisman," she warned. "It will allow you to remember. It will protect you from Xibalba, from falling back in. And, it will restore your strength, and your youth."

Alena, stiff with fear, constricted, although she felt strong, strength returning as Maleva said it would. "I…I don't understand. How can I not remember the past few years? It's like a blur across my mind."

Another thump on the ceiling, this time not as heavy or loud, this time it seemed someone was shuffling on the roof. Maleva's body loosened, the candlelight's flickering shadowy waves traveled across her skin.

"There are so many questions," said Maleva. "They will have to wait, I'm able to keep them from entering but not for long. Once they gain entrance I will be no more and you…you will be destined to a life of servitude and torture, just as I was; the only reprieve is to pass the dark torch. To select another to take your place. This is how it is done; how it has always been done."

Alena was shaking her head, "What are you talking about?"

"I am talking about Golem, Xibalba, and Baphomet. The dark trinity that has done this to both of us."

She wanted more. Alena remained silent to allow Maleva to tell her story.

Maleva cleared her throat. "Do you know the story of Pandora?"

Alena nodded, yes. She gripped the talisman. "Folklore," Alena said but Maleva shook her head, no.

"All folklore is grounded in truth." She paused. "What I am about to tell you requires a suspension of belief. Please understand that your acceptance of the facts is inconsequential; what is of consequence is that you heed the warning for what you must do to break the spell. I provide the story here only as a foundation for understanding."

Shuffling on the roof. Alena looked up, and Maleva just about jumped.

"Here, Alena," Maleva said. "Stay with me, don't allow what goes on outside to take your attention. It is meant to deter your understanding."

Alena was drawn to the ceiling; she had to force herself to turn away. Alena cleared her throat, "Go on," she whispered. Her heart jumped with a sense of urgency. Whatever was on the roof was doing a good job of distracting her. All she could think about was the roof.

"The box Pandora opened was not a box. It was an energy portal with a direct link to Xibalba."

Alena's eyes, wide with a fearful constricted gaze looked to the ceiling then back to Maleva. "Xibalba?"

"The Mayans referred to Xibalba, a place in the caves where they received direct contact with supernatural beings. This is what the Catholics refer to as hell. Xibalba is a place in the universe captured in the throes of dark energy, a dark gel-like planet locked within an evil vibration, a frequency with the single purpose to thrive and evolve, repeating the same pattern over and over until its dark vibration consumes all in the universe. These caves served as an energy portal from which the devils of Xibalba could gain access to this world. In the beginning, the earth was a haven for outside contact, and other worldly beings settled here on Earth. But after the Great War, thousands of years ago an energy field was placed around the earth for reasons too detailed and long for our current circumstances to reveal. When this field was laced across the earth, the connection to Xibalba was severed. But Baphomet was imprisoned on earth. Destined to roam for eternity he sought a way out, a way to reconnect with his hellish dominion. He discovered the rules and played them to his advantage. Choice being his weapon, ego his shield. Disguised as a god, Baphomet manipulated Pandora to open the portal. But this was met with a constriction because of the force field…and consequence for Baphomet. No longer were the evil lords of Xibalba allowed to roam free on our planet in plain sight. The human mind is how they exist on earth, only allowed when the mind invites them in. Electrical impulses in the human brain have the ability to connect instantaneously with the outside universe but the force field hinders this process, and the devils of Xibalba are subjected to match a polarized energy field. Think of magnets, when the magnets are the opposite polarization they attract but the same polarization causes retraction. The human mind must contain an equal and opposite polarization for the devils to arrive…the five gongs allows for this to occur, it is a frequency that once initiated binds the two opposite polarizations, one the human, the other a devil. This is how Golem is able to bring his minions to the planet to consume their earthly hosts. He feeds on the pain and tragedies of women. He is a slave to Baphomet and a uniquely masculine entity."

"What do they want?" asked Alena.

"What do all who have power want? More power. Control. Dominance over all. But this is its nature, what it wants is to consume, to repeat the same pattern of darkness and hatred until all is bathed in its embrace. Xibalba feeds on dark energy. Swallows fear. The fear brings them strength and growth. But Baphomet had become locked in a feminine vibration when he manipulated Pandora, his first female host. This is why he requires a female to exist in this world. Why he is illustrated in history with both female and male genitalia. He is a king in Xibalba, its ruler. And Golem is his minion, one of many in Xibalba who fight tooth and nail to appease Baphomet. Golem is his most ardent right hand; he has an uncanny manipulative disposition, an evil vibration human minds are attracted to. He catches them in his etheric talons, playing to their minds and their desires."

"Are human men not able to communicate with him, with these dark energies? Do they always require a female host?"

"For Baphomet, yes. But earthly men can invoke the devils of Xibalba and the power of Baphomet by pledging loyalty to him; it is only Baphomet who cannot exist physically without a female host. But there is always a requirement for the Xibalba devils to enter their hosts…" Maleva cleared her throat. "The human must give permission for the dark entities to enter. They must go willingly into the evil accord, and they must agree to it even if this agreement is due to manipulation or influence. Golem is an expert in this manipulation. He has existed on earth for thousands of years securing new hosts for Baphomet to consume time and time again, but his time is limited with each female host he secures. Baphomet feeds on the energy of his host. He depletes their life source. This, Alena, is why you have aged so quickly. Once the host is no longer able to contain Baphomet's energy the host must change, and Golem begins his decent into decay. He becomes the goat, the form Baphomet had taken when he first approached Pandora. It is part of the curse they must endure for opening the energy portal to Xibalba. Once the host's energy is depleted the frequency changes the chemical structure in the object Golem used to manipulate the female host to incarnate him. When the portal was first opened, Baphomet understood his devils could not enter the Earth without consent. He then manipulated Pandora to incarnate Golem into a statue gifted to her by her mother, the first incarnation of Golem here on Earth. To do so, Baphomet caused inconsolable pain and suffering to Pandora, destined to walk the earth without love, without touch or reason, until she wished for no more than one to love, to share pain and suffering. With Pandora by his side, Baphomet manipulated Pandora to ring the five gongs, the vibration necessary to encapsulate Golem's ether into the first statue. And so began an unholy trinity, a pattern forever continuing, devouring fear over millennia to bring to Xibalba. The only requirement is to pass the torch from one female host to the next. Until the torch is passed, Golem continues his descent into a goat. The drink you were given in this very shop so many years ago was from the goat's breast; it contained the essence that is Golem, his ether, his soul. The rape you endured planted his seed that destroyed your unborn, germinating in your blood and in the mind, willing you to manifest his ether into the statue. It was your tainted blood that allowed Golem's spirit to transfer from the goat to the statue; and your breath brought life to it, awakening Golem's spirit. Have you seen his hand, Alena? The hand you bit so many years ago. Why does he keep it wrapped? Because underneath he has already begun to change. He is no longer made of the marble stone you constructed; he is flesh and bone now, and he will turn into the goat until the torch is passed to another, a process that could take years to manifest, depending on the vitality of the host they procured."

"You did this to me," Alena said. "Why?"

"Because of the hell I was living in. The host is always kept in Xibalba, half out and half in this world. It is the most excruciating torture and suffering." She turned her eyes to Alena. "And I'm afraid, you will learn of this torture, too. You've already been to Xibalba although you will not recollect this happening. Not yet. Not until your energy is depleted. When you will be required to pass the torch, only then will you understand why I did what I did. Just like it was done to me."

Alena clenched her jaw. She squeezed the talisman. "Why do you look so different? How are you young again?"

"It is a gift. The same happened to the woman who passed the torch to me. We return to the age we were when Golem first captured our hearts. The energy returns our youthful appearance. But we have no heaven to look forward to, only Xibalba."

"What happened to the woman who passed the torch to you?"

"We don't live forever. We live a life of servitude and one day we do die and return to Xibalba, either as a subject or a minion, depending on the frequency the ether is vibrating on when the soul enters."

"Did she tell you this? The way you are telling me now?"

Maleva moved her head back and forth. "No. She told me nothing. She was the most evil witch. She loved torturing others. Some women's hearts are darker than any man who's ever existed. She took pleasure in my pain and deception."

"Why do you tell me this? If your fate is Xibalba then why tell me?"

"You are like me, Alena. Soft and kind and thrown into the evil that exists in this world. My heart still has some good in it and I cannot bear to see you suffering as you have."

"Why us? Why have we been chosen?"

Maleva continued, her eyes roaming over Alena. "Darkness is always attracted to the light it seeks to destroy. It is our light that was chosen. But sometimes, sometimes, Alena, a darkness exists in the human heart so profound Golem must catch it, latch on and carry it. Like the witch who passed the torch to me, this darkness thunders the reach of Golem and Xibalba, a force we do not want to unleash."

Alena pursed her lips, her face flushed red. "You wish redemption," she said. "And forgiveness. You are afraid of your fate and what you've done. You wish for God to forgive your sins. For me too." She stood. Her hands shaking. "I lost my child, my love, my life because of what you've done to me."

Maleva shouted, "I had no choice."

"Wrong," Alena shot back. "I would never do such an evil deed to another. You had a choice. You chose me despite your destined fate."

Maleva stood. Her head shaking. "I give you choice, Alena. You can end Golem's reign. You have that power, the power I was not told I had. You can end this. You have the heart to end this."

Alena shot back, "How?"

"Kill Golem. He is flesh and bone. Now is the time to end his life, and he will return to Xibalba. Before Baphomet has worked his evil hand against you. Before your energy source is depleted. There is a chance for you."

"He is so strong, how could I possibly. There must be another way."

Maleva paused. "There are two," she said. "Take your own life."

Alena looked down to the floor. Her eyes lost. "And the other?"

"Do not pass the torch," Maleva said. "I…I do not recommend this path. The horrors you will endure if you do not is an eternity of pain and torture. Xibalba will tear your soul to pieces for eternity, and you will continue to live, here on this earth, with Golem in tow and although you will want to drive a knife into his heart, you won't be able to. Not then, not after your energy is depleted. Xibalba will stay your hand." She looked down. "I know this more than any other. My refusal to pass the torch…Alena…" She looked up, and Alena caught her stare. "I am more than two hundred years old. I received the torch in 1745, a young gypsy at the age of sixteen."

Alena stepped away from the table to the dust-covered shelf. She looked down to her palm and the silver circle. She breathed deeply then clenched her jaw.

"What will you choose?" Maleva asked.

Alena saw her father and her heart squeezed in her chest. She thought of Jonah and the guests. Her throat constricted. Felt a baby kick in her stomach as tears swelled in her eyes. Her hand shaking, gripping the talisman. She nodded. "How do I kill him?" she breathed.

35

"With any means necessary," said Maleva. "Keep the talisman with you always, it will protect you. No matter what you see or witness, Alena, do not allow them to deter you and do not, for any reason, look into Golem's eyes."

Alena turned to meet Maleva. "Why not?" she asked. "What is with the eyes?"

"The dark part of the eye is a trap door. It draws the consciousness into Xibalba. It also serves as a branding in this world. All who have it have been taken by Xibalba. They are not to be trusted. The black eye is a looking glass for Xibalba to see in this world. No matter what, do not connect with it. Golem will have you then, and all will be for naught. Return to the ClairField; search the basement; you will find the children there. Those who have not been turned by Golem. Free them. Free them all then kill Golem, and his curse on us will be severed. Listen for the five vibrations. If you hear them leave immediately."

"What does it matter?" Alena said. "Baphomet is already within me, what use do those vibrations serve if he's already gained access?"

"The vibration is a direct link to Xibalba. The vibrations ring at a frequency that opens the portal, it is through this portal that Golem is able to bring his minions here to enter their willing hosts. It is also how Baphomet takes over your mind."

Alena saw the guest list with their black mad eyes.

"Should you hear the vibrations, leave immediately."

Alena nodded. "Are you not coming with me?"

Maleva moved her head back and forth.

"Why?" Alena asked.

"Because they are here. I'm afraid this is the end for me."

Alena heard the deep scrape on the roof. Her eyes turned to the ceiling as a rush of heavy wind erupted inside the shop. The candle lost its flame. Maleva went to the wall opposite Alena. She pushed over a book and a hidden door popped open.

"They will be here in a moment," Maleva said. "This door gives passage to the shop next door. Go out the back. Go to the ClairField. I will hold them here as long as I possibly can."

Alena hesitated. Breaking glass from the back room.

"Now," Maleva ordered.

Alena's eyes darted left than right. She went to the door as a heavy thump erupted from the back room. Alena squeezed herself in. Maleva closed door, leaving Alena in darkness as she draped the talisman around her neck. She was about to move when she heard Golem's voice.

"Maleva, my lady, so nice to meet you here."

Alena, breathing deep and hoarse, closed her hand over her mouth. Her heart constricted. Moonlight bathed the shop in blue silvery dark light.

"Why have you followed me?" Maleva asked. "You and your children of hell. This is my sanctuary, your gift to me. Take your fiends and leave."

Alena watched through the many splintered cracks in the wall. She could see Golem, red cane in his wrapped hand. He was looking over the room, searching.

"I said leave," Maleva ordered

Golem grinned, that sinister conniving grin. He stepped closer to Maleva, his heavy feet thumping on the wood floor, his red cane scraping against the wood as his eyes searched Maleva who turned from his stare.

"Honestly, Maleva, I'm disappointed," Golem said. "This is a deal breaker. You know that." His body tensed, his jaw constricted. "And you are aware of the penalty," his voice groveling and sinister.

Maleva did not waver under his heavy dark gaze.

Now more footsteps, behind Golem. Alena saw Jonah standing behind Golem as Maleva's eyes drifted hesitantly to the ceiling.

"Remove them from my shop," Maleva said. "Especially her."

Alena forced herself to look to the ceiling. Like a spider Sophia crawled above. Her mouth agape, long jagged fangs jutted over her lips, dripping saliva to the floor.

"Oh, please, Maleva, how could you treat them as such? They are as much your children as Alena's." He was smiling, enjoying Maleva's fear. "Not like you to be so timid." Golem cocked his head. "I wonder, Maleva, had it been there all along? I think so; I truly do, considering how difficult it was to break your spirit. My conclusion is that some lights, so bright, can never truly be extinguished."

"What're you talking about?" Maleva shot back, returning her stare to him.

"Your light. More often than not that flame is burned out with the treacherous and torturous consistency of Xibalba. But every once in a while it remains. Like the morning embers of a fire, they may be covered in ash. They may appear to be cold and dead but underneath, once you…" he pointed to Maleva's heart with his cane, tapping her chest. "…disturb the embers, hidden beneath is the fire. Just waiting to be reinvigorated." He dropped his cane, pounding the end to the wood floor. "I've seen this twice before." He leaned in to Maleva ever so slightly. "Usually the heart of a woman reaches a depth of despair no man can ever rival, which is more often the case." He looked down, contemplating. "What can we expect from a soul born from darkness?" Golem paused; he scraped the bottom of his cane against the wood. "But you, Maleva, have proven to be something of an enigma, and I do value your patience with your endeavor." His eyes found Maleva then, steady beady eyes imprinted with fire. "Must have taken you years of study and research. And while the rest of us were working for the common cause, you're running around cultivating and planning to take it all away. *Tsk tsk tsk*, Maleva." He breathed deeply. "I'm quite disappointed."

"You're a monster, Golem," Maleva shot back. "A true monster."

Golem grinned, staring, and gave a quick nod. "Thank you," he said, prideful. He stepped closer and

Maleva moved back. "Where is Alena?" His voice low although sinister and hissing.

Maleva shot back, "I've no idea where Alena is; that is your doing, not mine."

Golem stepped closer forcing Maleva against the wall as Sophia dropped down from the ceiling behind him, hissing and baring her teeth.

"I will ask only one more time. Your sole responsibility was to keep her mesmerized. We left the ClairField believing you would complete this task and when we returned...no Alena, no Maleva. So, where is Alena?" He thumped his cane.

Maleva responded, "I told you I do not know." Her jaw trembled.

Golem dropped his head, chin to his chest. He looked away then turned raising his chin to the ceiling. He stepped to Sophia. Touched her head, her cheek, then held her jaw. A small and admiring smug smile graced his lips.

"You gave her the talisman, didn't you?" Golem said, addressing Maleva. He turned to her. "You can tell me, my lady. I know it was you; makes sense, doesn't it? The ladies bonded together for a single purpose." He shook his head, his stare intense. "For the greater good. I do admit this was most unforeseen. It puts a wrinkle in my progress." He stepped closer.

Maleva stood erect. "I despise you and all you represent," she said. "Yes, I gave her the talisman. It's the only way to stop this madness. I know what you plan to do, Golem. Did you really believe human beings were like you, that we wouldn't try to defeat you? This is our planet, our humanity; you're nothing more than an uninvited guest. Back to Xibalba with you." She looked at Sophia. "With all of you. There's no way I'll allow your dark reign to sweep across this world. No way I'd stand by and be a part of your tyranny. You'll never stop; you'll never stop until you have this world in the clutches of your hand."

Golem rolled his eyes. "Your faith in your race blinds you from the truth. They are all dark hearts, Maleva. My hand has proven such for millennia. The heart of human beings is darkness. We are only meant to unleash it."

Golem thrust his fist into Maleva's chest, through the bone, and gripped her heart. Maleva constricted, her eyes wide and stiff. Alena couldn't help the stifled scream that escaped from her throat. She covered her mouth as her eyes darted to see Jonah, staring directly at her.

Can he see me? Alena pushed against the wall to her back. *Did he see me?* Her heart jumping like a rabbit in her chest; her body tense and shaking as she turned back to Maleva and Golem.

"There you go, my lady. Find my eye." Maleva's expression changed then, her bones and muscles fell limp. Golem smiled and tore Maleva's heart from her chest. "To Xibalba you go!" He raised the heart to Maleva's eyes and squeezed the organ, crushing it until blood ran down his arm, raining against the floor as the heart ballooned from his tight grip, between his thick fingers. He cocked his head to the left, gazing satisfactorily at Maleva whose body dropped to the floor by his feet with a heavy thud. Golem closed his eyes, and dropped the heart remains by her body. Turned his head up and his body shivered. "There you go, Maleva," he said. "Exactly where you belong."

He turned to Jonah and Sophia. Sophia gestured to the heart on the floor.

Golem shook his head. "Not that heart, my love. It's polluted poison." Then to Jonah, "We must find Alena. She is here or was here. I can smell her."

"We searched everywhere. Perhaps she returned home to Long Island," Jonah said, his voice cracked.

"Perhaps," Golem said. He tapped his cane twice. "Come, we must find out."

He led them through the front door, Jonah directly behind, Sophia on Jonah's heels. Alena, her body shaking, her breath stuttering, opened the door and crawled out. She could see through the window slits a limousine outside on the street. She watched as all three climbed in, first Sophia then Jonah. Golem glared at the shop, his body tense, before climbing into the limo that raced down the street once he closed the door.

Alena stood in darkness. She touched the talisman nestled close to her skin. Her breathing was heavy, and she turned to Maleva, lying in a pool of blood. Her chest torn open, her mangled heart lying beside her, and her eyes open wide. Alena went to her, kneeled beside Maleva's outstretched arm. She could see the eyes were dead, and although death had turned those blue pupils black, Alena knew they were only dead in this world. She could feel Maleva was in Xibalba.

She could hear those torturous painful screams.

36

Alena's head spun, so many thoughts carried on the wings of insecurity invaded her mind. She hailed a cab outside the shop once she was sure she could leave and that Golem was not returning. The cab driver was quiet, and Alena caught his stare in the rearview mirror more than twice.

"Am I surrounded by devils?" she thought. "Is he watching me everywhere I go? How many people has Golem turned over the last few years?"

She held the talisman in her palm during the cab ride to the ClairField. Her heart jumped as memories surfaced. She could taste the blood and heart of that newborn offering in the back of her throat. She felt the animal erection between her legs; the pulsating, dripping release of pleasure writhed in her stomach. She fought every sensation, every emotion, every longing and hunger that wrenched through her essence as if it were poison in a spiritual war.

Those sinister thoughts erupted in her mind like acid in the back of her throat as the cab pulled onto the ClairField drive. The inn was lit up like a beacon of light to the outside world. The city had planned to tear down the ClairField, this she knew was true, but Golem had persuaded them to deter that request, allowing his unholy ceremonies to continue under the veil of darkness. Alena's reaction to the ClairField carried mixed emotions. Her childhood home had become a house of evil. Even now as she gazed upon the inn, she could feel the anguish that replaced the inn's prestigious history.

"This is now a house of hell," she told herself.

"We are here, my lady," the driver said glancing at Alena in the rearview mirror.

Alena avoided his eyes. She paid him with a substantial tip then climbed out of the car. Her gaze turned immediately to the third floor—the only room in darkness—as the cab raced away. Alena paid no mind to the screeching tires. For the first time in her life she was afraid of the ClairField; it seemed to invite her in to its evil accord. A rushing wind at her back, fierce like a devil's hand pushing her to the steps as the front doors opened slowly.

"I'm sorry," she whispered as if the ClairField could hear the apology. She placed the necklace around her neck before taking the steps to the front door. The lobby was bright with beams of yellow light reaching to every corner where no shadows or evil eyes could hide. She stood in the doorway, her breath constricted. She looked out over the drive and saw red beady eyes glaring at her from within the dark of night. Wind, driving fury, blew violently forcing the doors to levy and buckle as if they fought off the wind that declared the doors should close in that instant.

"Perhaps the inn desires death," she thought. Perhaps the inn has become ashamed for what has transpired within its walls. She touched the door that continued to shake with the wind.

"Stay with me," she whispered to the talisman around her neck. "Be my eyes and ears. Give me strength. My God, please give me strength."

Alena entered the ClairField.

And the doors closed violently as if the inn had swallowed its redemption.

————————

Alena stood in the ghost town that had become the ClairField. Lights were not on as Alena supposed from the outside. The room smelled of dust and stale sweat. The furniture was covered with plastic; cobwebs were laced across the grand chandelier, in the corners and across the furniture.

The stench of death was everywhere. Blood and torn bodies beneath the putrid stink that now existed beneath the folds, raging and burning howls of sex and fear clung in the air like a stain on time. Maleva's voice in Alena's mind, *find the children and release them.*

She couldn't imagine, couldn't see the children Maleva spoke of although she knew they were here, huddled in corners and praying for death. Alena was certain that hope had run from them like a criminal evading the police. She went to the basement door and opened it. The room beneath pitch black with one exception. Her father's ghost stood at the bottom, his countenance pale and drawn. He lifted his hand, his finger stretched to his left. Alena gasped. She wanted to run to her father, fold herself within his embrace. His ghostly figure faded then, dissipated on the winds of darkness.

His ghost brought strength to Alena's heart. She wanted to cry but held back those tears. She reached for the candelabra on the wall to her left. "Matches," she thought. "I need to light the flame."

Her eyes went wide when the flames ignited on their own. She sensed her father's presence. She took the stairs down, her footsteps clunking against the wood steps. A foul stench of rotting human remains wafted into her nostrils, strengthening with every step down. She held her hand over her nose and mouth, fighting off the vomit that curled her stomach and nipped at the back of her throat.

When she took the last step down, she pushed the candelabra toward her left, the flames illuminating the room that had once been a speakeasy casino. She thrust the candelabra further into the room. On the floor she saw the dead bodies, a mass of children and adults, their torsos torn, split from navel to throat, their organs removed. And the peculiar manner these bodies were placed formed a circle that housed a pentagram. Beneath their bodies was that pentagram, painted red with blood. She couldn't help but notice the newborn from last night in the pentagram's center.

She tasted the baby's blood on her tongue. Felt the sting of the child's essence, its innocence burning in Xibalba. Alena threw up, her body shaking violently. Eyes wet with tears.

"My God, please forgive me," she cried when a loud heavy thud erupted down the hall to her right. Alena startled. Her eyes found her father again, although he disappeared quickly, behind him a door, thick heavy old wood. She went to the door. No handle to open it. She searched the door with her hand hoping to find a way to open it but there was nothing, no divots, no latch or keyhole, just a door sealed to the brick wall. Alena slammed on the door, frustrated and frightened.

She heard the scream that erupted beyond the chamber door. Alena's blood recoiled and turned cold. She stepped back holding the flames to the door. Her heart jumping.

Think, Alena, think.

She could hear low whimpering cries, filled with fear, behind the door. She lifted the candelabra above the door and saw a single key on a large, round silver ring. She went to it, grabbed the key, and placed the candelabra on the floor as she searched the door, her hands moving over the thick wood. Three metal slats lined the door, top, middle, and bottom.

If there's a key, there's got to be a way in.

She pushed on the middle slat and it moved revealing a keyhole beneath. Hurriedly, she twisted the key. The door popped open a few inches and a foul stench of feces, body odor, and rank decay, burned her nostrils with an imminent heat that beaded sweat on Alena's skin. She turned her head away as if the movement would cease the putrid odor, but to no avail. The smell was everywhere, like poison on her skin; she could feel it seeping into her flesh, and inside the pores as she took up the candelabra.

Alena went through the door.

Her presence drew another blood curdling scream. A young girl—she couldn't be more than four—sat in the room's middle, her wrists clamped to metal chains attached to the floor. A row of cells lined the wall to Alena's left, each cell held a child. Their eyes gleaming at Alena from the dark of their cells. Some stood, others barely moved. And the girl continued to scream pulling on her restraints. Metal scraping soft youthful flesh drawing blood with every frenzied tug.

The girl, eyes filled with tears and terror, recoiled when Alena stepped to her.

It occurred to Alena then that these children had seen her before, although not Alena exactly: they'd seen Baphomet in Alena's eyes. Alena went to the girl, put the candelabra on the floor beside them.

"I'm here to help," Alena said, her voice trembling, her hands shaking. Alena took the girl's wrists, looking over the restraints. Perhaps it was her voice that calmed the girl, Alena wasn't sure, although she ceased the loud screams. Now she whimpered and sobbed, stifling her screams in Alena's presence. The girl was pulling her restraints, frantic to get them off. Blood streamed down her arms, dripping on the concrete floor. Alena could taste the salty sweet blood on her tongue. She used the key to release the young girl who, once she was free, backed away from Alena in a hurried panic.

Alena noticed how the other children were standing in their cells, holding the thick bars, all with the same stare. They cowered under Alena's presence as Alena stood. The girl huddled against the wall, her eyes wide and stale, tears streaming down her face.

"Take me instead," a boy said. Alena looked at him. He couldn't have been more than ten, standing tall, his expression emotionless. Alena noticed a bowl had been set outside his cage, the same for all the cages. White bowls containing what Alena surmised was rice.

Alena stared at the boy. She moved her head back and forth. "I'm not going to hurt any of you," she said. Her eyes darting left then right, cell to cell. "We're all getting out of here."

The children paused, sharing perplexed, untrusting stares. Alena went to the cell doors, key in hand, twisting the key to unlock each cell. One by one, each door propped open but the children, all but one, remained in their cells. The boy who'd spoken rushed from his cell to the girl huddled in the corner, her arms cradling her knees. The boy wrapped his arms around her.

"You're ok," he said.

Alena looked down on them. "We must go," she said. "There isn't much time."

The boy, covered in soot and sweat, ragged clothes hanging loose from his frail shoulders, turned to Alena. His stare petrified. Alena looked over the cells. "Why aren't any of you moving?"

The children recoiled in their cells. The boy stood, glaring at Alena.

"Is this a trick or a test?" the boy asked.

Alena, her eyes in disbelief, shook her head. "No," she breathed. Her eyes fell on the girl's bloodied wrists, while droplets of blood dripped to the floor. Her body quivered. Her stomach lurched. Her mouth salivated. She wanted to wrap her lips around that soft wrist and swallow blood down her gullet, the insatiable thirst maddening. She shook her head to ward off the desire. To bring herself back to the task at hand.

The boy stepped back, his hand on the young girl's head as if he meant to shield her from Alena. She grabbed a handful of his pants, hiding her eyes behind him. Alena looked at him, at her, gathering her wits.

"I know you're all scared," she said, "I am too." She took up the candelabra and the key. Flickering shadows raged across Alena's skin. "The doors are all unlocked. They'll be coming soon." Her voice a low whining constricted hush. Alena understood these children were petrified by her presence; she was afraid herself.

"Come with me," she pleaded stepping back; her foot stepped on one of those white bowls which cracked under her foot. She looked down at the rice on the floor, drizzled with blood. She moved her foot quickly. Stepping over the spill, she shook her head.

This is mad, absolutely mad. She fought the tears, her throat constricted. The children then moved to the front of their cells, all eyes on Alena.

"Why aren't any of you moving?" She walked backward toward the door. "Why aren't you leaving? This is your chance to be free, why…why are you all standing there? Come with me, *please.*"

Drink the blood of the little lamb!

The voice slithered into Alena's thoughts. Her eyes darted to the blood droplets, then to the soft skin. Her eyes wide. The voice was soft and unsuspecting, low with a hiss. She forced her eyes away. The voice tempting, striking a chord Alena had never known existed. Her craving for the young blood was overwhelming. Her body shivered as if she could ward off the desire.

Little lamb, the voice said. Alena's eyes rolled to the back of her skull, grinding her teeth as her jaw tensed. *Little lamb. Blood so sweet and flesh so tender.*

Alena's hand floated to her chest and the talisman. The voice ceased. Her eyes shot open and the children were all standing, watching.

The boy standing beside the young girl spoke first. "She didn't change," he said. Then looked at the girl cowering behind him. "She didn't change."

"Not at all," Alena thought, although she knew the voice would be back. Baphomet wasn't giving up his host that easy. She held the candelabra high overhead, shedding light on those unsuspecting child eyes looking at her with trepidation. .

"No, I did not," Alena said. "And I won't, not ever again. I know you've all been through a nightmare but that is over now, too." She pursed her lips, swallowed the lump in her throat. "But Golem will be back. Please, we have to go now."

No movement. What do I do?

The boy helped the girl to her feet, and while holding her close to him, he walked her over to Alena. The rest remained in their cages.

"Come on!" Alena pleaded. "Why aren't you moving?"

The boy touched her arm, gentle and soft. Alena's body shook. She heard his heart. Felt the steady rhythm in her own heart.

"They are afraid," he said. "Golem said you'd be here, that you were coming to trick us as a test of trust."

"Golem said…," Alena thought.

"He told us if we go with you, he'd…." The boy's voice ceased.

Alena turned to him. Her voice trembled, "Kill all of you."

"No," he breathed. "We do not fear death. We fear Golem. We fear what those adults do to us. We fear…you."

"That's not me," she said.

He released her arm. "I know, but they don't believe you. They just want the pain to end. We welcome death. It would be the end to this nightmare called life. Golem promised us death if we don't go with you."

"What?" She shook her head. "You're choosing to die instead of being free?"

"Yes. What life is there for us? Golem will find us; he will never rest until he has, and we fear becoming adults. We are afraid we will do to other children what has been done to us. As Golem tells us, when we reach maturity he will turn us. The hearts of adults are corrupt; we witness this always. Even those sworn to protect us, as you do now, have handed us over without so much as a second thought. But we don't choose as they have. We keep our hearts hidden from them so that they can never touch us. They may use our bodies…" his breath caught and he forced a swallow down his throat. "But they can't take our hearts."

Alena closed her eyes, moving her head back and forth. She touched the talisman. *Give me strength!*

She shot her eyes open, stood erect. "Golem dies tonight," she declared. "By my hand he will die tonight." The children scowled at her. "He will not find you after tonight because he will be no more, but you must leave now. I can't fight him knowing you will all be down here. He will use you all against me."

"Where will we go?" a boy child still in his cage asked. "There is evil everywhere, no place is safe."

"Not everyone in the world is evil," Alena declared.

Another child said, "Everything contains evil, Miss Francon. Even you!"

"We've got to try," the boy next to Alena said. "It's worth it to try."

Silence. Then one of the children stepped from their cage. He looked down to the bowl of rice then stomped on it splintering the bowl, smashing the rice beneath his foot as a small puddle of blood seeped from beneath the foot. Alena cringed at the sight of blood.

The boy next to her said, "The blood, it's the blood of children," he told Alena. "Once it's consumed it's like poison that turns children into devils. We have all refused the rice."

Alena held the boy's chin. She brought him close to her. "Let's go," she said.

"Do you promise to kill him?" another child, a twelve-year-old girl, said.

Alena's body tensed. "Yes, yes I do promise." Although her heart jumped, Alena hoped she would deliver. She'd say anything to get them out. One by one the children stepped from their cages. All surrounded Alena. She breathed hoarse and stuttering as her heart calmed. "Thank you," she said.

"Can we go now?" the boy beside her said.

Alena looked at him. "Yes. All of us." She held up the candelabra and turned to the door. "Follow me."

She led them; ten children huddled behind, out of the chamber door, into the casino basement, to the stairs. Alena's heart raced faster with every step up.

"We're not gonna make it. We're not gonna make it," the four-year-old with the bloodied wrists started saying. Her voice shaking with terror.

"She's got to be quiet," Alena thought with mounting frustration. The girl was on the brink of hyperventilating, repeating over and over, *We're not gonna make it.*

"Here, take this." Alena handed the candelabra to the boy. She took up the young girl in her arms, hoping to calm her hysteria. "Look, sweetie," Alena said, she took the talisman from beneath her shirt. "This is for protection," she told her. "As long as I'm wearing this you can't be hurt, understood?" A lie, although a lie that was required. The girl calmed. Alena cradled the shivering girl in her arms as she continued up the steps, into the ballroom where she stopped to look for any possible sign of Golem.

The ClairField was quiet, eerily quiet. She saw no one. Moonlight bathed the ballroom with a silvery glow. Alena breathed deeply then rushed hurriedly into the ballroom toward the entrance. Her footsteps slapping against the tile floor with small successive and hurried footsteps following on her heels. They crossed the ballroom in a huddled mass. Alena could taste freedom. The entrance seemed to pull her toward it.

The sweet scent of the girl in her arms filled her nostrils. Alena closed her eyes. The girl's soft flesh salivated Alena's tongue. She didn't hear the screams erupting behind her. Alena stopped dead in her tracks. The need to feed was overwhelming. "Why deny what feels right?" Alena thought. Her body tightened, her head jutted to her left, then shook violently. She forced her eyelids open, peering through wet and narrow eyes.

The girl in her arms was smiling. "Told you," she said. "We're not gonna make it."

She yanked the talisman from Alena's neck. Alena dropped the child, her arms flailed by her side. Alena's throat ballooned then constricted, then ballooned again. Hot, scorching poison writhed in her blood then turned cold. Now she heard the frantic, panic-stricken screams.

Then the vibrating gong from a xylophone. One, two, three. The vibration erupted in Alena's chest, scouring through her bones. She tried to turn but dropped to one knee instead, the girl mockingly holding the swinging talisman. Her eyes were black to the core. Alena dropped to the floor, her head flopped across her left arm, and she could see why the children were screaming.

They were being torn apart. The boy who had helped Alena, long talons like a tarantula where his arms and legs should be, raced after the children.

Her body leapt off the ground then slammed back down. A fourth gong sounded, the vibration rang between Alena's ears. The screams echoed through the ClairField.

Fifth vibration.

Alena's body went limp. Her eyes, wide and staring, followed the approaching footsteps. Alena's eyelids growing heavy, her breathing shallow, witnessing Golem kneel beside her, his head cocked to the side. Jonah and Sophia were standing behind him.

Golem snarled and snickered. And then, darkness.

37

Alena's eyes shot open with a gasping breath. She was tied to a chair strategically placed in the middle ballroom. Her hands tied behind her back and her ankles were tied to the chair's legs. She immediately went to work, tugging and pulling at the rope, a reaction brought on by fear as she pieced together what had happened. The memory of the young girl holding the talisman rifled through her thoughts. She ceased pulling and tugging, and shook her head to shake the fog of tiredness as the scene before her became clear.

A pentagram had been drawn in blood. A rather large pentagram that consumed the whole floor. Alena's seat situated at the end of one of the five points of the five-pointed star. A body lay in the center, the child who had crushed the blood-rice bowl, his eyes open wide, not staring or looking forward but pinned in the corners. His body was stiff, although his chest rose with each breath he took. Waves of heat wafted off his body. The ballroom was hot, scorching heat slithered across Alena's skin. Her stomach twisted nausea up to her throat. The profound scent of burning sulfur consumed her nostrils with a suffocating grip.

"Be calm," Golem said. Alena's eyes shot to his voice. Golem leaned against the wall next to the cellar door, a large bowl cradled in his left arm, while his right hand mixed something in the bowl with a large wooden spoon. He stared at Alena through narrow eyes and Alena could see those flames flicker in his pupils. "You need to eat, Baphomet. Your strength is depleted."

"Let the child go."

Golem tensed, stopped mixing, his eyes narrow, staring at Alena. She could see that grin pull to his mouth's corner. He rolled his eyes and shook his head. "Oh please, Alena, as if you're so innocent. You're as much to blame for the child's predicament as I am." He pushed himself off the wall with his shoulder, continuing to stir the mixture.

Alena turned away. His presence was irritating. She despised everything about him. Her creation, born by her hand, heart, and blood. "All a lie," she thought. Everything was a lie with the purpose of manipulating means for power and control. She shook her head as sweat beaded on her forehead, dripping down her temple. She wanted to drive a stake through his heart. She could see herself doing it with a sense of pride to rid his evil off the face of the earth. To send him back to Xibalba. Cut his head off, too. She saw herself holding Golem's severed head, wanting nothing more than this wish to be granted. She could taste his death on her tongue and lips. *Isn't that how devils are dispatched, a stake through the heart and a severed head?*

"Those are vampires, Alena," said Golem.

Alena snapped her head toward him. *He can hear my thoughts?*

Golem continued, "A useful trick, those damn devils." He looked to his right, thinking, as if talking to himself. "I could never do such a thing. Taking dead human remains as a host." Then to Alena, "It's the smell, my lady. Vampires always stink to high holy hell. If it weren't for their powers of persuasion over the human mind, they'd never so much as get close to their prey." He cocked his head to the right, and his expression changed, as if some new idea had dawned on him, like a revelation he'd never thought of. He looked left then right before he turned to Alena. "What is rather interesting with vampires is their ability to transform those dead bodies, using the human mind against them. You see, Alena, they don't actually change form, it's merely a manipulation dropped into the mind of the victim. Ahh," he grunted. "But they're so easily dispatched, those dead bodies are too easily overcome. A stake through the heart!" He shook his head. Rolled his eyes again. "It's because they reside *in* the heart, it's their means of entrance, which, as a devil as you humans like to call us, is truly…disheartening. Carrying the previous life's memories of the heart for so long. It's why they're coined as hopeless romantics." He cocked his eyebrows. "I'd rather not."

"But turning into a goat is so much better."

"Don't mock, Alena, you're as much a goat as I am."

"Really, Golem? Take off that carefully wrapped bandage and let's see what contagious infection has taken over."

Golem ceased mixing. He grinned at Alena then walked quietly to the boy.

"Don't touch him!" Alena demanded, her voice hoarse.

Golem did not look at Alena, his stare almost sympathetic. "Not him, Alena. He's given himself over in honor of Baphomet. In honor of you."

"I am not that evil disgusting whore of hell. I never asked nor wanted such a fate."

Golem turned to Alena. "Oh, please," he said. "I'm sure what Maleva conveniently left out of your little inquisitive revelation, is that Baphomet cannot take a host without consent nor a match of the heart. Seriously, Alena, the heart of a woman is grounded in hell."

"You did that to me," Alena shot back. "You turned my heart to stone. None of this would have happened if you hadn't taken my child, my life. You turned my love into hate. That's not who I was or who I am. You manipulated me."

"No, Alena, I simply gave you a push; it was your choice in the end. Blame all you want on me, but it's you who made the final decision." And then his voice erupted, except it was not his voice, but Alena's voice from his lips.

"*DO YOU UNDERSTAND ME?*"

Alena remembered that moment, so long ago, when she'd completed her creation, the statue she'd slaved over, her masterpiece, screaming and praying for him to come to life.

"That's right, Alena. Remember. This is all your doing."

"Lies," she hollered. "If I had known who you were, I would never have participated."

Golem provided no response. He shook his head and looked down to the boy by his feet. He moved the boy's head with his foot, pushing down on the jaw and mouth. Saliva dripped from the corner of the boy's lips.

"I may have given him too high a dose," said Golem as if to himself. "No matter, he will awaken soon." Golem lifted the wooden spoon from the bowl. Thick, red liquid-Alena surmised it was blood-dripped off the spoon into the bowl. Golem carefully moved the spoon over the boy's forehead allowing thick red droplets to fall on his skin. The sight of blood ignited Alena with both anger and desire.

She tried to speak, to defend the boy once again, but her desire squelched her powers of speech. She pursed her lips and swallowed, attempting to stifle the craving to taste the sweet blood on her tongue.

"Enticing, isn't it?" said Golem. He dipped the spoon back into the bowl, cradling it in his arms as he stepped toward Alena. He held out the spoon, mere inches from her lips. "Drink?"

She turned her head, her body shaking.

"You will feel better once you drink."

Alena shot Golem an angry, disgusted stare. "So that Baphomet can surface? Tell me, Golem, is that what it takes, the blood of children? Is that what Baphomet feeds on? The essence of the innocent?"

"Unadulterated blood, Alena. Children are so sweet in their decadence. Tell me, would you rather dine on the flesh of an old diseased cow, or taste the delectable softness of a calf? It's really the same concept; our tastes are not different than any human." He stretched the spoon to her lips. Blood droplets fell on her lap. Alena looked away. "I know you want to, my lady…"

"I'm not your lady," Alena shouted, her eyes wide and staring with horrific intent.

Golem grinned. "Indeed," he said in a low hush. He looked into the bowl, dipped his finger in then smeared blood on Alena's forehead. "*AGIOS O BAPHOMET!*" he said with a sneer, his bloodied finger pressing into her skull.

Alena moved her head back, away from his hand. "Don't touch me," she ordered, tugging on her restraints. If she could jump up now and plunge her fist into his heart as Golem did to Maleva, his death would be satisfying. Golem clenched her jaw, squeezing the bone with such might Alena thought her jaw was about to splinter. And the look in his eyes, that fire raging in his pupils, revealed the devil inside. The bandage around his hand was saturated with crimson. And that strand of hair fell over his eye. She wanted to tear it from his skull. He stepped back, glaring at Alena when the thought dropped into Alena's consciousness.

She started laughing. Insanely laughing and Golem cringed.

"What's so funny, my lady?"

She continued to laugh before saying, "You can't kill me. That's what's so funny, Golem. You need me alive, or you return to Xibalba." She returned Golem's grin. "What's wrong, Golem, can't take the horror of your own home?"

Golem sighed with a slight laugh and slowly shook his head. "You'll go there soon enough, Alena. Soon enough."

He turned from her, and placed the bowl by the boy, then walked with his back to Alena. His eyes fixed on the statue of David.

"What do you think, Alena? David looks good here in the ClairField. Such a better home than withering away in the Hamptons." Golem's red cane leaned against the statue. He went to David. "This was your inspiration, wasn't it? To create something as equally masterful as David?" He glanced back at her, "Thank you," he said. "You really did create a masterpiece." Golem gazed at the statue, the solemn stare of David looking at him. Golem fixed his hair, brushed his fingers through those thick locks, as if he were looking in a mirror then winked and clucked his tongue. He took up his red cane.

"My opinion, Alena…" he turned to her. "David is by far a larger masterpiece."

"That's right," Alena shot back, "I forgot you prefer men." She gnashed her teeth. "Or should I say, young boys."

Golem leaned on his cane. "Indeed, Alena. Jonah has done me well in that regard. As did Sophia for you." His eyes turned to the ceiling. "Isn't it fascinating, Alena, swallowing innocence whole. It feeds our ether like no other deed allows. Nothing comes close." He shot a stare toward Alena. "In the future all will sacrifice their children to Baphomet. There will be no other alternative to gain power. All will come through me, Alena. All will bow before me. All will do my bidding should they desire fame and fortune. It is inevitable."

Alena's eyes slowly widened. Her stare stiff and horrified. *Sophia?* she thought. *Me? It can't be. It just can't be!* Her eyes filled with tears. Her lips quivered. Golem registered her response.

"Oh," he laughed. "You haven't dredged up those memories yet have you?" His grin was wide. Golem cocked his head, gazing at Alena. "I'll be sure you remember them, my lady. You and Sophia. Those memories will follow you to Xibalba to deliver an eternity of terror…and pleasure."

Alena saw the boy on the floor, he started to flap, his body jerking and twisting.

"What's happening to him?" Alena hollered.

"I gave him too much. An overdose may be imminent. Alena, take off those shackles and save this boy." He laughed.

Alena turned her eyes from the boy, hating Golem for the boy's demise. The boy ceased flailing and fell quiet. Alena looked at him. His chest continued to rise with breath.

"*AGIOS O BAPHOMET!*" Golem slapped his cane twice against the marble floor. *Tap. Tap.*

Alena pulled on her restraints.

"No use, Alena. Jonah is quite an expert at restraining others."

Alena looked over the ballroom. "Where is Jonah? Where are the others?"

"They'll be here soon." He cleared his throat. "For the ceremony. They are preparing. If you want this over, Alena now would be your chance."

Perplexed, Alena's eyes narrowed.

"Sophia will make a true bride for Baphomet. She is willing and more than eager to take the role."

Alena's brow furrowed, she looked around the room, understanding what was happening. The ballroom, the blood, the Pentagram, it all made sense. She moved her head back and forth, shaking her head, her eyes burrowing into Golem with a clenched jaw, gritting her teeth. "I'll never pass the torch, Golem. Ever! Especially to a child. Do you believe I would do such a thing willingly?" She started to laugh. "You really met your match this time, *Golem*."

"Powers of persuasion, my lady. There are many ways we can be certain such events do transpire."

"Never," Alena shouted, then, "Your reign dies with me."

"Please, Alena. There is always a lifetime in Xibalba that will deter your conviction. I've seen it many times, and it has never failed. No human being has ever escaped the thrall of Xibalba without passing the torch. Human hearts can only take so much horror until their hearts turn dark, soiled with catastrophe." He pointed his cane at her. "The same will be your fate." He stomped his cane on the tile. "But there is no need to engage in that circumstance. Pass the torch, Alena. Pass the torch tonight."

Another revelation dropped into Alena's thoughts in that moment, one she hadn't noticed until now. She was different than before. As if something evil had been vanquished from her heart, something sinister. *Baphomet!*

"He's not here anymore, is he?"

Golem's expression turned, as if he'd swallowed a ball of fear.

"That's why you need the torch passed, to bring him back. To provide another host." She looked at Golem. "If not, you will walk the earth without his blessing, without his power, destined to live and die as the animal you are."

Golem ground his teeth, his jaw tight. "There are levels of survival I am prepared to accept. The same as I have endured for centuries. It is inevitable, my lady, all have passed the torch, and so shall you."

Alena couldn't help but grin at him. "I will not. Not now or ever. You lose, Golem. And to my eternal satisfaction, you lose tonight."

Golem closed his eyes. He breathed deeply as his body shook and quivered and when he exhaled his eyes opened.

"Then let the ceremony begin!"

38

Those gong xylophone vibrations rang through the ClairField. Alena could now see that the vibrations emanated from a large crystal bowl on top of a wood pedestal on the opposite side from where she sat. Golem stood erect and thumped his cane against the marble floor. Alena's body shuddered, her heart jumped.

Standing in the cellar door was Jonah, a mirror image of Golem with his tight tuxedo; his eyes, black to the core, gleamed at Alena. After the fifth vibration the chanting began, "*AGIOS O BAPHOMET!*"

Jonah walked patiently to the pentagram. Behind him the boy Alena had trusted in the cellar—also in a tuxedo—then the little girl who'd torn the talisman from her neck wearing a disheveled pink bridesmaid's dress. Sophia emerged in the cellar door, wearing a white dress. They all held tiny thimble-sized cups.

"*AGIOS O BAPHOMET!*"

Alena pulled on her restraints fighting off the craving for Sophia. Her stomach twisted into knots. Each child took their place on a starred point on the pentagram, their bodies turned in toward the child flapping on the floor.

And the pentagram wavered as if it were coming to life. Alena caught Sophia staring at her, her mouth agape, eyes wide, directly across from where Alena sat. Alena turned her eyes from Sophia's burning stare.

"AGIOS O BAPHOMET!"

Golem slammed his cane hard against the tile and the children all raised their cups and drank. Blood trickled down the corners of their mouths. Sophia never ceased glaring at Alena who tried desperately to keep her own eyes from Sophia's. The pentagram wavered once again and then the ground beneath the pentagram cracked and trembled as a hurricane wind tore through the ClairField and the floor fell, plummeted into a void where darkness possessed its own bite and snarl. Alena could see stars in the darkness, spiraling to what seemed like an eternity to the fires and rage of Xibalba.

Although the fire was so distant, Alena could hear crackling furious flames. Heat, like sitting inside a fire, raged across Alena's skin as she turned to Golem, handing his cup to a girl who placed his crystal in a lead-lined box. Golem dismissed the young girl who went back to the cellar. A hideous growl erupted as a shadow raced across the ClairField walls, large and monstrous extinguishing the candles' flames that had illuminated the inn, now bathed in moonlight and the distant fires of Xibalba.

Alena watched Golem whose footsteps and cane tapped against the marble floor as he walked into the pentagram and although the floor had been torn away, he walked as though the floor was still there. The children remained as they were, standing dutifully in their place on the pentagram as the boy in the center continued to flap and convulse. Golem pushed the boy's head with his cane and his head flopped to the side, his eyes open, black and wide, towards Alena.

Inside the pentagram a barking snarling growl erupted. Alena could see a demon with gray scaly skin, long snout like a wolf but a human body, climb, crawl, and jump as if it were climbing on the stars like a ladder up toward the ClairField. The creature stopped when Golem slammed his cane.

Then all became quiet, as if time had stopped, the distant Xibalba fires the only noise. They crackled like a comforting fire on a cold winter night. Alena's stomach twisted as if a knife were gutting her hollow, wrenching her entrails. Her mouth salivated with the thought of the savory delectable taste of Sophia's fair flesh on her tongue. Her eyes burned with rage as she curled her lips in. Her throat swelled. Her chest tightened. Her jaw clenched shut as she gnashed her teeth.

"Residual effects," said Golem. Alena's eyes snapped to him. Golem cocked his brow. "In case you were wondering, the host always takes on some of the essence of Baphomet. It's like a stain beneath the skin." He shook his head. "It will never end. You will always crave blood…and the flesh." Alena turned away from his stare as Golem rolled his eyes then rapped his cane against the floor. "This demon wishes entrance," said Golem. "A willing host in this world." The demon barked as if agreeing with Golem. He pushed the end of his cane into the boy's skull. Golem's narrow eyes beamed at Alena. "This boy would do well with demon eyes."

Alena, trembling and shaking, glared at Golem. "Don't!" she said moving her head back and forth. "Don't," she repeated.

"What else would you have us do with him? It is obvious this boy is dying. Is that what you want, Alena? To see him perish?" Golem raised his head as if a revelation had occurred to him. "Oh, I've got it, we could hack him up. Grind his flesh and bones into food. A most delectable dish he would make for our prestigious ClairField guest list to dine on." His eyes settled on Alena, burning rage filled his stare. "A most delish pate'."

The children laughed and the waiting demon jumped toward the boy as if daring to claim the body without consent.

Golem slammed his cane down to ward off the demon. The pentagram wavered, rolling like an ocean wave. "Back!" he ordered and the demon froze, its lizard-like tongue lapping against its lips. "They're so impatient," Golem said. Then to Alena, "See, even the residents of Xibalba are leaping to leave. How long do you believe you will last?"

Alena forced her eyes away. Continuing to grind her teeth, she tried to ward off her desire for flesh and blood. The craving, unrelenting, kept coming in waves to rattle her senses. Golem knelt beside the boy and drew in a deep breath, capturing the boy's scent. He twisted the end of his walking stick and from it the hidden blade sprang free. Alena could see dried blood on the steel. Gently, he ran the blade across the boy's forehead. The demon snarled and jumped. Golem raised the blade over his head, threatening to strike down on the boy.

"NO!" Alena screamed.

Golem's hand froze, glaring at Alena. She refused to watch Golem indulge in the boy's death. Nor allow the demon to take his soul. Alena prayed silently, hoping this madness would somehow end.

"You agree to pass the torch?" said Golem. Then, after Alena's hesitation, "We have many children to welcome tonight, Alena. Courtesy of Mrs. McGovern. Spare yourself the torture; there's no reason for it." He looked at Jonah and bowed.

On cue, Jonah reached into his inside breast pocket, taking from it a wrapped package as Golem stood.

"To commemorate this passing, we've secured the appropriate gift, Alena."

Jonah unwrapped the package, rolling out the gift Golem spoke of. Golem stood in front of Sophia who looked on him with admiration, her chin raised, proud. Jonah placed the gift on the floor in front of Alena. The small gypsy statue Alena recognized as the gift Maleva had given her. Golem touched Sophia's chin and smiled.

Alena caught Jonah's stare. He appeared sympathetic. His hands were trembling as he took his place on the pentagram. Alena looked at the children. Her body constricted and she forced herself to sit up, arching her back and neck to lift her chin, eyeing Golem.

"Untie me," she said, igniting more laughter. Alena shot them all stiff stares. Golem stepped to her. "To present the gift you must untie me," she said to Golem.

The children all turned to him, anticipating Golem's reaction. He cocked his head to the side, inquisitively. Looked at the gypsy statue on the floor then back to Alena.

"Sure, Alena. I'll play along. Be it as it may, I invite you to not make haste." He pointed his cane at the boy. "This boy's fate is in your hands."

Alena looked down on the boy then back to Golem. She nodded her understanding.

"Very well," said Golem. "Jonah?"

Jonah moved swiftly, stepping to Alena while pulling a large crescent blade from his back, beneath his jacket. He cut Alena's restraints and she stood abruptly, blood rushing to her wrists and ankles.

Golem stretched his hand to Sophia. "Come, my lady," said Golem. "Take your rightful place by my side."

Sophia gracefully took his hand. Golem allowed her to pass in front of him as he handed his cane to one of the children. He went and stood behind Sophia, stretching her arms, her small hands lost within Golem's. If it weren't for the protruding fangs and devious snarl, Sophia would be the picture-perfect bride. Alena picked up the statue, and her body shuddered, those beady gypsy eyes staring at her. She squeezed the statue with trembling hands, as the pentagram fluttered, and the demon impatiently snarled. The children watching Alena with bated breath.

"Go ahead," Golem said. "Present your gift." His mouth agape, seething and huffing. He stood erect releasing Sophia's hands. "Now, Alena!"

Alena looked down to the statue then to Sophia whose eyes narrowed. Her jaw quivering, Alena gripped the statue tight.

"I said now, Alena." Golem's voice gruff. The candles and sconces all ignited in a wave across the ballroom.

Alena saw the scene as if it were in slow motion. The statue cracked within her tight grip. Sophia hissed. Golem's face constricted into a snarl. Jonah's footsteps echoed between Alena's ears as he swung the blade with a ferocious grunt, embedding the tip in Golem's back as the statue crumbled into tiny shards from Alena's hand to the floor. Golem's back arched as he hollered, immediate pain filled his eyes, replaced instantly with rage. The fire in his pupils ignited into a fury as the children covered their ears and started to holler, falling to their knees. The demon fell back as if its grip had loosened. Golem backhanded Jonah with a fierce and powerful thrust tossing the boy back to the crystal bowl that shattered on the marble floor.

And the pentagram wavered. The demon leapt for the boy, but the window closed before the demon could grab him. The pentagram now nothing more than painted blood on marble tile. The children's hollers and screams were ear piercing. Alena reached for the blade still lodged in Golem's back, but Sophia thrust her back with a powerful push sending Alena flying through the ballroom where she slammed on her back and slid into the stage with a crash. A single candle fell to the stage igniting the wood with flames that slithered like a snake toward the window where the velvet curtains roared with fire, licking at the ceiling, the walls, the ballroom igniting into fire. Golem fell to one knee, reaching for the blade in his back.

Alena could see Jonah was unconscious, and beside him, torn from his hand after Golem's dire punishment, laid the talisman. Sophia hissed and growled, her lips curled revealing sharp fangs as tentacles replaced her limbs, her eyes piercing through Alena as she raced toward her. Golem yanked the blade from his shoulder, blood poured from the wound. Alena's head gushed blood but she could see through a red veil as Sophia lunged toward her, teeth bared and ready to devour Alena's heart.

"That's right," Alena hollered, "Kill ME!"

Golem flung the blade toward Alena with both hands. The bloodied steel turned blade over handle across the ballroom. As Sophia was about to bear down on Alena the blade sank into Sophia's back igniting a scream and squeal from her throat. The demon inside her lurched from her body in a frenzy, squeezing itself from her throat as if it hurried in a panic to escape.

"I told you," said Golem. "She cannot die before she passes the torch." His lips curled in a scowl.

The fire reached the ceiling smoldering smoke, thick and black.

Sophia dropped into Alena's arms as the demon leapt from her body to the ceiling, its tongue lapping across its reptilian lips. It turned to Golem and like a pet cowered and whimpered before running off on the ceiling eyeing the other children.

When Alena looked down to Sophia, the fair, youthful innocence had returned. Those blue eyes gleamed as she whispered, "It's over."

Tears filled Alena's eyes. She cradled Sophia's limp body in her arms. Alena held the body tight and yanked the blade from her back, gently easing Sophia to the floor as she stood, blade in hand, glaring at Golem. The children's screams continued with ear piercing pitch. Golem gestured to Jonah then glared at the demon who leapt onto Jonah forcing itself into him through his throat. Alena stepped toward him but retracted quickly when the demon disappeared into Jonah. A moment later his body lifted off the ground, his eyes gleamed when he looked at Alena, standing, blade in hand, in awe of what had transpired. And the children all clambered in front of the weakened Golem, shielding him from Alena.

"What will you do, Alena, kill these children to get to me?" said Golem with that conniving grin across his lips as Jonah moved in front of him. "Even your prize, your Jonah is against you. Tell me, Alena, where do you think this will go? Hacking up children. I assure you they will fight to the death to keep me safe. Sophia is already dead, Alena. That girl's blood is on your hands, and now I'll need to find another suitable host."

Alena tightened her grip on the blade. He was right; she couldn't bring herself to hurt these children. No matter how evil they'd become, there still remained an innocence within them. Instead, she turned the blade on herself.

The ClairField was engulfed in flames, Alena watched as the flames licked up the staircase, tearing up the banister, consuming the second floor. Golem stepped from the children's shield, his wide and staring eyes on Alena, on the blade in her hands. Alena's hands and arms were shaking. The fire raging across the ClairField. Her home, by morning, would be no more. Behind Golem stood her father's ghost. Alena's breath caught. Her father bowed. Golem stiffened, his eyes wide.

"No," he huffed. "Do not do that!"

Alena gritted her teeth as her body shuddered, her hands and arms quaking and trembling. "You lose," she hollered.

And thrust the blade into her stomach.

39

Detective John Ashton sat back, chewing on his lip. Eyes narrow, lost in contemplation as he rehashed Alena's story. *So many holes in this story.* He didn't know where to begin. Alena sat across from him, eyes downtrodden, a single tear had fallen to her lap. Her appearance had changed, no longer the pent up, anxiety riddled and passion fueled patient he'd witnessed previously. She was sullen and, from what Ashton could surmise, couldn't care less what John himself thought of her story.

"Did she truly believe this Golem story?" thought Ashton. Judging by her demeanor and the passionate manner for which she'd told the story, this wasn't even a question; it was obvious she did believe. Of course, there was the last seven plus months she'd been at Bellevue, offering Alena the time to fit all the pieces together. To plug the holes in her story and tighten any potential gaps.

The story is filled with gaps, though. Namely the largest gap of all: statues don't come to life.

And let's not forget the implications she'd suggested concerning the district attorney, the mayor, and the police captain, not to mention most of New York's elite society. All part of an elaborate satanic pedophilia ring that would put McCarthyism to shame. Although she'd been correct with the police captain. New York's police department had been shaken to its core a few years ago; police scandals included mafia implications streamlined with prostitution, gambling, and money laundering. *But this could just be a part of Alena's morbid curiosity.* The police scandal was all over the front page, all she had to do was read the article and insert said story into her own.

Had she ever actually seen the DA's daughter? Ashton thought not. Although this would beg the question why, why would Alena report she had? As far as Ashton could see there was no benefit to Alena. She wasn't getting out of the hospital any time soon, not with her erratic behavior and this Golem story would keep her here indefinitely.

It was Alena who broke the silence. "Well, detective, what do you have to say? The anticipation is killing me."

John sat forward leaning against the table, his arms folded. He cleared his throat. Went to speak, but no words arrived. He looked away, pursed his lips.

"That bad?"

"I hope she doesn't think I believe her story," thought Ashton. He took a deep breath. "Well, yes and no," he said. "There's so many holes I don't know where to begin."

Alena rolled her eyes. Her body tensed. "Holes?" she said. "Of course there are holes, detective. All stories have holes, but that doesn't make them any less true."

Ashton cocked his head. "Understood. But you said you stabbed yourself and that's the last thing you remember. The world went black then, right? Those were your words." Alena, eyes downtrodden, gave a slight nod. "Ok, but there's no report of you going to the hospital for a stab wound. I've read all the reports.

Surely if you stabbed yourself, Alena, you would have either died that night or would have been in the hospital. At the least there'd be stitches and a scar after."

Alena tensed, jumped off her chair, and yanked her hospital gown up, revealing her stomach. Ashton snapped his head away. Held his hand up. "Don't do that!"

"Why, detective, afraid to look? It's just a scar. Look, detective!"

"There's no reason for that. I'll take your word for it that there is a scar, Alena. Please…put your gown down." That would be all he needed, for Deshawn or the doctor to walk in while Alena's gown was hiked up to her breasts. Alena dropped the gown. "Thank you," said John. Alena took her seat. Ashton sighed. "That scar could have come from your miscarriage. Or another operation when you were a child."

Alena moved her head back and forth, tears forming on the bridge of her eyes. "No," she said. "It came from that night."

"So, Golem is a doctor too. He healed your stomach and left you in the rubble to be found the next morning?"

No response, her eyes downtrodden

Ashton sat back, tipped his hat up. "Would you like to know what I do think?"

Alena closed her eyes before turning her gaze to Ashton. "Go ahead, detective. I'm brimming with anticipation."

"What I think is if there's any truth to your story it is this: After your break up with John Astor, you met this Golem person. Maybe that's not even his name, but

I do think whoever it is you're protecting him, for one reason or another. I think this Golem person took advantage of your weakened mental state. Convinced you to reopen the ClairField so he could meet all your friends. In the interim he took over your father's company, drained the bank accounts and was trying to blackmail good people. I don't doubt that these…rituals or ceremonies took place, but honestly, I think they were innocent. Maybe people getting a bit too drunk, maybe gambling. And this Golem person took advantage of the situation. Probably set it up right from the start." Alena rolled her eyes. "There're people like that in this world, Alena. Con artists that take advantage of people who are in dire straits. They feed off of misfortune like parasites."

To Ashton the concept that Alena was taken advantage of by a con artist was a viable explanation. The result was Alena's refusal to believe such a concept - *no one likes to admit when they've been conned* - hence the elaborate story.

"Of course Golem is a con," said Alena. "Haven't you been listening to anything I've said?"

"Yes, Alena, I have. But we could do without the alien from outer space version of your story, which, by the way, releases you from all implications."

She shot John a stare that burned through his heart. "You're implying I had a hand in this? That I was a part of it?"

He sat back. "I'm only pointing out alternate possibilities."

"Then how, detective, do you account for him being here, in this locked down hospital? How can he get in without being seen if he was just human?"

"Because he hasn't been here, Alena. It's just a part of your delusions." Alena's jaw dropped. "I hate to have to point this out to you," he said. "Perhaps you should at least consider the possibility."

She tightened her jaw. Ground her teeth. Her eyes, wide and staring, twitched uncontrollably until Alena closed her eyes as if to ward off the erratic movement. Ashton leaned on his left hand as Alena breathed deeply, opening her eyes.

"What you could tell me, Alena, is where the DA's daughter could be? Where to search? Do you think this con man would actually stay in New York? Is there a possibility he went out to California?"

Alena's voice was low. "I told you already. Try the Hamptons and the ClairField basement…"

John shook his head. "The ClairField is no more, Alena. There's nothing there but grass and dirt."

"Search underground, detective."

He leaned back. "Is it possible Golem goes by another name?"

Alena shook her head. "No, detective. Not to my knowledge. He has always been known as Golem."

He sighed while nodding. "Ok," he said, standing. "Thank you for your time."

Alena looked at him, puzzled. "But don't you want to know why I requested for you to come here?" her voice trembling.

"More like demanded," said Ashton. "But please, go on. Why did you summon me here, Alena? Something to do with your nighttime delusions I'm sure."

Alena's face shut down. Her body tensed. "Thanks for the support, detective."

"Maybe I shouldn't have said that," thought Ashton. "She is obviously a sick and deranged mind." John widened his eyes and cocked his brow. "Go on," he said.

Alena paused before answering. "I brought you here, Detective Ashton, because Golem came to me last night. How he does it I don't know, but he knows about you, detective. And he's got his eye on you. He's waiting for you to come to him. I told you my story to prepare you so you know what you're dealing with." She pursed her lips and swallowed her breath. "I brought you here to save you, detective. To save you from Golem."

––––––––

Ashton had thanked Alena and promised to keep her informed on any discoveries or progress with the DA's daughter. He left Alena alone, and informed Deshawn that their conversation was over so he could collect Alena.

Ashton wanted to speak with Dr. Elliot prior to leaving and went to the nurse's station. The crazies were on the prowl, too. Seemed it was crazy night at the crazy house. Patients pacing frantically, some sitting and rocking, their arms confined. "Lost eyes and lost hearts," Ashton thought.

And there was Wanda, who Ashton saw in the room's corner, staring at him. The grin she wore revealing those yellow jagged teeth. She was drooling too, her mouth agape.

"Full moon," said a nurse behind the station desk. "Happens without fail," she continued then gestured over John's shoulder. "Looks like you've got a number one fan."

John stretched his neck, looking over his shoulder. Wanda's smile turned to a frown. Her eyelids drooped and John could see how her eyeballs fluttered beneath. She drew in a deep breath then shot her eyes open, glaring at John.

The nurse cringed. "Maybe not," she said.

John had no reaction. "Is Dr. Elliot here..." he asked catching her name on the tag pinned close to her shoulder. "Melissa?"

"Unfortunately not, he's on the fifth floor talking to the powers that be. Probably more budget cuts..."

He cut her off mid-sentence, said, "Can you let him know I've received all possible information from Alena and will contact him if necessary."

"Of course," said Melissa. "Anything else?"

John shook his head. "No, that'll be it." He tipped his hat. "Thank you."

He was on his way to the elevator when he heard that familiar sound. Three xylophone vibrations, one after the other, followed by a pause, then two more. He stopped in his tracks. His chest tight, and his blood turned cold. John Ashton turned on his heels.

Where did it come from?

He searched over the ward. Patients moving restlessly across the floor. His eyes scanning each and every one of them, when he found Wanda. Her head was down.

Three more vibrations.

Ashton could see the xylophone on her lap, a mallet in her right hand.

Two additional vibrations.

John's bones rattled with the vibration. His stomach turned. Wanda looked like a child who'd received a new toy she wasn't aware how to work properly. But why would she play that exact tune? Is there a connection? Is this where Alena received the information? John stomped over to Wanda. She paid him no mind, keeping her head down.

"Wanda?" said John. She gave him no response. "Wanda, why do you play the xylophone like that?"

"Like what?" she said, her voice soft and unassuming.

"Three followed by two. Why? Is there some significance?" Silence as John waited for a response. "Wanda, did someone tell you to play it like that?"

Wanda said nothing. She passed the mallet from her left hand to her right then shifted in her seat, cross-legged and keeping her head down.

"Wanda? You ok?"

She sat motionless.

"It's ok, Wanda, you're not in trouble or anything. But I would really like to know."

John knew all eyes were on him, watching. He could feel those stares roaming over his body, wondering what he was doing. Wanda made no movement.

"No worries, Wanda. Thank you," he said then went to leave.

"In my dreams," Wanda, her voice just above a whisper.

John stopped cold. He turned to her.

"I hear them in my dreams. Always three then two. Always."

"Did Alena play them like that?" he asked. "Did she show you?"

Wanda chewed her lip, shaking her head.

"Ok," John replied. 'Thank you," he said.

"The devil's in the details, detective," said Wanda as John was once again about to leave.

He curled his brow. "Come again?"

Now Wanda looked at him with a stare that turned John's stomach.

"The devil," she said. "The *devil* is in the details."

John shook his head. "Why would you say that?"

Nothing. Wanda clasped her hands behind her back and starting swaying, her eyes lost.

"Did someone tell you to say that?" Johns voice just above a whisper.

Wanda nodded feverishly.

"Yes? Ok, who, Wanda? Who told you to say that? Alena?"

Wanda shook her head violently.

"Who then, Wanda? Who told you?"

Wanda's hair whipped from one side of her face to the other. John could hear the growl erupting from her throat and his chest constricted, his whole body tensed. Wanda cupped her hands over her ears and Ashton moved back as if she were about to explode.

"*G-O-L-E-L-E-E-E M-M-M!*" she screamed. "Golem! Golem! Golem! Golem!" Her head was shaking so violently phlegm and drool whipped across the room, splattering Ashton's lips.

"It's ok, Wanda, the officer was just leaving," Melissa took hold of Wanda's shoulders and shot John a stare that could have stabbed his heart. "Aren't you, detective?"

John wiped the drool off his mouth. "Yes," he said. "I'm sorry."

Wanda calmed at that moment. She put her head on Melissa's shoulder, started whimpering like a child. Started muttering beneath her breath. As he was leaving Wanda caught his attention once again.

A solid holler. "At night, detective. The devil comes at night."

The elevator door opened.

"Let it go," John told himself, his heart jumping in his chest. He wanted to get the hell out and as quickly as possible. He entered the elevator and caught Wanda's stare through the veil of blonde locks covering her face. Thought he was slipping, being drawn into Wanda's stare. Quickly he shook his head, snapping his focus then his eyes settled on Wanda's lips. Her voice a whisper but John heard her clearly as if she were whispering in his ear.

"*AGIOS O BAPHOMET!*"

Part III

Annette Flemming
40

"Insanity is an infectious disease," thought John Ashton. He had gone to the state planner's office to look over blueprints for the ClairField, conveniently located on the twelfth floor in the police precinct. It was quite obvious to the young detective that Alena had spread her insanity to Wanda. He tried to push Alena's story from conscious thought, mindlessly staring over the blueprints.

The ClairField was so old the original blueprints were non-existent. Instead, he was able to locate the plans used for the ClairField's redesign from the 1930s. Now, John Ashton wasn't an expert in blueprints or design, however he was searching for a specific reference, anything to give plausibility to Alena's story. Namely the basement.

The truth hides in plain sight. This thought kept surfacing, creeping, and slithering into his mind with every remembrance of Alena's fantastical and horrific story. One point was for sure, Alena believed her story. She saw it as fact. And she seemed so sincere.

The devil is in the details. Wanda again. He tried to shake her from his thoughts. His body shuddered and quivered. Those eyes, John thought. They seemed to jump out and grab him, even when hiding behind the veil of Wanda's blonde hair. He shook his head, focusing on the blueprints and the geometric shapes that all seemed to meld one on top of the other. He'd gone over it over and over again and one thing was certain.

He could not locate a basement.

He'd even asked the clerk, a young man named Tomas LeChilds, for help. Tomas took one look at the blueprint and confirmed John's suspicion; there was no basement in the ClairField.

Strangely, he wanted the basement to be there. Not that he believed Alena's story but nonetheless Wanda had been correct. The devil *is* in the details, and the truth does hide in plain sight. Take out all the fantastical details, and John was confident this Golem was a con; Alena was just too proud to admit it. And after all this time he was sure Golem had left New York. More than likely with the DA's daughter in tow. Perhaps Captain Knowles was correct; this assignment was a wild goose chase.

It now seemed to John that he was chasing a ghost.

"Detective Ashton," Tomas said, standing in the door.

Ashton looked up from the blueprints to Tomas.

"A call from the precinct. There's a lady wishing to speak with you. Said she has information on the missing girl."

"Really?" A break, he thought. Might be my lucky day. Tomas nodded. "What's her name?" John stood, fixing his hat and straightening his tweed jacket.

Tomas looked at the paper in his hand, reading the name he'd written down.

"Annette Flemming."

———————

She seemed nervous, this Annette Flemming. John had introduced himself as the detective assigned to the case. Of course she mentioned his youthful naïve appearance but John dismissed the comment, offering Annette a seat in one of the interview rooms. She sat with her left leg crossed over her right, clasping her collar over her throat. John surmised she was a part of New York's elite, or at least on her way there, considering the jewelry and high-quality clothes she wore. Although she appeared slightly disheveled, her jacket was wrinkled and her hair was nappy as if she'd been sweating, the cold wintry weather not helping with every out of place strand of hair.

"Thank you for coming, Mrs. Flemming," John started, pen and notebook ready to go. "You said you've seen the DA's daughter?"

Annette nodded then looked over the room, her eyes nervously twitching from one corner to the next as she clasped that collar even harder.

"Are you ok, Mrs. Flemming?"

She nodded again and cleared her throat. "I'm sorry," she said. "My dog passed away today." She gave up squeezing her collar and folded her hands over her lap.

"So sorry," John said. "I'll make this as quick and painless as possible."

"Thank you," Annette whispered.

Ashton paused, studying Annette whose eyes were downtrodden. Something about her reminded him of Alena.

He cleared his throat. "Where did you see her?"

Annette looked at her trembling hand. "My house," she said.

John dropped the pen. "Your house? When?"

"Two days ago."

John's eyes widened. He sat back. "Two days ago?" he repeated. Annette nodded. "Halloween?"

"Yes, detective."

"What was she doing at your house?"

"It was Halloween; she's a child. What do you think she was doing there?"

"Understood," he said. "Was she with anyone? An adult? Where do you live?"

"Long…" Annette cleared her throat. "Long Island," she said, stretching her back and moving closer to the table. "No adult but she was with a young boy."

"How old was he?"

"He looked about twelve to me."

"Ok," John wrote in his notebook. "How can you be sure it was her? The DA's daughter? How did you make the connection?"

"My housekeeper…Camilla…after the dog passed, she went to the garage for a shovel and newspaper. I recognized her picture in the paper."

John paused, thinking. "You're certain it was her? There had to be a ton of kids out that night; how could you be so sure? Did something happen to make her stand out? Anything out of the ordinary? What costume was she wearing?" His heart was jumping. *These high society people sure are strange.*

"I'm not sure if it was a costume," she said. "At first I thought they were homeless. The clothes they had on were tattered. They could have been dressed as Raggedy Anne and Andy, but I don't think so."

She seemed lost in thought. "Was anyone else at home? Your husband maybe or your housekeeper…Camilla?"

She shook her head no. "Just me. Camilla only comes during the day, and my husband has been away on business."

"Understood." He sat back. "Trick or treating, that's it? Did you notice anything else about them? Anything at all. Maybe when you handed them their treats for the night…"

"I never opened the door," she said, her voice monotone.

John stared at her, confused. "Why not?"

"I was afraid to open the door. They didn't ask for candy. They asked…to come in, detective. They wanted to come into my house."

"For what purpose?"

"They asked to use the phone. They said their father would be along soon and wanted to use my phone."

"Did they?" he asked. "Did you let them in?"

No answer.

"Mrs. Flemming, did you let them in your house?"

"No," she said. "I mean…I don't think so. I don't remember."

John cocked his eyebrows. "You don't remember if you let two kids into your home on Halloween? How is that possible?"

"These last few days have been a blur. There's a lot I don't recall."

"Do you drink, Mrs. Flemming?"

She looked at John, shameful. "On occasion," she answered.

"Was Halloween night one of those occasions?"

She shook her head no. John decided to change direction.

"Have you ever been to the ClairField? Have you had associations with Alena Francon?"

"Alena?" Annette tensed. "Poor soul. What's happened to her is a catastrophe."

"So you know her?"

"An acquaintance really. A friend of a friend, but yes, I've met Alena. I've had lunch with her on several occasions…not us alone but with friends."

"Has she ever mentioned a man named Golem?"

"Golem, of course. He's the ever so kind gentleman who runs the ClairField. He hired my husband for some renovations he needed done prior to the ClairField reopening."

"When was that? How long ago?"

"At least a few years now."

"And Golem…who is he? Where did he come from? How did Alena meet him?"

"No idea, detective. I never had time to ask him about his family tree. From what I learned he's from Jersey."

"New Jersey?"

"Is there another?"

"New Jersey," John thought. "A bit far off from Xibalba."

"What kind of man is Golem? What was your impression?"

Annette thought a moment. "Kind. Graceful. Always helping others. I mean, I don't know him intimately, just passing moments at the ClairField but he's never given me any reason to think otherwise. My husband thought the world of him."

"How so?"

"Noel enjoyed working at the ClairField; he always said Golem was a man with backbone and integrity. Such behaviors go a long way in the world of business. Noel was confident Golem would be a success for many years to come."

John's perplexed stare caused Annette to second-guess herself. "What's wrong, detective?"

"You're the first person, outside of Alena, to admit seeing this person Golem." He paused then added, "Tell me, were you ever a part of the after-party festivities at the ClairField? I heard they were…to die for?"

Annette shook her head. "My husband likes to be in bed early. Work, work, work. We never stayed longer than dinner."

John chewed his lip. "Is there a basement in the ClairField?"

"A basement?" She seemed reluctant to answer.

"Yes, a basement. Alena mentioned a basement but there's no basement on the blueprints and, as we all know, the ClairField was torn down soon after the fire."

Annette nodded, "My husband was in charge of the construction in the basement. He told me that during prohibition the basement was used as a speakeasy. Bathtub gin and all that. Gambling too, so, I'm not surprised the basement was left off the blueprint."

"Noted." John cocked his brow. Something finally made sense in this story. Time to redirect. "On Halloween, was there anything about these kids' appearance? The way they looked, other than the tattered clothes. Anything about the way they talked or anything about…their eyes?"

John noticed how Annette's expression tightened, as if she remembered something. John was hoping she'd mention the eyes.

"No," she said. "They looked just like the children they are."

"Ok. And the father they spoke of, did you ever see him? How did they get home?"

"I told you, detective, I don't remember."

"Duly noted. Where do you think they are now?"

"Isn't that your job, detective?"

"Indeed," he said followed by a long uncomfortable pause. "Well, I'd like to thank you for coming in. I would like to speak with your husband when he returns, and I'll also need to come out to your house, probably tomorrow."

Annette nodded. "Of course."

John led Annette to the door.

"If you think of anything else before then, please don't hesitate to call. You can leave a message at the front desk if I'm not here. If they show up again, please call emergency services."

"Thank you, detective."

John forced a smile.

"What happens now? Do you believe you'll be able to find her?"

"I truly hope so, Mrs. Flemming. I won't rest until I do."

Annette smiled. "Nice hat," she said then walked away.

41

Kind and graceful. That's how Annette described Golem. Kind and graceful.

The description continued to loop through conscious thought as he stood where the ClairField's garden had been, his back to the Hudson, holding and looking over the ClairField blueprints.

Kind and graceful is a far cry from sick and deranged. But not so far off from the typical con man. They made their living on being kind and graceful; that's how they rope in their prey.

Using the blueprint as a guide he traced his steps across the barren ground to where the ballroom doors would have been then stopped to study the blueprint. He was looking for the cellar door. Ashton stepped through his imaginary door, into the ballroom. His stomach constricted, and acid burned the back of his throat. He despised this place. Knowing what had truly gone on at the ClairField shook him to his core. The famous inn was a cesspool of crime and debauchery. No wonder his instincts were on heightened alert; although the inn had been decimated John could still sense the crime. It left a sour stain on the earth.

Following the blueprints John turned left, walking across that barren ground. Although the blueprint reported no cellar door, John recollected Alena's story. According to Alena the cellar was beyond the staircase and after the kitchen entrance that was clearly shown on the blueprint. His feet and ankles tingled, as if the blood flowing to these limbs were cut off. Ashton paid it no mind. The weather was cold and the wind off the Hudson chilled his bones as if he were encased in a block of ice. Overcast skies threatened to rid New York of daylight. He did not have much time before the sun would be gone and with it his natural light.

He followed the blueprint.

"Staircase." He moved forward following the geometric shapes and spacial coordinates. "Kitchen door." The air turned thick and heavy and his temples twisted and pulled with a cold sting. He squeezed his hat over his temples then walked a few more feet and stopped. Standing on barren ground Ashton imagined the ClairField.

"Has to be here," he whispered studying the blueprint and retracing his steps. "Definitely here." Ashton folded the blueprint into a thick wad of paper he stuffed into his inside breast pocket. He then reached out his cold chapped hands to feel the air. Noticed how he could now feel his toes. "The air is warmer here," he told himself. "Not by much but in this cold weather a few degrees makes a big difference."

He bent down, his hands a foot above the earth. A cold breeze ran across the grass as if it attempted to capture the underground heat. Ashton closed his eyes and breathed deep. He could see in his mind's eye children locked in cages as Alena described. Ashton sighed and stood, then walked the grounds as if he were taking the steps to the basement. The air turned thick around him tingling with a burning sensation.

Muffled whimpers and fear tore through him. He could sense pain.

Kind and graceful. Annette's voice in his mind. He shook his head.

There's no such thing as ghosts and demons, he told himself. The heart of man is evil enough.

He could see them clearly now, as he walked across the ground where he presumed the cells would have been. His chest tight. These children huddled in their cells, emaciated and weak. Waiting for death because life had turned its back on them.

"Golem," John breathed, shaking his head.

One thing was for certain: he needed to see what was underground.

————

"Are you out of your mind?" Captain Knowles said after hearing John's request for a bulldozer to pull up the earth at the ClairField grounds. He opened his desk drawer, pulled out a bottle of bourbon and a glass, and poured himself a drink. "Based on what?"

Ashton cleared his throat. "Gut instinct," he said, immediately regretting his declaration.

"Gut instinct?" Knowles cocked his eyebrows before taking a drink.

"Annette Flemming," Ashton said.

"Who?"

"Annette Flemming came in today. She's a socialite who claims she saw the DA's daughter at her house on Halloween. She's also been to the ClairField on several occasions and confirmed there was a basement there. It doesn't show up on any blueprint though. I'm thinking it was kept off because the cellar was used as a speakeasy and gambling racket."

Knowles took another drink.

"According to Alena the cellar is where this guy Golem kept the children he was kidnapping."

"Alena?" Knowles shot back. "Golem the statue? Come on, rookie, you're being strung along by a psychopath. Can't you see that?" Then after a moment, "Please tell me you're not falling for this crap?"

"No, sir," John said. "Just looking between the lines. I have a hunch this Golem character is a real person…a con man and a pedophile. Alena made up the story to spare herself from the shame of being taken advantage of. But this Annette confirms Golem is real."

"Annette Flemming? She saw the DA's daughter on Halloween? Where?"

"At her house, trick or treating. She arrived at her door with another child, a male around ten or twelve years old, acting strange, even for Halloween. She swears it's the DA's daughter. Take that and Alena's claim that Golem was hoarding kids by the truckload and we've got ourselves a very sordid tale to tell."

Knowles was silent, thinking.

Ashton huffed, "Captain, there may have been children underneath the ClairField that died in the fire and were buried by the construction crew. Not knowing, of course, that they were there."

Knowles put his glass on his desk and sat forward. "So, here's a question, rookie. If this statue is kidnapping kids why hasn't anyone reported it? Where's he taking them from?"

"They're street kids mostly, Captain. He's getting them from the orphanage."

Knowles cocked his brow. "Orphanage? Mrs. McGovern would have reported it."

"According to Alena, she's in on this. Sold those kids for money."

Knowles slammed his fist on the desk. "Not a chance," he scolded. "I've known her for years. I investigated her husband's murder after a home invasion, and I've been a part of the yearly fundraiser for the orphanage. You're telling me she's selling kids to a pedophile? I don't believe it. Won't believe it. You're about to smear a good person's reputation based on what exactly? The ravings of a lunatic? That's preposterous!"

John went to speak but swallowed his words, cowering under the Captain's sinister gaze as if John was the fool the captain was claiming he was. Perhaps it wasn't the time to bring up Alena's claim about the death of Mr. McGovern.

Seeing his restless and undermined demeanor the captain jumped in. "Listen, John," he began. "You received your promotion based on good cop work, but this is an easy assignment; that's why I gave it to you. Take Alena's statement and follow up, that's all."

"But Annette Flemming, sir, she confirms the girl is alive; we've got to take Alena's story with a grain of salt but the truth hides in plain sight, in between the lines. There's more to follow up."

"She was probably drunk and never even seen the daughter. It was Halloween; who's to say it wasn't a dozen other possibilities. You say Annette knew Alena?"

"Acquaintance is how she described the relationship. Her husband did some construction on the ClairField."

"Ahh, there you go," Knowles proclaimed. "Probably got stiffed on the bill and is looking for retribution." He sat back. "Don't underestimate the lengths people will go to to destroy someone else. Especially when said person is already deemed a fruitcake. She's probably looking to bill the city for the work her husband got stiffed on. Have you followed up with the Hamptons address?"

"Not yet, sir. I plan to head out there in the morning. Was going to go there today but I'd like to talk to Mrs. McGovern first."

Knowles shook his head. "I'll meet with her. That conversation will go a lot smoother if she's not being hounded and ridiculed by a rookie."

"What about the ClairField?"

"Wild goose chase, for now at least. Plus getting a bulldozer is like moving a mountain. Let's see what you find in the Hamptons. We can wait on the ClairField. Go out tonight, hopefully by morning this matter will be settled." He eyed Ashton. "And I can give you your next assignment."

"Assignment?"

"Yes, just came across my desk." He shook his head. "Friggin' scandals in this city keep mounting up. I swear if I didn't know any better I'd say Pandora's box just reopened."

"What scandal?"

"Seems the former mayor resigned for a reason other than his health. He's been implicated in a prostitution and mafia scandal. This is big time, boy, don't make me regret it."

"Yes, sir," said Ashton.

Knowles eyed him, and John hoped he hadn't come across too excited.

"Well, rookie, why are you standing there? Go!"

42

Why didn't I tell him about the eyes?

Annette Flemming kicked herself for leaving this point out. The detective had asked very specifically about the eyes as if he knew and was anticipating her reaction, observing how she responded. How could he know? It was impossible for him to know. It's just a dream. A figment of imagination brought on by stress and...Lovecraft. Too many scary stories warp the mind. Noel had warned her against indulging in fantasy and horror, the supernatural, and paranormal.

"Those stories turn good hearts dark," Noel had said. She could hear his voice repeating the same over and over again as she sat in the backseat of a car service taking her back home. She despised driving in the city; it turned her anxiety on high alert. Of course, she had refused to take the train, *too many people, too close for comfort.* The city's being handed over to criminals and junkies. She feared for her safety if she were to take a train. All too ripe for the picking for any manipulative degenerate to snatch her purse off her shoulder. Or even worse. The thought of those disgusting vagabonds creeping their dirty little fingers across her skin drove her to the brink of insanity. No, it was better to take a car service. Safety was always the first line of defense.

"But those eyes," she thought. "Those eyes were in your house."

What did they do?

Another lie to the young detective, although she could not be one hundred percent certain that she did let those kids in. There was no concrete recollection that she had, only scattered fragments that could be and more than likely are the result of a programmed mind, filling in the gaps in her memory with…Lovecraft and Poe.

She cursed herself for those indulgences. No one should read such tales. It brings the devil to your doorstep. They should be banned. No child should have the opportunity to read them.

Annette's stomach churned. Her jaw trembled with the taste of acid in the back of her throat. Elbow on the window, jaw in her right hand, and she caught the driver's eyes in the rearview, he immediately looked away. Annette clenched her purse closer to her stomach.

"People," she thought. "Like wild animals. Heathens really. Little children not knowing a damn thing about how to live appropriately. With dignity. Stay in your lane. Know your role."

In times like this Annette breathed a sigh of relief that Noel refused her children. Not that she wished to carry a bundle of weight around for nine months either. Some man's seed, even if it were her husband's, turned her stomach, brought her to the brink of vomiting. The world's gone to hell in a hand basket. She couldn't fathom raising a child now, not in this age. All decency has gone out the window. People have no clue how to live or where they stand, reaching to crime to get what they want. Could anyone imagine what the world would be like should these heathens climb the ranks? They wouldn't know what to do with it. It would be the beginning of the end times.

She could see the city landscape in the side mirror, calmly drifting out of sight. Bright lights smeared by an overcast and dark sky.

Maybe we are *in the end times!*

43

The train sped over the train tracks toward the Hamptons. Ashton sat alone, frustrated for not grabbing a newspaper prior to boarding. He could be reading about his next case instead of mulling over for the hundredth time the sentiments of Alena Francon and Annette Flemming.

"Captain Knowles was correct," Ashton thought. "Close the case and start a new one." This all seemed to be getting away from him. Of course he'd have to take a larger look into Annette and Noel Flemming. Nonetheless, the Captain had an instinct for these sorts of assumptions and proclamations. Ashton was sure Knowles' conversation with Mrs. McGovern would shed a brighter light on Alena's story.

"But what if the most basic parts of their stories were true?" Ashton thought. "What if the DA's daughter is alive?" How would he be received if he were to find her, and bring her back to her parents?

Ashton could see the headlines already: WAR HERO COP FINDS DA'S DAUGHTER.

He'd be hailed as a hero once again.

"High profile cases," he thought. "My specialty."

And he smiled, thinking of himself and all the good he could do. How his career would skyrocket high above the Empire State. "No limits," Ashton told himself.

He could taste success on his tongue.

First order of business, focus on the task at hand. Alena's mansion in the Hamptons was a simple cross the "T" and dot the "I" part of his investigation. Search the house for any signs of living. Since Alena has been behind locked doors for the better part of the year, Ashton was sure he'd be greeted by a neglected home, barren and desolate.

A ghost town, for lack of a better phrase.

He made a mental note to thoroughly comb through the basement. Golem's sanctuary, according to Alena. He shook his head, rehashing Alena's story. Read between the lines, he told himself.

The devil is in the details.

He saw Wanda's eyes behind those strands of oily matted hair.

Insanity *is* an infectious disease.

"Poor souls," he thought. "Just a bit too high strung." Ashton braced himself as the train came to the final stop. The last train back to Manhattan departed just after midnight.

His thorough investigation would need to be in high gear if he was going to make it back in time. Ashton disembarked, searching the string of cars waiting outside the train. Cabs, civilian vehicles, but no black and white, no Hamptons Police Department escort he'd been promised earlier would be waiting for him, assisting Detective Ashton with his search.

Where are they? How could they forget?

Ashton located a pay phone outside the train station, picked up the receiver and shook his head. The wire was cut. Ashton would not be making a phone call.

What to do? They know I'm here. He slammed the receiver onto its cradle then snapped his head around and hailed the first cab he laid eyes on.

————————

"Where we goin'?" asked the cab driver. His heavy foot propelled the cab forward.

Ashton braced himself as the cab jumped through traffic. The cabbie eyed him through the rearview mirror as John fumbled through his pockets for the piece of paper he'd written the address on. "Francon Mansion," he said. "I've got the address…"

"I know where it is."

"Even better."

John noticed how the cabbie squeezed the steering wheel. He looked at John through the rearview. "Question is, why?"

"What do you mean?"

Silence. The hum of the road beneath the wheels.

"You ok?" John asked. Again nothing. "Cat got your tongue or something?"

He gripped the wheel again. "What business do you have there? No one goes to that house anymore."

"Not surprised, since the owner has been under lock and key for the last seven months."

The cabbie's face tightened, eyes wide.

"You ok?" John again, this cabbie was beginning to bring some anxiety to the situation at hand. Very weird, thought John.

"Yeah, I don't like going to that place."

"That bad?"

"You can say that."

John thought the cabbie was holding back. "It's ok, I'm a detective with the Manhattan Police Department."

"Detective?" the cabbie hollered.

"Correct."

"You're going to investigate the Francon Mansion?"

"Once again, correct."

"Are you expected?"

Ashton cocked his head. "What'd you mean?"

"Do they know you're coming?"

"Who?"

The cabbie shot him a look as if Ashton were a confused wet behind the ears fool. "The people who live there?" he breathed.

"What people? Alena Francon is a patient at Bellevue."

"Doesn't mean no one lives there." His voice a whisper.

"Who lives there?"

The cabbie eyed him in the rearview then turned his attention to the road.

John's blood pumped, hot. "Sir?"

"No one knows really, but the lights are on and sometimes there's cars by the truckload on the weekends. Strange things go on there. Are you sure you don't want to come back during daylight hours?"

"I'm sure I'll be fine. What's the concern?"

He looked in the rearview, turned his eyes to the road, then back in the rearview. "Many people say it's haunted, and some God-awful things go on there."

John shook his head. "People's imaginations," he thought.

"I'll be fine," John muttered.
The cabbie shook his head. "Ok then."
And sped down the highway.

44

Annette slipped through the front door cautiously, then closed and locked the door with shaking hands. Her breath constricted and stuttered. Looking out the window she watched as the cab pulled away from the curb then turned around and headed down the street.

All was quiet. The house was cold, Annette's breath like smoke off her lips. She continued to hold her purse close to her chest. Now that the cab and, more so, the cabdriver were gone, she could breathe a sigh of relief.

He had kept eyeing her in the rearview. The cab driver's stare was unsettling. Annette's body, her blood and veins, continuously constricted during the ride home.

Why did he keep staring? There was lust in that man's eyes, I know it.

Annette leaned her head against the door, and closed her eyes, breathing methodically, attempting to calm her rapidly beating heart. The same heart that jumped with thick rapid beats into her throat.

The house was quiet. Quiet and dark and cold. Empty! And Noel hadn't called, at least not that she knew. Annette had given specific instruction to Camilla that should Noel call to relay the message to call her after nine tonight.

The house creaked under the weight of winter wind.

"Get it together," she told herself, breathed easy, and cleared her throat. "All is well," she whispered, flipping the light switch on when she caught the silhouette out back, outside the back door, in the moment before the room filled with light. Her heart jumped. There was no one there; she was positive now that the light was on. Her thoughts went to Sam, buried beneath the earth.

Camilla had wrapped the body in a blanket. Camilla, who, Annette was sure, was cursing her at this very moment. Probably complaining how Annette stood nearby as she dug the grave. The ground was cold; it had taken hours for Camilla to complete the task.

Annette shook her head. "Why didn't I help her? I should have helped her."

She started to cry, her hand over her face, purse still clutched to her chest. Annette wiped her eyes and looked over the house. All was motionless, nothing moved, no one called to her, no dog barking, no Sam, no Noel, not even Camilla; she was alone, alone with her thoughts and stories. Alone with the nightmare, human spiders crawling across the ceiling, and the eyes, those black eyes forever plastered in her thoughts. She pursed her lips and her heart sank into her stomach. Not right, she thought. She felt off, angry and alone. And Annette despised being alone. At least Sam had provided comfort in Noel's frequent absences. She looked to the stairs, where Sam had so often sprang down the steps to greet her. Hoping, wishing he would spring from the bedroom. Annette's skin crawled when her eyes fell on the upstairs hall, leading to the master bedroom.

She thought there were eyes up on the second floor, anticipating and waiting her ascent. Her jaw and lips quivered. She went to the kitchen, flipped the light switch, and dropped her purse on the counter.

Camilla had left a note. Noel did call and would call again after nine. Annette checked the wall clock. Twenty minutes to nine.

She wanted him home. No matter what other business he had mattered not. Annette needed Noel to come home. She was scared to death of being alone. Always had been since childhood when she'd come home from school to an empty house. Her parents both worked to make ends meet. No siblings, it was just Annette. Annette and her books and magazines to help pass the days and lonely evenings.

She should have been used to loneliness by now; nevertheless, Annette Flemming couldn't stand being alone. A phone call from Noel would put her right for the night. And a stiff scotch would do her nerves good. She went to the sitting room and poured, quickly swallowing the first heated sting. Then poured again, filing the glass by more than half, replaced the bottle, and stood in the dark sitting room. The only light was from the hall. Drink in her right hand, her left arm draped across her stomach, watching the outside.

"They won't see me with the light off," she told herself. "If they come again I'll call the operator. No hesitation." She almost welcomed another visit from the "black-eyed kids."

Why didn't you tell him about the eyes?

Annette saw those metallic, black eyes. In her thoughts and memory she could see them and hear those monotone voices. *May we come in?*

What was it about those eyes? They seemed to take hold of her, to draw her in.

Annette was watching the other side of the street, where she'd first seen them. They were watching her that night, in the bathroom. What were they doing? Why did they come?

Why me?

Because I'm lonely was Annette's answer. Lonely, tired, and most of the time, inebriated. Scotch was a good friend. It passed the time and softened the paranoia that raged on during daylight hours. She took a long sip.

Maybe it's because I am alone. *They think they can take advantage of a lonely woman alone in a big house.*

Annette took another sip that turned into a gulp. Scotch trickled down her chin. She wiped her jaw, gritting her teeth and staring, glaring through the window to the dark cold night and the barren trees that swayed ever so slightly under the breath of winter wind. Shadowy branches crept along the sidewalk to where the children had first been seen.

She sensed their presence and her heart tensed.

"I'll wait all night if I have to," she thought.

She checked the time on the grandfather clock. Ten minutes to that phone call.

He better call! That cheating cesspool of manhood.

I'll wait all night if I have to.

She finished her scotch.

All night!

45

"Sixty-two bedrooms," said the cabbie. He was explaining to Ashton the Francon Mansion's history. "Every brick was imported from all over Europe. Right down to the marble tile." He added, "From Italy." Ashton surmised the cabbie was Italian by the prideful way he expressed "Italy".

They were driving down a barren road lined with red cedar trees. Every so often they passed a gate and driveway leading to a house or mansion tucked back off the main road.

"It's the biggest house on the block," said the cabbie as he eyed Ashton in the rearview mirror. "We're almost there."

"You seem to know a lot about the house."

"Lived here most of my life. One tends to pick up history as the years go by."

"Have you ever been inside?"

He shook his head. "Not at all. A guy like me has trouble getting invites." He laughed. Then a moment later, "Here we go."

Ashton perked up. The gate was old steel and wide open attached to two stone pillars on either side. The cab stopped outside the gate and Ashton looked up the long winding drive to the house that stood in darkness. *Colossal*, was Ashton's first thought, his eyes wide taking in the sheer volume and size. A single light flickered in the mansion as if a candle had been lit in the foyer.

"No party tonight," said the cabbie. "Your luck must have run out."

Ashton caught the cabbie's smile.

"You're not gonna drive up?"

He clucked his tongue and shook his head. "No," he said. "This is as close as I get."

"Superstitious?"

"You might say that. I don't invite devils into my life, detective. That's your job."

"Indeed," Ashton breathed staring at the long walk up to the house.

The cabbie added, "I feel like I'm dropping off Rhenfield to meet his doom. Be careful in there, detective. Evil spirits are everywhere around this place."

"Rhenfield?"

The cabbie eyed him in the rearview. "You don't read, do you?"

Ashton shook his head. "No time."

"You should. Great books are like a blueprint…a survival manual disguised as fiction. As folklore. Because the truth hides in plain sight and those that see have to hide and those that can't see…well, they're just a part of the plan."

Ignoring the comment, Ashton stepped from the cab into the bitter cold evening. The cabbie draped over the passenger seat, rolling down the window.

"You sure you want to do this? Maybe come back tomorrow. During daylight."

The sheer size of the mansion hovered in the distance. Ashton had never seen such a big house.

Ashton shook his head, "No, I'll be fine." He looked at the cabbie whose eyes rolled over the mansion, back to the street behind them then to Ashton. "Are you able to wait?" Ashton asked. "I won't be more than an hour."

"Wait?" The cabbie curled his brow.

Ashton handed him a twenty. "I need to make the midnight train home. You'll be doing me a great favor."

The cabbie grabbed the twenty. "That's how people get killed but I got you. I'm not parking here though. I'll be down the road, not too far but definitely out of sight." He looked at the mansion and his body quivered. "This place gives me the creeps. How do you know anyone is in there? Honestly, detective, this all seems a bit strange to me. Late at night like it is, and you're walking into an abandoned mansion."

"You said you've seen people here," said Ashton.

"I said I heard about the parties. Doesn't look like anyone's there now."

"There's a light on. Looks like a candle, which means someone is home. Besides, they're expecting me."

"They?"

"The staff. Captain said he called ahead and they're waiting. Must be them."

"Who? If you were here during the day the first thing you'd notice is the grounds. If there's a staff in there, they're not doing a very good job." His eyes darted from mansion, to driveway, then behind them. "What if you find something? Isn't that why you're here? You're searching for something."

"Formality really. Crossing the I's and dotting the T's. If I do find something you can keep the twenty."

He shook his head. "This seems ludicrous. What about local law enforcement? Shouldn't they be here with you?"

"They're aware I'm here. Refused to come over until I find something, I guess."

"Smart move," he breathed. "You're going to search that house in less than two hours?"

"My primary concern is the basement."

"The basement? All that house, and that's where you're going?"

"Something like that, yeah."

The cabbie put up his hands. "Ok, detective. I'll be down the road but I'm only waiting an hour. After that you're on your own."

Ashton nodded. "Seems to be that way," he whispered. "Thank you."

"No problem…*Rhenfield*. Be careful, detective."

Ashton watched as the cab turned around, and drove down the street not too far off. The headlights faded to black. John then stared up the drive blowing warm breath into his hands before beginning his ascent to the Francon Mansion. One thought was on his mind.

Why am I alone? Seems almost unnatural.

————

The cabbie was right. The grounds were desolate. He would have surmised the foliage would have been overgrown, but nonetheless everything was dead. The lawn was devoid of grass. Skeletal bushes dipped like an old cackling and gagging man who'd seen better days. Perhaps dying from dehydration. The mansion loomed in the distance, standing erect as if it attempted to stand tall against the wind.

Ashton could hear the ocean waves in the distance. The air turned thick with a heavy veil of cold.

"I'm a long way from home," Ashton whispered. He eyed the candle in the window and for the first time noticed the silhouette standing behind the flame. Ashton's body tensed. The person, bathed in darkness, was watching him intensely.

Ashton's lips quivered. "Check the basement," he told himself. "Check the basement and go." He looked back, over his shoulder, hoping to see the waiting cab. Too far or too dark, he thought. "He better be there."

He rounded the drive to the front door. Ashton's breath was heavy. His legs ached. "No seeing tonight," he ordered as if that seeing part of him were an entity he could demand and command. "Just police work. Keep your wits about you."

He stepped up to the double doors, noticing the person and candle were no longer in the bay window. He knocked on the door.

"Keep your wits about you," he thought as the front door creaked open.

46

At the same moment John Ashton was being received at the Francon Mansion, Annette Flemming's phone rang.

She was on her fourth scotch and took note of the time. Almost ten.

An hour late, she thought, stomping into the kitchen. She answered on the fourth ring.

"Noel," her voice cracked.

Silence.

"Noel, is this you?" She placed her glass on the counter, waiting to hear his voice. Instead, static cut through the receiver pressed to Annette's ear. "Noel, can you hear me?" Waiting, she squeezed the receiver.

"Hello. Noel?" *Damn phone company will never get it right.* "HELLO!"

The phone cracked and cackled. Annette clenched her jaw, shook her head. "I can't believe this. Can you hear me? Sam is dead, Noel, you need to come home NOW!" Her heart jumped. Jaw tight. The receiver on the verge of cracking in her fist.

More static and cackles. She reached for the glass, took a sip that warmed her throat and stomach.

"*Sonofabitch!*" Annette slammed the receiver on the hook, her body wrapped in the receiver's curled wire. Her vision blurred from the sudden movement. Her body swayed. Annette held the counter to steady herself, closing her eyes to ward off the dizzy spell of scotch. Breathed deeply, her head heavy, the room spinning. Pressure in the back of her eyeballs.

Annette vomited in the sink and yanked the receiver off the hook that bounced on the tile floor, recoiled, and slid to the wall. Her eyes were wet, beads of sweat on her forehead and a stabbing pain between her temples. Her brain twisted inside her skull. Annette coughed and gagged on the last bit of vomit and the string of bile that dripped off her bottom lip.

A busy signal raged from the receiver with short and loud blips that echoed in the kitchen. Annette turned on the faucet, swished water in her mouth, and spit then splashed the cold fluid over her face. Her eyes, dry, floated from left to right. Annette slid down the counter hoping to ward off the spinning sensation. She had a fleeting thought her brain was hemorrhaging, twisting nasty in her skull. She didn't dare open her eyes. She knew the world was spinning; she'd been here many times before. *Keep your eyes closed. It'll pass if you keep your eyes closed.*

Acid belched from her burning throat. Warm liquid ran across her top lip. She wiped her nose, opened her eyes a bit, and peering through watery slits she recognized the blood on her fingertips.

Another bloody nose, she thought through a haze of jumbled, painful and rapidly cycling thoughts. The busy signal was relentless, although muted within a background of foggy thoughts.

Annette's breathing, heavy and labored, was the last sound she heard before falling unconscious.

She never heard the rapping on the front door.

47

Ashton was surprised by the man who welcomed him inside the Francon Mansion. He was no taller than five feet nine with a medium build, a sparse goatee, and dressed in a black suit. He held a candle and greeted the detective with a warm smile. His dark eyes complimented his short black hair. When he talked he carried a European accent.

"Welcome, detective, I've been expecting you."

Ashton could see over his shoulder the large expanse, how the mansion opened as if inviting him inside. He noticed the marble floor Alena had spoken of. His body tensed, standing by the door, feeling like a child not knowing what to do.

"Please, do come in. Would you like some tea or something to eat? You must be hungry, I'm sure, after your trip."

Ashton tried to move, but his feet refused the thought. Dumbfounded, he opened his mouth but his words escaped him. The man in the door staring, devouring John with his eyes.

It was as if the seeing part of him attempted to keep him out of the mansion. Wrapping its proverbial arms around Ashton's body, safeguarding the detective in a protective bubble.

"No need to be frightened, detective, we've had several issues with the home since Miss. Francon's tragic circumstance. But we make do, don't we?"

Ashton thought himself a fool. The man's mouth, Ashton was certain, curled ever so slightly into a grin.

"Infectious insanity," thought Ashton.

John cleared his throat. "Excuse me, it's been a long day." And he stepped through the door. "I didn't catch your name." His eyes widened, taking in the sheer expanse of home. This is where Alena grew up? No wonder she's worse for the wear; a person can get lost in this place. Mentally and physically. The man turned on a dime and Ashton's heart skipped a beat. The stare in the man's eyes was dark, hypnotic even, staring at Ashton as if he were his next meal. The candle flickered in his pupils.

"Herbert," said the man. "Herbert West."

"Strange," thought Ashton. His gut told him the name was fictional. "Trust no one."

"Good to meet you, Mr. West."

Herbert closed the door. Ashton gasped for breath after the door sealed in its frame, as if the air had been locked out with it.

"Do believe me, detective, the pleasure is all mine."

Ashton forced himself to look away from Mr. West; his stare was menacing. Is this Golem? John thought. Can't be. Golem, according to Alena, was tall and bulky. Herbert did not fit the profile.

"What happened to the electricity?" asked Ashton, looking over the mansion once again.

Herbert moved past John. "Unfortunately, we've done without power for the last month, lucky for us the staff is only here in the day…current circumstances excluded of course. And the lawn, oh, my lord, Mr. Ashton, the grounds were at one point the most beautiful on Long Island, now, without appropriate funds to tend them, and the awful drainage issue a few months back, all has turned cold and dead. But Mr. Golem assures all of us these issues are being settled. And settled quickly and urgently." He stood proud, arching his back and shoulders. "By spring the Francon Mansion will be reverted back to its glory."

John cocked his head. "Excuse me, did you say…Golem?"

"Of course, Mr. Golem has taken over the Francon estate including day to day operations for the Francon Investment Group. He has done a fine job replenishing the good Francon name. He has our utmost respect, detective. We don't mind current circumstances; we make do knowing all will be reset soon. Unfortunately, Miss. Francon in her fragile state had left matters unattended for too long. Poor thing, she's befallen so many tragedies, we can only hope for the best resolve to her situation."

Ashton thought, "Con man, just like I thought. Has the whole business under his thumb and Herbert here is fooled just like the rest of them. A grand con indeed."

"Have you seen Alena?" asked Herbert.

"Today actually. She tells a rather unique story about Mr. Golem."

Herbert pursed his lips, nodded. "Unfortunately, psychosis reaches to those who are closest to the psychotic. Mr. Golem has done nothing more than care for Miss. Francon with dignity and utmost respect. It is a shame the stories she has conjured."

Silence and the air seemed to stiffen as if the mansion were alive, holding in its proverbial breath.

Ashton snapped the tension, looking over the home. He glimpsed the statue in the far room.

Pointing, Ashton said, "Is that…"

"David? Good eye, Mr. Ashton. You have a good eye for recognizing great art."

Ashton dropped his arm. "According to Alena, the statue was destroyed in the ClairField fire." He turned to Herbert who appeared to freeze, staring at the statue as if he'd become lost in its beauty and awe. "Mr. West?"

Herbert cleared his throat. "Sorry, detective, my remembrances of the ClairField sometimes get the better of me. Truly the family's greatest downfall to date." He appeared to hold back tears.

"Understood," said John. Things were now adding up to the young detective, his thoughts were clear, surmising Herbert played a part in Golem's grand con. "How long have you been employed by the Francons?" he asked.

Now there *were* tears in Herbert's eyes. "All my life," he said. "And proudly too."

"I can see your emotional connection to the family is strong."

"Indeed, detective. Those who have dignity and integrity take pride in their work, no matter how minute or insignificant said work may seem to the outside world." He paused as if expecting Ashton's response, then added, "The statue has always been here, detective. Mr. Francon would never allow such an important piece to be taken from his home. It is the real David and a testament of genius talent."

Ashton surveyed the statue, its glowing white marble softened by darkness. "It's only a statue," Ashton thought.

"Now come, detective, your captain informed me your investigation is concerning our basement." John turned to him. Herbert's grin glimmered behind the candle. "It will be my honor and then you will see...see that Alena's mind has turned on its heels."

"After you," said Ashton. Herbert bowed and turned, leading the way.

"Through the kitchen, detective, this way."

Ashton followed noticing how Herbert limped. Such a rickety old man, Ashton thought, but he looks so young. Upon entering the kitchen Herbert reached for something behind the entrance. John noticed Herbert's right arm was finely wrapped with gauze. He watched as the same hand had captured a red cane that he used to steady his limp. John's eyes narrowed, looking over the cane. Thick gnarls spiraled down the cane from the top to the bottom; they looked like wide opened mouths on the verge of a scream. "Souls," Ashton thought. "That's how Alena described them."

"You use a red cane?" said Ashton continuing to follow Herbert through the kitchen.

"A necessary extension of the body, detective. I was born pigeon toed; my ankles have never healed properly. Unfortunately, the effect of a poor upbringing. Alena herself purchased this cane for me. It is my pride and joy. A remembrance of all things good and past."

The cane tapped the floor with every step.

"The devil is in the details," Ashton thought. Alena's story was coming into the light, those little blips in the story conjured by real and actual events lent credibility. Yes, Herbert is a strange and odd character, but then again aren't all of them who live a life such as this. Ashton referenced the Francon Mansion. Living like this, even as an employee, must warp the mind and values.

"How did you hurt your hand?" Ashton asked.

Herbert stopped at the basement door, and handed Ashton the candle. "Please," he said. "The door is locked; I must use the key."

Ashton took the candle. Now a scuttling erupted over his shoulder. He snapped his head around. His body tensed. Nothing but darkness.

"I cut myself a few days ago while cooking," Herbert said.

Ashton could feel hot breath on his neck. He heard the basement door unlock behind him. His eyes searching the home, darting from corner to corner, left to right. Nothing!

The basement door creaked open.

"I assure you we are alone, detective. Old houses have their noises now, don't they?"

John turned to Herbert, standing in the open doorway, leaning on his cane. The stairs drenched in pitch black. Ashton's jaw gaped open.

"You're more than welcome to search all sixty-two rooms if you don't believe me. Although, the time it would take, you'd never make your train back home in time."

"How did you…" Ashton stopped himself. It was obvious he would be taking the train back to the city.

Herbert grinned. John could feel the candle's heat on his skin. The flame flickered in Herbert's eyes.

"After you, detective," said Herbert. "It's difficult for me to take the stairs with my condition. Always best to walk behind someone, that way I have a shoulder to hold onto."

Ashton stared down the stairs. His thoughts turned blank as if his wits had escaped him.

"Please, detective, *I* would also like to get home tonight." His voice rose, on the brink of anger.

Ashton saw himself shrinking beneath Herbert's stiff gaze.

Herbert rolled his eyes as he shook his head; apparently frustrated as he turned towards the stairs. "Follow me, detective, if you're too afraid for me to walk behind you. Please keep the candle steady. It's quite dark down there."

————————

The wood stairs buckled and creaked beneath Ashton's feet.

Herbert waited for him at the bottom, steadying himself on his cane. The candle shed no light past Mr. West, whose skin resembled smooth porcelain in the candlelight. Ashton's hand shook casting flickering shadows across Herbert. The air grew hot, smug and thick carrying a profound scent, sweat, rancid decay, and sulfur that curled and burned Ashton's nostrils.

"That's right, just keep steady, detective, the stairs are old. Very difficult toward the bottom." Herbert offered his hand. Ashton waved him off. "To each his own, detective."

"Not much to see," said Ashton as he took the last step down standing close to Herbert. He pushed the candle into the room. The light offered little comfort in the darkness.

"I rather enjoy the dark, detective. It has its place in the universe, doesn't it?" Herbert wore a grin on that thin face, watching Ashton reaching into the darkness. "There are more candles, though."

Ashton looked around. "Where?" He turned to face Herbert whose eyes stared stiff and menacing, candlelight flickered in those dark pupils. Ashton forced his eyes away.

Mr. West stretched his hand. "On the walls, detective."

Ashton could see nothing. No end and no beginning. Only darkness.

"Perhaps I should come back in the morning." Ashton's lips quivered. Sweat on his upper lip. Difficult to breathe with the air so thick, constricting his lungs.

"Nonsense," said West. "All this way for nothing? Captain Knowles assured me you would handle this situation with the utmost and swiftest dignity. We are here, detective, please take a look around. See for yourself Alena's vast and uncommon delusion."

"Captain Knowles," John repeated, his voice monotone and soft.

"Yes, detective, your superior. You do understand, don't you, detective, the sensitivity in this situation? Alena has caused havoc for many people. All wish for her story to be swept under the rug for what it is. Insanity!"

John closed his eyes; he could feel the sensation in his gut, trembling and unsteady. That *seeing* part of him, his senses running in all directions, spinning and dizzy.

"Take my hand, detective," said West. "Lead me to the candelabra so we may shed light on this darkness."

Ashton snapped his eyes open. His body wavered.

"The ground down here is all dirt, very difficult to move with the cane."

John looked at Herbert's feet and the cane beside them.

"Don't you want to *see*, detective?" His voice trembled. "Is that not why you're here?"

"Why I'm here," John repeated.

"Yes, why you're here. Honestly, detective, I find your demeanor and lack of dignity quite disturbing. A crippled man stands before you, and you refuse to lend a hand. What gives with you, detective? Did your mother not teach you basic manners?"

"What's wrong with me?" Ashton thought.

"What is wrong indeed?" West whispered.

John looked at West, confused. *Did I say that out loud?*

Herbert raised his hand again and Ashton took the offering. West's eyes closed, a small grin graced his lips.

"Thank you, detective," West breathed. "Thank you."

Now the basement was illuminated. The wall sconces burst into life. One after the other, like dominos across the walls. Ashton stepped back, releasing his hand.

"So naïve, detective," said West.

Ashton's heart jumped, gazing over the enormous basement, following each sconce, his eyes jumping to each light. He could feel West's breath on his neck, Ashton's hand shaking, trembling, as the candle he held shook violently. On the far wall across from Ashton a pentagram was drawn in what John surmised was blood, in front of it, more than a few feet from the wall a crystal bowl sat on a tall marble stand. In between the stand and pentagram was a waist high marble slab. Ashton's eyes continued to roam, witnessing dead bodies scattered across the ground. Some half buried, others that have yet to be.

Ashton's eyes widened, startled and confused, his jaw hung loose. He stepped forward, a jerk reaction, realizing his foot was inches away from the first body, a skull, mouth ajar as if whomever this person had been their last breath had come in astonished surprise. Black slime stained the skull down to the eye sockets. Ashton's defenses dropped; he could hear the screams, feel the fear experienced by the lives that had been taken. That seeing part of him was overwhelming, paralyzing. The candle he held dropped from his hand, the flame gone once it hit the ground, as Ashton dropped to his knees and West moved cautiously to the marble stand, carefully pacing each step, every drop of his cane to not disturb the dead.

He heard screams; cries of pain and torture, pleas for life, and wishes for death spiraled and pounded in Ashton's mind. His eyes followed the bodies. Some weren't complete, simply the skull and spine. Flies and maggots scurried and squirmed on bodies yet to be decomposed. Some bodies large, fully grown, others presented a life cut short, prepubescent. In that moment John realized the dead were conveniently placed to form three circles, one smaller than the other. Ashton was in the center of those deathly rings. He realized he was huffing, gasping for air. The screams, the cries, the wrenching, twisting pains swarming like moths to the flame all leading like a red carpet to the curdling shivering newborn screams that pounded in John's ears, relentless and blood curdling. Cry, wail, cry, wail. SCCCRREEEAAAMMMM!

Ashton clenched his hands over his ears. The baby's cries slamming and rattling in his skull. He could sense the terror in his gut as he rocked back and forth with whimpers escaping his throat.

"It's the seeing part of you, detective," said West. "When you bury it down the way you have it arrives with a vengeance."

John could hear West's voice as if it snuck into his brain. Ashton forced his eyes to West. Screaming souls ripped through Ashton's skull, realizing this was not a servant named Herbert West. He knew then he was in the presence of Golem.

His brain twisted inside his skull. Compounded pressure churned and hemorrhaged. Blood swelled in his nostrils. His lips quivered, shivered, and jumped. He couldn't cease the whirlwind that captured his chest, his heart now caught in an iron grip, suffocating the air from his lungs. Blood from his nose now pooled into his mouth, and dripped down his chin. Now Golem raised a mallet and pelted the bowl that rang with a heavy vibration. Ashton could see the vibration floating above the bowl, lifting and widening into the folds between Ashton and Golem, expanding as the vibration consumed the screams. The vibration shot through Ashton tumbling him over onto his back, and the screams and howls ceased although John's skull continued to twist. Low and muted, he heard Golem approach, heard the cane crunch into the earth.

He'd landed inches away from a skull, the empty sockets staring when he noticed he'd fallen on top of and crushed the dead bones of another body beneath him.

Golem now consumed his vision, squatting beside him. And his emerald eyes flickered with fire.

The trap door in the back of the eye.

Ashton heard Alena's words. Golem placed his hand over John's chest, and his heart squeezed and wrenched then calmed in unison with his breathing.

He could hear his heartbeat echo between his ears, and the thick, slow breath emanating in his lungs. Felt himself drifting, saw stars spiraling within a dark glow. Heavy eyelids, they opened and fell with every thick breath.

"You're not going to die, John," Golem's voice like thunder facilitating the storm. "There is too much work to be done."

48

Annette had been dreaming, a dream where anger had ushered in suffering. Beneath her hand were millions of people hoping and waiting for Annette's approval. From her hand were strings, one tied to each finger, and when she twisted her wrist the people moved. She found them repulsive, these people who beckoned her worship.

The sky above burned with fire. The ground piled high with skulls where those people puppets stood. Raging winds lifted death's putrid scent. Annette breathed it in, like ecstasy that drove pleasurable quivers raging in the veins. Her neck shivered. Fear, like a dense fog, surrounded Annette, and turned to ghosts with black eyes baring sharp teeth, circling around her. There was comfort being with these ghosts, she opened her arms to them, welcoming all.

She saw her face drawing in the ghosts with a deep inhale.

Her eyes shot open.

Blurred vision with bulbs containing white light moved across wide eyes. Annette clamped her eyes shut, shook her head, then snapped her eyes open. Her body ached when she rolled on her side. She saw the receiver lying beside her, noticed how the wire coiled around her body. Her head pounded with a foggy haze. The linoleum floor was cold, comforting to the alcohol heat that pumped through her veins.

She wished for death. For death to replace the hollow sensation wrought with pain. The hole inside where the soul should have been. She had no reason to rise, to get up and brush herself off. To do away with the cobwebs strung across her mind. Her eyes were staring with numb surprise. Annette knew any sudden movement would strike pain through her skull. She'd been here before, so many times before.

Always lonely, Annette Flemming was. All her life, alone.

"Get up," she thought. "Don't just lie here. Get UP!"

She did just that, forced herself to her ass, leaning against the counter. She was correct, her head spun, burning heat between her temples. Acid churned inside her stomach. She breathed deeply.

Her mouth and throat were dry. "I need water," she thought as she stretched her eyelids so the eyes could focus. She reached for the countertop and yanked herself to her feet, then leaned against the counter, turned on the faucet, and dipped her head in, gulping down water. Cool liquid soothed the alcohol-heated skin, washing crusted blood off her nose and mouth. Satisfied, she leaned back, drew in another deep breath, then turned off the faucet, wiping her mouth with her hand.

The clock on the wall ticked a few minutes past midnight. The phone was still on the floor. The moments before she passed out were a blur. Did Noel call? Did she speak with him? No, she remembered. The connection was bad. She couldn't hear him.

I don't give a shit!

Annette brushed her hand through her hair, and placed the receiver on the hook, then went to the stairs, her bed beckoning for her to rest her head. She could hear Sam's bark. Loud, ferocious, relentless.

"Oh, Sam," she whispered. "I'm so sorry."

His bark was everywhere now and Annette stopped cold. Upstairs, downstairs, in the kitchen, in the sitting room, his bark was relentless. Suddenly ceased, like tearing off a warm blanket on a cold, cold night.

Annette stood in the sudden silence, her eyes darting left to right. Heavy short breaths. Tension gripped her chest, constricting the throat.

She jumped, startled by a sudden knocking. Someone was rapping on the front door.

49

He was back in the war, hearing whistling bombs dropping, ripping, and tearing away building after building. Gun fire, close, too close for any reprieve, breath, or indignation. Zipping close to his head in white flashing streaks. John Ashton, his arms pulling his knees tight against his chest, spilled tears and propelled fearful screams.

"You're not a war hero…"

Allied soldiers, hustling weaponry and acting instinctively, ran passed him.

"You're just a frightened boy."

He could hear heavy footsteps, boots in the dirt; scuttle forward and out of sight. Behind them the ghosts, fresh souls, weary and bleak, frenzied and delusional, walked aimlessly, listless. The dead lay all around Ashton, bodies dismembered and torn. "This was the place," Ashton thought, "where nightmares exist, propelled into the future where the free sleep restless."

"You've always resented the *seeing*. You stuffed it down hoping it would leave…"

Another bomb exploded, tore through the building where Ashton sat, ripping concrete walls to ashes around him. John couldn't move, pinned to the ground.

"Hell is nothing more than truth revealed, detective. We all have our truths. There should be no shame in them."

Ashton shook with fear, beneath the rubble, breathing concrete dust.

"Hell, Detective Ashton, exists in those moments when the truth turns on us. And they do come so very viciously."

Something tore at John's skull, a hand full of his hair. He could feel his skin tearing off his skull. Quickly he was propelled from the ground, lifted into the air and thrown. Landing inside the building's remains, every organ in his body squeezed with pain. His vision blurred, his head bleary.

"Why didn't you admit the truth, detective? You're no war hero; you hid like a frightened child. Hell, to compare you to a child is an insult."

In front of John was the ghost, a fellow soldier with his stomach torn open, and his innards dripping down his legs. "There it is, John, that seeing part of you. Should you have listened to your mother, you would have been prepared."

The ghost jumped on Ashton, knife in hand.

"Don't," Ashton cried. "Please don't."

He eased his knife into John's chest.

"You should have died in the war, detective. So many brave men and women would have been better to take your place."

The knife tore through bone, constricting John's breath. He could feel that blade inside him, inching deeper. The ghost's eyes oozed green bile.

"You're no war hero," said the ghost pushing the blade further.

Another explosion, tearing away the broken walls around them. And Ashton screamed.

Screamed and found himself in the Francon Mansion. On the marble slab, Golem or West or whomever, hovering over him. His wrists and ankles tied to the stone, naked. Sweat beaded across his skin, head to toe.

"Just a taste," said Golem running his hand over John's forehead. "A small taste of Xibalba." He closed his eyes, breathing deeply. "We can take an eternity to feed on that fear."

John, wide eyed, staring, glaring, yanked on his restraints as low, struggling whimpers escaped his throat.

"Pull all you want, detective. The restraints will not give. I've had men much stronger than you attempt their freedom. The more you struggle the tighter they get. Best to save your energy; you will need your resolve for what is to come."

John tried not to listen, but Golem's voice was hypnotic, carried on the wings of doves to his ears. His thoughts flipped across conscious thought, raging, shameful. How did this happen? What is happening? He saw the red cane; saw the crippled Herbert West with his wrapped and bandaged hand leading him to the cellar.

How could I have been so foolish?

"Because you're frightened, detective. You chose not to believe Alena, at least that fantastical part of her story. You tried, no, forced, rational thought onto something that clearly has no rationale, not in this life, and not in this world."

John despised Golem's voice. Hated knowing the truth.

"You followed your programming to the letter. Stuffed down that seeing part of yourself, like your father told you to. This world…this planet continues to constrict. To tighten reality like the atoms in this marble. Keep the world under control by disregarding outdated thinking. Such thoughts are necessary, for us. All part of the programming, Mr. Ashton. Loose associations play no part in the future. Convince the world we don't exist, and they play right into our hands. God is dying in your world, detective. The death of the light quickens to meet the desire of the wretched and corrupt. Soon, all humanity will be bathed in darkness."

John started to laugh, and Golem raised his chin, staring inquisitively at Ashton.

"I hadn't expected this reaction, John. Whatever could be so funny?"

"Alena said you enjoy giving speeches. She hit the nail on the head with that one. Don't you ever shut the fuck up?"

Golem grinned. He moved his head back and forth. "Of course, truth is always the best ally. You will see. See for yourself how people disregard the truth. How they throw it off in favor of a more common reprieve. No one wants the truth. They desire lies. The truth forces them to look, to see with wider eyes. So much easier to dismiss the unknown than to think through it."

John turned his head to the side, away from Golem. He thought of his wife and their unborn. Thought about how he got here, how he allowed himself to be deceived. "Alena," he thought, "I should have listened. I'm sorry I called you insane."

"Don't be so hard on yourself, detective. Any rationally thinking human would have thought the same of Alena. It's good she's in safe care, such crazies are apt to hurt themselves and others."

John snapped his head to Golem. "You won't hurt her, you can't. You need her to stay here. To pass the torch." He shook his head. "She will never pass the torch. Alena's resolve is stronger than all of us. You chose the wrong counterpart, Golem. Your time here is limited. You speak of the future. You have no future." He motioned his head to Golem's wrapped hand. "You're already going goat. Tell me, Golem, what is that like? Nipping and tugging like a goat?" He laughed. Laughed because there was nothing more to do. "What's next, Golem? More torture? More visits to Xibalba? Whatever. You lose this round, Golem. Alena's got you pegged for an ass kickin'."

Now the basement door creaked open. Wind rushed into the basement and John's eyes shot wide open as he screamed for help.

"Still holding on to hope, detective? There's no use really. No one is coming for you. No one cares that you're here. Not even that sadist Captain Knowles."

Ashton's jaw dropped.

"That's right, detective. Knowles wasn't as taken by your heroics as you thought. It was I who forced his hand to make you detective. Knowles was simply the messenger. He sent you here, to me, on his orders. And you followed dutifully as we expected." Golem raised his head. "I wonder if he and Mrs. McGovern are enjoying their time together? I think so. In fact, I would stake a bet on it. Although Knowles does prefer

Charles, sometimes Mrs. McGovern needs some love, too."

"Sick fuck!" Ashton shouted. Tried pulling himself free. He heard the steps buckle and creak. His eyes darted to the stairs. He could see the tiny feet and small legs standing on the third step; the body and head still out of view. "What is this? Who is that?" his voice hurried.

"Come, darling," said Golem. His left hand leaning against his cane, his right hand stretched toward the stairs. "Show the detective his prize."

Emerging from the steps was the DA's daughter. John recognized her from the picture. She took the steps cautiously, one after the other, her tiny hand holding the rail for safety.

"Come, Isabelle." She came into view, stepping down onto the dirt floor. "Mind the bodies, please," said Golem. Isabelle looked to the floor. She raised her dress to watch her feet, being sure not to crush any decaying bones as she walked with a child's spring in her step to the marble slab; her eyes always fixed on Detective John Ashton, never wavering. Those beady, dark, and menacing eyes revealing the devil within. Golem put his hand on her shoulder and stepped behind her.

Ashton's eyes grew wide. Isabelle was thin, sickly thin. The skin beneath her eyes dark and sunken. Blonde hair matted and greasy, short and cut above the ears. Her dress, tattered and torn, brushed across the floor.

"She's become one of my greatest assets, detective."

Ashton curled his brow, his eyes roaming. Isabelle's lips pressed tight in a soft grin.

"Let her go!" Ashton demanded.

Golem rolled his eyes. "That's up to you, detective." John's scowl turned inquisitive, confused. "But honestly enough, it is a time for celebration. You have found the DA's daughter. Good detective work." He started clapping, right hand slapping against the wood cane in his left hand. And John could now see how those gnarls moved and slithered across the cane with red eyes gleaming and mouths opening and closing, revealing pain and torture. "Bravo! Bravo!" Golem's cackle echoed through the basement. Isabelle's grin opened revealing rows of jagged teeth. She looked up to Golem then back to John.

"What did you do to her?"

"Come now, John, I think you know where this little morsel has been. A gift from the new DA, a very…ambitious young man. Now my gift to you, detective." He forced Isabelle forward, pushing at her back. John looked at Isabelle then to Golem. "The moment of truth, detective. What will you give to save this little child? To deliver her home to her parents?"

Isabelle snapped her head to Golem, her stare stern, disappointed.

Golem reached his hand to her chin. He smiled. "No worries," he told her. "We will find a new body for you."

John's heart jumped. He started pulling, tugging, yanking, willing himself to be free. Short grunted breaths raged with every pull.

"Please, detective. Please, please me. This is all for the best. For all involved. You, the young detective solves the case. Delivers the missing child to her parents. You'll make all the papers. *War hero and prominent officer brings in the new DA's missing daughter.* You'll be celebrated your whole career. Although we will know the truth now, won't we?" He placed his hands on Isabelle's shoulders. She nodded and smiled. "Yes, we will." She looked up to Golem. "Detective Ashton is no war hero, any more than he is a police hero. Isn't that right, John? *Fancy shooting*, isn't that how the papers wrote it up for you? Dropping down to the ground to deliver the perfect shot." Golem shook his head and clucked his tongue. "You tripped, didn't you, detective? And the gun went off when you hit the pavement. Nothing more than luck, Mr. Ashton. The same luck that found you a war hero when it was fear that helped you survive. Now look at you. Frightened out of your wits without an inkling of what to do next. I'll make it simple. Take the girl, Isabelle. Leave here with her. Deliver her to her parents. Force the reality driven news to blame Alena for the bodies and the girl. Then we all go on our merry way."

Isabelle stepped closer to John.

"What other alternative do you have, detective? Considering present circumstances, I'd say there is no other option. Other than keeping you here with us. Let the Xibalba devils take over your body. Lock your consciousness in Xibalba." He moved his head back and forth. "Not a fitting end to the world's greatest detective."

John forced himself to turn away. Tears in his eyes.

"Oh, Isabelle look, we've made the tough detective cry. Do you think we'll go to hell for doing so?" Golem laughed. "Go ahead, Isabelle. Give the detective a kiss."

Isabelle mounted the marble slab. John's body cringed. Her mouth opened, she snapped her head to his and those sharp teeth tore into Ashton's mouth. His deafening screams echoed inside Isabelle. Blood streamed from the puncture wounds. Ashton could feel his blood, leaving his veins, pouring down Isabelle's throat.

"Not too much, my lady. We don't wish for the detective to lose too much blood."

She snapped her head back. Her mouth wide, swallowing blood and fear. Pain shot to Ashton's skull. He could taste her lips, like putrid stink, sulfur in his throat.

"Come now, detective, please tell me you're not holding on to that sliver of hope. It doesn't exist, Mr. Ashton. Never has."

"This can't be real," Ashton cried. "I'm not here; this is just a nightmare. This can't be real, it can't."

Isabelle went into Golem's arms. They both watched as Ashton continued to cry and wail.

"Can't be real. I know it. It can't be real."

Golem and Isabelle locked eyes. They touched foreheads.

"Can't be real. Please. It's not real. Please get me out of here. Please let me wake up." He tried his restraints. Still no give to them. "Can't be. Can't be real. Can't. Can't be real."

"Possible," Golem said to Isabelle. "He may crack." Isabelle looked to Golem, inquisitive as if she sought understanding. "The human mind, my lady. So fragile. It cracks under the pressure."

Ashton continued his raving and lunacy. Blood dripping down his face to the marble stone.

Golem breathed deeply. "Is the alternative in place?"

Isabelle smiled and gave a quick nod.

"Good," said Golem. "If he doesn't completely crack, we will need them."

"Can't be real. Can't be. Can't. Can't be real."

Ashton continued to flop and pull on the stone, his eyes wide. His brain twisting, body shuddering, jumping.

"Why not just eat him?" asked Isabelle, watching Ashton, her finger raised in front of her face.

"Too much effort has been put into Detective Ashton, my lady. I'd hate to have to begin all over again. We are too close to make haste."

Ashton started hyperventilating. His heart constricted, eyes bulging from their sockets, suffocating.

"Besides," said Golem. "He's the perfect catalyst to meet our needs."

Ashton couldn't breathe. His body lurched off the marble, gasping for air.

"He needs a bigger push than I expected."

Ashton fell silent; his eyes bulged from their sockets, labored breath swelled in his lungs. His throat ballooned, his bloodied mouth gaping, gasping. His head pounded as if his brain swelled inside his skull.

And Detective Ashton bid hello to darkness.

50

Annette Flemming experienced a sudden drop of relief. Her body loosened, stiff shoulders now free as if the weight of the world had gone. She was lighter, her heart calm, breathing easy.

Again, the rapping, and Annette smiled. She would not be alone any more. A new life waited behind that door. She could feel it, in her bones, flowing through her veins.

She went to the door when relief washed over her, sweet exquisite relief. She unlocked and opened the door without looking through the long rectangular window beside it.

"There's no need," she thought. "All is well."

She realized in that moment, the door opening, the anxiety was gone, replaced with confidence. Camilla stood in front of Annette, in the door, her purse tucked close to her stomach, held by both hands.

Annette noticed, perhaps for the first time, how Camilla looked radiant under the moon light, delightful and glowing.

"Camilla?" Annette had expected the children but gave no second thought to it.

"Oh, my lady," said Camilla. "I have been so worried about you. All alone here. Mr. Noel not coming home for a few more days, and Sam…" She chocked back her words. Tears in her eyes.

"Camilla," Annette, her voice sympathetic. She offered her hand and Camilla took the offering, stepping into the foyer.

"I couldn't sleep," Camilla said, looking over the house. "Just kept thinking about you being alone in this big house." She peeled off her jacket, switching her purse from one hand to the other, then draped the jacket over her arms with her purse. Now she faced Annette. "I can't stand to be alone, Mrs. Annette. I think you feel the same."

Camilla's eyes roamed over Annette, a stare Annette enjoyed as her body tingled from her chest to her navel. Camilla put her hand to her mouth. One of those tears welled in her eye, and cascaded down her cheek. And Camilla shivered, the icy air rushing into the house. Annette smiled, smug with sympathy.

"Looks like you could use a drink," Annette said, and she closed the door.

"Si," said Camilla.

Annette paused, noticing Camilla's skin, how the flesh glowed in the darkness.

"You know what we'll do?" Annette moved past Camilla toward the sitting room. Camilla followed. "We'll open Mr. Flemming's reserve scotch. Why not, right? Toast to Sam, to celebrate the joy he brought to us."

"Si, Mrs. Flemming. Sounds good."

"Annette, please," she said, scuttling across the sitting room to the china cabinet. "Just us girls here, Camilla. Call me Annette, please."

Camilla draped her coat across a chair, and placed her purse on the cushion. Annette opened the cabinet, took out the reserve scotch, and placed it on the counter, then took two crystal glasses. She uncorked the scotch.

"Play some music, please." Annette poured while Camilla went to the window. The streetlight across the street shed light on the soft wind where leaves danced on the sidewalk.

Camilla began to sing, at first low as if embarrassed, her voice like sweet jasmine that paused Annette's hand. Annette turned to Camilla.

"Your voice is beautiful."

Camilla regarded Annette from over her shoulder. "Gracias," she said. "My mother teach."

Annette finished pouring, corked the bottle and replaced it on the shelf. Carrying both glasses, she stepped toward Camilla. She handed her the glass then raised hers.

"To Sam," said Annette.

"To Sam," repeated Camilla.

They toasted then drank, Annette swallowing her scotch in one gulp. Camilla followed suit. During a comfortable pause, Annette's eyes danced over Camilla. She couldn't help but smile.

"Now that's good," said Annette. She took Camilla's glass and returned to the cabinet.

"Thank you, Mrs. Annette."

Annette raised her finger. "Just Annette, please. After all, we are going to be together a long time. Might as well maintain a first name basis."

"Si, Annette, ok."

"That's better." She uncorked the bottle and poured, this time filling each glass by more than half. "You can stay here tonight, Camilla? I hope so. It's awfully late, and it wouldn't be safe to go out at this time." No need to cork the bottle again, Annette was confident the bottle would be empty by morning. She handed Camilla her glass.

"Si, Annette." She locked eyes with her, and Annette drifted into those dark pupils. "But where would I sleep?"

————

The first rays of the morning sun reached through the bedroom window. Annette brushed her fingers through Camilla's hair, silky smooth long black locks while Camilla's lips caressed between Annette's legs.

She'd never experienced such a tingling, the exacerbated release from tension that had lain dormant for what seemed like forever. Annette held in her groan. Hold it in a moment, hold it there, just right, hold it, feel it, jaw tight, teeth chattering. Breathe in pleasure, the tantalizing absorption filled with ecstatic elation. The moment right before explosive release. Annette remembered from when she was a teenager, how all was right and natural.

She caressed herself, her hands clenched over her breasts, pinching her nipples. Her legs wide, she pushed herself closer as Camilla's tongue lapped Annette's release, gyrating her pelvis to usher in what she'd always desired. Her knees buckled, toes curled. Annette's orgasm filled the house, absorbed by the walls and thrown back into the house like an echo of desire and jealousy. She was sure the neighbors had heard them, and she was pleased.

People love to talk, so why not give them something to talk about? To whisper as they walked by the house? To give that smug, knowing smile every time they saw Noel.

No one wants to tell the truth anymore, thought Annette as she embraced Camilla. They'd rather gossip than tell the truth.

Gossip gives small minds purpose.

51

Ashton's head throbbed, his eyes hurt. He could feel the back of his eyeballs, constricted and painful.

Behind the darkness—his eyes still closed—he could hear hustling and typing, phone's ringing and hurried footsteps. He lifted his right eyelid and the overhead light brought down a fury. His head swelled although the fog began to lift.

Ashton was lying on a couch in the police precinct. He jumped up, almost fell, caught himself and straightened his back.

His fellow officers began to cheer and clap.

"Rookie's got his first sofa city," said an officer.

"What happened, your wife kick you out?"

"Too much to drink, rookie?"

"We've all been there."

"Kidding me? I think I spent a month on that couch."

John stretched his eyelids, trying to get some air into those dry gelatinous balls. Breathed deeply to shake off the fog and cobwebs. Trying to piece together the how and the why.

How did I get here? What happened?

For the life of him he could not piece together any event after the train. *The train! They never picked me up*. He clamped his eyes shut, an effort to bring back a memory.

"Looks like he went slumming."

"Nasty bitch bit you, huh?"

"Tell her it was a dog…always works for me."

"Looks like chewed up dog shit."

Ashton, puzzled by the accusation ran his hand over his mouth and lips. Indentations, bite marks. In his mind's eye he saw blood, and felt the strangle of teeth over his mouth.

"Holy shit, rookie, lay off the sauce."

And the officers belted into unison laughter, cut short by Captain Knowles, standing in the door to his office.

"Cut that shit out," he ordered. "*Now!*"

John then caught a memory, flashes of Golem, no West, Herbert West, and Isabelle.

My God! Ashton thought, his hands feeling over his eyes. He ran to a window, the blinds closed on the opposite side. He could see his reflection and he checked his eyes. His jaw was quivering. He studied his pupils for a sign, any sign of…

The trap door in the back of the eye.

Nothing but those dark, brown eyes. No trap door. No segmented black corner.

"Ashton!" Captain Knowles said.

But John never heard him, the Captain's voice muffled to his ears as if he were speaking under water as Ashton's thoughts raced, breathing heavy. *What happened?* He looked down at himself, his clothes, his suit, wrinkled, disheveled. And his fedora? Gone. He spun around, searching. His fedora was on the couch, scrunched from his own weight. With trembling hands, he reached for it. His body tense and shivering.

"ASHTON!" Knowles hollered.

John snapped his head to Knowles and his body constricted. As he looked around he could see his fellow officers had gone back to the day's work. Ashton's eyes darted from one officer to the next. His breath was shallow, constricted. His hands began to shake.

"Trust no one," he thought, although the voice was not his own. The declaration dropped into his mind, behind his eyes. Golem's voice. His lips began to quiver.

"Jesus, what's with you boy?" said Knowles. Ashton, staring untrusting at Knowles, tensed. "Get in here, rookie."

Ashton forced his breath down his narrow throat. The look on Knowles' face reaped disgust and disappointment. Or was that empathy? Ashton wasn't sure.

If what Golem said was true, Captain Knowles is as crooked as a politician. But how could he accuse Knowles? Accuse him of what? There's nothing, nada, zip, zero, zilch. Nothing but the raving lunacy of a mad woman locked away for insanity. Start throwing out accusations and you'll be sharing a room with Alena swapping Golem stories and praying around a pentagram. Ashton squeezed his fedora over his skull, his movements slow and cautious. He focused his breathing, listening to his breath like an echo between the ears, like listening under water. Drowning. He smoothed his hand over his suit. He had a lump in his throat, and his hands were unsteady.

"I already look insane," he thought.

Ashton walked to Knowles' office, and the world started spinning. He stopped, steadying his feet and legs, equilibrium out of balance. His eyes rolled. He was on the verge of dropping down and passing out. He closed his eyes and breathed deep, warding off the dizzy spell, and entered Knowles' office. He had to turn away from Knowles' stare. Turning, Ashton closed the door, looking over the detectives, chattering, and phones ringing. The sound softened when the door shut.

"You look as pale as a vampire," Knowles said. He lit a cigarette and inhaled a deep drag. "Looks like you got bit, too. I'll tell you this once, son, if you're on something and I find out, you'll be thrown in the street on your ass so fast your head will spin."

"On something?"

Knowles paused. Puffed his cig. His expression changed, his eyes staring at Ashton, sympathy in his stare.

Knowles cleared his throat. "Drugs, son. Drugs."

Ashton shook his head. "I've never taken a drug in my life."

"Then lay off the liquor for a while. You're a detective, for Christ's sake. We need to maintain some semblance of order. You know all the controversy; the press sees you looking like that they'll have a field day with you."

Ashton tilted his head, inquisitive. *The press*, John mouthed the words. Isn't that what this is all about, people protecting their reputations from slander and accusations? Doing anything to keep their names clean.

Knowles dropped his shaking head, his cig burning between his fingers.

Ashton pursed his lips and pain rose in his swollen cheeks. "Did you meet with Mrs. McGovern?" His voice was desperate.

Knowles nodded. "Of course. The Governor's ball was last night. You've no idea what I had to do to keep her rage down. She did not welcome the accusation. So, there's a dead lead. Thank God Alena's under lock down. Loons like her accusing good people. Christ, next we'll have just anyone making false accusations." He looked up to Ashton, his face tightened. "Look at you." Knowles shook his head. He pursed his lips, swallowing his words. "Go home, detective. Take a nap. Take a shower. Put this out of your mind for an afternoon. Go home, rookie." Knowles paused as his voice constricted. "Go see your wife." His voice cracked. His stare intense, dire, and empathetic.

Ashton repeated, "My wife," studying the captain's stare. Knowles' eyes were stiff, sad. John cocked his head, following the outline of Knowles' pupils. The captain had dark eyes, but Ashton could see it. Knowles' right pupil, the segment in the right corner, discolored, dark.

The trap door.

"You hear me, rookie?" Knowles' voice raised. John blinked, and looked up. "Go see your wife."

Ashton's eyes narrowed.

My…*wife!*

52

He needs a bigger push than I expected.

Golem's voice, his words, his declaration, looped through Ashton's thoughts. His heart jumping, pumping, thumping in his throat, he hurried like a mad man to his apartment, his home.

A bigger push!

Fury, rage boiled his blood. Not my wife. My baby.

His efforts seemed futile. What was he going to do? He saw the captain's eye, the trap door. This is insane! How can it be? Can't believe it. I can't.

Go see your wife. A bigger push. McGovern at the governor's ball. Alena. My God, Alena. I should have gone home. I should have made sure Laura was safe. Insane. All of it is insane. There has to be a different explanation. A real explanation. This is all insane. Fucking insane. Laura, please, please tell me you didn't let anyone in. They can't come in unless you invite them. Isn't that what Alena said? They have to be invited.

He mounted the stairs to his apartment. Hurried footsteps from above. Ashton drew his gun, slammed his back against the wall, head up, looking. Three kids scurried down the stairs, raced past him, too involved in their own game to notice him.

He took the steps two at a time until he arrived on his floor. Noticed his door was ajar. The smell of bacon wafted in the hall. He heard humming in his apartment. Cooking, singing. Ashton breathed a sigh of relief. Laura always sang when she cooked.

You're losing it, John. Absolutely fucking losing it.

Ashton holstered his weapon, all too happy to be home. The scent of cooking bacon, the humming like food for his heart. He went through the door, and closed it behind him.

"Laura," he said stepping into the kitchen. "You'd never believe…"

Ashton froze, his jaw dropped, eyes wide.

Golem stared at him.

"Detective," Golem called, "Too happy to see you." He flipped the bacon in the pan then glanced at Ashton. "We've been waiting for you."

Ashton's eyes went to his bedroom door. Closed. Scanned the tiny room. The kitchen table set with a fork, knife, and napkin. Golem's cane leaned against the back of one of the chairs. Golem scooped a wad of bacon onto a plate beside scrambled eggs.

"One thing I do enjoy most of all is cooking." He placed salt and pepper shakers on the table then eyed Ashton. "We all need a hobby to calm our hearts." And he grinned then cocked his head. "You ok, detective? You look like you've seen a ghost."

Ashton couldn't take his eyes off his bedroom door. Laura was in there, he was certain. Golem dipped his head entering Ashton's view, standing between the detective and the bedroom door; the door an arm's reach away from Golem.

"Detective?" He arched his back, looked to the bedroom door then back to Ashton. "It's ok detective, she is fine… and safe. Unharmed. Resting too. A pregnant lady needs her rest," he declared. "Sit, John. You look like hell. Food will do you good."

John's eyes narrowed, glaring at Golem. His stomach twisted. His head burned. He pulled his gun. "Get away from that door."

"A gun, John? In your own home? Please, detective, don't make decisions based on anger. I assure you…"

John fired. One, two, three. Bullets ripped into Golem's torso. A dog barked from somewhere in the building.

"Jesus, John, you must be angry." Golem brushed off his suit where the bullets entered. "You can't kill me, detective; you know at least that much. Only Alena has that right."

Ashton aimed at Golem's head. "Back away from that door."

Golem closed his eyes. "Of course, detective," he said, his voice soft, caring, opening his eyes to John with a slow shake of his head. His eyes narrowed. "But do you really want to see your wife's current condition? What could you do about it? Call the police?" He burst into a laughing fit.

Ashton cocked his revolver and Golem silenced. He shook his head, then dipped his chin to his chest, his arms extended, eyeing John. "Go ahead, detective. Shoot all you want." Ashton's hand trembled. "Do what you will, detective but I assure you some Good Samaritan has already contacted the police. Those cohorts and confidants you have so much respect for. Which gives us limited time; and then your wife will be dead along with your unborn child. Is that what you want? To lose your family over this nonsense?"

Laura, why did you let him in? Ashton's anger raged in his chest, boiling blood to his skull.

"You still can't see, detective. You think she let me in *today?*" Golem laughed. Moved his head back and forth. "No, no, no, your poor wife, alone all day, her back hurting. Pregnancy, detective, takes a toll on the body."

Puzzled, Ashton's eyes narrowed, thinking.

Salesman was here today.

He saw Laura in his thoughts. How her back ached. The salesman. The salesman at the door, bringing...gifts.

Ashton's head bobbed, his brain twisting in his skull, trying to piece it all together, to see, to know, to accept that...

"The cream, Ashton. She's been using it for days now. What do you think I used in that ailment, detective? What do you think is happening to your unborn child right now, as we speak?" Golem's voice turned to rage. "Will you let him slip away? Honestly, detective, I don't even have to do any more than I already have. If you lock me up, the seed of that cream will manifest inside the blood of your child. Only I can stop it from happening. Lower your gun, detective, and let's get this over with. We've only moments, and time keeps ticking."

John, lost in contemplation, lowered his gun, his eyes staring into space.

"Good, detective," said Golem. "There is still time to save Laura and your child."

Ashton's mouth agape, his breath stuttered.

"Take refuge, detective, knowing you never had a chance," breathed Golem. His voice a calm hush. He tilted his head, glaring at the lost detective. "When one is unknowingly surrounded by the corrupt, there is nothing one can do to make good on noble promises."

Blood dripped from Ashton's nose. Stiff, wide, and dry eyes carried sadness and distain. The blood ran across his upper lip, down the side of his mouth. And Golem grinned.

"Sit, detective," said Golem, gesturing to the table. He took the breakfast plate off the counter along with a handful of napkins, and put the plate on the table. "Wipe your nose," he told Ashton. "You're bleeding, although when the police arrive you can tell them you took a punch…while rescuing the DA's daughter." Golem tapped the napkins he placed by the plate before sitting down. Ashton furrowed his brow.

Isabelle? His hand went to his mouth and his chest cringed remembering the bite, his relentless screams echoed in the child's chest.

"Sit, detective. Let us hash this out like men."

Ashton saw blood on his fingers. He glared at his bedroom door, feeling, sensing the darkness that existed beyond the door. Golem traced his stare, looked at the door then back to Ashton. "I SAID *SIT*, DETECTIVE!"

Ashton closed his eyes. His head shook; his body just about screamed. He looked at Golem, sitting sideways on the chair, his left leg over his right, his hands resting on his lap. He gestured to the seat.

And John, defeated and on the brink of a dizzy spell, took his seat, holstering his weapon.

"Eat," said Golem as he stretched his back, sitting closer to the table, resting both feet on the floor.

Ashton studied the plate in front of him and his stomach lurched. "Pate'," he thought. Acid boiled into the back of his throat. He took the wad of napkins and wiped his mouth.

"I'm sure you haven't eaten anything in a day or two. You should eat; get some fuel in that stomach. You're going to have a very long day, John." Golem's voice was close to sympathetic, caring even. John hesitated. He saw maggots and human remains, remembering Alena's story. Golem shook his head. "The food is clean, detective. I haven't any reason to feed you humans." Golem cocked his eyebrows. "No?" He stretched his arms, snapping his elbows. "Very well then." He shook his head, stretched his back, then stared at Ashton. Sirens now, outside the window.

"Let us begin, detective."

53

At the same time Ashton was sitting down with Golem, Annette Flemming's phone rang.

She was wrapped in a towel after a hot bath. Beads of water glistened off her skin. Annette flipped a towel over her head, and twisted her hair within. On the third ring she picked up the phone, sitting on the bed. Outside the window children ran hollering down the street, some on bicycles.

"Hello, Flemming household," she answered. Annette knew Noel would be on the other line; her voice carried a relaxed sarcasm.

"Annette," Noel muttered. "It's me."

"I know," she said. "How's your trip going?"

"Trip is good. Great actually. What happened to Sam? Are you ok? I tried calling last night. I think we got a bad connection. Long distance and all."

Annette smiled. She cleared her throat. "I'm ok. I don't know what happened to Sam. I think maybe he ate something in the backyard he shouldn't have."

Noel grunted. "Poor Sam. I can't believe it. Are you ok though? I know you don't like to be alone. Do you want me to come home today? I can get a flight out this afternoon…"

"No," Annette said, abrupt. "I'm fine. Camilla is here."

"Camilla? On a Saturday?"

"Yes, I asked her to stay. She's been a great help, really."

From the bathroom Camilla began to sing, her voice sweet, calming. Annette smiled.

"Is that her?" asked Noel. "I hear singing. Is that Camilla? I didn't know she could sing."

"Rather well, too. It's comforting." Then, after a pause, "Very comforting indeed."

Another pause.

Annette spoke first. "When will you be home? Where are you headed next?"

"Back to California. They've really got things going out there. Lots of big things happening. I can't get into all of it on the phone. Too complicated to explain. But it's all good, Annie. Excellent really."

Annette grinned. "Perfect," she said. "Just perfect."

Camilla's voice raised an octave. Her sweet melody funneled off the bathroom tile and walls. Hypnotic! Annette felt Camilla calling to her.

"Yeah, it really is perfect. We're taking the world by storm, Annie. It feels so good."

Annette stood from the bed, and stepped to the window. Her thoughts focused on the playing, running, fumbling children outside. All but one. A child she had not recognized before. He was staring, she was sure, standing beneath the streetlight.

"You there?" Noel asked.

Annette snapped back. "Yeah. I'm here, just doing a few things is all."

"Reading those books? You always get preoccupied when you're reading."

"Of course." She cleared her throat, comfortable under the child's gaze. He couldn't be more than twelve. *Can he see me?*

"I hate talking to you when you're like this."

Annette rolled her eyes. "I'm sorry. A lot has happened. I'm trying to put my thoughts at ease."

"Understood. Listen I'll let you go. I'll call later tonight. Are you sure you're ok?"

Annette turned from the window. Camilla's voice melodic.

"Yes," she said. "All is well, right?"

"Right," Noel said. "Are you sure you're ok? You sound different?"

She answered with conviction. "I'm fine, Noel. I'm just ready to take the next step. Put the past behind us."

"That's the spirit," he said. "Are you up to plan a dinner party? Invite the socialites. It'll be good. We need to network. So many big things happening. Having the right friends is paramount. Everyone's up in arms about Senator McCarthy, and a rumor he may be holding hearings within a few years. They're all looking for fresh blood to sink their teeth into."

Camilla came out of the bathroom. Continuing to hum she wrapped a towel around her body. She locked eyes with Annette.

"I think that's a wonderful idea," said Annette, eyeing Camilla. "I'll get started on it today."

"Perfect," said Noel. "I love you and I'll call you later tonight."

"Ok," said Annette. "I love you, too."

Camilla rolled her eyes, and Annette held in her laugh.

"Ok. Talk later."

The call disconnected and Annette gazed at Camilla. The two ladies shared a smile. Annette replaced the phone on the hook then glanced outside.

The child was gone.

54

Detective John Ashton was trembling, shaking with fear. Police sirens were growing louder with every passing second.

Golem began, "Your wife will live, detective. This I assure you, however, your unborn will be stillborn. Think of it, detective. Think of living a life under such duress." He pursed his lips, moved his head back and forth. "Although this does not have to happen. I can help you, detective, I can make sure your child lives." Golem cocked his brow. Fire burning inside his pupils.

John cringed. His stomach twisting.

"But I need something from you first, detective. I need you to visit Alena this afternoon."

"Alena?" Ashton's face pinched in confusion. "Why?"

"I have my reasons. Alena will be undergoing a procedure today, as recommended by Dr. Elliot. I need you there for that procedure."

"To do what?"

"Just to look at her. I want Alena to know, detective. I want her to know before the procedure where she is going."

"That's it?"

"Yes, detective."

John looked to the window then the bedroom door. He shook his head. "I…I don't get it."

Golem sat forward. "Insignificant what you understand. This is what I need you to do."

John raised his eyebrows. "And then you'll go? You'll leave me and my wife alone?"

Golem tilted his head right then left. "Not exactly. From time to time I'll ask you to do something. Nothing too out of left field, detective, I understand you have a fragile ego." He grinned and Ashton cringed. "In return, your wife and child will be protected. Your career will skyrocket. Detective…" Golem dipped his chin to his chest, glaring at John. "Isabelle is in that room with your wife. The police will be here momentarily. This is your chance, detective. Think about it. Either you lose your unborn and go to jail for kidnapping…"

John shook his head. "They'll never believe it."

Golem rolled his eyes. "Please, detective, truth is simply a matter of who is telling the story." He paused. "Or you walk out of here with Isabelle in tow, deliver her to her parents. Be hailed—once again—as a hero. Although you and I will know the truth. We will always know the truth."

He could hear commotion on the street. Sirens blaring.

"Yes or no, detective. Yes…or no?"

John hesitated. His chest constricted, difficult to breathe, his lungs tight.

"This is the last chance, detective. Now is the time. NOW!"

Ashton's breath stuttered. The world, it seemed, was raining down on him. He could hear the police circling his building. He thought of Laura. His baby.

Ashton closed his eyes, nodding as his eyes wearily opened.

And Golem grinned. He stood up, gazing at John.

"Very well, detective." Golem pushed his seat in to the table. "Go into your room. See your wife. Isabelle will require you for a brief moment and then all will be well. Deliver her to her parents, then go see Alena." John hesitated. "Go now, detective."

John stood, stifling his tears. He went to his bedroom door, Golem watching him as he put his hand on the doorknob.

"Take refuge, detective, knowing you never had a chance. You were outwitted and outmatched the moment you were born."

John looked at him, really looked at him, and his heart burned with rage.

"I'll be seeing you, Golem. Sometime, somewhere, I'll find you."

Golem laughed. "Not really, detective." Then, after John paused, "Go!" he said, "And don't forget to thank Isabelle for returning your hat."

Ashton opened the door. The room was dark, blinds closed over the window, allowing thin streams of sunlight into the room. Laura was lying on the bed, breathing shallow. John entered and the door slammed shut behind him. He went to Laura, his breath catching, almost tripping over the body lying on the floor. Ashton, eyes wide, studied the body. Three bullet holes in the man's torso. Blood poured from the wounds, pooling beneath the body. The man was older than John, middle aged. He'd never seen him before, but

Ashton thought he knew this man, somehow. In John's gut he sensed he was a cop.

Something stirred above his head, in the corner.

Ashton's eyes widened. Isabelle, her eyes a cold sinister red, clawed on the ceiling. John screamed when she pounced on him.

———————

Golem was whistling. He pushed Ashton's chair to the table then took up his cane. He could hear Ashton's heavy fearful breath and whimpers. Golem paused by the front door, listening, a wide grin across his lips, before leaving, using his cane and holding the banister as he took the stairs down.

Two officers, guns in their hands, rushed up the stairs towards him. "Did you hear gunfire?" one asked.

Golem paused. "Yes," he said. "Thank God we have a detective in the building. I saw him in the hall. Told me to get out. There's a kidnapper he said." His voice hurried with a sense of urgency. "Some sick and twisted detective Reilly."

The two officers stared at each other, confused.

"That's all this great city needs," said Golem. "Another scandal. You just can't trust anyone anymore."

"Thank you, sir, get out of the building. We'll take it from here."

Golem cocked his brow. "Indeed," he whispered beginning to whistle once again, taking the stairs down cautiously as the officers rushed up the stairs.

He found his way into the street, where Golem disappeared within the thicket of watching and curious with all the commotion bystanders.

Whistling all the way down the street.

55

The official story told in the Sunday paper was that Detective Reilly never went to California. He was the head of a pedophilia scandal that rocked the city. Having kidnapped Isabelle, he'd held onto her and had come to Ashton's home—the detective assigned to the case—to kill him and his wife Laura. Nonetheless, the war hero took down the older detective. Three shots and Reilly was dead, after which Detective Ashton delivered Isabelle to her parents. An event captured by reporters, flashing, popping cameras, and a tender moment. The paper also issued a warning.

A warning to the criminals of New York City. Be careful, Detective John Ashton – *the war hero* – is here to clean up the city.

It was an article Alena would never see.

––––––––––

Now Ashton arrived at Bellevue. He'd called ahead to have Alena waiting for him. A request Dr. Elliot had been waiting for.

"Alena's become too much of a harm to herself and the other patients," Dr. Elliot had informed Ashton. "We've scheduled her for surgery this afternoon but will wait until after you've talked with her."

Ashton had thanked Dr. Elliot for his understanding. He was humble when Elliot offered congratulations on finding the DA's daughter.

A congratulations Ashton would not piece together, not at first in the least. John was preoccupied, his thoughts on Alena.

————————

She seemed nervous, even for Alena. She jumped off her seat the moment Ashton opened the door like she was sitting on a spring.

"Thank God," Alena shouted. "Are you okay?" She wrapped her arms around John. "I've been so concerned about you." John did not return her sentiment. His body stiff, his heart tense. "He was here again last night," Alena's voice shook. She tightened her grip on John. "I don't think it's him in the flesh. I think he's using someone here. Maybe multiple people. He's more like an apparition. I...I don't know what to do."

His jaw quivered. What was he to say to Alena? Her story is true, every claim, every intricate, sadistic detail. True!

And he had been her last hope.

What were they about to do to her? Ashton had not one clue as to what would be Alena's fate. But Golem's instructions were clear, *just look at her.*

Before the procedure. At the very last second. Until then, berate her. Turn the moments before into a frenzy. Curse her! Scream at her. Turn her story on its head.

His stomach turned. Throat constricted. *I'm sorry, Alena.*

John clamped his eyes shut. Clenched his jaw. Forced Alena's grip off him and stepped away. Alena, confused, watched him stand behind the desk.

"Are you ok?" she said, folding her arms across her chest.

John couldn't look at her.

"What is it, detective? What did you find at the house?"

He shook his head, turned from Alena's eyes, looking down.

"Did you see the basement?" Nothing from John. Alena tilted her head, attempting to capture John's attention. "Detective?"

"Nothing," John huffed. He looked at Alena. His expression changed, angry, disgusted. "There's nothing in the basement, Alena. Nothing at all. Nothing at the ClairField, there's not even a basement. Everything about your story is as I first suspected. Insane!" His voice raised. "This has all been a waste of my time and tax payer dollars."

Alena's jaw dropped. She stared wildly at Ashton who clenched his jaw, and turned his eyes away, moving his head back and forth.

John continued. "I have done some investigating into you, Alena. And you know what?"

"Tell me. Go ahead, detective, this your big moment isn't it?"

John shot her a look. "You're a sick woman, Alena." Alena's eyes widened, furrowing her brow. "It's good you're in here, locked up. This is where insane people need to be. Under lock and key to keep those above ground safe."

Alena reached out and slapped the detective; her nails cut his cheek drawing thin streams of blood.

"How dare you!"

John touched his face. Saw the trickles of blood on his fingertips.

"He got to you, didn't he?"

"This is insanity."

"Look at your face. Who bit you, detective? Was it Golem himself, or did one of his minions do it? Look at you. You're trembling with fear. My God." She shook her head. "My Lord."

"You know what I think, Alena? I think you killed Bill Astor."

Alena shook her head. "Not true. I told you what happened."

"No, Alena, that's your insanity. You killed him. Maybe it was an accident or maybe it wasn't. But you did kill him. Then covered it up. I'm not sure when you had your psychotic break, either right before or directly after. Maybe you took those kids, too, so you wouldn't feel alone. To make up for the child you lost. But you did kill Bill Astor and made up the story about Golem."

"I wouldn't hurt anyone." She kept shaking. Trembling.

"Yes you did, Alena. Yes you did!"

"No, I loved Bill, I'd never hurt him."

"I don't believe you." She put her hand to her forehead. Ashton could see her tears. "No one believes you."

She moved her hand, crossing her arms again as if she held herself. Held herself up. Tears beaded off her jawline. Her eyes lost, defeated. She turned her back to Ashton, shaking her head, looking over the room. "What do I do? What do I do?" she repeated.

He wanted to reach out to her. To tell her the truth. To let her know she wasn't insane. To tell her, how truly sorry he was. That he wasn't strong enough. That he should have believed her. That he knew she was telling the truth from the beginning. That he could feel, no, see that she had always told the truth. That he was too...

"There's only one option left," she whispered.

The door opened. Although there was no need for Ashton to hear Alena's last option, he knew she was stronger than him. Knew he was her last hope before the final alternative. Now he understood, at least half of the last part. What Golem had in store for her after this meeting he was not sure, nevertheless he knew now Alena would take her life. That's why she's been here so long, to keep her safe from herself. Because she had the courage and will to do away with Golem, even if it meant her own life. Alena would kill herself. She'd made her mind up before Ashton had even walked through the door three days ago.

And this act of suicide was what Golem had wished to prevent.

Two large orderlies and a nurse were in the door. Alena glared at them.

"What?" she said, shaking her head.

The main orderly gestured to Ashton's face and the trickles of blood streaming down his cheek. Alena cleared her throat forcing her breath down.

The nurse spoke first, "We can't have this anymore, Alena. You're a threat to everyone here."

Alena moved her head back and forth, her mouth open. "What does that mean?"

The nurse stepped forward. "Dr. Elliot is waiting for you. You're going to have a procedure, Alena. It'll be fine, no need to worry. This will all be over very soon."

Alena backed up. The orderly reached for her hand. She snapped her wrist away.

"What procedure?" she looked at Ashton, his mouth agape, confused.

The orderly snatched her wrist, hard, squeezing her wrist bone as the second orderly took hold of Alena's free arm.

"What procedure? What are you doing?" Alena was frantic, panic setting in and raising blood to her flushed face. She started kicking and flailing. Screaming as the orderlies rushed her out of the room.

The nurse glared at Ashton. "Are you coming?"

John's eyes narrowed.

"Follow me."

Ashton did follow, nervous and confused. Alena, screaming all the way down the hall. Ashton looked back. He saw the other patients gathered and huddled at the end of the hall. Wanda crossed herself and dropped to her knees.

"Here, detective," said the nurse. She pulled Ashton's arm forcing him to follow.

The orderlies forced the kicking and screaming Alena into a small surgical room where Dr. Elliot waited, a surgical mask covering his face. They strapped Alena, panic-stricken and screaming, to the bed by her wrists and ankles.

"Stand here, detective," the nurse hollered over Alena's screaming and pleading to be let free.

Ashton's eyes darted over the room. Dr. Elliot was watching him. He held a thin iron pick, like an ice pick, in one hand, in the other a small hammer. Ashton's face pinched in a nauseating cringe.

Just to look at her. I want Alena to know, detective. I want her to know before the procedure where she is going.

Ashton put his right palm on the glass separating him from the room. The orderlies, those large mitten sized hands, gripped Alena's head and chin silencing her screams that now turned to whimpers, forcing her to look at Ashton whose eyes, stiff and wide, stared back at Alena.

He could feel her. Could hear the shallow breath. Felt her heartbeat as he stared into her pupils. The orderly forced her eyelids to remain open. Ashton sensed Alena's eyes roaming over his pupils. She tried to buckle, to lift her restraints. Her body jerked and jolted.

Ashton felt it then. Saw how Alena's body loosened, fell limp. Saw how her eyes turned black and blank.

Knew she'd found it. The trap door in the back of Ashton's eye.

"Now, doctor," the nurse hollered.

And Dr. Elliot drew his iron pick across Alena's forehead, and with a quick snap of his wrist he slammed the hammer down, cracking Alena's skull.

56

Ten Years Later
October 1961

Ashton always remembered the blood, his hand on the glass window and that sinking feeling, as if he were standing in quick sand, slowly swallowed into the void.

This was followed by Alena's blank expression. The light in her eyes gone in a blink. Those emerald pupils had faded to black. On the surface, and to any casual observer—if there was any observer who came to pay Alena a visit—the lobotomy Alena endured by the hand of Dr. Elliot had turned out the light. Captain John Ashton knew differently.

He felt Alena's descent into Xibalba, as much as he felt his son in his arms after his birth. And he knew she was trapped in that demonic hellish realm of torture and fear.

A thought he'd blocked out for more than a decade, cutting off that seeing part of him, stuffed down and forgotten after so many plagued nightmares. Ashton was successful in his efforts to forget Alena. Successful until this morning when he'd received a phone call prompting his current walk to the precincts records room.

The department had issued a statement that all records were to be transferred to microfiche, a new state of the art electronic method for record keeping for any case that exceeded the statute of limitations. Alena's case file was included in the bundle.

The phone call he received broke open all those suppressed memories. He recognized the voice on the call immediately. Golem was of course his natural charismatic self, making light conversation with Captain Ashton, inquiring how his wife and two children were and, of course, congratulating him on his promotion to Captain. Unfortunately, Knowles had slipped on black ice last winter, cracked his head on the sidewalk and died from a brain hemorrhage. Those who knew him had whispered how the drink finally caught up to him—Captain Knowles was drinking at his favorite bar, his fall occurring outside the front door on his way home.

Now Ashton's hands were shaking, his palms sweating. Golem's voice turned his stomach; old familiar feelings choked his throat. He'd thought it was over, had wished he'd never hear from Golem again. But do we ever truly leave behind unresolved issues? The Captain had never entertained the thought. Now what stuck in Ashton's thoughts was the name, not Golem, but Herbert West, to which Ashton could not shake.

Not in the time he rifled through the records room, searching for Alena's file. Memories, thick and surreal kept rushing at him as if they had a mind of their own. Dr. Elliot had hung himself shortly after Alena's lobotomy. The DA was implicated in a mafia scandal and run out of the city. And Alena, her heart still beating, confined to a bed for all her days.

Ashton couldn't think about Alena. He refused to allow those thoughts. She'd told him what Maleva had said—that living with Golem, his transformation before the torch was passed, could last centuries. How long could Alena last in Xibalba before she cracked?

To Ashton, Golem's phone call was proof positive that time was coming. And that sinking feeling came on its heels.

Sinking into the void Ashton had so diligently forced from his thoughts, now back with a vengeance as he scoured through box after box searching for his much-needed file.

Ashton knew what Golem was doing. Erasing any and all mention of the name Golem.

57

While Ashton was buried in boxes and files, a man no one had ever seen before—no taller than five feet, wearing an Armani suit and using a red cane, his hands covered with black hair jutting from the cuff's of his suit, his face, so thin and narrow, fashioned a thick goatee—went to pay Alena a visit.

He provided proof to his connection with Alena Francon - executor to the Francon affairs and multiple businesses. He came to survey Alena's state of mind, to provide a decision at the bequest of city officials as to the humanity concerning Alena's condition. He brought a bouquet of flowers—lilies, Alena's favorite.

"You do know she does not have the ability to recognize the lilies," said the nurse escorting him to Alena's private room.

To which this stranger responded with a grin and, "She will know they are here. I can guarantee it."

A sentiment the nurse found endearing although naïve.

"I do have one question, if you don't mind."

The nurse responded, "Of course."

"Does she know?" he asked. The nurse looked puzzled. "Has Alena been informed of the state's decision?"

The nurse, eyes narrow, stared as if the question were ludicrous. "What good would it do? She's in a vegetative state, unable to process even the simplest thoughts and cognition."

The stranger smiled, dipped his chin to his chest. "Understood, however, do you know if anyone has said anything to Alena, yourself included?"

The nurse shook her head. "Not to my knowledge and if I had to guess I'd say absolutely not. There would be no reason for it."

"Thank you," he said then entered the room.

————

Golem waited for the nurse to disappear down the hall. Slowly, he closed the blinds to lock away prying eyes then turned to Alena lying on the hospital bed, comatose, although her eyes were open, seemingly staring at Golem. Cane in his right hand, lilies in the left. Alena's heartbeat bleeped on the EKG beside the bed.

"Awful hot in here, isn't it?" He paused, and a thin smile graced his lips. "One would think within this hospital setting the room would be ice cold." He looked over the room, right to left. "Come to think of it, the hospital is quite cold in the hall." His stare found Alena's eyes. Blank, dark, half open, staring not only at Golem but through him. "Perhaps Xibalba's heat turns the temp up a bit." Golem cocked his head up and to the left, contemplating. "Yes, that seems right to me."

He looked back to Alena, searching those stiff pupils. Titled his head to the right, examining Alena's shallow breathing, her chest rose slowly with a slight wheeze in the back of her throat.

Golem raised the lilies. "Brought your favorite. A gift for you, Alena."

Golem walked to Alena's bedside. Placed the small floral pattern vase on the tiny dresser by the bed.

He noticed Alena's eyes moved with him. Golem fluffed the flowers.

"I know you can hear me, Alena. All the way from Xibalba. Peering through those dark eyes." He paused, looked to the ceiling then cleared his throat, swallowed his breath. "Tell me, how is my Sophia?" And then that grin. He couldn't help his devious nature. "Spending much time with her I'm sure. Ahh, Alena, we had so much fun, didn't we?"

Alena's breath constricted, her body jerked.

Golem smiled. "That we did." He glanced over the room to a chair in the corner opposite the bed. He went to it, his cane tapping the linoleum floor, and pulled the chair against the wall beneath the window directly across from Alena, and sat. Their eyes met. He crossed his right leg over his left. Cane in his right hand, left hand on his lap.

Golem sat in silence. Sat a long while—spinning his cane—before beginning.

"I have a truce for you, Alena." Staring into Alena's eyes, he thumped his cane on the linoleum. His heart was racing. He drew in a deep breath. His face flushed. He pursed his lips. "Ten years in Xibalba and no sign of the light." He moved his head back and forth, pointing at her with his right hand still holding his cane. "And no possible way to it. Never to come, not without my help. I've heard Xibalba has become quite taken by you." He lifted his head. "Taken, indeed. What a nightmare, Alena. So many tortures, so many cuts. Over and over again." His voice trailed off, and he looked to the floor. "I know, I remember that eternity."

He turned away, gave a quick shake of his head, then gritted his teeth. "I'll try cutting to the quick. Of course, you know how I enjoy my speeches, although I will spare this moment for you." He paused, put his leg down locking eyes with Alena. "My transformation, Alena, and I know Maleva allowed this point to be known, will take a considerable amount of time for which you will be locked inside Xibalba. Although what Maleva did not know is what happens to you, should the torch not be passed." He clucked his tongue, moved his head back and forth. "Although I turn, Alena, you…you will turn with me, into something that no longer resembles Alena Francon. You will become what you despise the most, Alena. Is that what you wish? To be the devil you so hate? I know you can feel it too. The change, that is. Tell me you don't?"

Alena's chest sank, her breath constricted. Her body jerked, struggling to draw air into her lungs.

Golem nodded. "I know. I know. But none of that is required, Alena, not if you pass the torch." He smiled, a toothless smug grin. Alena's throat wheezed. "Of course, of course." He paused then stood up, left arm behind his back, leaning on his cane while he stepped around the bed to the right. "It's taken me a long while to truly understand your heart. Trust me, I've spent many a night in dire contemplation." He looked to the ceiling. "What does Alena want, I've asked myself, over and over and over again." He drifted off as if drowning in thought. "My conclusion eluded me. Perhaps it was because the answer was foreign. Thinking like a good human is not only putrid, it's nauseating." He shook his head. "If humans would just give up trying to be so good and accept their dark nature they would truly be a force to reckon with." He turned to Alena, not looking at her but listening. "And vice versa."

He sighed. "There goes one of my speeches. I do apologize, can't help it really. I love to rant and I love to rave." He grinned, as if to himself, and walked around the bed. "All things aside, the answer dawned on me quite recently after Jonah had completed a small task. He's grown to be quite the young devil, Alena, this is true." A small chuckle escaped his throat. "And that's when it hit me." He stood erect, shoulders back, and slapped his cane to the floor. "Releasing Alena from Xibalba is not good enough. I must give something too. Sophia, my dearest minion whose human heart runs the corridors in Xibalba with you." He stepped closer to the bed. "Do you hear me, Alena? Do you understand what I'm saying? I am offering to release *you* from Xibalba, but not just you…Sophia, too. Release you into that…other realm where your mother resides. Your father too. Disgusts me it does, that place, although it does have its purpose."

Alena's eyes floated, finding Golem. His face cringed. Her eyes seemed to mock him. Golem's heart jumping in his chest as he gnashed his teeth.

"*DO YOU UNDERSTAND ME?*" Golem screamed, breathing heavy. He could feel Alena smile, all the way from Xibalba. Golem searched the room, listening for any patter of footsteps in the hall. Nothing! All was quiet outside the room. Golem rolled his eyes and shook his head. "I apologize; I do get ahead of myself sometimes."

He stepped to the chair, dragged it, metal scraping linoleum, to the bed and sat. Alena's breath struggled, her chest constricted. Her eyes closed.

Jonah!

Golem heard Alena; her voice hovered in the room.

"Jonah, not Sophia," said Golem. "Why, Alena I hadn't expected this deviousness."

Both.

Golem's eyes widened. "Both?" His jaw tightened. Clamped his eyes shut.

Yes.

When he opened his eyes, Alena was staring at him. "You do realize that Jonah may not want to go? He's been with me for so long he'd be lost without me."

Both.

Her voice carried the weight of resolve, absolution.

Golem turned his head, thinking.

Clucked his tongue before he said, "Very well, Alena. Both. But I require your absolute declaration." He reached into his inside coat pocket, and took out a folded paper and quill, then opened the paper. The heading read: LAST WILL AND TESTAMENT. "Your signature is required." Golem placed the paper on Alena's chest, then took her hand, and punctured her finger to draw blood onto the quill.

"No worries, Alena," he told her.

"*I* will guide your hand."

———————

The orderly opened the door to Alena's room. His eyes shot open by the apparent noise; the EKG machine buzzing with a relentless flat line. He hollered for help and within seconds the nurses were there. They attempted to resuscitate but the heart wouldn't allow it.

Alena Francon was pronounced dead.

Strange, the nurse thought, later that evening after her shift.

She'd never seen it before, not from a patient who'd received the now illegal lobotomy.

Alena Francon had died with a smile on her lips.

The image had been so baffling to the young nurse she'd forgotten to contact the patient's benefactor. A person with the name, Herbert West.

58

At the moment Alena Francon was pronounced dead, Captain John Ashton arrived home.

To his wife, Laura, he seemed distracted. Not that a cop under the throes of deep concentration was anything new; she'd become used to his lost gaze over the years. Nonetheless, there was something different about today's distraction.

She saw shame in her husband's eyes. And an incessant need for his family to know how much he loved them.

Her eyes narrowed when John had taken Samuel by the wrist. The boy had wanted to return to his room after dinner—comic books, always comic books—but John had a dire need to question him, face to face, about his day at school.

She watched while John studied Sam's eyes, not hearing Sam recounting the day's events. His gaze investigating the boy's eyes resulted in John's further shameful stare although prideful and loving.

After dinner, he took his nightcap outside their home.

————

John Ashton lit a fire in the backyard. The metal garbage can raged with heat. He enjoyed the crackling and popping, flames devouring a month of newspapers.

He warmed his hands, breathing deeply the autumn wind. He searched for prying eyes—nosy neighbors had little to do. The Queens brownstone's backyard was surrounded by numerous windows, all offering an opportunity to watch the Ashton's backyard.

Satisfied he was not being watched, John reached behind his back, beneath his jacket. The thin Francon file was wedged between his jeans and t-shirt.

No more than a brief hesitation. Then he watched the flames devour the file, putting an end to the name Golem and Alena's fantastical and depraved story.

Captain John Ashton sucked back his tears, and turned his gaze up. The sun—fighting dark clouds—would be sleeping soon. John feared his dreams would be torturous tonight. Knew the nightmares were coming. Understood many sleepless nights were in his future. How long they would last he did not know but he knew he deserved much more than nightmares. No matter how many crimes he'd collared. How many criminals he'd put away. How many innocent people he'd kept safe.

Captain John Ashton was guilty.

Responsible for opening the proverbial door—inviting the devil into the world.

59

The office was a hive of activity, hectic, lively, and humming with thick and heavy conversation. Salesmen and secretaries were finishing deals, last minute phone calls, and hustling paperwork from desk to desk and office to office. The Francon Corporation was taking on new ventures, stretching their hand across the country and in fact the world at large.

Changes were on the horizon. Great big changes that would send an army into the world.

Despite all the distractions, new deals and hustle, Annette Flemming was escorted to the president's office without a moment's hesitation or wait. Her trusted confidant, Camilla, by her side. They were driven into the city from their mansion in the Hamptons, at the request of the president.

Annette Flemming had been mentioned in Alena Francon's will. Golem greeted them, graciously, and escorted the ladies to his private office, then offered them the two seats in front of his desk while he stood, leaning on the oak desk in front of them.

"Mrs. Flemming," Golem cupped her hand in his. "It has been such a long time, has it not?"

"Too long, unfortunately," said Annette. "My condolences for Alena. When did she pass?"

"This afternoon. Although we have been aware for some time now. Her health had taken a dire turn over the last few months. There was nothing any one could do for her. So unfortunate. Unfortunate for everything Alena had been through," he paused. "It's disheartening."

"Alena was the best of all people," Annette said. "I often think about our times at the ClairField with fond memories."

"As do I. Time certainly has a way of changing all that is good." He looked over the ladies settling his stare on Annette. "How is Noel? Haven't seen him in a day's age." He grinned.

Annette cleared her throat. Pursed her lips. Camilla reached her hand to Annette's. "He passed last winter." Annette folded her fingers between Camilla's.

Golem tilted his head. "So sorry. I hadn't heard."

"Heart attack," Annette recalled.

Golem shook his head. "My condolences. To you both."

It was Camilla who responded next. "Do you have the papers for Mrs. Flemming to sign? We have a dinner party tonight and so many loose ends to tie up before our guests arrive."

"Understood. Time is always of the essence." He took his cane off the desk, walked around, and sat forward, close to the desk. He eyed Annette. "By signing these papers, Mrs. Flemming, you are acknowledging acceptance of Alena's last will and testament. Once signed I'll have the statue brought to your home immediately." He pushed the papers across his desk. "Simple enough really. I remember so many years ago how Alena had wanted to give you the statue. She spoke so highly of you. I thought it best the statue go to you once she passed."

Annette looked up to Golem. "Do you have a pen?" She seemed to not care for Golem's small talk.

"Indeed," he breathed, passing the quill on his desk.

"Old school?" Annette said regarding the feathered pen.

"I have an affinity for nostalgia." He grinned; eyes darted from Annette to Camilla.

Annette read over the papers, her eyes glancing across sentences, paragraphs, and headings. She flipped the page and took up the feather, then dipped the quill into an ink vial. She signed her name in red. Her hand now shaking, she replaced the quill. Golem reached for the paper, flipped to the second page, staring at the signature. He looked at Annette, and cocked his head.

"Oh, my dear, your nose is bleeding."

"My lady," said Camilla handing Annette a handkerchief from her purse.

"Thank you." Annette used the handkerchief to soak up the blood.

Camilla responded on Annette's behalf. "She suffers from nose bleeds. Has now for a long time."

"We all have our ailments," said Golem. "Would you like a glass of water, Mrs. Flemming?"

Annette laughed. "How about a scotch?"

"Oh Annette, not yet," said Camilla. She helped Annette to her feet while addressing Golem. "When can we expect the statue?"

Golem stood with them. "This evening," he said with pride. "In anticipation of your arrival I dispatched a moving van prior. It may be there before you return home."

"Thank you, Mr. Golem," said Annette, the bloodied kerchief squeezed in her fist.

Golem bowed his head. "You are most welcome, Mrs. Flemming."

He walked them to the door, cane in hand.

"You're so kind," Annette said. "Perhaps you can help myself and Camilla. Noel's affairs have been in disarray since his passing. We just can't keep up. Maybe you can help us with a few of his newest ventures."

"Of course, of course," said Golem. "What are these new ventures you speak of?"

Annette thought for a moment. "There's so many but the one that has the most pressing matter is the production company in California. A few films have been placed on hold and we really do need to get them into the theatre if we're to recoup our investment."

Golem raised his chin. "California," he said. "I would be delighted. New ventures are my specialty." He grinned.

"Excellent," said Annette.

"We can go over the details tomorrow if you'd like?"

"Better yet," Annette said. "Come to the dinner party tonight. We can discuss the most pressing matters."

Golem's eyes gleamed. "Mrs. Flemming, consider me there." He leaned into Annette. "I can guarantee it."

"Thank you," Annette said. "I...we..." she gestured to Camilla, "Have been so inundated lately. It's overwhelming. Noel built a great empire; I don't want to see any part of it go to waste. He worked so hard."

"As have you, my lady."

Annette shook her head. "No, Noel deserves all the praise, not I."

"Not at all," he said. "I've heard always how you've placed your husband on a pedestal, hosting so many guests of influence. In fact, I've often heard how gracious you have been. Your work has not gone unnoticed, Mrs. Flemming. You have been as much a part of Noel's success as he has." He locked eyes with Annette. Her body shuddered then tensed as if something locked into place in her stomach. Her stare unblinking, thinking, thoughts churning.

"Ok," said Camilla, breaking Annette's concentration. "Let me get this young lady home."

Golem opened the door.

"Thank you once again," said Annette.

"You are most welcome. I look forward to our meeting tonight. And to visiting my old home; it has been a long time since I've been there."

No response. Camilla took Annette by the elbow, escorting her through the busy office.

And Annette's mind started to race with thoughts toppled over, one on top of the other, while riding the elevator.

"Oh," said Camilla once they exited the elevator. The ladies stopped walking. "I left my purse."

Annette looked at her wristwatch. "We haven't time," she said. "If we're to make it to…"

"It's ok, you go ahead. I'll take a service home and begin preparations."

Their driver stepped to them. "All well, ladies?" he said.

"Camilla forgot her purse."

"It's ok," said Camilla. "Take Annette to Tiffany's; they will close soon. I'll meet you home."

"Yes, ma'm." The driver snapped his shoulders, and offered Annette his arm.

Camilla and Annette shared a caring stare. Annette closed her eyes and gave a slight bow. Camilla caught the elevator before the doors closed.

"Follow me, Mrs. Flemming."

He escorted her outside where the limousine was waiting. He opened the door for Annette and she stepped inside as the driver went around to the front, and took his seat. He eyed Annette in the rearview — the glass window was down.

"Everything go ok up there, Mrs. Flemming? You seem a bit distracted."

"Just thinking is all," said Annette and then laughed. "Seems I've got a lot on my mind at the moment."

He gave a quick bow. "I'll leave you to it then. We've a long ride back to the Hamptons. Plenty of time to process those thoughts."

Annette offered him a smile before he closed the window, allowing Annette her privacy.

60

"Absolutely splendid," said Golem once Camilla had closed Golem's office door.

Camilla approached his desk; a smug smile graced her lips.

Golem began to clap. "I've never seen such precision. Bravo, Camilla. Bravo!"

He offered his hand and Camilla took the offer, taking the same seat she'd sat on not a few minutes before. She sat beneath Golem's stare.

"All for you," she said. "All for Baphomet."

"So decadent," Golem said. "A decade of decadence. I'm sure you were able to bowl her over with that sweet, sweet voice. I knew from the first time I laid eyes on you, *Niyah*, that you would accomplish such exceptional goals."

She bowed. Her stare then turned inquisitive. "Have all preparations been made?"

"Indeed," Golem gleamed. "That's what all the hustle and bustle has been about. By tomorrow morning all the Francon assets and businesses will be in the name of one man. Herbert West."

He raised his chin. "Do you believe Annette has suspicions?"

Camilla grinned. "Not a thing." Now Camilla raised her chin, prideful. "That Noel," she laughed. "A heart attack," she laughed again. "The poison took years to build in his system. No one gave notice or suspicion. And Annette..." she closed her eyes. "So sweet, she is." Eyes now open. "You were right about her. She only needed a friend, someone to share those lonely nights."

Golem grinned. "And the bed, too. I've always said, play to their desires, give them what they want most, and they'll be forever loyal," he scoffed, shaking his head. "Humans." He rolled his eyes.

Camilla took her purse off the floor and stood, eye-to-eye with Golem.

"It will be good to see you in your new skin." She touched his chin. "This body does not suit you any longer."

"Indeed."

Camilla closed her eyes, then went down to one knee, bowing.

"*AGIOS O BAPHOMET!*"

Golem placed his hand on her head, repeating, "*AGIOS O BAPHOMET!*"

Annette watched the city disappear.

"He is right," she thought. "Noel would have been nothing if it weren't for me. All those parties, playing goodie goodie with those insipid guests. How every moment irritated me. How he irritated me."

She looked at her hands, folded on her lap.

Undeserving people. All of them. How they want what I have. Desire me!

She moved her head back and forth. Clenched her jaw.

They only exist to serve me, and they don't even know it. How arrogant of them. They get nothing from me other than to further serve my interests. Hand them a plate of food and they'll love you for it, without even understanding the food is also mine, the plate too. No, no, they must be kept under the thumb. Look at them, disgusting vermin. Make me want to puke knowing how truly disgusting and stupid they all are. They need to be told what is good for them. Told what to think and how to behave. Like little children without an inkling of what's good for them.

Her eyes went wide, grinding her teeth.

Want what I have? Of course but they are undeserving, wretched fiends. If they do desire more, they will have to bow for it. They will be required to offer themselves for it. To bow in my presence and give all they have in my honor. If not, they get nothing but the scraps from my table. And they'll be grateful for those scraps. Makes me cringe to even think of them.

Those stupid, putrid and vile little minds.

61

John Ashton sat on his stoop outside his front door, lost in contemplation. The sun had departed minute's prior and with it night had arrived, bathing the city in a veil of cold and darkness. Children on the street, Ashton's son included, engaged in a tireless game of stickball. But Ashton didn't see them, couldn't hear them; he was thinking, trying to remember. To remember what Alena had said. Maleva's words, her description of Golem's chosen female host for Baphomet.

What were the traits?

Every time he came close to locating the memory, it ran from his mind like a child playing a game of hide and seek.

He closed his eyes, turning on that seeing part of him, restoring thought and memory.

————

"Where is everyone?" asked Annette to Camilla upon her arrival home. Annette had been confused when the driver awakened her in the car's backseat. How had Camilla arrived home before her? Why had the sun already retreated? Had she lost time? Did she even go to Tiffany's? The car ride home was a blank slate on her memory. She'd been losing time recently, believing stress had taken its toll on the mind.

Camilla took Annette's purse off Annette's shoulder, and dropped it on the floor. She seemed hurried, jumpy.

"In the basement," said Camilla. "They wait for you."

Annette looked at Camilla, puzzled. "Are you ok?" she asked.

"Of course, of course." Camilla smiled, and leaned in to kiss Annette, her lips soft and delicate.

"Why the basement?"

Camilla straightened her shoulders. "For the ceremony."

Annette paused and shook her head. "Ceremony?"

"Yes, David has arrived. We had him placed in the basement."

Annette snapped her head back and curled her brow. "You put the original David in the basement? Camilla, what has come over you?"

"Do you trust me?" Camilla breathed as two sounds echoed in the basement, vibrating the floor. A clunking bell coupled with a xylophone vibration.

Annette looked at Camilla. "Of course I trust you. More than anyone, you know that."

"Then trust me now."

Camilla took her hand, and walked her through the kitchen to the open basement door. The scent of sulfur drifted into the kitchen.

Annette freed her hand. "You know I don't like going down there."

Camilla stiffened and Annette stepped away. Camilla took her hand, soft and gentle. "Look at me," said Camilla.

"What?"

"Just look at me. Follow my eyes. So much love in them….all my love for you."

————————

John could see Alena, in the office at Bellevue, sitting across from him. The scene muted, like listening under water; Ashton focused on Alena's mouth, studying the words formed by her lips.

"Why us? Why have we been chosen?" Alena's voice, revealing her eye-opening conversation with Maleva.

Ashton kept his attention on Alena's lips; it was as if she were speaking to him from the netherworld.

"Darkness is always attracted to the light it seeks to destroy. It is our light that was chosen."

————————

Annette was taken by Camilla's dark eyes. She followed the pupils, and her brow cringed. Something about her eyes. Annette looked closer. She found the trap door. Her body fell limp, calm. Annette's eyes filled with black.

"Now," said Camilla. "Come with me."

She escorted Annette to the stairs. And the chanting began.

AGIOS O BAPHOMET!

They took the stairs down. Candles illuminated the basement. The newly paved, smooth concrete floor reflected those flames. A pentagram had been painted on the floor, David in the center.

AGIOS O BAPHOMET!

The bridesmaids stood on three points on the pentagram, all of them in white robes, hoods covering their heads, each of them holding a candle. Camilla brought Annette to the statue.

AGIOS O BAPHOMET!

She cut her palm, and reached Annette's hand to David. Blood fell in small droplets to the base.

"The blood is the life," hailed Camilla, her eyes mad and wide.

AGIOS O BAPHOMET!

————

Ashton went deeper into the *seeing*. Apt focus and concentration, seeing Alena's lips move, hearing Maleva's declaration off those lips.

"But sometimes, sometimes, Alena, a darkness exists in the human heart so profound Golem must catch it, latch on and carry it."

Ashton leaned forward, listening, drifting.

"Like the witch who passed the torch to me, this darkness thunders the reach of Golem and Xibalba, a force we do not want to unleash."

————

Camilla escorted Annette to her point on the pentagram, then stepped to her own. The ladies lifted their chins. The room thundered around them.

AGIOS O BAPHOMET!

The chanting reached a fevered high pitch. The gong, the xylophone vibrations rang through the basement. One, two, three...

AGIOS O BAPHOMET!

Four. Five.

AGIOS O BAPHOMET!

———————

John's eyes snapped open as a thick rush of wind ripped through every pore in his body. The words hung in the air, floated and stained on the wind.

"A darkness exists in the human heart so profound Golem must catch it, latch on and carry it."

Ashton, eyes staring, downtrodden, and lost, turned numb inside, thinking about the world around him, all he'd witnessed, all he'd taken part in, all the people all the world over. He lifted his chin, seeing the dark night, tiny blinks of stars and a black cloud that raced across the full moon. He clucked his tongue then rolled it inside his mouth.

But that could be anyone.

In today's world, there's so many who fit that description.

Where do I begin?

———————

The basement turned quiet, maddening quiet. The vibration dissipated. The chanting stopped. Breath constricted.

All looked on David as his thin lips gasped open with his first breath.

And Golem opened his eyes.

Epilogue

Captain John Ashton spent his morning out back, distracted, and pleading for retribution. He couldn't face his wife, couldn't look at his children. Couldn't stand to be in his own presence.

Ashton stepped to the metal garbage can and thought about Alena. The morning air reminded him about their conversation. Something in the wind he couldn't put his finger on. A nagging sensation in his gut. His throat closed. His fedora in his hands. He searched it over. Ashton had not worn his precious hat in over a decade. Not since his last meeting with Alena.

And Captain John Ashton, meaning to toss his fedora into the trashcan, gasped when he looked inside. The ash from the night before formed a word.

The word was unmistakable.

WEST

And he could hear Alena's voice whisper the same on the heels of the wind. And John Ashton thought,

It's not over!

Author Note

Writing Golem was a labor of love, a story I've wanted to write for a very, very long time. Some of the most major literary influences in my life have ranged from *Frankenstein* to *Dracula, Dr. Jekyll and Mr. Hyde* to *The Legend of Sleepy Hollow*, and so on and so forth with *Frankenstein* continuously taking the top spot on my favorites list still to this day. These are the books that ignited a fire in my gut that has never waned nor diminished and I am thankful for the gift of literature that these stellar classics have provided.

I have always been intrigued by the psychological component that horror novels have contributed to the human psyche over the long history of literature, probably beginning with Dante's Inferno-now there's a motivated insight into the human condition and society if there ever was one. Additional major influences over the course of my reading obsession have been, of course, Stephen King, Clive Barker, Anne Rice, and books like *The Silence of the Lambs, Something Wicked This Way Comes*, and even Batman comic books, all of which weaved its way into an appreciation of classic characters. Frankenstein and Frankenstein's Monster, Dracula, Pennywise, Lestat, Hannibal Lecter, and of course, one of my personal all time favorites, the anarchic Joker. A great character not only drives a brilliant story, but also breathes life for eternity, as the aforementioned literary characters have proven time and time again.

As you can imagine I'm sure, my obsession with all things classic and iconic related to horror and anarchy began at an early age, culminating in the story that is now Golem. But let me slow things down a bit, because I need to clarify a little bit more about influence. In early 2003 I was enrolled in a college course on Theatre and was lucky enough to have a great teacher who was kind enough to include in the curriculum the story of *Pygmalion* along with a viewing of the iconic musical, *My Fair Lady*. I know, you're probably thinking *My Fair Lady*? Well, other than foaming at the mouth over Audrey Hepburn, I was intrigued by the origins of the *Pygmalion* story in Greek Mythology, which is essentially about a sculptor who wills his statue to come to life. Loved the concept that's for sure, but even more a seed had been planted that would take root some years later, some years being fifteen years later when I had officially decided to write my monster book, as I have always referred to Golem.

When one begins to write such a book there are very specific needs the story requires within its pages. The first was the monster, of course. At some time in 2014 I watched the silent film, *Golem: How He Came Into The World*. Yes I enjoy silent films and if you are brave enough to sit for a good hour and a half to marvel over a stellar work of film noir, I'll give you a tip that'll boost your enjoyment. Hit the mute button on your television and ask Alexa to play Pink Floyd's album's *The Piper at the Gates of Dawn* followed by *Animals*. Trust me it's a good way to go.

For those who don't know about the legend that is Golem, here's the long and short of it: Golem comes from Jewish folklore where a demonic force is incarnated into an inanimate object, or a clay statue, then wreaks havoc on society. A Golem is supposed to protect society-at least that is the original reason why the presence is incarnated into the statue-but instead, destroys the society he was supposed to protect. Once the legend was discovered, coupled with my appreciation for *Pygmalion*, I had my monster, although I always saw Golem's personality as a cross between Hannibal Lecter, the Joker, Lestat and an ace con man.

Unfortunately, I've had more than my share of con men in my life, although, fortunately, I've had more than my share of con men in my life; people who know how to push the buttons, gaslight, and hit that nerve none of us want pushed. Considering that I've been a practicing therapist in the field of psychology for the better part of the last two decades, my psychoanalysis on these con men was crucial in developing the Golem character. Golem needed to be cerebral, manipulative, cunning, treacherous and anarchic, using those dirty little secrets against his foe in order to achieve his desired result: power and control. The Golem folklore was the perfect catalyst to write my monster story and hence I ventured out to begin writing.

Choosing the perfect setting was paramount. My roots are in New York-my family emigrated from Italy to Brooklyn, NY in the early 1900's and I've always been intrigued over the ambience and mystery that is New York City. So, when I was deciding on the setting New York was always on my mind. The biggest question I had was regarding time. I wanted the story to have an old world type of feel to it, however, I wasn't content with going too far into the past-there's been so many books, movies, and plays written about witches and woods and I wanted to get out of that time period. This is when the 1940's came into my mind as a possible time for the Golem story.

My grandfather was a fighter pilot in WW2 before he returned home to Brooklyn, NY and having heard so many stories about that time in our history-including the people and supposed sophistication during that time, and yes they wore Fedoras-I began researching the time period. Also, I do have to give a shout out to Ayn Rand and her book *The Fountainhead*, for being the catalyst that drove me to think about my grandfather and that time period. If you haven't read *The Fountainhead* I do recommend the book, which, I do consider, to be a truly exceptional piece of literature. For those who are Ayn Rand haters, I always say, hate the artist, not the art. Nonetheless, I was intrigued by the time period, sparking my interest to learn more.

Golem is a story about loss, isolation, contempt, division, and fear, as are most of the monster books previously mentioned. Plus, in the Golem folklore Golem is a master manipulator who seeks to destroy society, so what I required was controversy. It really is amazing how far down a rabbit hole one can tumble when they begin to look. Just about every scandal and controversy mentioned in the Golem story is true. From the district attorney to the mayor to the police, all real scandals that rocked New York during that time, not to mention the fact that McCarthyism spread like wild fire a few years after the Golem story-I did hint to that in the final chapters-although McCarthy gave his initial speech on communists in our government in 1950, resulting in a blotch on our history that pushed playwright Arthur Miller to write *The Crucible*. McCarthyism fit perfectly into the Golem manipulation and was the perfect distraction to thwart John Ashton's belief in what Alena was warning him against. I enjoy it when society reflects what I need to accomplish in a novel. Should you be intrigued enough about the time period take a tumble down that rabbit hole, you won't be disappointed. New York has always produced the most stellar controversies and scandals, unfortunately the same continues in our current time.

During my rabbit hole tumbling I came across what would become the ClairField Inn, and yes the ClairField was a real hotel, although the official name is the Claremont Inn-when I first came upon the Claremont I kept thinking it was the ClairField and the name stuck. Every detail about the historic Claremont as told in the Golem story is true and accurate according to the research. From its prestigious roots to the offering of cheaper meals and yes, the Claremont burned down at the exact date reported in the Golem story and yes, the official story was that the fire was started by hot coals left unattended. And yes, there is now a park where the Inn had resided, it's in Harlem just off Riverside Drive. Originally the story was going to take place solely in the 1940's but after reading about the Inn I changed a few things in the story to weave the fire into the fabric of the narrative. Fit perfectly, if you ask me, as did every other researched detail making Golem the first historical fiction novel I've written, if it could be called historical fiction.

A few other details I'd like to throw out there. The winter blizzard that erupts on the night Golem is born also happened, although the blizzard hit New York City like a tornado, the storm never made its way to Long Island, as the Golem story suggests, however, I thought it was cool beans and wanted to keep the storm in the story. And yes, the blizzard began at just after three in the morning after Christmas as the story reveals. Microfiche was the new rave in 1961 and yes Charleston Chews were a popular candy provided during Halloween in 1951. I could go on and on but maybe that's just another book in waiting or perhaps that is up to you dear reader, to assess whether you'd like to go down that rabbit hole or not.

Now I believe I may have taken up a bit too much of your time with this long author note so I'll wrap this up now. Simply put, overall, writers write what they know and what they see and, as Nina Simone so eloquently stated, "An artists duty is to reflect the times," and I do hope I've accomplished that mission. Nothing changes if we aren't aware there's a problem to begin with. Golem is a story about isolation, paranoia, and division, and, as unfortunate as it is, reflects our current society in a nutshell. Who opened the front door and invited the devil in? Well, we all did now didn't we? We need to be celebrating our differences, not creating additional ways to categorize, label, and segregate any particular group.

We need to look to each other for answers and change, and not give up our freedoms and liberties to the few who live in mansions and fly private jets while telling us all how to live. Maybe try to see and understand your neighbor's perspectives instead of listening always to people who portray themselves as an authority when all they have is their own interests in mind? Or you could just continue to argue, bitch, moan, point fingers, and call out derogatory names all because you think you're right and everyone on the planet should bow to your will. Choice really is up to you and the choices we make determine the lives that we live, mold our daily thoughts and concerns, and determine our basic daily frequency. Not everyone is always going to agree with you and there is nothing wrong with alternative opinions; they just add spice to this beautiful thing that we call life. The wise and brilliant William Shakespeare once said, "Trust few, but love all." These are beautiful words to live by, just make sure the few people you choose to trust are chosen wisely.

And remember that if you always believe that you're right, you couldn't be more wrong. Do you want to be right or do you want to be peaceful?

With all things being equal, I choose peace.

~ PD Alleva
Florida, 2021

Coming Soon From PD Alleva

<u>Horror</u>

Jigglyspot and the Zero Intellect (2022)

<u>Sci-Fi/Fantasy</u>

The Rose Vol 2 (December 21, 2021)
The Rose Vol 3 (Summer 2022)

<u>Urban Paranormal Fantasy</u>

Girl on a Mission: The Dead Do Speak (February 2022)

About the Author

PD Alleva writes thrillers. Sometimes those thrillers are Sci-Fi Fantasy's about Alien Vampires attempting to subjugate the human race, and sometimes they're steeped in a haunting psychological horror story, or an urban paranormal fantasy. But here's the best part, PD always provides readers with a profound, entertaining, and satisfying reader experience in a new genre he has coined Alternative Fiction. His novels blend mystery, conspiracy, psychology, and suspense with the supernatural, horror, fantasy, paranormal, metaphysics, and science fiction. Alternative fiction is PD's attempt at describing what readers uncover in any one of his books, a new discovery towards mainstream storytelling.

He's been writing since childhood, creating and developing stories with brash and impactful concepts he describes are metaphors for the shifting energies that exist in the universe. PD lives inside of his own universe, working diligently on the Sci-Fi/Fantasy series, *The Rose Vol. II*, the urban paranormal fantasy series, *Girl on a Mission*, and *Jigglyspot and the Zero Intellect*, PD's upcoming horror novel.

Also by PD Alleva

Sci-Fi/Fantasy

The Rose Vol 1: A masterful, dystopian science fiction thriller of telepathic evil greys, mysterious rebellion, martial arts, and Alien Vampires.
ASIN: B089JTPJ8G

Dark Fantasy

Presenting the Marriage of Kelli Anne & Gerri Denemer: One known terrorist. A protest about to erupt. A family on the brink of collapse. Is the bond between husband and wife strong enough to defeat evil?
ASIN: B07HFJGJQR

Twisted Tales of Deceit: Three supernatural tales of horror (*The Calculated Desolation of Hope, Somnium, & Knickerbocker*) chronicling evil's influence on innocent hearts and our uncontrollable desire to give in to their calculated transgression. Features Knickerbocker, a novelette and reimagining of Washington Irving's classic tale, *The Legend of Sleepy Hollow*, with a modern day twist; all characters are recovering addicts employed as teachers at the prestigious Sleepy Hollow Private School. And yes, heads do roll.
ASIN: B07GBJP2BL

Literary

A Billion Tiny Moments in Time…
ASIN: B077LVS67G

Indifference
ASIN: B072KNXG4P

Find all of PD Alleva's books on his website at:
pdalleva.com

Ingram Content Group UK Ltd.
Milton Keynes UK
UKHW040016200423
420333UK00030B/472/J